To Frankee,
It has been so
nice to connect with
you on facebook! May
you be blessed as
you read this ~~book~~ book.
Sharon
March 12/11

Antipas: MARTYR

Antipas:
Martyr

SHARON DOW

Scripture taken from the *Holy Bible, New International Version.* Copyright © 1973, 1978, 1984 International Bible Society. Used by permission of Zondervan Bible Publishers.

Deep River Books
Sisters, Oregon
http://www.deepriverbooks.com

ISBN-10 1-935265-53-9
ISBN-13 978-1-935265-53-5

Library of Congress: 2011920160

Printed in the USA

Cover design by blackbirdcreative.biz

Dedication

This book is dedicated to my husband, George. Without your love, care, and encouragement, this book would not have become a reality. Your faith in me never wavered, even when I was struggling to make revisions. You always knew we could make this happen.

Antipas: Martyr

"These are the words of him who has the sharp, double-edged sword. I know where you live—where Satan has his throne. Yet you remain true to my name. You did not renounce your faith in me, even in the days of Antipas, my faithful witness, who was put to death in your city—where Satan lives."

REVELATION 2:12B AND 13

Prologue

Antipas, Antipas…" The ghostly call drifted in and out of his dreams. "Antipas—ha, ha, ha, ha, ha!"

He awoke, disoriented and sweating.

It was only a dream, he told himself, a nightmare sent straight from hell. He sat up on the edge of the hard cot, wringing wet and shivering violently in the predawn chill.

He was in prison. Held for what reason? When did the local authorities ever need a reason? The events leading up to his arrest began to flood his memory. Faster and faster the images flashed across his mind, until he put his head in his hands and wept.

One

Pergamum: his hometown, the place his family dwelled, the place he learned to worship Zeus, the place he trudged up the long hill to serve at the altar, the place he watched the caravans coming through on their way to Ephesus or the Aegean Sea. Pergamum: capital of Asia, center of Roman emperor worship, the very house of Satan.

It had rained during the night, but morning dawned bright and clear with raindrops sparkling on the grass around his home. The air wafting through his window was fragrant with the scent of flowers from his mother's garden nodding their vibrant heads in the soft breeze. He watched lazy clouds gliding overhead. Without was peaceful; within was turmoil and he was reluctant to begin his day.

His servant slipped quietly into the room.

"The master awaits your presence," he spoke respectfully.

"I'm not ready." Antipas crossed his arms and rested his head on the window ledge.

"I wouldn't keep the master waiting," the servant warned. When Antipas did not respond, the man exited as quietly as he'd entered.

Antipas knew his father would not be pleased but still he lingered.

Finally his father, Julian, made an appearance in his room, an unheard-of occurrence. He glanced around before he fixed his gaze on his son.

Antipas heard him enter the room but kept his back to the door. His shoulder muscles tightened and he gritted his teeth. Fear knotted in his stomach.

"Antipas, you delay." The words were stern and harsh.

"Yes, Father." His shoulders slumped as his head went down.

"There is no more time. We must leave at once. I would almost think you didn't want to go."

"I don't want to." Antipas spun around to face his father, chin held high. "I'd rather play with my friends, or go for a walk, or chase the dogs, anything but this." He flung out his arms as he hurled the words at his father.

"Antipas, you shock and shame me. You will go and you will not disgrace me or the family. You will make your first offering to Zeus and become a man just like your friends and your brother before you. We've been preparing you for this. You know how important it is. I don't understand you." Julian turned with a swish of his robe to leave the room.

As he reached the door he turned again. "There will be no further talk about this. You will present yourself, fully clothed in your ceremonial robe, or face the consequences. Believe me, the consequences will not be to your liking." Another swish of his robe and he was gone.

Antipas slumped onto his bed. He wasn't even sure he believed in Zeus, but he wouldn't dare mention it to his father. In Julian's household, worshipping Zeus and the emperor was the only permitted faith.

He wished he could believe like everyone else. His older brother, Marcus, had become a man this time last year and told him wild tales about the ceremony.

As he sat dejected on his bed, Marcus stuck his head in the door.

"Just wait, Antipas, you'll be scared when you see what you have to do," Marcus taunted him.

"You always tell tall tales. I don't believe half of what you say."

"Just wait," he jeered as he disappeared.

Antipas made a face at Marcus's retreating back. He tossed a cushion across the room, jumped from his bed, and kicked at his wall. He thought about the consequences his father had mentioned. He remembered that once Marcus had been sent to stay with an elderly aunt while the family vacationed after he had defied his father. He finally decided it wouldn't be worth it. He picked up the cushion and turned back to his bed.

He donned the white robe that his mother had laid out for him and placed the scarlet turban on his head. The simple yet elegant gold chain he wrapped about his waist was a gift from his father. He knew it cost far more than the family could afford, but his father was all about appearances.

When Antipas joined the family, his father ignored him. But when Julian was looking the other way, his mother put her hand on his shoulder and squeezed it gently. No words were spoken between mother and son, but he felt sympathy in her touch.

The sun was directly overhead as the family left their home and began the long trek to the temple, many other families joining them on the way. The group swelled as it progressed along the Roman road.

The Roman Road stretched through the city and joined the well-used caravan trails to the north and south. It had been constructed many decades earlier when the Roman legions made their way to the East. It was no wonder the people worshipped the emperor—life was easier after the influence of the Romans.

But his grandfather had told him differently. He had told him about the freedom the citizens of Pergamum had before the coming of the Romans. This was seditious talk. If his father knew the things his grandfather told him, the old man would be imprisoned for treason.

He could see his grandfather ahead of him, thin shoulders bent beneath his dark turban. It pained him to see how old he looked. Gradually his grandfather slowed until he was beside Antipas.

"Remember the things I've told you," the old man whispered. "There's more to life than Zeus and the emperor."

Julian's cold, glaring eyes scanned both of them. Antipas looked away quickly.

"We'd better not talk about it right now," Antipas breathed.

"I wish I could tell you more, wish I knew more. Don't ever forget. Look for the truth, Grandson. Look for the truth. "

Julian moved away from the group of men he was with until he was on the other side of Antipas. Without a word he fell into step with him. Grandfather kept silent, but Antipas kept hearing his grandfather's words. *Look for the truth.*

Grandfather soon fell behind and Antipas walked with his father. He could see the stiff back, the haughty tilt of his head, whenever he glanced sideways at him.

"I expect you will not disgrace the family today with your foolish ideas," his father said to him in a low voice. Antipas felt fear slide down his back. "I spoke to you, Son. That requires a response."

"Yes, Father," Antipas replied.

"Remember what I've said." Having made his point, Julian once again joined the group of men.

Antipas steeled himself for the ordeal ahead as he mingled with the families of friends who were also to become adults today. His best friend was Cleotis. They had been friends forever, sharing interests and ideas. He had hinted to Cleotis a few of the things his grandfather had told him but was frightened to share all as it might compromise his friend. The things he had mentioned were received with interest, not shock.

Cleotis joined him, high with excitement.

"I can't wait," Cleotis blurted. "Just think, we'll be men in a few hours."

Antipas didn't respond, but Cleotis was far too energized to notice.

Soon they could see the temple at the top of the hill, its white marble exterior glowing in the noonday sun. Its lofty pillars looked sinister to him, as though it beckoned him to enter its evil presence. He needed to get control of himself. His mind was running wild. His father said he had an imagination that would scare Zeus himself.

The crowds had swelled until they filled the entire street. Laughter and bantering could be heard as people jested with the boys. Rough tunics rubbed shoulders with the finest of materials as they pushed on to the temple entrance where the priests, clothed in their elaborate and colorful robes, waited to receive the boys. When the moment came for Antipas to leave his parents, fear gripped his insides, but he resolved to show no indication and obediently followed the long line of boys behind the priests.

After the heat of the sun and the press of people, the temple felt cool as they walked along the marble corridors. At length they turned into a dimly lit room. There appeared to be about thirty boys and just as many priests. The boys were instructed to sit on the floor around the perimeter of the room while the priests stayed in the center. Cleotis and Antipas found places together. An ancient priest stepped forward to address the boys. He was bent and frail and his hands were shaking as he lifted them in worship to Zeus.

In a high whispery voice he began to speak about the rite that was to take place. As he droned on, Antipas stopped listening and escaped in his imagination to green fields and flowing streams. He occasionally heard the words *blood sacrifice*, *penance*, *service*, but had lost the old man's meaning. He decided he should be able to follow Cleotis and the others when the ceremony started.

Finally the old priest finished and several of the younger priests prepared for the next part of the ritual, the shedding of blood. Each boy would have a small incision made in his arm for the drawing of his blood to swear fealty to Zeus. The young priests, resplendent in fresh white tunics with deep purple turbans, arranged small, gleaming knives on a wooden tray. Antipas wanted to run away, but priests blocked the exit. Cleotis beside him was tense with excitement.

He whispered to Antipas, "It's even better than I imagined."

Antipas didn't reply.

The older priests, moving rhythmically in a slow circle, began to chant, "Zeus, god of thunder, hear us. Zeus, god of thunder, hear us." Over and over the chants swirled around the boys in a mesmerizing ring, pulling them into the ceremony.

He watched as several boys were cut and repeated the oath to Zeus in shaky voices. Two of the boys swayed as the knives sliced their skin. Their eyes rolled back and they slumped to the floor. One of the other boys tried to help.

"Just leave them," a young priest said tersely. "We'll continue without them."

When the two revived, the process started again and they, too, swore allegiance.

If a boy could not complete the ritual, he was returned to his parents in disgrace and could never become a full citizen of Pergamum. Antipas determined that when it was his turn, he would not faint but would make his parents proud of him. Even though in his heart he felt this was wrong, he would not disgrace his parents.

The cut was less painful than the oath. A quick slice of the priest's ceremonial knife and it was over. The sting was sharp but not as sharp as the prick to his conscience. He had lied to the priests and to himself, but what could he do? He was only a boy caught in his culture.

"Now swear the oath," the priest intoned in a voice that promised punishment if not obeyed.

Antipas swallowed, tightened his muscles, glanced once into the priest's penetrating eyes, and began to recite the oath.

"Oh, Father Zeus…"

The blood oath was finally over and they moved out into the courtyard, the boys jostling each other in their haste to continue the ceremony. As they entered the room, the bleating of lambs and goats filled the air. The holding pens lined one wall. In groups of two the boys were to select a lamb or goat, slaughter it, capture the blood in a vessel, and then place the animal sacrifice on the great altar.

Antipas and Cleotis easily caught their goat and together slaughtered it. As the animal twitched and warm blood covered their hands, they glanced at each other, Cleotis smiling with glee, Antipas with a more sober look. All had soon accomplished the kill, as every boy was accustomed to slaughtering animals for the family food supply.

As they stood in pools of blood on the tile floor, they were instructed to drink a portion of the blood of the sacrifice. The boys cheered. This was what they were waiting for. Cleotis cheered along with the others. Antipas gagged and struggled to control himself as the metallic taste of the warm blood touched his tongue. The smell of dead animals and fresh blood was smothering him. The bright, slick blood on the floor was darkening as they walked through it.

And the chanting continued, "Long live Zeus, long live Zeus, god of thunder…"

Over the chanting, the stern voice of the priest explained that the drinking of blood was the most important part of the ceremony. They could not become men in the eyes of the law without this. The boys eagerly grasped at the cup and drank. At last even Antipas managed to consume his portion. This year, no boy had to be sent back to his parents in shame.

They were now ready for the final ritual. Servants appeared with basins of water and new robes. The boys shed their bloodstained white robes, were washed with the clean water, and donned blue robes as an indication of achieving manhood. All that remained was to light the altar under the sacrifices. The smoke ascending skyward would signal the waiting families that the boys had passed the ordeal and would soon be appearing on the temple portico.

As the column of smoke climbed upward, a great cheer rose from the people.

"Zeus has been honored," they cried. "Hail Zeus!"

The wild cheering continued as the boys filed from the temple. Fathers and mothers scanned the group looking for their sons. Sighs of relief could be heard as each boy was spotted. Fathers began boasting about their sons, Antipas's father among them.

Antipas rejoined his family amid backslapping and cheering. He approached his father, hoping his distress at the ceremony wouldn't show on his face. His father greeted him with his arms spread wide.

"You've done it, Antipas. This morning I was sure you would shame me. You're different from your brothers and I don't understand what goes on in that head of yours. But you didn't disgrace the family today."

The parties were about to begin. Each household with a new man was ready with a feast for family and friends. The main thoroughfares quickly cleared as people dispersed to the parties. Antipas was relieved now that the ceremony was over and joined the party atmosphere. He put aside his thoughts to be entertained later and focused on the attention he was getting from his father and on the coming feast. It felt good to be in the center of attention. He stood tall and walked with pride through the streets of Pergamum.

Two

Life settled into a pattern after the ceremony. Antipas, along with Cleotis and their friends, attended classes at the temple to prepare for success in business in Pergamum. He quickly became the most promising student, eventually being recommended for further training in Rome.

Rome! Antipas didn't want to go to Rome, the seat of emperor worship. He had not forgotten the teachings of his grandfather and had no desire to become involved in all the practices of Rome. He approached his father, who had become a successful business man without having to go to Rome, and whose opinion he highly valued.

"Father, I need to talk to you in private."

His father frowned, drawing his eyebrows together. He sighed audibly. Antipas had heard that sound before and felt a tightening in his stomach. "Then come to my trading office this afternoon. I'll meet with you then." His father turned back to what he had been doing. Antipas knew he was dismissed.

He left the house after the midday meal and walked through the city to his father's place of business. He usually enjoyed strolling through the colorful marketplace, exchanging greetings with the vendors, but today he was focused on only one thing: his talk with his father.

On arriving, he was greeted by Ostis, his father's old clerk.

"Your father is expecting you." He bowed deeply and shuffled to the back room, leading Antipas to where his father was waiting. He greeted his father with a nod of his head. Julian was standing in the center of the room, arms folded, face expressionless.

"Is this going to take long?" The words seemed like a cold wind blowing in from the desert.

"I hope not, Father." There was a quiver in Antipas's voice as he glanced at his father.

"Well, you'd better sit." Julian indicated a low couch at the side of the room. There was little furniture in the room beside the couch. A desk that had seen better days was resting against the far wall and was cluttered with scrolls. The room had an air of abandonment.

Antipas was beginning to think he had made a mistake coming to his father.

It was too late to back out now. His father would insist he explain why he was here. His knees felt weak as he lowered himself to the couch. He couldn't speak yet, so he sat in silence, his eyes on the floor.

"Why don't you begin and tell me why you requested this meeting?" Julian remained standing, his back stiff and straight.

Antipas looked up, hoping to see encouragement in his father's face. Instead he saw nothing. He gulped and swallowed a few times. His hands were gripping each other. He could feel dampness gathering on his palms.

He looked up at his father. "I know it's a great honor for you that one of your sons has been chosen to go to Rome. I know you only want the best for us."

"Yes, that's true." Julian remained unmoving. He stared into his son's face. He gestured with his hand indicating he continue.

"Well, I've been thinking about it and—"

"That's good." His father shrugged his shoulders as he unfolded his arms. "It's a privilege to be chosen for this."

"I know that, and I want to please you," Antipas stammered. His hands were beginning to feel sweaty. He wiped them on his robe.

"I think I hear some doubts in your voice." His lips curled unpleasantly as his eyes narrowed. Is it that you will miss your friends and family?"

"Yes. No."

"What does that mean?" his father asked irritably.

Antipas began to sweat profusely as he looked into his father's impassive face and felt the chill in his tone. Here, away from home, his father was formidable. He was aware that his father wouldn't be pleased but hoped Julian would consider his feelings and rule in his favor.

Honesty was his best weapon.

"Father, I don't want to go."

"I'm not hearing you correctly, I'm sure." His shoulders lifted, increasing his height. He turned his back on his son then swung around to face him again.

"Your hearing is sound. I'm not comfortable with the idea of going," he continued, eyeing his father for his reaction.

"And you have a valid reason for this strange feeling?" His father pulled over a wooden chair and sat facing his son. His forehead was creased and a puzzled look crossed his face.

"Father, you remember that Grandfather and I used to talk often."

"Did that old man fill your head with his crazy ideas?" Julian's neck and cheeks flushed.

"I don't think his ideas are crazy. I believe them." There, he'd said it.

No response so he continued.

"You know I didn't want to take part in the ceremony when I was twelve. I'm afraid to go to Rome. I will not worship the emperor." He lifted his head higher, thrusting his chin out. His father sat staring at him. No comments, no change of demeanor. There was nothing in his eyes to indicate what his father was thinking. Antipas sat, waiting for his father to speak.

Julian stood, hands behind his back, and paced the room. A frown creased his forehead. He was so quiet that Antipas began to tremble. This did not bode well for him. Usually his father was quick to respond when he didn't approve of something his sons had said or done. His silence was much more terrible.

At last his father came and stood before him. In a quiet, controlled voice, he said, "You are no longer my son. I have no son named Antipas." He focused his gaze on the wall over Antipas's shoulder. "There is no such person." Each word was spoken deliberately, with finality.

Antipas stared in horror at his father, his mind frozen.

"You will not return to my house, you will never seek to see me or the members of my family again. What you do and where you go will be totally your concern. You will leave my presence now."

His father turned his back on him as Antipas slowly stood. He tried to speak but no words would come. He knew not to argue or try to say good-bye. His feet were heavy and his knees weak as he left his father's presence.

He drifted to the marketplace. He had to think, had to make some plans, but nothing would come. He was numb. He had known his father wouldn't be pleased, but he had not expected this. He slumped down close to a vegetable stand and watched his surroundings with disinterest. As night drew near, the vendors began to gather their wares and close their shops, chatting loudly with each other. Finally he was the only one left. In the sudden silence, he felt that all the world had deserted him.

As darkness settled, he felt fear like he had never known before. The moon rose and the stars displayed their shimmering beauty, but it was all lost on him. He became aware of a tremendous physical hunger and pulled himself up out of his slumped position. Surely there would be a few morsels left over from the day's market.

He searched around some of the now empty booths and managed to find a few wilted vegetables, which he threw away in disgust. He wandered back to his earlier position and sank down in dejection. Then the tears came in great gulping sobs. At last, alone, he fell into a troubled sleep.

Gradually the jingling of harnesses, snorting of camels, sharp orders from camel drivers as well as cooking pots clanging filtered into Antipas's mind and he awoke. At first he didn't know where he was, but soon complete realization came. He listened intently to the noise and ascertained the source of the sounds. A caravan had stopped on the other side of the market. They would not be able to carry on their business until daybreak, so were setting up camp to await sunrise. He carefully lifted his cramped body from the ground and slowly began walking toward the caravan. An idea was forming in his mind.

He had a distant cousin who had run away with a caravan and was never heard from again. His parents had cautioned at the time that caravan drivers were always looking for young boys to assist with the goods and camels. Perhaps this was the answer for him.

He knew he could never go home again. His father didn't make idle threats. But how could he leave Pergamum and never see his family again? But if he didn't, how could he live? Like a beggar on the streets? Maybe this was the way out for him. Maybe. If they would take him.

Three

As he cautiously approached the caravan, swarthy men were moving back and forth carrying supplies and talking with each other. Turbans in deep reds and purples dotted the heads of the men. Long robes of many colors belted with pieces of rope swished around their ankles as they walked. Never had he seen exotic dress like this. His pulse tripped at the sight.

From somewhere deep in the camp wafted strong smells of a meal cooking. The odors were not recognizable but whetted his raging appetite. About now, he would eat anything no matter how strange or foreign.

He crouched low to the ground to observe the supper activity and to decide how best to approach the group. His heart was racing as he contemplated leaving his family forever. The face of his mother rose in his mind, beckoning him home, but he couldn't go. His mother must be wondering where he was. What had his father told her? Julian's word was law in the household. No one would acknowledge Antipas. His mind was dizzy with the thought of leaving.

"This is it," he decided.

He rose from his place and walked toward the blazing fire where supper preparations were underway. What he would say and who he would say it to would be decided by their response to him.

At first he was not noticed. Then a young boy saw him and raised the alarm.

"Horatious," the boy called, "you need to come. "A big, burly man materialized and looked in the direction pointed out to him by the boy. He moved toward Antipas, his scimitar glittering at his side.

A new fear gripped Antipas as he stared at the man. He was huge, towering over six feet with long, tangled hair and a beard and mustache of ebony. White teeth gleamed from between protruding red lips. Antipas wanted to run but couldn't move.

An awful roar erupted from the giant's throat. Antipas shuddered. He could not understand the words pouring forth from his mouth. Horatious pressed on until he was inches from Antipas. He grabbed him and unceremoniously dragged him into the camp. He led him away from the fire to one of the wagons near the center.

An old man was seated on a red cushion in front of the wagon, eating his meal. When he saw the duo nearing, he called to Horatious.

"Release the young man."

Antipas found himself promptly deposited on the hard ground at the feet of the old man, who continued eating his meal undisturbed. He finally motioned for Horatious to leave them alone. The huge man backed away from them, a snarl distorting his lips.

At last the old man finished his meal, wiped his hands on a cloth, and sat back to contemplate the boy. A serene expression lingered on his face and he gently smiled at Antipas. He leaned forward and spoke in a soft voice.

"I am Claudius of Terra," he said, "and who might you be?"

Hesitant, he mumbled, "Antipas of Pergamum, sir."

"Why are you here?"

Claudius's voice was so gentle and kind, and Antipas was so lonely and forlorn, he found himself pouring out his whole story. The words tumbled over each other in such a hurry that he had no idea whether he was making sense. The tears began to fall as the story progressed, and he sobbed out the ending in a desperate plea to be allowed to join the caravan.

Finally he stopped, exhausted. For the second time that day, he sat and waited for a verdict that would decide the direction of his life. When Claudius did not answer right away, he began to think he had made a great mistake sharing his story. He should have made something up rather than tell the terrible truth, but it seemed less than noble to lie. If there was a god above, he would decide his fate.

Claudius had looked steadily at him while his story was unfolding. He lifted his hand and beckoned the boy closer to him. Antipas arose and knelt before him.

"Antipas of Pergamum, on the trail we do not care what a man believes, only if he does what needs to be done so that the caravan reaches each destination on time. As it happens, we lost two boys on the trail and need extra help with the camels." He paused, bowing his head, his lips pressed together. "I would recommend that you not share your story with anyone else, as other ears may not be as tolerant as mine.

"Unfortunately, you will be under the command of Horatious, captain of the guard, who seems to have taken a dislike to you. Watch yourself, as he can be a brutal master. You will receive your meals and a small wage for your work. Work hard and you may succeed. Go now and find Horatious. Tell him I wish to speak to him."

Antipas stood up slowly. He tried to thank Claudius, but Claudius ignored him, so he slowly backed away. He turned and tried to get his bearings. Where would he find Horatious? He began to wander through the camp until he came once again to the roaring fire. Here there were several people cooking the meal and making preparations for the night. All ignored him. He decided to approach a boy about his age who was stirring something in a big pot over the open fire. The smell was tantalizing and hunger began to clench his insides. He figured he would get nothing to eat until he had completed his mission to find Horatious and send him to Claudius.

The boy stirring the pot had a surly, unkempt look, but still seemed the most approachable to Antipas. He stole up beside the boy.

"Do you know where Horatious is?" he asked in a halting voice.

The boy lifted his gaze to Antipas.

"Wherever Horatious is, I hope he stays there and never comes back."

Then he went on stirring his pot.

Antipas tried again, explaining his dilemma. The boy grumbled directions to the guards' wagon. Antipas scurried away in the direction indicated.

But it was not that easy. When he arrived at the guard's wagon, all was silent within. He continued his search until he felt he had been all over the camp. No one paid him any heed so he kept turning in new directions.

In the end he heard Horatious before he saw him. He was scolding a young boy, and when Antipas approached, Horatious grabbed his robe and slapped his face.

"What do you want?" demanded the guard. "I thought I was done with you."

"Claudius wants to see you." He choked out the words, holding his hand over his stinging face.

"Don't move until I come back," the guard roared. He stomped away.

As soon as he was out of sight, the other boy ran away. Antipas decided to stay where he was, fearing that to leave would only bring more trouble on his head. Hopefully Horatious would have a job for him to do and an invitation for supper.

Horatious eventually arrived back with a swagger in his step and his head held high.

He bellowed at Antipas, "Get a move on and help water the camels."

With a blow to the side of his head, he sent him on his way to find the camel enclosure. It wasn't hard to find as the smell drifted on the wind and the groaning and cries of the boys mingled with the night breezes.

It seemed supper would have to wait. Antipas was gathering some courage and approached a young man working with the camels.

"Horatious sent me to help with the camels."

"Welcome. My name's Artus, and who are you?"

"Antipas."

Artus proved to be a hard but fair taskmaster. He had a heart for the beasts and for young boys. He made Antipas feel welcome and showed him how to water the camels and care for them after the grueling day of travel.

"We wipe the camels at the end of each day. It improves their disposition." Artus chuckled, the sound coming from somewhere deep in his throat. "Here, take this cloth, don't be afraid, they like their bath." He tossed the wet cloth to Antipas. He caught it and reached out his hand to touch the camel. A shake of the head and a shudder from the camel was the response. Antipas jumped back. "Don't worry, Antipas. That means he likes it." Another rumble of laughter came from Artus as he watched Antipas.

They led the camels to the grassy area behind the caravan. Once the camels were hobbled for the night, Artus showed Antipas where he would sleep. A tent had been erected between two trees and fastened to form a cover against the elements. He was given a blanket that would be his bedding for the journey.

A number of boys and men of all ages began to congregate in the area to settle down for the night. A caravan was on the move early in the morning so no one was anxious to extend the evening activities. Blankets were unrolled amid much laughter and bantering among the group. Antipas spread his blanket on one of the outer edges of the tent's shelter and lay down to sleep. In all the hustle, no one had thought to give him something to eat. In fact, no one paid any attention to him at all, so it was a hungry Antipas who closed his eyes on the hard ground.

Instantly, his thoughts turned to his family. Was his mother mourning the loss of her second son? Had his father told her the truth and related all that Antipas had said? That seemed unlikely as it would appear as a mark against his father that he had been unable to influence and instruct his son in the correct manner. More likely the family had been told that Antipas had disappeared and any attempts to find him had proved futile. They would probably assume he was dead.

What does the future hold for me? What did I accomplish by sharing my deepest thoughts with Father? What would Grandfather do in this situation?

He had no answers to his questions and eventually fell into a troubled sleep.

The moon was still in the sky as he regained consciousness to the sounds of the camp stirring. The others in the shelter were stretching, moaning, yawning, and folding blankets as he opened his eyes. He had somehow hoped that it had only been a bad dream and he would be safe in his own bed. But he was still here with the caravan.

A young man close by looked his way.

"What's your name?" he asked in a low voice.

"Antipas," he responded shakily.

"I'm Demos," he said. "Come, you must break your fast before we break camp. It may be a long time before you get the chance again. Because we were late arriving last night, we need to do business with the city merchants before we begin our day's journey."

Antipas folded his blanket, clutched it closely, and followed Demos through the camp. He had time to observe his companion as they wandered through the sights and sounds of early morning. Demos was probably in his early twenties, with dark curly hair and a massive mustache. When he smiled it came alive on his face. His body was lean and muscular, his face and arms darkened from long hours of exposure to the sun.

There was so much activity going on around him that Antipas could hardly take it all in. He hadn't realized there were so many people in the camp until he saw all of them preparing for the day. As he and Demos approached the big campfire, breakfast preparations were underway. The smell of the cooking food overwhelmed him as he realized he had not eaten since noon the day before.

Demos handed him a wooden bowl and grabbed one for himself. They helped themselves to the thick porridge and poured a cup of strong black tea. Antipas was accustomed to much finer fare, but the smell and taste were like nectar to him. He gulped down his portion and would have taken more, but the crowd of people had increased around the fire and food kettle and he was too shy to push in.

Demos had been called away and Artus soon found Antipas and gave him his assignment for the morning.

"You are to assist in leading the camels into the center of the city and help unload them when the goods have been sold. Come, I'll take you to your camel."

A heavy, musky smell was prevalent in the air as they neared the waiting camels. Demos told him to grasp the lead of one of the beasts and follow the others already lined up to go. The camel flung its head away from Antipas and snorted angrily, but long hours on the trail had bent his will and with Antipas holding the lead steady, he fell into formation behind the others.

Antipas walked with dread as he realized the implications of heading into the marketplace. What if his father or brothers were to see him? Maybe his uncles would be present to buy precious goods from the caravan. As the stalls of his childhood came into view, he had to cling to the bags on the side of the camel to keep from sinking to his knees.

Over the next hour he learned something he had not known before. Caravan workers were to all intents and purposes invisible. No one acknowledged his presence or even looked his way. He kept his head down and hung onto the lead rope as tight as he could. The buyers quickly purchased their wares and soon the camels' bags were lighter and the money pouches bulging. The word was passed along that it was time to join the main body of the caravan and head out of the city.

As they were traversing the main road through Pergamum, off to the side Antipas thought he saw his friend Cleotis and his father. Antipas raised his head quickly and made eye contact with him. It was Cleotis.

"Cleotis!" A cry of joy broke from his lips and he started to move toward him.

Cleotis began moving at the same time, but Cleotis's father grabbed his son's arm, yanked him around, and rapidly moved off in another direction. Cleotis looked over his shoulder, his mouth open and his eyes squeezed together. Antipas could see the anguish in his look. He could feel the hurt inside as Cleotis was led away from him. They quickly lost sight of each other in the gathering crowd of spectators watching the camels plodding steadily forward.

Antipas felt pain in his chest. His shoulders slumped as the separation from his past became real. His father had obviously spread the word that Antipas was gone and there was to be no communication with him. His only hope in all of this was that Cleotis had acknowledged him. Antipas felt in his heart that one day he would be able to make contact with him again. There had to be a brighter future. There had to be.

Four

Dust! Who would ever have believed there could be so much dust? It filled his nostrils. It clung to his clothes and coated the inside of his mouth. It flavored the meals. It crept into the trail blankets. It clouded the air he tried to breathe. But the camels continued their slow steady pace, padding their way across the barren sand.

"This can't last forever, can it?" Antipas wiped the sweat from his forehead with the back of his hand. Artus just laughed as they plodded on.

They had been on the road for three days now. After Antipas saw Cleotis, the market group had joined the main caravan just outside the city and they began their journey. Excluding the dust, it was an exciting time. Antipas knew how to look after the camels by now and had met many of the men and boys traveling in the caravan. Nothing had prepared him for this kind of life, but despite his grief, and when he could avoid Horatious, he was enjoying himself.

He loved waking in the early dawn hours and watching the sun rise. The early morning bustle around the fire stirred his blood and whetted his appetite. They ate well as the owners knew that well-fed trail workers worked harder and took better care of the animals and goods.

Demos raced up from behind him.

"Antipas, follow me," he yelled, turning and heading away again.

Antipas realized that something was wrong and quickly fell into step behind him. They hurried toward the back of the caravan where the slower camels trudged along. He saw right away that one of the camels was in trouble. He was limping badly and shaking his head from side to side. As they neared him, Antipas grabbed his lead and pulled him to a stop. Demos began checking his feet and soon found an irritation above the foot. They knew they could not go on until it was treated and the camel was rested. Camels were too valuable to have one hobble on a sore leg. Demos left to tell the others that he and Antipas would catch up as soon as they could.

They went to work with the salve all camel drivers carried, but it was slow going as the camel did not appreciate their interference. It struggled and snorted and finally sank to its knees in defeat. Demos was finally able to clean the irritated spot and smear it with the salve, but then they were unable to convince the camel to get up again. The caravan was out of sight and even the cloud of dust that followed it had blown away.

It was an eerie sensation to be alone in the wilderness. As Antipas stood and looked around him he felt the loneliness of their situation. He scanned the horizon all around, but there was no person or animal to break the endless monotony of the landscape. He looked at Demos and realized he was thinking the same thing.

"This is not the first time I've been alone like this, but I never get used to it." Demos stretched his back as he swept the area with his gaze.

"What if we can't catch up to them?" Antipas shaded his eyes with his hands as he stared down the trail.

"If we haven't rejoined the caravan by sunset, someone will alert the leaders and they will send a search party for us at first light."

"First light? Anything could happen to us during the night out here."

"That's true, but we'll hope to catch up."

They continued their ministrations to the camel, putting on more salve and trying to encourage him to stand. With great reluctance and much noise, he struggled to his feet, only to drop to the ground once again.

"Let's let him rest awhile. After the salve begins to work he may be more cooperative."

The two sat down beside the camel and a long silence stretched out before them. Antipas, as usual, thought about the home he had left. He wondered over and over if he had done the right thing in talking to his father. But as always, he felt he had no other choice. Thoughts of home always led him to his grandfather and the things he had learned from him. Someday, he was determined, he would find the answers.

Demos at last broke the silence.

"When I was young, my father was a camel driver with a large outfit that traveled the routes from Antioch to Jerusalem. My mother died when I was born so my father was everything I had. On nights like this, far away from everyone and everything, I think about him. We spent many nights alone on the trail, because when he had to stay behind with a camel, he always kept me with him. He said it was dangerous for me, but it was more dangerous to leave me with the others. He didn't trust many people and he trusted no one with me. I was all he had. I get lonely for him and the life we had and the plans we made together."

Antipas was silent. He was becoming more comfortable with Demos but not enough to share his story, not yet.

Darkness fell quickly and cut off the two from their surroundings. Demos pulled himself to his feet, approached the camel, and lifted a small pack from its back.

"We keep an emergency pack on each camel for times like these. Too much can happen to take chances."

He withdrew a thin blanket, some dried dates, and a flask of water. It wasn't much, but enough to keep the two of them alive through the night. It was too dark to look for fuel for a fire, so they huddled close to the camel and shared the water, the food, and the blanket.

As he leaned against the camel, Antipas could feel the even breathing of the beast. The vibrations were regular and lulled him into relaxation. Even the rancid smell was tempered with the cool night air. The warmth derived from the camel was worth the roughness of the hairy side.

The stars soon spanned the heavens in their magnificence. A week ago Antipas would never have imagined he would be sitting on the cold ground in the dark with a lame camel and a young man his family would consider far below their station in life.

"How do you happen to be with the caravan?" Demos asked him.

Antipas wasn't sure how to answer. As he was thinking of a good reply Demos spoke again.

"You seem different from the rest of us. I've been watching you and my guess is you've run away from home."

Antipas was startled at his guess. His throat was dry and he didn't respond. Again the silence stretched out.

His mother's face filled his mind. He remembered her coming to his room each night and talking to him. The memory was warm and poignant.

"Take your time, we've got all night." His voice sounded loud in the still space around them. The only sound was an occasional snort from the camel. Antipas got lost in the visions of home.

Demos relaxed against the camel and finally drifted off to sleep.

Antipas watched the night sky awhile longer and then dropped into a restless slumber.

Before sunrise the boys were up and ready to begin the catch-up trek. The camel was ornery this morning. When Antipas tried to get him to his feet, he bellowed, shaking his head until the harness bells rang.

"Don't worry, Antipas, camels are often like this. I'll show you how to handle him." Demos grabbed the harness, then he bellowed back at the camel until it began to rise. It grunted, again shaking its head from side to side, but finally rose to its full height.

"There. Don't be afraid to get rough with him. Sometimes it's all he understands."

"I'll remember that," laughed Antipas. "I've never seen someone bellow like a camel before."

Both boys laughed and bellowed at each other while they gathered their belongings, stuffing them in the camel bags.

As they set off in the direction of the day before, they soon saw a couple of riders approaching. It was the search party coming to collect them. They mounted with them and came upon the main group shortly. Breakfast had never tasted so good. They had to tell their story over and over as everyone wanted to hear it first hand.

The next few days proved uneventful other than the routines of the caravan. Antipas and Demos deepened their friendship and found they could talk for hours on various subjects. Antipas was still reluctant to share his past but Demos didn't mention it again and Antipas kept it to himself.

While Demos had only the training his father had been able to give him, he soon deduced that Antipas was well educated.

"Antipas, I want to learn everything you know," Demos told him.

"Ask me questions and I'll tell you anything you want to know," Antipas replied, pleased that his keen-minded friend had asked.

After the day's work was done and they had set up camp for the night, they spent long evening hours discussing deep topics. Antipas shared some of his earlier doubts about the worship of Zeus.

"I know nothing about religion of any kind," Demos admitted. "My father never talked about it and the other men in the caravan never mentioned it either."

They pondered the heavens and studied stars trying to find answers to the universe. They came to the conclusion that there had to be a power beyond human power, a supreme being of some sort, but emperor worship and the gods like Zeus were not the answer. Antipas determined in his heart that he would search until he found the source of all life.

The days became long and tiring as they cared for the camels, walking league after league with no end in sight. Their next major stop was Pisidian Antioch. Antipas anticipated their arrival with some excitement as he had never been to

Antioch. He had heard of it from his father, who had travelled there on business. The marketplace was exciting, he had told his family. The thought of his father brought painful memories. He determined to put them aside, as he wanted to enjoy Antioch.

One morning the camp awakened at its usual early hour and breakfast was underway. Demos and Antipas were preparing the camels for the day's journey. The packs had to be loaded; a difficult, time-consuming job. The camels were getting tired of the journey and were not in the best of moods. The camel in Antipas's care that morning was more fractious than usual.

"Come on, stay still," Antipas muttered to the camel as he yanked its lead.

As Antipas lifted the first pack, the camel staggered to its feet, snorting and moaning.

"Enough, you stupid beast," yelled Antipas in frustration as he jerked the lead harder. The camel lunged away from him, which threw Antipas off balance, and took off through the camp. Antipas leaped up frantically and began to run after it. People were jumping out of its way, clothing and bedding strewn aside as the camel plowed on. It reached the cooking area and charged through the fire pit, shrieking in terror. The meal was upset, the boy tending the fire was trampled, and everyone was running and screaming, adding to the pandemonium.

Antipas finally caught up with the camel and struggled to get it under control. Almost as quickly as it had bolted, it fell to its knees in defeat. Antipas collapsed beside it, both of them panting and sweating. Horatious appeared in front of them, rage distorting his face. Every muscle in Antipas's body trembled as he saw the fury on his face. He wanted to look away but his eyes refused to move. Horatious seemed to swell in size before him.

"I knew the day you arrived that we should have sent you on your way. I told Claudius to throw you out, but no, no, he had to give you a chance. Look where that got us. You've probably killed the camel, which we can ill afford to lose, not to mention the boy at the fire, or the damage done in the whole camp. You are a worthless piece of scum, an upper-class Pergamum boy who doesn't know how to live. Get out of my sight before I get my hands around your neck."

Horatious turned on his heel and stormed off through the camp. Antipas lay still, trembling with dread as he contemplated the words just poured over him like liquid fire. The camel beside him shuddered once and then lay still. He could hear its ragged breathing. This was somehow all his fault. If the boy should die, he would never be able to forgive himself.

A group of people were surrounding him but he was hardly aware of their presence. Someone gently pulled him to his feet and led him away.

"Come on, Antipas. I'll take you back where you can lie down," one of the other camel hands murmured.

As they passed the fire area, he could see the boy lying on the ground with someone working over him. He could see that he was still alive, which lifted his spirits a bit. The trail of the camel was evident through the camp. What a mess!

"How will I ever survive this ordeal?" he whispered to himself. This was his last conscious thought before he sank into a heap on the ground.

He awoke to cold water sliding over his face. He sat up sputtering. His whole body started to shake as he looked at Demos.

"What will happen to me now?" he asked.

"We'll get you on a camel and ride at the back of the caravan for the day. By tonight Horatious will have other things to think about and we'll stay out of his sight," Demos answered.

"What about the boy? Will he live?"

"We'll have to wait and see. Someone will bring us word soon."

Around them the camp was in a frenzy to get everything cleaned up so they could get on the road. Enough time had been wasted on the delay and the chiefs were anxious to get underway. Eventually the order was given to prepare to leave. Demos led Antipas to the back of the caravan where he talked Artus into letting Antipas ride on one of the camels.

Soon the lead camels were shuffled into position and the entire caravan fell into line behind them. It was a hot day, dry and dusty. Antipas had ample time to think and worry. Would the boy live? If he died, would he be sent away from the caravan? What would his future hold then?

The break arrived at last, and Antipas slid down off the camel. He had to find out what had happened to the boy. Demos was nowhere in sight, having been called to unload the supplies for the noon meal. Antipas began his search through the camels and men. Most of the men stared at him as he went by. He became uneasy as he reached the center of the caravan. There was a group gathered around something on the ground. As he came closer, he could see it was wrapped in a cloth.

Clarity came to him suddenly. It was the boy. He was dead.

Antipas sank to the ground as the world spun around him. He had caused the death of another.

Five

When he opened his eyes, he realized he was not alone. Nor were his hands and feet bound. He looked around him. Camel drivers were shifting loads and tightening straps. Camels were jostling back and forth with their usual snorting and complaining. Artus and Demos were bending over him. He watched them, a puzzled frown on his face.

"Don't move too fast," Artus said.

"What happened?" He sat up and stared at them. "I know the boy died and it's all my fault. I'll never be able to forgive myself. My life should have been over."

Demos sat down beside him and put his arm around his shoulder.

"It wasn't your fault. I've heard others talking and they all blame Horatious for pushing the camels too hard. Claudius has asked all of us to meet at the campfire. I think he's going to investigate. We need to hurry so we won't miss it."

Antipas stood up on shaky legs but refused help from his two friends.

"I guess Claudius will ask me questions about what happened."

"I'm sure he'll want your side of the story. Who knows what Horatious may be saying." Artus shook his head as he spoke.

The three hurried through the camp. Antipas could hear voices as they neared the campfire. Everyone was already there. Many were sitting on blankets around the fire; some were leaning on packs or standing in small groups. There was an air of excitement and expectancy as they waited for Claudius. The boys found places near the back of the group.

Antipas could feel the muscles in his stomach tensing. Even though the day was warm, he felt a chill shudder down his back. Would Claudius blame him, maybe send him away from the caravan?

As he sat brooding, a shout went up from the group nearest him.

"Here comes Claudius."

With the shout, quietness fell on the group. All eyes turned to watch their leader emerge from the tent area. A sullen-looking Horatious accompanied him. His customary swagger was gone but a fierce gleam of hate and rage spilled from his eyes. Antipas wanted to look away, but he couldn't take his eyes off him.

Someone quickly arranged stools for Claudius and Horatious, and the two men sat.

"An unfortunate incident has taken place today." Claudius looked over the group gathered before him. "I know all of you are upset by the mishap. A young boy has died needlessly. My reason for gathering all of you is to determine the progression of events that led to this situation." He made eye contact with each man as he turned his head slowly. "As the crisis started with the unruly camel, I would like Antipas to tell us what led up to the camel's getting out of control."

"He's irresponsible and stupid. That's what happened," Horatious lashed out the words.

"I will ask you to remain calm, Horatious. You'll have your chance to give your side of the story."

"Just let me at him. That's the only side I want," he roared, jumping up and knocking over the stool.

"You will be quiet or I will have you removed," Claudius spoke firmly.

Horatious hunched on his stool, lips silent, but eyes speaking clearly his words of hate.

With a deep breath, Claudius turned his attention back to his investigation. "Antipas, we'd like to hear your story. Don't be afraid, just tell us what you can remember."

Antipas stood where he was. At first his voice was shaky, but he gathered confidence as he spoke.

When he came to the part referring to the boy, he spoke more quietly.

"It was my fault that he died. I'll never be able to forgive myself."

"Now, now, we haven't established who is at fault. Don't blame yourself. We'll arrive at the truth in the end." He sent a smile toward Antipas. "Thank you for your honesty."

Claudius had several others speak, giving their view of what had happened.

When it was Demos's turn, he spoke candidly.

"Claudius, the camel had reached the breaking point. Horatious should have let it rest for a day or two until it was past the crisis stage. The caravan is supposed to have a dozen extra camels on each journey just for times like these. Camels are strong and have great endurance, but they all have their limits. Usually they carry the packs for five days and then are given two days off to move with the caravan unfettered and free. However, Horatious in his greed, is always trying to save expenses. This time he went too far. He brought no extra camels, gambling that he could make these ones bear all the burdens and save the expense of the extra camels and the boys to look after them. It failed him this time."

Horatious lunged from his seat. "How dare you make accusations against me? You're a know-nothing, too." Spittle flew from his lips as he flung his words at Demos.

Others jumped up and started shouting, "Demos is right."

Claudius motioned the guards to get the men under control. Two of them grabbed Horatious and forced him back onto his stool. The others soon settled and all looked to Claudius.

His usual calm demeanor was distorted with anger.

"Horatious, is it true that we do not have extra camels?"

Sullen silence.

"Answer me, Horatious. These are serious accusations."

Still silence.

"I think your lack of response speaks guilt. If you can prove these accusations are false, I will punish the men who spoke them."

Horatious only stared at the ground.

"Then I think I know the truth. Guards, flog him."

Horatious fought against the guards, filling the air with foul language and flying fists. But in the end, the guards overpowered him. Two guards held him down while a short lash appeared from under the robe of a third. As the strands of the whip struck his back he went limp but made no sound. The blows continued to rain on his body, one after the other until a rhythm was established. Finally a fierce scream pierced the air. Horatious fought back, thrashing and groaning under the heavy blows.

Antipas watched in stunned disbelief. He had never seen a flogging before. He swallowed hard, trying not to be sick. He turned away, his hand over his stomach. He had been sure he would be the one receiving the flogging. His skin prickled, and in his mind he felt the blows and knew Horatious would want revenge. With his heart beating heavily, he closed his eyes.

When Horatious was lowered before Claudius the air was tense with expectation.

"You are no longer the leader of the guards. You are now assigned to the cleanup crew. If there is any more trouble, you will no longer be needed in this caravan."

As he staggered to his feet, he turned to face Antipas. "I blame you for this. You can be sure I'll never forget. I'll have my revenge." He shook his fist in the air and stumbled away from the campfire.

Antipas stared after him. He felt fear from Horatious's threat, guilt that he'd been unable to control the camel, and relief that no one blamed him for the boy's death. It was almost too much for him to take in. He still felt responsible and knew he would bear the scars on his soul for the rest of his life. Artus and Demos pulled him away from the group.

"Let's get some soup and take it back to our area," Demos suggested.

They sat talking while they ate their soup. It helped to take Antipas's mind off the events of the day. The one piece of good news was that after all the delays they were approaching Pisidian Antioch. Claudius had declared they would travel no further today, as they had been delayed by the investigation.

Caravan gossip said they should reach the fabled city by noon of the third day. There would be much buying and selling once they reached the marketplace. After the rigors of this stretch of the journey, it was rumored that they would have a three-day stopover before setting out on the next section.

Several of the men and boys wandered by to see how he was faring. Many of them spoke of the trouble with Horatious and how they were all glad the man was receiving his just rewards.

One of the seasoned caravanners spat, "He has been nothing but trouble since he joined the caravan three years ago. The only reason Claudius agreed to take him was because he's the stepson of his oldest sister. The way I heard it, his mother ran away and his father took a second wife, Claudius's sister. He's caused her grief ever since and his father doesn't care. She finally talked Claudius into giving him a try. He's an evil one if ever there was one."

"What will happen to him now?" Demos asked.

"If he's lucky, Claudius won't hang him or turn him loose in the wilderness. My guess is he'll disappear when we get to Pisidian Antioch. He'll probably join some outlaw band and cause trouble for someone else. It can't happen too soon for my liking," answered Artus. "The main thing is for all of us to stay out of his way as much as we can. He's in a mean mood these days. You, Antipas, should be particularly careful after the threat he made to you. He's trying to shift the blame to you, but no one's buying it, which is making him rage at everyone."

Antipas felt fear creep over him once again. It was getting to be a familiar feeling and he didn't like it. After the others drifted off, Demos and Artus assured him that one of them would always be in sight of him until they were on the move away from Antioch.

The stars once again moved across the heavens. Antipas expected to have a restless night, but his youth overcame him and he slept.

The camp stirred as usual before first light. Breakfast would be frightening as there was a good chance he would see Horatious. Both Artus and Demos accompanied him to the main campfire and sure enough they could hear him before they were even close to the fire. He was ranting in great style and hurling pots and pans at anyone who came near. The young boys in charge of the fire were terrified and consequently were dropping things and generally creating chaos. Antipas held back, thinking it would be better not to break his fast than to encounter Horatious at the fire. His friends urged him on assuring him that he wouldn't try anything with so many people around.

As they approached the fire, a disturbance occurred on the other side. They saw an unusual sight. Claudius was being escorted into the center of the meal area. He never appeared there, always taking his meals in his tent. His expression was serene as usual, but Antipas could see the steely glint in his eyes. He knew some people thought he was a weakling, but Artus had told Antipas of times he had seen him in action.

Horatious spotted Antipas and bellowed a filthy stream of abuse. He took one threatening step toward him when a loud command filled the camp.

"Stop."

Horatious did stop. He slowly turned to face Claudius. His face went ashen. Claudius had been clear what was expected of him and what the consequences would be if his orders were not followed.

Horatious fell heavily to his knees, begging for another chance.

"Get up on your feet," Claudius said in his calm, serene voice. "You have gone too far, and the consequences will be binding and final. When we leave this morning, you will not be accompanying us. We will leave you with your blanket and enough food and water for three days. You may walk to Antioch or join another caravan if one happens to pass this way, it doesn't matter to me. You will not be a part of this caravan again. If I see your face, or hear your voice, or hear of you being seen by any of my people, you will be executed within the hour. Have I made myself clear?"

Horatious rose slowly to his feet. A great calm had come over him. Antipas knew that a deep rage was seething within him, but he was defeated for the present. He surveyed the scene surrounding him and scanned each face as though memorizing the features for future reference, lingering at length on Antipas. With some magnificence, the giant strode off through the camp, heading for the back of the caravan. When he was at a distance but still within earshot, he stopped and turned to face the group.

"I will not take anything that belongs to you or yours, Claudius. Your water and food are poison to me. But I will survive, you can be sure of that."

He stopped short of threatening revenge because he would quickly be surrounded by the guards and executed. But Antipas suspected there was not a person present who would not watch his back for a long time.

He watched in stunned silence as Horatious stalked off through the camp and disappeared behind the last of the caravan.

Claudius broke the spell. "Get back to work. The caravan needs to get underway as quickly as possible."

The camp sprang into action as camels and drivers worked at feverish speed to put distance between them and the scene just witnessed. An extra guard was posted at the rear of the caravan, but the day passed uneventfully.

≋ ≋ ≋

As they broke for the evening meal and nighttime preparations, Claudius met in secret with his remaining guards.

"Men, it is necessary for me to speak with each of you to determine if any are still loyal to Horatious. I know it will be hard for you to tell me if you suspect a fellow guard, but loyalty to Horatious will be a risk to each of us and to the goods."

Janus, who had been appointed leader after Horatious was expelled spoke up, "I can assure you of my loyalty to you, Claudius. Each man can speak for himself, but I have heard of no dissension today among the guards."

One by one, they spoke their loyalty to Claudius. It became abundantly clear that each could be trusted.

"Thank you, men. Let me remind you of the severe consequences of disloyalty. You have seen the result today. I want a double guard posted tonight. Good night to each of you."

≋ ≋ ≋

Excitement overruled Antipas's fear tonight as he realized there were only two more nights on the trail, and they would enter the city for a well-deserved break. He was feeling much safer tonight. He joined the others around the fire and ate his first full meal since the awful experience with the runaway camel.

The talk around the campfire was all about Horatious.

"I've heard lots of stories about him."

"Yeah, I heard he killed a man with his bare hands once in a rage."

"My cousin's uncle's friend worked with him and told him about beatings he gave to anyone who wouldn't do what he wanted."

"I heard he used to beat up on his own mother. Beat her so hard one time she nearly died."

The stories continued. His reputation was well known. His ruthlessness was exaggerated, no doubt, but there was enough truth in it to put everyone on alert.

"Be sure of one thing, we haven't seen the last of him."

"What do you think he'll do now?"

"One thing for sure, he won't just go away without a fight. He'll be up to some trouble. We'll all need to watch our backs."

As the flames died to embers, the men drifted off to their tents, as tomorrow would be a long, tiring day. Antipas left with Demos and Artus, who had agreed between them that they would not leave him alone for a minute. He was the most likely target if Horatious should strike. Darkness deepened and silence descended on the camp.

The wind came up during the night, pushing in a thick cloud cover that hid the moon and stars. A drizzly rain began to fall as night reached its darkest hour. Antipas tossed in a fitful sleep close to Demos and Artus. He stirred in his sleep and opened his eyes slowly. Something had awakened him.

As he stared into the night, unable to see anything in the oppressive darkness, he thought he heard a sound. Before he could react, burly hands closed around his throat. Instantly wide awake, he fought with fists and feet. The scuffle alerted the others, who were instantly beside him. The grip relaxed around his neck as grunts rumbled from his attacker.

"Light a torch so we can see," yelled one of the men.

"I think I've got him," he heard over the scuffle.

As the torch gained in brightness, the men looked at each other.

"It's Horatious. Who's got him?"

"I thought you had him."

"No. I thought I did, but he slipped out of my grasp."

A voice drifting on the wind could be heard.

"I'll get you yet. I'll be back."

"How did he get past the guard?"

From the other side, Demos gave a startled cry, "The guard is down. Come quickly."

Several men hurried to his side. The torch was lowered and horrified faces looked on the body. His throat had been slit and blood was pooling beneath him.

"Check the other guard," someone called.

The search soon located him, unconscious but alive. They brought him to the fire that one of the men had started.

"Get water to bathe his face."

He gradually regained consciousness.

"What happened?" he gasped.

Demos leaned over him with a drink of cold water and a cool cloth. He spoke quietly to him as he bathed his face.

"It was Horatious. You're okay. Just try to relax."

The men looked at each other over the fire in stunned silence. The wind rose with a wail, adding to the bleakness of the scene. There was no more sleep that night.

As the wind shrieked across the desert sands, Antipas was sure he could still hear,

"I'll get you yet...."

Six

Pisidian Antioch. Through a haze of dust the fabled city shimmered in the noon sunlight. The braying of donkeys was insistent as they approached the gates. The cries of other animals housed in pens just inside the gate assaulted them. The babble of voices raised in anger and frustration permeated the scene as tempers flared. A whole flock of sheep struggled to pass the caravan with the shepherd's voice calling over the din.

Shouts were heard as they neared the gates.

"A caravan's arriving! It's a huge one!" A flock of little boys rushed out to surround them, shouting and laughing. The men threw coins to them, laughing with them. The boys pushed and shoved each other, trying to get as many coins as they could. They wore ragged tunics and tramped the dust with dirty, bare feet. All had the dark, curly hair so prevalent in the area. More and more children appeared until the camels could barely move through the push of small bodies.

Artus worked his way to the front of the group and attempted to make a way for the camels.

"Make way! Make way! Move to the side, we're going through."

Gradually the caravan eased its way through the gates and into the narrow alleys leading to the market. Antipas gazed around him, trying to take in everything. The colorful tunics and turbans drew his eye again and again. Purples, reds, and intense blues clothed the people all around him. They all seemed to be talking at once and with an accent unfamiliar to his ear. Artus soon became the spokesperson for the group and answered the barrage of questions fired at him. Everyone wanted to know what the caravan had brought for the market.

Soon the unmistakable fragrance of incense mixed with the odor of live animals assaulted their nostrils. These smells were familiar to Antipas and he felt a wave of homesickness. But there was too much to take in to dwell on his personal problems. By now there were several people accompanying the caravan as it neared the market. A great shout went up as the merchants became aware of their progress through the press of people.

They found a suitable place on the north side of the market to halt the caravan and begin unloading their goods. Claudius made his appearance to begin the bargaining. He was dressed for the occasion in an ornamental red robe edged with gold thread. He was an imposing figure and commanded respect from the local merchants. All dealings would be conducted with him as the owner and leader of the caravan. The guards kept the local people back to make room for the serious buyers.

Claudius's tent was quickly erected and all business was conducted inside the tent and by invitation only. He was known in these parts as a shrewd businessman but a fair dealer with superior merchandise. The local merchants all clamored to do business with him. It was considered a great honor to be invited into the tent to begin the transactions.

When all was ready, four merchants were invited to enter. These were the leading men of the city and were considered to be the best business heads. Antipas waited by the opened packs. His job was to carry samples into the tent for perusal by the merchants. Artus was nearby checking the cargo to make sure everything was in good condition. At the least sign of inferior or damaged wares, the local merchants would withdraw and spread the news not to bargain with Claudius. Claudius would be ruined and they would all be without jobs.

Demos was rounding up some of the camels to lead them to the famous waterfall in the center of the city. The camels would linger long near its cooling spray and drink copiously from the lower basin designed especially for them.

A lone figure slid through the crowds toward Artus. He was on the short side, with a dirty gray robe clutched in his gnarled hand. His turban was pulled low over his bushy eyebrows. He kept his head down but his eyes never stopped searching and scanning the scene. He finally materialized just behind Artus and in a rusty voice spoke close to his ear.

"Where can I find Horatious?" he croaked.

Artus stumbled over the packs. He whirled around to face the stranger. The stranger quickly turned his head, spitting on the ground.

"Why do you want him?" whispered Artus.

"None of your business. Just tell me where to find him."

"I haven't seen him for a long while, so you're wasting your time," Artus replied in a voice meant to be strong but which betrayed him with its shakiness.

"I can make it worth your while. I have connections. You could leave this lousy operation and join with Horatious and others in a much more profitable venture. But you must lead me to him."

"I don't know where he is."

The gnarled hands quickly came around his neck and the dirty face was inches from his own.

"Don't give me that story. You find him or else." The man spit in his face.

Artus howled in outrage and began wiping his face with the edge of his tunic. When he opened his eyes again, Demos and others were running toward him and the stranger was gone. Artus told his story. The others tried to see where the stranger had gone, but by now he had mingled with the crowds and there was no sign of him.

"We'll have to tell Claudius, but we'll wait till the buying is over. I wouldn't dare interrupt him," said Artus.

"Our best plan is to keep on working as if nothing had happened," Demos declared. "I'll get the guards and double the watch again. The good news out of all of this is that Horatious hasn't made contact with his cohorts, so he probably hasn't made it to the city yet."

"That's only partial comfort, because now we have new enemies. We don't even know who the others are or how many are involved. Keep a close eye on Antipas, as he could well be their target."

Demos found the guards and a double watch was set. He returned to work beside Artus.

"I'm having trouble concentrating," he muttered to Artus. "I keep wanting to look over my shoulder."

"I'm having the same problem," Artus replied. "I'm so glad Antipas had just taken some samples into the tent before the stranger appeared and missed the whole thing. After talking to Claudius later, we'll have to decide how much to tell Antipas. He has a right to know he might be in more danger, but I don't want to scare him so badly that he won't enjoy his stay in Antioch."

"Well, once we tell Claudius, he'll decide what to tell Antipas."

"That's true. Let's get back to work. Thinking about it isn't going to make it any easier."

As the afternoon wore on, the heat became intense. Inside the tent it felt like an overheated clay oven. Bargaining was sharp with voices raised in conflict. One merchant left the tent halfway through the afternoon, only to be replaced by the next in line. After what seemed like an age, the group broke out in smiles, bowing to each other with great glee. The first stage of the bargaining was over.

Claudius sent for his assistant, and orders were given for the disbursement of goods to the various merchants. Bargaining was over for the day but would commence early the next morning. This evening, all the goods remaining would be counted and checked again in preparation for the morning. Claudius looked pleased over the results of the day's transactions.

The sun was descending in the western sky when Claudius gave the order to move the caravan outside the gates once again. They would find a secluded place close to the gates where they could bed down for the night. Men and camels needed a good rest, and all were ready to do his bidding.

As they made their way back through the city, there was no sign of the stranger and their progress through the gates was uneventful. Before they arrived at their campsite, Artus approached Claudius.

"I need to speak to you once we're settled," Artus spoke softly.

Claudius looked puzzled but said, "Of course. Come when the evening meal is being prepared."

"Thanks," Artus replied, making a slight bow to Claudius turning to join the the others.

Not far from the gates, they found a small grove of trees with a little stream flowing through it. They directed the camels to it and began unloading the cooking utensils, the tents, and whatever else they would need for the night. The camels were unharnessed and allowed to drink in the stream. Artus, Demos, and Antipas were kept busy while making sure the camels were properly cared for. Artus left Antipas and Demos preparing their sleeping quarters for the night and sought out Claudius.

Claudius was sitting outside his tent deep in conversation with his assistant. They were discussing the day's transactions and calculating the profit made. Plans for tomorrow were in place and Claudius looked pleased with their efforts. He spied Artus and called him to come closer. Artus approached as the assistant prepared to leave.

"We'll talk again just before we depart in the morning," said Claudius. "Until then, a good night to you."

"And to you too, master," replied the assistant as he backed away from the tent, leaving Artus alone with Claudius.

"Come closer, son. I know you have something pressing on your mind. I observed you this afternoon and saw that you were greatly troubled, although you were trying to hide it. Come, sit here by me and tell me what troubles you so much."

Artus found himself recounting the whole story, going back to the days on the trail and the events that happened there. Claudius listened carefully, asking questions for clarification now and then but generally not interrupting the flow of words. At last, exhausted, Artus came to the end of his tale and sank back in his camp seat and waited for Claudius to break the silence.

Several minutes passed. Artus could hear the sound of the camp in the distance and the night insects hammering out their evening rituals. At last Claudius leaned forward and spoke carefully.

"What you have told me troubles me deeply. I feel responsible because I allowed Horatious to accompany our caravan. However, regrets don't solve anything. We need to decide how best to handle this to protect our young friend as much as is humanly possible. Let me think on these things and come up with a plan. Can you keep silent for another hour or so?" asked Claudius.

"I can and I will if that is what it takes to protect Antipas. Since he joined us, he has become like a younger brother to me."

"Then go back to him now and return when the camp has settled down to sleep."

Artus thanked Claudius deeply, receiving a wave of the hand in dismissal. He made his way back to camp, practicing a smile as he went. He would try to speak with Demos when Antipas was busy elsewhere and apprise him of the situation. Everything seemed so peaceful and normal as he made his way past the fire with the men enjoying the evening meal. It was hard to believe they were in any danger, but he knew that danger lurked behind every shadow.

"Hey, Artus, where've you been?" called Antipas in greeting. "Demos and I have been looking all over for you. The cook got lots of fresh food at the market and has prepared a feast. You should go get some fast before it's all gone."

Artus gave him a smile as he turned to head back to the camp center. The food did smell wonderful and he realized suddenly that he was starving. He took his seat close to the fire with a group of men he knew quite well. The talk tonight was all about the sights and sounds of Antioch. There was much planning and boasting as to how they were going to spend the next few days of liberty. Artus listened but did not participate in the conversation. He had heavier things on his mind and couldn't focus on frivolous plans. He ate slowly and deliberately, hoping to fill the time before he would return to Claudius. The less time he spent around Antipas the better so he wouldn't say anything before he should.

The night was like soft velvet. The heat of the day had lessened and a slight breeze had stirred. The smells of cooking blended with the scent of unknown foliage, making the night air fragrant. Men drifted off talking quietly as Artus stayed seated, thinking. Were their lives about to end? Was he ready for such an event? Was anyone ever ready? Somehow Claudius had to come up with a plan that would protect them, especially Antipas.

After another hour Artus approached Claudius, who was waiting for him in his tent. He was wrapped in a large, colorful robe and appeared ready for the night.

"Come in, Artus. I've been waiting for you. Have you met Lucian, the goldsmith from Antioch?"

"No."

"He's outside the tent waiting to make your acquaintance. He came to me an hour ago and we have been deep in conversation since that time. It seems he knows Horatious quite well and thinks he knows the stranger you described. He wants to meet you to ask you some questions." Claudius rubbed his jaw thoughtfully. "Evidently there is a gang in Antioch preying on unsuspecting merchants, with the intent to rob and kill. It is his suspicion that Horatious used his relationship to me to become part of this caravan for the sole purpose of furthering the plans of the gang."

"This is far worse than we thought." Artus shook his head and sighed.

Claudius shifted to a more comfortable position. His hands were restless as he told the story. "There was apparently a plot to rob us once we reached Antioch."

"Whoa, this is getting more disturbing." Artus looked stricken.

"The stranger who approached you looking for Horatious was the messenger. When Horatious failed to show up at the contact place, the leader must have sent the stranger to find him. They probably think he's betrayed them. We're in grave danger, as the gang may still decide to strike."

"What can we do?" Artus twisted a corner of his robe with his hand; lines deepened on his forehead as he looked at Claudius.

"Lucian has come to us to warn us and offer his help. Antipas is in particular danger if Horatious has made contact with his cronies. We have no way of knowing if that has happened. If it has, he will blame Antipas not only for his disgrace, but also for foiling the plans.

"He's a dangerous character. Can we protect Antipas?" By now Artus was chewing on his lip.

"Lucian wants to talk to you as well as to Demos and Antipas. Would you be so kind as to get them? Try not to give away any hint of what our conversation will be about. I don't want to alarm Antipas unnecessarily."

◈ ◈ ◈

Antipas asked Artus countless questions as the three walked together to meet Claudius, but Artus remained silent. Claudius rose when the three came into view.

"Sit, my friends. We have much to discuss. Demos, you know what happened today, and it is now time to provide Antipas with the information."

With a gentleness in his voice, Claudius briefly told Antipas the details of what had happened in Antioch. Antipas sat in stunned silence. It was much worse than he had imagined. While he sat along with his companions, Lucian slipped into the tent. He was completely covered in a tattered brown robe and headdress. When he spoke his voice was low and urgent. He questioned all three, who answered his questions haltingly, not being quite able to shake the shock of what they had just heard.

Antipas was overcome with the news.

"I need to leave the caravan." He stood as he spoke. "I've put all of you in danger. If I go away, Horatious won't bother you. It's me he really wants." He stood tall, looking straight at Claudius.

"Sit down, Antipas," Claudius instructed. "We need to protect you, not you protect us."

"If I may interrupt here," Lucian ventured, "I think Antipas has a good idea. I was about to suggest something similar. I have people in the city who will not only receive Antipas, but who have determined to meet to plot the downfall of this gang."

"If Antipas goes, I go with him," said Artus emphatically.

"I would like to go as well," stated Demos.

Antipas looked at both of his new friends. Their loyalty touched a deep place in his heart. He reached out his hands and touched both of them. It was a small thank you gesture. "I can't spare both of you but I appreciate your loyalty to Antipas. Artus, why don't you go with him?"

With little further discussion, the plan was set. Claudius rose to speak once more.

"Lucian will meet both of you at your tent. Go in peace and may you survive this ordeal. I hope to see you again once this danger has passed. If all goes well, we will depart in three days' time. If you can, join us beyond the city gates on the road heading west out of the city."

The three left swiftly to make their preparations. Antipas and Artus rolled up their belongings in their sleeping mats and were ready to leave when Lucian arrived. Demos left to report to Claudius and the other two followed Lucian's leading.

The world caved in on Antipas as the night noises of the caravan faded behind him. What was in store for him now?

Seven

Lucian had given Antipas and Artus dark robes to warp around themselves as they left the camp. They needed to look like the local shepherds to go unnoticed as they traveled through the night. They had been warned not to speak as their speech would betray them. Antipas walked bravely in line with Lucian and Artus. Their walking had settled into a steady pace as they put distance between themselves and the caravan.

Soon they could see the gates of the city rising sharply to their right. Lucian had told them they would not be entering by the main gate as that would be closed and barred for the night. He knew another way in. They wound their way along the hillside skirting the walls, three dark figures moving silently. The stones of the wall were still warm to the touch after the hot sun of the day. The wall seemed immense this close. It seemed impossible to find an entrance.

At last Lucian slowed his pace and silently glided behind a row of bushes. The other two followed him.

In barely a whisper Lucian breathed into their ears, "Silence is absolutely necessary."

The path dipped suddenly and Antipas tripped but caught himself before any noise was made.

Another careful whisper, "Take care."

Deeper and deeper they went until their heads were below ground level. Lucian made an abrupt stop and pushed heavily on one of the stones. It fell away quickly and he shoved Artus and Antipas through, following them closely. The rock was replaced by strong hands while Artus and Antipas were surrounded by more men in dark robes and hoods. Antipas could hear the shuffle of hooves on the ground. The odor of animal sweat mingled with a whiff of manure was enough to turn his stomach.

"Follow the front rider," instructed a soft voice as they were guided to donkeys and clambered aboard.

The path went along the edge of the wall before rising again and surfacing among small enclosures that housed the city's misfits. The night was still except for the occasional bark from a market dog as it navigated behind the ruined sheds and mounds of garbage. Eventually they moved away from this part of the city but still kept close to the wall. They drew up beside what appeared to be an abandoned shed. All was dark and silent within.

They dismounted from the donkeys and were ushered inside. Once the dilapidated door was shut and barred, a small lantern was lit and a group of shadowed faces appeared. Lucian nodded to the group and asked for wine to be given to the travelers. A bent ancient brought a wineskin and passed it to Lucian. He handed it to Artus, who drank deeply, then passed it to Antipas.

By now the men were gathering on mats in the center of the structure.

"There is much to discuss," said Lucian. He recounted the story as told to him by Claudius. "These two are in danger and must be protected. But we must also set our plans carefully to trap Horatious and his gang. Horatious has much blood on his hands and must be brought to justice."

"What are we waiting for?" growled one of the men. "Let's get on with it. We've sat around for days doing nothing. If they aren't caught and brought to justice soon, there won't be an honest merchant able to do business in this city. I say let's just move out and get them."

"Not so fast, my friend," replied Lucian. "All in good time. If we move too quickly, we may be compromised and the whole plan fall through."

Artus and Antipas sat huddled on damp mats some distance from the others. The day had been long and Antipas struggled with weariness.

The voices droned on and on through the night. Some were raised in frustration while others argued for a more moderate approach. As the first flush of morning stained the sky, they reached an agreement. Each slipped out of the enclosure and headed to fulfill his part of the preparations. They had agreed to meet an hour after sunset this night. Meanwhile, Lucian would gather as much information as he could as to the whereabouts of the gang, including Horatious. All had agreed that Horatious would have survived and had probably even arranged matters so that he would be sent away from the caravan.

Antipas must have fallen asleep, for he awoke and it was daylight. He and Artus were alone except for the ancient one. He shuffled over to them and informed them that he was David.

"Ye're to stay here for the day with me. I have me orders and you'll get yers," he mumbled.

Both Artus and Antipas stared at him in bewilderment. What did he mean, orders? Artus tried to engage him in conversation but all he would say was that he couldn't tell them anything but they would get their orders.

The long day dragged on. It was hot and uncomfortable. There was little talk between the three. David slept fitfully, snoring intermittently, but whenever Artus or Antipas tried to move, he jumped up and threatened them to stay put or else. On one occasion, David seemed to stop breathing and they held their breath, waiting. He gasped and sputtered, moaning and groaning in his sleep.

As midday approached, Antipas whispered to Artus, "What do you think is going on?"

"I can't figure it out, but I trust Claudius and he sent us with Lucian. We'll just have to wait and see. I think we'll see some kind of action by nightfall."

The afternoon seemed even longer than the morning. They absorbed their surroundings but could make nothing of where they were. There were stacks of nondescript items along the walls, but all were covered with coarse material. Where they could see through, they couldn't determine what was there.

"I feel sure these men are local merchants," declared Artus. "Lucian is a goldsmith and I think I recognized a couple of the others from the marketplace. The voices sounded familiar. They must have reached the end of their tolerance with all the stealing that goes on. I think we're in the middle of something much bigger than Horatious's revenge."

"Do you think they'll let us be part of the plan, whatever it is?" asked Antipas.

"It's highly unlikely. We don't know the area well enough."

Silence fell again. At last shadows began to appear in the corners of the enclosure and they knew someone would come soon. David stirred and brought them a skin of water. It was tepid and tasted terrible, but they drank it anyway. Grumbling, he opened a pack left by one of the others and laid out bread and cheese. As he finished, a low knock came along the wall. He shuffled over and removed the bar from the door and several men slid into the room.

Once they were in, the bar was quickly put back in place and the group gathered around the food that was laid out. Almost without a sound they began to grab at the food. There was a feeling of urgency in their movements. Antipas counted seven men plus David and Lucian. As they eased their hunger, they beckoned for Artus and Antipas to join them. They sat down within the circle. The men stared at Antipas, causing a quiver of fear to surge through his body. Lucian was the first to speak.

"We have located Horatious and know the whereabouts of his cohorts. From what we were able to discern, they plan to move on the caravan tonight. We have roused a number of merchants who are willing to fight if necessary. The big problem is, of course, that we are not trained in this. The local legions can't be trusted and may well be in league with them. We have only one chance for success, but it will depend solely upon you, Antipas."

Antipas held his gaze. "I will do what is necessary."

Artus spoke up. "You promised Claudius you would protect him."

"That's true, but things have changed since then. There is no other way."

"Then tell me what I have to do," Antipas said.

"We need you to be bait to catch Horatious."

Antipas swallowed.

"Where? How?" Artus asked in defiance.

"Back at the caravan. We think Horatious will strike there again."

Artus protested vehemently, but to no avail. This was the only way, they were emphatically told.

At length Antipas spoke in a whisper. "It's the least I can do after all Claudius and all of you have done for me. I'm willing."

"No, Antipas," pleaded Artus. "It's suicide!"

"To live a life of fear at every turn is no better choice." Antipas drew back his shoulders. "No, we must settle this once for all and I agree, there's no other way."

Eight

Darkness had settled in seriously when they slipped out of the cold enclosure and drifted along the city wall. It seemed like forever since they had come in, though it was only yesterday that they were looking forward to a few days in Antioch. Only yesterday life seemed so good. And now, life could be over in the next few hours.

Antipas pulled his robe closer around him. He was shivering but he wasn't sure if it was from the cold or from fear. Probably some of both.

The group had reached the gate and huddled in the shadows until a noisy group was pushing its way out. They mingled with the others and passed through unnoticed. Once outside they glided to the left and reformed to head out toward the camped caravan. When they moved away from the gate, everything was still. Even the night seemed to be holding its breath as they moved slowly into the unknown.

Presently he could see the light from the campfires beckoning them forward. There was no turning back, no chance to change direction. They had passed the decision point. Antipas felt fearful yet ready. The future once more was beyond his control, but he had the sense that there was a purpose in whatever the outcome tonight.

When they reached the camp, all was quiet within. Where was everyone? Usually there would be at least a few of the men still sitting around the fire talking over the events of the day and making plans for tomorrow. Now all was deserted as they silently approached Claudius's tent, where a light still shone within.

Lucian lifted a hand to indicate they were to wait while he entered. He raised the tent flap and glided into the light. Once he was inside the light was extinguished. Antipas felt Artus put a hand on his shoulder. He felt rather than heard Artus whisper in his ear.

I would do this for you if I could."

"I'm ready, Artus. I'm not afraid," whispered Antipas. The grip on his shoulder tightened.

Time dragged on and Lucian did not emerge from the tent. The night air felt cooler than when they had left the city. They huddled together, not daring to talk anymore.

At length the tent rustled and Lucian emerged. Claudius was with him and they took the lead away from the central part of the campsite. The others followed in careful formation until the order was given to halt just before the outer camp-fire.

Antipas knew what was required of him. He squeezed Artus's hand, felt Lucian pat him on the back, and casually strolled into the light of the fire. He tossed his blanket on the ground near the flames and dropped down onto it. He stared into the fire for some time, humming to himself. Finally he lay down on the blanket and closed his eyes.

He did not go to sleep. With closed eyes he was totally aware of all the night sounds. Every nerve in his body was alert and ready. He went over the information brought back by the merchants earlier in the evening. All signs pointed to an attempt by Horatious and the gang to approach the camp tonight to steal the costly cargo. Antipas would be the bait to bring Horatious to where the merchants and guards were hiding, ready to defend the camp.

Minutes seemed to be hours and he tried to lie perfectly still. If Horatious was watching, he would want to be sure he was asleep. Greed and rage ruled the heart of Horatious and the men were counting on him not being able to pass up the opportunity to get Antipas as well as the goods. This is where the hard part came in. If all went well, nothing would happen to him. Sometimes plans did not go the way they were intended. He could die tonight. Was he ready? He knew he wasn't, but his choices were limited. He began to remember the words of his grandfather. He knew he had believed in a God who was greater than all the gods of Rome and Pergamum.

In his heart he had believed it too, but that seemed so long ago.

"God, if you're there, and if you can hear me, please spare my life. I will spend the rest of it searching for you."

The calmness came again. Then he heard sounds, quiet sounds; someone was approaching. He became aware that someone was standing over him. He willed himself not to open his eyes. Whispered voices reached him. He knew it was Horatious and others with him. He must not move. His life was totally depend-ent on Lucian and the others. He had to allow them enough time to circle the thieves to assure victory.

Suddenly the night exploded with sound. He heard screams, felt himself lifted from the ground. His eyes flew open and stared into the raging eyes of Horatious.

"Hah, you thought you could escape me, you little scum. I swore I would get even with you and now you are in my power!"

A scream froze on his lips as Horatious threw him over his shoulder and started running. There was the sound of many feet and voices raised in angry cries. Someone tackled Horatious and they both went down hard on the earth. Horatious did not loosen his grip on Antipas. As they rolled together on the ground, something in Antipas roused itself and he began struggling. He balled his hand into a fist and lashed out. Over and over he punched. He wasn't sure where the punches were landing but eventually he felt the grip lessen.

"Stop…umph…arhhh…stop."

"Over here. I need help."

Antipas grabbed a handful of hair. Twisting it around his hand, he yanked.

"Ahhhh. No you don't."

Horatious hit him once more. Antipas moaned as his nose started bleeding, but there was no time to pause as another swipe just missed his head.

"He's getting away. Help."

A final punch landed on the side of Antipas's head and brilliant lights flashed before his eyes.

Out of the haze in his mind, he became aware of the fight again. He drifted in and out of consciousness as his body was trampled, kicked, and finally left alone as the fight moved away from him. The sounds were still terrible, but slowly the screaming eased and finally the night was quiet once more.

He lay still. Everything hurt, but he was still alive. He couldn't move. He could only wait, but for what? For Horatious to find him and finish the job he started? Or would Artus and Lucian find him and take him to safety?

He heard his name whispered softly, too softly for him to distinguish whether it was friend or foe. He decided his best option was to play dead until he could tell for sure. The sound came again, closer this time.

"God," he breathed, "you spared my life through the attack. Please don't leave me now."

He could hear quiet footfalls along the path near where he lay. A dim light penetrated his eyelids. Two sets of feet shuffled by his side. He dared not open his eyes. Then gentle hands began to probe his head and body. A low voice whispered his name again.

He slowly opened his eyes and looked into the face of Artus. Artus quickly covered Antipas's mouth with his hand.

"Not a word."

He removed his hand and slid both hands under Antipas's aching head and shoulders. At the same time, someone lifted his feet. He was limp in their arms as they picked him up and began a slow journey back into the center of the caravan. The torch had been extinguished earlier so the path was dark and foreboding. Reaching Claudius's tent, they entered and lowered him onto a soft pallet.

More whispers reached him as he settled into a less uncomfortable position. He was safe, at least for the moment. It was dark in the tent, but he became aware of several people around him. Skilled hands examined him and bathed him with cool water. Soon they left him alone to sleep.

Dawn was creeping through the tent flap the next time he opened his eyes. He looked around in puzzlement at his surroundings; soft bed, big tent, low chairs. He soon recognized he was in Claudius's tent.

There wasn't a place on his body that didn't hurt. He tried to sit up, but he was so stiff he fell back on the pallet. Questions began to circle in his head. What had really happened last night? Was a victory won?

He eventually managed to achieve a sitting position, and finally he stood. His whole body screamed in pain, but he had to find someone, find out what had happened. He steadied himself then slowly pushed his way through the tent flap.

Demos was sitting outside the tent, on guard, he guessed. He jumped up when he saw him and put his arm around him for support.

"Antipas, you're awake," cried Demos. "You are the bravest person I know. How did they ever talk you into such a plan? I wish I had been there, I would have made them stop their foolish talk—"

"Stop. You're talking so fast I can't follow you." Antipas reached out his arms to steady himself, then looked at Demos.

"Sorry, Antipas. I got carried away when I saw you. Let me get you something to drink. Lucian left a drink with herbs to sip when you awoke."

He mixed the herbs in hot water brought from the fire close by. He stirred the mixture, then urged Antipas to drink it slowly. As he drank, he could feel strength returning to his body.

"What happened, Demos?" asked Antipas. "It all happened so quickly that I couldn't tell what was happening."

"Artus will be here in a few minutes and he wants to tell you the whole story. I'll get some water to bathe your wounds while we wait for him. Your nose looks like a camel's hump."

"Thanks, Demos. I think I'll live."

The next few minutes passed in silence while Demos held the wet cloth to his nose. It hurt when the water hit the cut, but he wouldn't let Demos know. Artus arrived when they had finished and greeted Antipas.

"Artus, what happened? I have to know the outcome."

"I'm so sorry, Antipas. We let Horatious escape. It shouldn't have happened that way. The plan was to capture him and bring him to trial. That will now have to be done all over again at another time. We're hoping to get some valuable information from the prisoner."

"The prisoner? What prisoner?'

"Well, Horatious and his gang fled into the wilderness, leaving one of their number seriously injured. Claudius and Lucian are questioning him now.

"He escaped." Antipas's shoulders slumped and a painful looked crossed his face. "All that and he's still out there. We're still in danger, then?"

"I'm afraid so. Claudius has cancelled our stay in the city. We leave within the hour."

Nine

They had been on the trail for several hours. Artus had helped Antipas onto the camel, which had been outfitted with extra blankets to help ease the beast's swaying stride until his bruises healed. Artus led the camel to line up with the others and then had to leave him to make his own preparations.

Antipas sensed the usual excitement of a caravan on the trail. The men were good sports about losing their two days of leave in Antioch, having been briefed by Claudius, who had plotted another route with his assistants. It would take them out of their planned way but would ultimately bring them back on course.

A few of the men and camels had set out on their original route. Lucian would make sure it was known in the city that they had left on the planned route. The hope was that Horatious would give up the search and be content to stay with the gang in Antioch.

Their next scheduled stop had been Iconium, which was known to Horatious, so they had decided to travel to Colosse and then veer cross country to Lystra, leaving Iconium until the trip back. Antipas didn't care where they went as long as they soon stopped so he could get off this camel.

On and on they jogged, the day getting hotter and hotter. Antipas felt the sweat pouring down his body. He dozed for a while until he felt himself slip from his position. He quickly righted himself, determined to stay awake for the remainder of the day.

The shadows began to lengthen, but still they traveled on. Claudius wanted to put as much distance between them and Antioch as possible. The guards were traveling at both the front and back of the caravan, ever alert to danger. But the weary day dragged on and nothing disturbed their journey.

As darkness began to gather in the east, pale starlight softened the evening. The order was given to halt for the night. A stopped caravan has more protection from attack. They found a grove of trees suitable for the night and filed into the area. The guards moved into strategic positions before they started to prepare for the evening.

Antipas dismounted from the camel as it obligingly sank to the ground with groans and snorts. He sat on a patch of grass then stretched out for a few minutes. There was much activity going on around him as the great fire was started and supper preparations got under way. Fortunately, Claudius had instructed several of his men to purchase supplies the first day they were in Antioch, so there was sufficient food for the next several days. The smell of the food began to revive Antipas and he was sitting up by the time Demos and Artus located him.

Once the meal was over, the three friends approached Claudius.

"Claudius, we'd like to talk to you," Artus began.

"Of course. What can I do for you?"

"We know you're posting a guard through the night. We'd like to volunteer to take part of the watch." Antipas spoke boldly, shoulders back, making eye contact with Claudius.

Claudius observed each of them in turn. Then he gave a positive shake of his head.

"You've been involved in this almost from the first. Yes, I think it's time you took a turn at guarding. You've proved yourselves to me."

The three grinned at each other.

"For tonight, I'd like the three of you to stay together. The first watch is already in place. Take the second watch. Report to the guards to find out where you should be stationed. Go now and get a couple hours sleep so you'll be alert."

"Thank you, thank you," they responded, grinning again.

"Young men," he spoke sternly, "this is serious business. I expect you will conduct yourselves accordingly."

"I promise you, we will," Demos spoke for them.

They set off back to their sleeping area, still grinning and pushing each other in fun.

The sliver of the new moon was hovering above the horizon when Antipas awoke. He roused the others to begin their watch. As they quietly moved through the camp, clouds scudded across the moon, blocking its feeble light. The guards on duty welcomed their arrival, reported that all was well, and left for their beds.

The trio found places to sit on the cold ground and began their watch.

"We'll have to depend on our ears," Antipas whispered. "I can't see a thing."

"Me neither," Artus replied in a hushed voice.

"Don't worry, our eyes will adjust." Demos's voice was almost inaudible. "We need to be quiet as our voices will carry farther than we think."

"Do you think they'll attack tonight?"

Demos replied in the same muffled voice, "You can be sure Horatious will be out there somewhere. I don't think he'll be fooled by any change of plans."

They fell silent and watched into the night. It was quite cool by now. They could still hear stirrings from the camp, camels and men trying to find comfortable positions for sleep.

Antipas was wide awake. He still felt responsible for the disruption of the caravan and was glad Claudius had allowed them to stand watch. He watched the moon appear again as the clouds traveled on. He tried to pick out stars he had studied in the temple at Pergamum. How long ago those days seemed.

His body felt cramped and he moved to change his position. He thought he heard a soft noise coming from the trail. It was almost imperceptible, but sounded different from the camp sounds. He was suddenly alert.

No one spoke, but he was aware of the others also coming to attention.

"I'm going to rouse the others." The low-pitched breath in his ear might have come from either Artus or Demos.

He heard nothing for several minutes. His ears were attuned to every nuance in the air. Someone brushed by him, returning from the camp.

He became aware of others behind him, felt their presence rather than saw or heard.

The soft sound came again. Maybe a sandal touching rock. Every fiber of his being was on high alert.

Then a blood-chilling scream split the night air and they were upon him. Someone snarled in his face. He fought with fists and knees and the knife he always carried. It was impossible to see what was happening. The rough texture of his attacker's robe ground against his cheek. The biting smell of sweat and fear hung between them. The attacker was aggressive but Antipas was agile and ducked some of the blows. A rough hand grazed his throat just as one of the guards joined him and together they overcame the attacker. Antipas lost his grip and the intruder twisted away from them with a guttural hiss.

Antipas turned to see what was happening with the others. The camp had swiftly become silent. The attackers had fled into the night. Only the heavy breathing of the guards could be heard. Someone lit a torch and they began to assess the damage. No one seemed to be hurt seriously, just minor cuts and bloodied noses. Demos was straightening his robe, and Artus—

"Where's Artus?" Antipas asked with alarm.

"He was right beside me." Demos looked around puzzled. A quick survey of the area proved fruitless.

Artus had disappeared.

Ten

The battle-weary group staggered into camp. The fire had gone out but was quickly lit with the torch. They crouched on the ground in a circle.

"Is there nothing we can do?" Antipas hugged his robe to him as he appealed to the group.

"It's too dark to try to locate Artus tonight. The guards on third watch will listen for any further activity or any sound from him or Horatious."

"Do you think they've taken him captive?" Antipas asked in a worried tone.

"It's quite likely," Claudius responded. He had been awakened and told of the attack and had just now joined the group.

"At first light I would like to take a camel and try to retrace their tracks. He may have been able to get away in the dark." Demos's voice was thick with emotion.

"I'll go with you," Antipas stated resolutely.

Others joined in the discussion and plans were laid.

"It's only about an hour to first light." Claudius got to his feet and turned toward the rest of the camp. "You need to eat something and be prepared to leave. I'll rouse one of the cooks."

A cold meal was quickly assembled and they broke their fast. Antipas didn't feel like eating but knew he would need the energy.

When the early streaks of dawn lightened the horizon, a party of four was already mounted, watching the trail away from the camp. The guards reported no disturbances or sounds of anyone approaching. The camels slowly swung onto the trail, riders alert to any sound or sight.

They had only traveled a short distance when the lead rider, Demos, gave a shout.

"To the right. I thought I saw a movement behind those rocks."

The riders cautiously dismounted, never taking their eyes off the spot.

"Help me…"

"It's Artus. I know his voice." Antipas looked at Demos, excitement in his eyes.

Demos and Antipas raced toward their friend's voice. Artus emerged from behind a large rock.

"Are you all right? What happened? Did they capture you? Are you hurt?"

"Give me a chance to talk, Antipas." Artus was gasping for breath while beaming a wide smile at them. "I'm not hurt, not too much anyway. I was grappling with one of them when he grabbed me and flung me over his shoulder. He started running along with the others, all whispering how they'd won, and wouldn't it be great when Claudius realized they had stolen one of his men." He took several deep breaths.

"I was bouncing up and down on his back, grabbing at his robe. He started to lose his grip on me and I managed to get my head close to his ear. So I bit down hard and didn't let go. You should have heard him yell. I was able to drop to the ground and roll to the side. Fortunately there were rocks all along the trail, like here, so I was able to sink down behind them. They weren't able to find me so they finally just left without me."

"We've not seen the last of them, I believe." Antipas squinted in the direction the gang had gone, his head swimming with thoughts of what might have been if Artus had not been able to get away.

"Let's get back to camp and report to Claudius." Demos pulled Antipas back to the present. He turned and patted the nose of his mount.

"Climb up behind me, Artus." Antipas beckoned to him. "I want you to ride with me.

Helping hands boosted him up on the camel, and the group rode back to the camp in triumph.

∽ ∽ ∽

Soon after the attack, Antipas began to have dreams. Sometimes they were comforting but more often they were frightening. Most mornings he could not remember the substance of the dreams, only that he had been disturbed by them during the night.

One night he awoke with his heart racing and his whole body shaking. He cried out before he was fully awake. Artus heard him and rushed to his side.

"What is it, Antipas? Are you in pain?"

Antipas sat up on his blanket, trying to remember what had awakened him.

"I think I was dreaming again, but I can't remember what it was. I only know I was terrified."

"I'll get you a drink and maybe you can go to sleep again."

Antipas sipped the tepid water and tried to let his body relax. He told Artus he thought he would be all right and for him to go back to sleep. Artus quickly fell asleep again, but Antipas stared into the night sky for a long time. What had the dream been about? He wished he could remember. Maybe if he could recall it he could face whatever it was. The dreams came every night after that. He would awaken in a sweat, terrified, but unable to remember anything about the dream.

The caravan stopped mid-afternoon, sheltering before the approaching storm broke. The sky was slate gray with huge menacing clouds piling up in the west. By all the signs it was going to be a bad one. As Artus located Antipas, there was already a low growling of thunder in the distance.

"Antipas, you look tired. More dreams last night?"

Antipas rubbed his eyes and yawned. "Oh, yes. I woke up several times and then couldn't get back to sleep right away."

"Look, there's a fellow traveling with the caravan who might be able to help you."

"A doctor?" Antipas opened his eyes wide and put his hand over his mouth.

"No, not quite... ." A shrug of the shoulders accompanied the comment. He adjusted his turban, looking at the ground by Antipas's feet.

"What don't you want to tell me? Go ahead, I'm desperate enough to try anything." He reached out his hand and gripped Artus's shoulder. "Look at me. Tell me."

"Well, he claims he can see the future and interpret dreams."

Antipas laughed as he saw that Artus was serious. "Do you really believe he can?"

Artus plopped his hands on his hips and glared at him. "You said you were desperate enough to try anything."

He stopped laughing when he saw he had offended his friend. "You're right, I am. Where do we find him?" He gestured with his hands.

"Demos will arrange a meeting with him for tonight if you want." Artus rubbed his hand over his face.

"What harm can it do? I can't go on like this. Will you and Demos come with me?"

"Sure. I'll go find out the time and come back."

Artus strode off through the camp, leaving Antipas contemplating the coming meeting. Something didn't seem right about it. While he sat there thinking the wind sprang up, blowing dust and debris through the camp. The sky was more threatening than ever as the storm rolled closer. Antipas shivered and clutched his blanket around his shoulders.

Artus returned with Demos a while later and said they had a meeting with the man right after the evening meal. He had a tent on the far side of the camp and asked them to come there. Antipas was to bring a personal belonging with him.

"Why does he want that?" asked Antipas.

"He didn't say," replied Demos, "but he was adamant that you must bring something."

The only thing he had of any value was the gold link belt his father had given him on the day he made his first sacrifice to Zeus. He knew it was valuable, but he had nothing else. He kept if stuffed in the cloth bag that contained all his worldly goods, not much of anything. He slowly pulled it out as memories flooded his mind. He wouldn't dwell on them now. He couldn't. The past was well buried but still painful when probed. Artus and Demos admired the belt when they saw it.

"This is worth a lot of money," exclaimed Demos.

Artus whistled softly as he touched the links.

"Where did you get this?" questioned Artus.

"It's a long story and too painful to tell at present."

Artus and Demos asked no more questions. They watched as Antipas slipped it on under his rough tunic. When he was ready they headed for the main fire to eat their evening meal.

Antipas could hardly swallow he was so tense, but he knew he needed to eat something. The other two enjoyed the excellent stew and unleavened bread. There was no time on the trail to make real bread, but it was hot and fresh. Dipped in olive oil, it made a great companion for the stew.

When they had finished, they washed in the pool nearby and then walked to the other side of the camp where they knew the guest was located. As they approached, the storm broke furiously, drenching them in an instant. Lightning bolts lit up the sky as the wind whipped the rain in their faces. Fear rippled Antipas's insides as they neared the entrance to the tent.

There was a feeble light burning inside. They called out and then bent to enter. The interior was smoky from the torch and the air felt oppressive. The man, who called himself Ivor, beckoned them to sit on the ground in the center. He crouched in front of them, and closing his eyes, began to moan. Shadows leaped up the walls of the tent from the flickering torch as the storm raged outside.

Antipas was mesmerized. He had the urge to run, but seemed rooted to the ground. The moaning increased in volume and Ivor began to sway back and forth. The sounds coming from him intensified until he stopped abruptly and opened his eyes.

"Antipas, Antipas. Much is required of you. What have you brought with you?"

Antipas unhooked the belt and removed it. It gleamed in the weak light as though it were on fire. He slowly passed it to Ivor, who took it in his hands, stroking the golden links. He wrapped it around his hand and slowly began to lift it into the air, chanting in a singsong voice.

The air in the tent became cold as the voice of Ivor droned on. Antipas felt the chilly sweat of unease on his back. Something did not feel right. It felt like there was a presence in the tent with them. Antipas struggled inside himself, fighting off the oppression. He stood, then took a step backward. The move seemed to release the tension in the tent. Ivor stopped and stared at Antipas. In a normal voice he began to ask him questions about his dreams.

Breathing slowly, Antipas answered as accurately as he could. Above all else, he wanted the dreams to end and their awful oppression to lift. The atmosphere in the tent seemed more peaceful now and he was able to relax for the first time. Even the storm seemed to be passing on and the night felt normal again.

After listening carefully, Ivor told him, "I'm certain I can reveal the substance of the dreams and can bring them to an end. I'll need to administer some medication to you and observe you while you sleep."

"I'm ready to do whatever needs to be done." Antipas's fear and distrust had drained away.

"I'll need to keep you here with me for the night." Ivor nodded toward Artus and Demos. "You two will need to leave as I must have complete silence and concentration for my observations."

"We would really like to stay," pleaded Artus. "We promise to be quiet and still."

"No." Ivor shoved his face toward Artus's. "It must be this way. If you want a cure, you must follow my directions in every detail." He stood tall with fists clenched at his sides. "You may return for your friend at sunup. By then I will know all I need to know."

Reluctantly, Artus and Demos rose to leave. They conferred with Antipas as to whether he wanted to go through with it. He said he had decided he must do so and that he was convinced that Ivor knew what he was doing. They would have to do it his way.

Once the others left, Antipas turned back to face Ivor. The old man was stirring a mixture in a bowl and heating it over the feeble torch. Antipas sat on the ground and watched him. Ivor had become distant again, almost like he was alone. Antipas sensed a foreboding but brushed it from his mind. He was determined to find the meaning of his dreams.

Ivor indicated a blanket in the corner and told Antipas to sit there. He handed him the potion to drink.

"All of it," Ivor said.

The drink was sweet with an unusual odor. Antipas didn't recognize the smell, but it was not unpleasant and he soon emptied the cup.

"Lie down now. Sleep will soon come."

The medicine took effect rapidly and Antipas sank into warm, dark sleep.

He woke up gasping for breath, his heart pounding. Sweat poured from his body while he struggled to breathe. Gradually his heart slowed down and his breathing returned to normal.

It was dark in the tent. The torch had been extinguished at some point. He wondered if Ivor was even in the tent until he heard the low moaning sounds again. He struggled to stay awake, but the drug took over and he slept again.

He was walking in a cave deep in the earth. Ahead of him he could see figures gliding around the next bend. He felt compelled to follow their leading. Behind him he could hear feet pounding. Somehow he knew they were after him. He increased his speed in an attempt to catch up to the ones ahead of him but he never saw them again. He decided they must have gone off a side passage that he had missed. He ran on and on but still the pounding feet came behind him. He knew they were gaining on him but he could push his legs no faster. He slipped on a muddy section of the path and felt himself sliding to the left. He could not see the terrain but it was steep. He began to scream as his rate of descent increased. He screamed until he once again awoke gasping for breath.

Ivor's voice rose out of the darkness.

"Tell me where you were!"

"I don't know," he gasped.

"Think, don't let the dream slip away."

But it was gone, just like all the other ones.

He sensed another presence in the tent with them, then he heard whispered voices. The new voice drove a coldness deep into his heart. Something told him there was evil in the tent. He tried to sit up but felt a heavy weight on his chest. Again he had the sensation of not being able to breathe. The coldness increased as he felt a slight breeze pass over him. Someone or something was close. He fought with everything in him but it was not enough and he fell once more into an uneasy sleep.

This time the dream took on bizarre proportions. It was oppressive and evil. A quiet thought penetrated the darkness and he sensed rather than heard the words "Call on me." He didn't have time to analyze it before he was deep into the dream again.

The shrieking from the shapes and figures intensified in terrifying waves until he could no longer bear it. He became conscious again and realized that the shrieking was going on in the tent. He lay still, hoping it would not be noticed that he was once again awake. It was then that he remembered. "Call on me."

Silently he said, "God, if you are there, I ask again for my life. What should I do? There is evil here. I'm scared."

Leave.

He had to get out of the tent. The shrieking and moaning were all around him. More presences swept in and raised their voices in a cacophony of horror. He knew he would have to move quickly if he were to escape. He took a deep breath, jumped from the ground, and made a dive for the opening.

Eleven

Muted sunlight was filtering through the leaves, making patterns across his face when he awoke. He lay blinking in its light, unable to focus his thoughts for a few minutes. He stretched, closed his eyes again, then sat bolt upright as comprehension dawned on him. He was alive! He had survived whatever had happened during the night.

His eyes finally found Artus and a slow smile spread across his face.

"Are you okay?" inquired Artus.

"I think so." He ran his fingers through his hair then shook his head.

"What happened in there after we left? We stayed for a few minutes but couldn't hear anything so we finally came back here. When did you get back? When we got up this morning we were surprised to see you. We tried to wake you, but you wouldn't budge."

Antipas looked around with a puzzled frown on his face. He was back under their tent. He shook his head again, trying to remember how he got here.

"I'm not sure," he finally said. "I need some time to sort it all out in my head."

"Well, here's something else to sort out. At breakfast I heard that Ivor is gone. His tent and all his stuff is gone, too. No one saw him go or heard anything out of the ordinary. When the cooks got up this morning, he was already gone. What do you make of that?"

Antipas rubbed his head in confusion. His mind wasn't functioning properly this morning, the after effects of the drug, no doubt. He got to his feet gingerly as his knees felt like water. "We need to find Demos and then the three of us need to talk. I'll try to fill you in on what happened last night. In the sunlight today, it seems like a nightmare."

"Let's go. I think he's with the camel drivers repairing harnesses."

As they moved across the camp, Antipas began to feel more alert. He was beginning to process what had happened and to draw a few conclusions. The conclusions scared him as much as the actual experience. It was going to be good to be able to share what happened. He had doubts as to his state of mind. He needed someone to tell him he wasn't crazy.

They found Demos busy with two other men and asked him to take a break and walk with them. They found a quiet area and Antipas told the whole story. The other two didn't say anything until he was finished, but he could tell by their faces that they were shocked by what he had to say.

The questions tumbled out when he finally stopped talking.

"We need to take this story to Claudius," Artus exclaimed.

"He might think I was making it up to cause more excitement," exclaimed Antipas. "I have caused him enough trouble already. I really don't want to tell this to anyone else. You say Ivor is gone, so let's just forget it."

After much discussion, the other two agreed to keep it to themselves.

"When are we leaving?" asked Antipas. "What I need is to get back to work and try to forget all about last night."

"I heard the men say we would leave once all the harnesses are repaired. Claudius wants to put more distance between us and Antioch today."

All three headed for the camels and joined in the preparations. It was late morning when they set out. The sky was clear after the storm of the evening before. They should be able to make good time for the remainder of the day.

～ ～ ～

Claudius rode his prized donkey and wandered up and down the caravan, checking the progress of the camels and the goods. He had heard rumors of the happenings of last night and wanted to keep an eye on Antipas. He knew the boy would come to him when he was ready. In the meantime, he would observe and listen.

"Something's not right," reflected Claudius. "Where has Ivor gone? I felt a repulsion when he approached me and asked to join the caravan, but I couldn't think of any reason why I should say no. I should have refused. All this talk of demons, and potions, and strange noises and smells, nothing substantial, but where there are rumors there's usually some truth. The men are a superstitious lot but essentially honest."

Everything seemed routine through the length of the caravan and Claudius soon put his mind to other matters requiring his attention. Later he would return to the problem and give it more thought. For now, he had a caravan to run and a detour to navigate.

Twelve

Colosse seemed a long way away as one monotonous day followed another. The land lay barren and rough along their seldom-traveled route. Heat and humidity continued day after day with monotonous repetition. The sun was a brassy disc flaming in an empty expanse. Vetch and glastum were stunted from the heat of the sun and showed no blossoms. Everything was coated with sand ground so finely that it lay as a thick layer of dust.

The men were restless as they longed for the end of this section of the journey. With each passing day the camels got more ornery. Only yesterday a nasty brute had bitten its driver. Fortunately the skin hadn't been broken and no infection had set in. A camel bite could be dangerous, especially this far from civilization.

Demos appeared, his black, curly hair soaked with sweat and his entire body filthy.

"I hate this feeling," he groaned as he wiped his face with the edge of his tunic. "I can't believe we haven't found water in three days."

"I guess we should be thankful we're still carrying enough to slake our thirst, but it would be nice to have enough for our hands and bodies." Antipas rubbed his grimy face, taking off his turban to shake out the grit. He kicked his sandals from his burning feet. As he stretched his tired body, a listless insect buzzed around his head. He swatted at it lazily and it drifted away.

Antipas sank to the ground where they had paused for the midday meal. There would be no fire today as they needed to cover more ground before nightfall.

Demos dropped down beside him without a word. They were both too tired even to talk. Antipas leaned back and closed his eyes. Though hot, he was relaxed. Since the night in Ivor's tent, he hadn't had one of his dreams. Either Ivor had cured him or the prayer he sent up to God had made a difference. Even Horatious was a distant memory today. Nothing had been seen or heard of him since the night of the attack. As each day passed, Antipas felt more at ease. Maybe things were going to work out for him after all.

All too soon, the call was given to prepare to leave. Artus, who had been called to repair a camel pack, returned and the three friends were soon ready to go. Just a few more hours on the trail and there should be a welcoming pool and some shade. Tonight should be good. Claudius had said they would stay at least a day and allow the camels and men to get some extra rest and to check the whole caravan for any needed repairs.

They would then be ready for the next section of their journey. The stories being told indicated this would be the worst leg yet. The old trail wound through rocky outcroppings before ascending into the mountains. It would be rough going and they needed to have everything in the best possible shape. The camels would protest vigorously when they had to traverse the rocky path. It would take all of the men's skill, not to mention patience, to get them safely through.

Just before nightfall the trees were spotted and the call was sounded. The camels could sense water and food and picked up their feet in anticipation. The men, too, felt a lifting of their spirits as they forced the camels to slow their pace to avoid a stampede. The camel packs would need to be unloaded before the animals were led to water and allowed to wallow and drink.

The caravan came to a halt beneath a grove of trees with a good-sized pool. The shade lessened the heat of the day and was a welcome relief to men and beasts. The men hurried with the packs, and with much bellowing and shoving the camels splashed into the water. The men would have to wait a while before they, too, could sink into the coolness of the pool.

A fire was soon blazing in the center of the camp and the fragrance of cooking stew wafted through the air. It would be a feast tonight. There would be time to cook a proper meal, as they would not be traveling tomorrow, and a day of rest would put them in a better mood for facing what lay ahead. No one wanted to venture on the trail with tired, hot, nasty camels.

Once the tents were set up, the signal was given for the men to head for the water. By this time the camels had been led out to feed and the men were free for a time. Antipas sighed with pleasure as his body sank into the water. Demos ran in beside him and started splashing. The fight was on. Several of the men joined in. After the long days on the trail, they were like children. Laughter and shouting rang through the camp as one after another they were dunked.

The call for the meal ended the play, and they came out of the water to approach the fire. Bowls of hot stew, flavored with ginger and turmeric, were snatched from the hands of the cooks and eagerly devoured. Antipas licked his lips to savor every bit of the fragrant ginger. They were relaxed tonight. They lingered around the fire after the meal, telling stories. As the evening wore on the stories became more fantastic as they tried to outdo each other.

One of the older men, Jonas, said he had heard a story from a man he met a couple of years ago in Ephesus.

"Tell us the story," begged one of the others.

"Well, okay." Jonas curled his robe about his legs, grinning at the group. He wiped his mouth, cleared his throat, and threw out his arms to begin. "This man was a traveler and had been everywhere. He said he was born in Jerusalem, but his father immigrated to Ephesus when he was a boy. He was a Jew and always wanted to return to Jerusalem to see the temple where he had gone as a lad."

"Yeah, all the Jews I know talk about going to Jerusalem as if that were something great," growled one of the men.

"Don't interrupt," demanded another. "Go on with your story, Jonas."

"So when he had the chance to go on business, he was delighted. When he got to Jerusalem, there was some kind of a celebration going on. If you know any Jews, you know they are always celebrating something."

"Yeah, I know some Jews and you're right, they have holidays all the time. I never could figure out what they were all about," said one of the others.

"Well anyway, there was something going on when this guy got there. He had a hard time finding a place to stay but finally got one, then set out to see the temple. He said there were hundreds of people in and around the temple, all pushing and shoving trying to get in. He joined the throng and was moved along with the crowd. He heard some of them talking about a messiah who was supposed to come and save them. Some of them were saying he had already come. Others were mocking them and saying they were crazy. Before he even got inside the temple, a stampede of animals came bounding out of the temple and through the crowds. People were knocking each other down trying to get out of their way. The noise was horrific what with the cattle, goats, and birds all squawking and bleating as they fled the temple. Their owners were chasing them shouting for them to stop. Can't you imagine the fun watching that?"

"Might even be worse than our camels," laughed Artus.

"He decided he would keep moving on into the temple to find out what had happened. He kept asking questions of everyone who would listen. He heard a strange story. It seems like this man they claimed was their messiah had come to the temple that morning and upset the tables of the money changers and released the animals and birds and driven them all out. I would love to have seen that. He apparently told them they were making his father's house a den of thieves. That's a good one. I know a few Jews I'd call thieves, too."

When Jonas finished they all had a good laugh. No one being able to top his story, they soon drifted off to their tents. The moon was high in the sky, casting shadows in hidden places as Antipas reached his tent. He had not laughed at Jonas's story. It had touched something deep inside him.

Thirteen

The once great city of Colosse had over the years been reduced to a much smaller market town. The trade routes were now passing it by. But to the men of the caravan, on the trail for weeks, it looked spectacular as they neared the entrance.

Their arrival caused a stir in the town as the local folks were not used to seeing a large caravan arriving in their midst. Most of the traffic these days went to Laodicea or Hierapolis. Children and dogs surrounded them as market people thronged them.

Cries of "caravan coming" could be heard up and down the road. Men and women came out of houses and places of business to witness the sight.

The warm welcome was received with laughter and good humor on the part of the caravan men. It had been so long since they had seen anyone other than themselves that they felt like kings as they progressed into the marketplace.

An elderly man approached.

"Welcome to Colosse." He bowed low to them. "I'm the head elder of Colosse and would like to wish your leader a formal welcome to my town."

Claudius was called and accepted his welcome.

"I would ask you for permission to set up camp for a few days and engage in trading."

"That would bring much pleasure and delight to us as we have few opportunities for outside trading." The elder bowed low again, touching the edge of his turban with his fingers.

"Then we will seek a suitable place and set up for business." Claudius returned the bow.

The caravan began to move again, into the town.

The scene before them was bright with sunshine, smiling faces, and much coming and going among the citizens of the town. Dogs barked and the occasional cat could be seen avoiding the commotion, while the little boys danced and begged for treats.

They were soon directed to a shady spot along the river. As they began to disembark, many of the residents who'd followed them offered their assistance. It was a chaotic scene but exciting after the rigors of the trail. A young man introduced himself to Antipas and offered his help. Antipas was grateful and the two were soon in conversation as they helped with setting up the camp. The young man's name was Epaphras, a trader himself who lived in Colosse but traveled between Ephesus and Laodicea.

Once the camp was established, people began heading for home with the promise of good trading and buying on the morrow. There was much merrymaking around the campfire after the evening meal, but it ended early as the men were tired and tomorrow promised to be a busy day. Antipas's last thought before going to sleep was a sense of anticipation that his visit to Colosse would be a memorable one.

That night, he had another dream. He was standing on the bank of a great river, looking for a way across. A man on horseback approached, riding fast. Antipas was afraid the man would hurl himself and his horse into the fast-paced river and drown. He called out, waving his arms to alert the horse and rider. At the last moment the rider pulled on the reins and the horse came to a sliding halt just shy of the steep bank.

Instead of being thankful for being saved a terrible fate, the rider jumped off his horse, shouting at Antipas to mind his own business. He was in a tremendous hurry and could not spare the time for unscheduled stops. He turned quickly before Antipas could speak and leaped back on his horse, plunging into the torrent.

Antipas gazed in horror as the man and horse were swept away in the rush of tumbling water. He awoke drenched in sweat and trembling. Whatever could it mean? Why would someone not accept being saved from a certain death? The man was crazy, whoever he was.

It was a long time before Antipas got back to sleep. He couldn't get the image out of his mind of the horse and rider disappearing under the gray swirling water. The dream had been so explicit. He could still picture the cut of the man's tunic and robe and the twist of the turban he wore. He had seen a ring of gold with a red stone on the man's left hand. Everything spoke of wealth and education. But the man was a fool. A dead fool.

A restless sleep overtook him at last and he slept until he heard the first stirrings in camp. It was his turn to help with the breakfast so he quickly rose, splashed cold water from the river on his face and hands, and presented himself at the campfire.

The three friends had managed to arrange the camp schedule so they would be on breakfast duty together. Antipas relaxed as they bantered back and forth over the preparations. Soon water was heating for the morning hot drink and meat was sizzling, ready to be placed in the flat bread baking over the fire. The smells were tantalizing and as they curled over the camp, men began to appear in anticipation of the morning meal.

The talk was all about what the day would hold. As usual it was work first and leisure later. They made plans for where to set up the goods to be traded, and jobs for the day were given out. Claudius joined the group for breakfast. He would do the trading with the town officials and merchants. The men would deal with the housewives and old men looking for bargains for their households.

Before the meal could be cleared away, the townspeople began to arrive. The crowd swelled amid much laughing and talking. The men jumped to their jobs and sharp trading was soon in evidence. As was usual, there was much haggling over prices.

"Ha. You think I'll pay that price, young man? That cloth's hardly more than a rag," cackled an old crone come to purchase.

"But I assure you, this is the finest of linen," Demos's smooth voice answered.

"I'll give you half the amount you ask, young man, and fortunate you'll be to get it."

The bartering continued until finally the woman bought the cloth and left, hugging it to her closely with bright eyes sparkling.

Antipas overheard her say, "I've struck a good bargain today. The young man wasn't sharp enough for me."

As the morning proceeded, Antipas found himself dealing with an old, wrinkled man. He reminded him of his grandfather and therefore he had trouble pushing a hard bargain. But soon he realized this was an insult to the old man and he tightened up his approach. The man visibly brightened and Antipas could see he felt he was still of some worth to his family. He left with his shoulders high, knowing he had won a hard bargain.

Antipas looked up in time to see his new acquaintance of yesterday entering the camp. Epaphras scanned the crowd until he spied Antipas. He waved and headed in his direction.

"Antipas, I was looking for you. Are you free later in the day? I'd like to spend some time with you, if you are."

"We should be through by late afternoon."

They made plans to meet at sunset. The rest of the day passed quickly as men, women, and children came and went with a steady pace. By late afternoon, the camp was once again quiet.

Claudius gave the word for the men to leave their posts and spend the rest of the day in leisure. "All I ask is that everyone appear for breakfast, as tomorrow we will assess the needs of the caravan, supplies and repairs, and portion out the work. He promised them that they would only work part of each day, allowing time to explore the town.

Antipas returned to his tent to prepare for his meeting with Epaphras. Demos and Artus had opted to spend the rest of their time catching up on sleep. As Antipas exited the tent, he saw his new friend approaching. He called a greeting and moved to meet him.

Epaphras asked, "Would you mind coming to my home for the evening meal?"

"I would be honored to do so," replied Antipas.

"There will be a few others there and you will hear some interesting discussions."

Antipas had only heard caravanners' discussions around the campfire for the past several months so he eagerly looked forward to educated conversation. As they approached the house, Antipas felt almost shy. He had not been in a house for a long time. He was not sure he would remember how to act. But his anticipation was high as they entered through the gate.

Fourteen

The same as that of Jesus Christ," a fiery young man was exclaiming as Antipas and Epaphras entered the coolness of the home.

The speaker stopped as he saw Epaphras entering with a stranger.

"We were wondering when you would arrive," the young man said. "While we were waiting, we were discussing Paul's last letter. There's some weighty stuff in there that needs your interpretation. But I talk too much. Please introduce us to your guest."

Epaphras smiled as he approached with Antipas behind him.

"You do like to talk, don't you Gaius? I'm not sure what I would do without you and your enthusiasm. Meet my new friend, Antipas. Antipas, this is Gaius. Who else is here? Greetings my friends. Rueben, Clement, Zirca, Levi," he said as he made his way around the room, greeting them individually. He introduced Antipas, adding a personal encouraging word to each man present.

A servant slipped silently into the room and indicated the meal was prepared. As they entered the dining area, another group arrived, this one containing two women. When they finally took their places on the mats around the low table, there were twelve in attendance.

The talk centered around Epaphras's last visit to Ephesus and his meeting with someone named Paul. Antipas listened intently. They almost seemed to worship this person called Paul. The lively conversation swirled around him. He began to pick out the name Jesus. They spoke the name with reverence.

The meal was reminiscent of his home in Pergamum. His father's table was well known and it had been an honor to be invited to partake of a meal there. Several familiar dishes were being served by the servants as well as a large number of enticing concoctions he had never before sampled.

The conversation flowed as they ate. He sensed an excitement in their voices and a passion he wasn't used to hearing. What was it that so excited them? He wanted to hear more.

As the meal progressed and his appetite was assuaged, he started observing the guests and the host. It was obvious the host was a wealthy man. The home was rich and the meal beyond compare. But the guests. Some of them were obviously not of Epaphras's class and standing, yet he treated each one with an equal respect. Something was wrong here, and yet everything felt right.

"Now that doesn't make any sense," he thought.

Gaius spoke again, "Epaphras, please explain this letter to us. How are we to consider others better than ourselves, and how could we ever have the attitude of Christ? I don't get this whole letter. It seems contradictory to say Christ was God but didn't consider himself equal to God. What is Paul saying?"

"Let's take it one step at a time and digest what Paul is writing. I wish all of you could hear him for yourselves. Just hearing my reports and reading a few letters isn't the same as actually sitting at his feet hearing it from his own lips. But I will do the best I can to explain things to you."

For the next two hours, Epaphras talked while the others listened, asking questions frequently, inserting comments. There were a few arguments as some did not agree with each other, but Epaphras patiently explained things to them.

Antipas was overwhelmed. He understood only some of what was being said, but something inside of him was saying over and over, "This is what you have been looking for." He heard about Christ's coming and what that meant to each of them. He heard about His death and resurrection. He heard about sin for the first time in his life.

"Epaphras, may I ask a question?" Antipas ventured.

"Certainly, Antipas."

"Why did this Jesus come to earth? I don't understand why one man would die for people he didn't even know."

"That's a good question. Let me answer it this way. When God created the world, he created man with the ability to choose. Unfortunately man chose to disobey God. That broke a beautiful relationship between man and God. The only way the relationship could be restored was for a sacrifice to be made. The only one who could make this sacrifice was Jesus, God's son. Does that help to answer your question?"

"It certainly gives me much to think about," Antipas replied. "This is new thinking for me." He lapsed into silence again and continued to be absorbed in the conversation. He kept going over in his mind that Christ had died for mankind.

"That includes me. Can it really be true?" he thought.

Things his grandfather had said to him began to come back. There was a better way to live life, more to life than titles, riches, idol worship. Before the evening was over, he had made the decision that he had to go to Ephesus himself and talk to this man Paul.

Fifteen

His mind wandered away from the talk around him. He needed to get away and think about things. He once more became aware of what was being said as Epaphras closed his speech by saying, "Brothers and sisters, that is why we must love one another, because love is from God, and He first loved us by sending Jesus to free us from our sins.

"We need to talk to God before we leave this place. I want you to pray for Paul, as his health has not been the best and the persecution is heating up again. Pray that he will be strong and put his whole trust in the Lord.

"Now, I know you have some requests. I know that Joanna has not been feeling well. What other things do you have that you need to bring before God?"

The next several minutes were spent in sharing about hurting people, sick relatives and friends, and personal requests. Antipas was touched by their concern for each other and by their confidence that God would be interested in these concerns.

The meeting broke up soon after the prayer time. All the people present came to him and told him how happy they were that he had joined them this night. They even asked him to come again. When the last one had gone, Epaphras told him he would accompany him back to the caravan.

The two slipped out of the house into the cool evening air. The sky was clear and full of stars. There was such peace in the air that Antipas could feel it. They walked without speaking for several minutes. Epaphras finally broke the silence.

"Antipas, you heard many things tonight. Did any of it make sense to you?"

Antipas wasn't sure how to respond. He had so many questions he didn't know which one to ask first.

"I truly have never heard anything like this before except for things my grandfather told me when I was young. I have so many questions, but also so many fears. I would like to know more, but I don't think I'm good enough to be a part of this."

There was a sadness to his words as well as a deep longing.

"That's a good start, friend." Epaphras began to explain the message of Christ to Antipas, just as Paul had explained it to him.

"Do you think I could go to Ephesus and hear Paul for myself?" asked Antipas.

"I'm going again on business in a few days and you are more than welcome to come with me. But what about the caravan?"

"I would like to leave the caravan. I have a little money put aside and we will be paid again in a couple of days. It will be enough to keep me for a while. I must see Paul!"

"Then it's settled. I will come for you in two days at sundown. We will stay here for the night and leave just before sunup. I have horses and wagons so transportation will be no problem. My friend, it will be good to have you along. We can speak more of Paul and his teachings on the trail."

So it was decided. Another chapter of Antipas's life was closing but the future seemed to hold more hope than had been his share in the last several months.

Sixteen

The morning dawned bright and chilly. The sun had not yet risen, but the sky was streaked with pinks and purples as they departed Colosse. Antipas gazed around him with a profound sense of wonder. He was no longer with the caravan. He was on the road to an entirely new life, one that was completely unknown to him, but felt so right.

As they journeyed they talked, discussing the things Epaphras had learned from Paul. Antipas was filled with a hunger to know more. He was convinced he had made the right decision to find Paul and hear for himself.

He dozed in the saddle as the horse plodded along. He hadn't felt this relaxed since he was a boy. That seemed a lifetime ago. The life he had led for the last while had aged him far beyond his biological years. Experience is the great teacher in life. As he drifted in and out, thoughts of his family filtered through his conscious thoughts. It was doubtful he would ever see them again, especially if he should become involved with this Paul and the new teachings he had been hearing. His father would never relent. Paul—and Antipas by association—would be considered a criminal in his father's mind.

The day had begun cool but quickly reached sweltering heights. Heat shimmered in the distance, encompassing everything in its embrace. A swarm of insects buzzed around the horses, making them irritable. Antipas glanced at his companion, wondering when they would pause for the midday break. Epaphras seemed to be deep in thought as well, but he looked up at Antipas's glance and indicated there was a good stopping place just ahead.

Within a few minutes a welcoming grove of trees could be seen in the distance. The horses picked up speed and headed for the shade. Antipas gratefully slid from the saddle when the horse stopped well within the trees.

His anticipation was mounting even though he was tired. He had a million questions for Epaphras, who answered patiently to the best of his knowledge. It wouldn't be long before they reached Ephesus. Epaphras had a few stops to make on the way as business still had to be conducted. Antipas understood and tried to help Epaphras whenever possible. Epaphras told him he was a quick learner and was welcome to join him as his helper if he would like. Antipas appreciated his offer but decided to wait until he met Paul and talked to him. Somehow he felt his future was tied in with Paul.

Once the horses were watered and rested and Antipas and Epaphras had partaken of a small meal, they were on their way again. The sky blazed its coppery hue and poured down waves of heat. Antipas had never experienced heat as intense as this. Always on the caravan trail there had been places to climb in the wagons when the heat was overwhelming. Epaphras assured him that it would not be long before they would stop again. There was a village coming up where business was always conducted.

Silence fell between them as they traveled the remaining distance to the village. The barking of dogs was their first indication that they were nearing their destination.

"What's the name of the village?" inquired Antipas.

"It's the old town of Selçuk," replied Epaphras. "It has a long history as a stopping place between Colosse and Ephesus. I have tarried here many a day resting and visiting with the locals. They are simple folk but steeped in the art of hospitality. Many of them are of Jewish origin whose ancestors arrived here too long ago to remember. You can't get away from them without a cup of their famous sage tea."

"Sage tea? I don't believe I've ever encountered it before. Is it drinkable?"

"It's not only drinkable, it's delicious. They grow and dry the sage themselves. It would be an offense to them if we refused their offer of tea."

"I would not want to offend them, so I will drink the tea even if it's undrinkable." remarked Antipas.

The clamor of the dogs had increased by this time and huts were visible in the distance. Small boys accompanied the dogs to escort the pair into the village. There was evidence of poverty everywhere, but the children looked healthy and energetic. They stopped beside the village well and rested their horses.

From one of the nearer huts, a young woman appeared bearing a pitcher. She approached them and spoke shyly to Epaphras.

"Would you like water for yourselves and your horses?"

"Yes, please, Eunice. Thank you for thinking of our welfare. Have you been well since I was last here?"

"Yes, thank you."

"Is your father well?"

"Yes, but he is out with his sheep in the far pasture and won't be home until dark."

This seemed like a long speech for Eunice and she promptly stopped talking. She was graceful, with an arresting face. It was delicate in structure with large dark eyes. Her clothing was simple but colorful, becoming to her obvious beauty. A pink tinge brightened her cheeks, and she kept her eyes averted as she drew water for them and their horses.

They drank gratefully, making sure the horses had their fill as well. When they had slaked their thirst Epaphras once again began talking to the girl.

"Eunice, I would like you to meet my new friend, Antipas. He is traveling with me to Ephesus to hear Paul speak."

The girl glanced surreptitiously at Antipas and mumbled a greeting. After telling Epaphras that he was welcome to wait for her father, she fled into the hut.

Epaphras assured him that it was acceptable to await the return of Eunice's father, so they turned and walked toward the home. Epaphras suggested they mount the stairs on the side of the hut and wait on the rooftop terrace. There were low seats along the sides where they soon made themselves comfortable. Small shade trees struggled to grow in clay pots but managed to provide some relief from the heat.

From this perch, they had a good view of the entire village. There were not many people visible in the heat of the day. Eunice, Epaphras said, would be preparing the evening meal for her father and brothers and they would be expected to stay.

As the afternoon wore on, they dozed on the shady side of the roof while awaiting Abdullah. Antipas awakened as the sun began to slant to the western horizon. He stretched himself awake and rose to watch the road. In the distance he could see a flock of sheep led by a shaggy shepherd. He turned quickly and shook Epaphras's shoulder.

"Someone's coming."

Epaphras sat up, looking over the edge.

"It's Abdulla." He jumped up, shouted, and waved until he was seen and recognized. Abdulla waved as he hurried toward the house.

"Epaphras, my friend, you are welcome beyond measure."

"Greetings, friend Abdullah, allow me to present Antipas to you, a new friend."

The customary greetings took place, making Antipas feel comfortable and welcome in his home. Abdullah needed to see to the sheep before he could enter his home for the evening meal. They awaited his return and entered the humble abode with him.

The meal was prepared and delicious smells were emanating from the cooking pots.

"Eunice has become skilled with her cooking pots," reported her father. She lowered her eyes in embarrassment.

Extra mats had been placed around the low table so both family and guests were seated together. The two brothers had arrived prior to their father and further introductions were made. They weren't exactly hostile, but certainly reserved in their responses to the greetings of the visitors.

Eunice brought the food to the table. She had prepared fresh bread and a savory dish with lamb, rice, and vegetables. The travelers hadn't been aware of how hungry they were until the food was placed in front of them. They did justice to the repast and many compliments were given to Eunice.

After the meal the brothers said they had business in the village and quickly withdrew from the house. Abdullah invited his guests to the rooftop again, accompanied by Eunice. They arranged themselves on the low seats and prepared for an evening of keen discussion. Eunice sat back in the shadows where she could listen but not be observed. She sat leaning forward with her hand supporting her head. Her gaze was intense as she attended.

Abdullah began by asking, "How can you know for sure that Jesus is the Messiah?"

Epaphras excitedly began to answer the question. He cited many reasons why this was true. The questions and answers rapidly volleyed back and forth between the two men, one young and filled with a wisdom from God, the other aging but with a heart that had been opened to the things of the Lord.

Antipas once again soaked in the words. In the depths of his being there was a response. He was starting to believe that Jesus was God. Everything that was said rang true in his heart. But deep feelings of unworthiness closed over him and although he felt stirrings in his heart, he knew he was not good enough to be a part of this. Surely a worshipper of Zeus, even though a reluctant one, would not be accepted by Jesus. Sadness filled his whole being as he recognized how much he wanted this. He glanced once at Eunice and her face seemed to glow with an inner beauty as she quietly listened to her father and their friend.

"None of us is worthy of Christ and what He has to offer. You remember how we've talked about the faith to believe that Jesus took all our sins—past, present, and future—on Him when He hung on that Roman cross? Not one of us could ever reach our God without Christ's sacrifice. Some people find it a stumbling block, thinking they aren't worthy. Of course they aren't worthy. No one is. That is why we need Jesus. He makes us worthy. Oh, if only everyone could see how easy it is just to throw everything on Jesus. Why, one man who follows Paul was once a

Roman guard and was responsible for the deaths of several slaves. Even Paul himself used to persecute the Christians before meeting God face-to-face."

The atmosphere seemed to be electrified. Antipas could barely breathe. From somewhere inside of him he heard a whisper saying again, "This is what you've been looking for all your life."

He moaned softly but caught the attention of Epaphras and Abdullah. Epaphras slid over beside Antipas and said, "Brother, you are ready to commit your life to the cause of Christ."

Antipas knew beyond the shadow of a doubt that this was it. It was to change the whole direction of his life.

"Yes, yes, I am."

"Then we need to talk to God about it." And Epaphras bowed his head.

"Father, I'm rejoicing in You. Another child has come home to You. I praise Your wonderful name, the name above all names, the name of Jesus, Your only son. Accept Antipas into Your kingdom.

"You need to talk to God too, Antipas."

Antipas slid down onto his knees on the rooftop, head bowed before Almighty God.

"God, I believe, I believe." There was laughter in his voice, joy beyond comprehension.

"I believe in You. I believe in Your Son, Jesus. I believe He died for me. I know I'm not worthy, but You are worthy. Thank You, oh, Jesus, thank You."

When he opened his eyes, Eunice was wiping tears from hers. He realized he was seeing with new eyes. Everything looked different. He felt different; lighter, unburdened, clean, free.

Later Antipas could never say what happened for sure, but he only knew that from that moment he belonged to Christ and a fire was burning within him that nothing would ever quench.

Seventeen

After a long night of talking, morning seemed to come incredibly early. Antipas awoke to the sounds of a meal being prepared. Eunice was already at work. She smiled shyly at him as he entered the open area of the cottage.

"You'll be able to break your fast in a few minutes. There's water in the clay pitcher just outside the door if you wish to use it."

That was a long speech for Eunice. He thanked her and entered the sunlight. He was amazed to see that everything looked brighter this morning. His heart felt light and he shivered in the early morning air, partly from the coolness of the day, but also from the events of the night.

Abdullah had already left to take his sheep to pasture before the heat became oppressive. The brothers had also been gone for some time so it was only Epaphras and Antipas to eat the morning meal. Epaphras asked Eunice to join them, which she reluctantly did. Epaphras kept the conversation alive by asking questions of both of the others, who had a lack of things to say.

They finally made preparations to move on to the marketplace and do a little business before they returned to the road to Ephesus. Antipas helped Epaphras unload the saddle packs as customers started to arrive. Business was lively and soon Epaphras felt they had met the needs of those customers who regularly dealt with him.

Before the sun was overhead, they had packed up and headed out of the village. The same dogs who welcomed them yesterday saw them on their way today, following them until they were a distance beyond the last hut.

"Ephesus by nightfall, my friend, then we'll stay at the home of an ancient Jew who says he's lived too long to make changes. He's sympathetic to the Christians but refuses to hear our message. I pray for him daily because he believes in God so fully and thinks all is well if he only keeps the law."

The talk of prayer and laws was foreign to Antipas, not having been brought up in the Jewish religion. They passed the next several hours discussing the Jewish laws and traditions. Antipas asked question after question. Epaphras was visibly thrilled to answer all his questions. They were truly brothers in Christ. Epaphras told him he'd been drawn to Antipas the first time they met and had prayed the Lord would use him to bring Antipas to Him. As they talked, Epaphras exclaimed over Antipas's story and announced that Christ had been drawing Antipas to him for several months, even years.

"I have so much to learn," sighed Antipas.

"But you have the rest of your life to learn it," replied Epaphras. You are well ready to sit under Paul's teachings. You're like a camel heading for a refreshing pool after many days in the desert."

"That I am," agreed Antipas.

They stopped for a few minutes under a rocky outcropping. The land was hilly near Ephesus. The hills looked barren other than the olive trees dotting the slopes. Their gray-green leaves were a contrast to the brownness of the landscape. As they neared a village, they could see local olive grove owners working among the trees. Sheets were laid on the ground under the trees to catch the olive harvest as the farmers beat the trees. Donkeys moved to and fro carrying baskets of the harvested olives.

The scene was peaceful and fit with the mood Antipas had been experiencing since last evening. He could hardly wait to meet Paul. He felt unworthy to meet the great man, but he also was filled with anticipation. He knew his life had changed forever. He didn't know what the future held, but he knew he wanted to serve this God he knew so little about.

After a short rest they resumed their travels, expecting to reach Ephesus by nightfall. As the afternoon wore on, conversation diminished as they grew weary from travel. It was already getting dark when Ephesus came into view. They were both so tired they could hardly navigate the laneways of the city. The usual hustle and bustle met them along with the smells and noise. Epaphras led the way out of the main town into the gently rolling hills to the north. Eventually he turned into a property that bespoke wealth and prosperity.

The old man was awaiting them at the door.

"Epaphras, you are welcome, my friend."

"Mordicai, meet Antipas," he cried as he greeted the old man.

"You are welcome, Antipas. A friend of Epaphras is a friend of mine."

He instantly made Antipas feel welcome. He turned them over to a servant equally as old as his master. The ancient led them through a dimly lit hall into the back of the building. The rooms were spacious and comfortable.

"The meal will be served shortly," he advised them in a quivery voice. "As soon as you are refreshed from your travels, I'll escort you to the eating area."

All Antipas wanted to do was to fall on the bed and sleep, but he knew that the old man wanted company and it would be rude not to appear. He found warm water in the basin along with soft towels and soon felt much better.

Epaphras was ready as well and the servant led them back through the house and out to a tiled courtyard in the center of the home. Here it was brightly lit with lanterns, and fountains tinkled with a flow of water. The place spoke of peace and tranquility. Antipas had not seen so beautiful a setting before. His father's home was well appointed, but this surpassed all.

"Welcome, my friends," Mordicai greeted them. "I have long awaited your return, Epaphras. An evening of stimulating talk will be most appreciated."

"Thank you, Mordicai." Epaphras moved to stand beside Mordicai. "I, too, look forward to an evening in your company. Antipas is in for a special treat both in the meal being served and in the conversation to come."

Antipas soon decided there was no way to describe the meal except splendid. The appetizers and dishes came one after another, each one more delectable than the one before. There was plenty of space between the courses to digest the food and be ready for the next one. The talk around him centered on the deep teachings of Moses and the other prophets. All was new to him and most fascinating.

"Tell me, my friend, why was Moses not allowed to enter the Promised Land?" Mordicai asked Epaphras.

"He disobeyed the direct command of God," answered Epaphras.

"It has always seemed to me that God could have made an exception for Moses, seeing he was such a great character."

"But you see, it's a picture of Christ and the way of salvation. Just being a good man isn't enough to get to heaven," Epaphras ventured.

"I have a deep faith in Jehovah God, and nothing will change what I believe. My entire life has been intertwined with the Holy Scriptures and I believe that God will honor my faithfulness."

Epaphras wisely moved on to other topics. He would continue to pray for enlightenment for his friend but would not jeopardize their relationship.

The talk ranged from politics to economic situations to current events. Antipas was amazed at the knowledge possessed by Mordicai. Even though he was well on in years, he kept abreast of happenings locally and farther afield. He had an opinion about everything and expressed it concisely and with strength. Antipas recognized that he must have been a leader in his prime. Even though Antipas was exhausted, the talk was so interesting he wouldn't have missed it for anything.

From time to time a question would be directed to him. At first he was afraid to answer, considering himself far beneath the other two in both knowledge and experience, but they insisted on hearing his opinions, so he gradually became engaged in the conversation.

Finally even Mordicai began to tire and suggested they retire and continue the discussion in the morning. The servant mysteriously appeared carrying a small torch to lead them back to their rooms. Antipas wondered about him and if he had any life of his own. He seemed to be available to serve Mordicai at any hour. The strange thing was, he seemed perfectly content.

When Antipas reached his room he found the bed prepared for him and a candle burning in a silver holder. Warm water was again available along with soft towels and fragrant soap. He prepared himself for bed and slid under the covers. In the early morning he felt warmth on his face as the sun appeared above the horizon.

Patio doors opened into a garden shining with early morning dew and fragrant with the heady blossoms of an abundance of luxuriant flowers. Antipas stepped out through the doors into the brilliance of the sunrise. Birds chirruped from the branches of tall evergreens, bending and dipping from branch to branch. Exotic white swans glided among the lilies in the circular pond in the center of the garden. Stone benches and tables were scattered around the grounds, making a welcoming picture.

Antipas sat on the nearest bench, drinking in the beauty around him. He let his thoughts drift to this new commitment he had made to Christ. What would his future hold? He had the feeling he was about to embark on an incredible journey such as he could never have imagined. Once again the longing came to him to get to Paul to learn everything he could teach him. Maybe even today he would meet the great apostle.

He was aroused from his reverie by the sound of another set of doors opening. Epaphras appeared and greeted him.

"What a wonderful morning. Did you sleep well?"

"Incredibly well," replied Antipas. "I've never experienced anything like this house or ever met anyone quite like Mordicai."

"Now you know why I always stay here when I'm in Ephesus. We can come and go as we please. Mordicai's house is our house for as long as we wish. All he asks in return is that we take a few meals with him and spend some time in conversation. He says that we make an old man happy when we do."

"Have you ever brought Paul here with you?"

"I have approached the subject with Paul, but he refuses to come. He says Mordicai is not yet ready for him. I've never been sure why he feels this way, but I trust his instincts. He feels quite certain Mordicai will come to the Way before he is gathered to his fathers."

"I'm so anxious to see Paul. Do you think we'll be able to see him today?" asked Antipas.

"He's usually to be found in the temple area late in the afternoon. We'll go there to greet him. If he's not there, I know where he lodges and we'll visit there. I think…"

They looked up as the sound of running feet echoed through the house and out onto the patio. The ancient servant was panting as he appeared.

"Come quickly, sirs. My master is sick. I found him lying on the floor when I went in to take him his morning water for bathing. Oh, please come, come."

Antipas and Epaphras left the old man catching his breath as they rushed into the house. Epaphras knew the way to Mordicai's room so they wasted no time getting there. Mordicai's eyes fluttered open as they arrived. They knelt beside him to see what they could do.

Mordicai whispered, "Epaphras, get Paul. I need to see Paul."

"Yes, we'll get Paul, but first we'll send for your doctor."

By this time the old servant, Rufus, had made it to the room. He gasped out that he had already sent the young slave boy to get the doctor. He should be here any minute.

"Please help me up to my bed," begged Mordicai.

"We'll try, but only if you are strong enough to move," said Epaphras.

Antipas and Epaphras gently lifted the old man. He was so light, Antipas wondered how he had lasted this long. They easily lowered him onto his bed. He gave a long sigh as he sank beneath the covers.

"Thank you, my friends. I would like you to stay with me while the doctor examines me, if you would be so kind. Epaphras, you are like family to me."

"Of course we'll stay if that's what you desire," replied Epaphras.

The sound of the doctor's voice could be heard coming through the house. As he reached Mordicai's quarters, the old man raised his head to greet his old friend.

"Mordicai, what's this, what's this? You should be out checking your roses, not lying in bed at this hour," boomed the doctor.

"That's why you were sent for, to get me up and out of here."

The doctor's large hands were surprisingly gentle. He began checking over the old man and murmuring to himself. At last he was finished and sat on the edge of the bed.

"It's your heart again. We've known this was coming for a long time. You once told me to be blunt when the time came, so now I'm telling you to make sure your affairs are in order. This time you will not be up again, short of a miracle."

"Thank you for your honesty. That is indeed what I wanted. I've lived a long life and my financial affairs are all in order. Epaphras, I need you to go on that errand for me as quickly as you can." His voice faded away. His face was gray and drawn but a weak smile graced his lips as he looked at those around him.

Epaphras motioned to Antipas to follow him and they left the room. The doctor was going to give him something to help him sleep awhile.

"Get your cloak and sandals, my friend. We have some walking to do," instructed Epaphras.

Within a few minutes they were leaving the house behind and walking into the morning sun: destination, Paul.

The air was fresh and invigorating as they wended their way through the countryside to Ephesus. The shadows were still long and dew still shimmered on the grass along the way. Neither spoke as they walked the distance. The usual dogs greeted them along with a shepherd or two gathering the sheep for their morning trek to green pastures.

The streets of Ephesus were quiet as Epaphras made several turns in and out of alleys until they arrived at a shabby house with an upper room. They could see someone walking around on the roof in the early morning sunshine.

"There's Paul now. Wait here and I'll ask him to accompany us back to Mordicai's."

Antipas waited with dread and anticipation. He had not wanted to meet Paul under such sad circumstances. He wanted to talk to him, but knew he couldn't ask his questions this morning. Paul must concentrate on Mordicai.

He watched as Epaphras entered the house. He soon appeared on the rooftop and greeted Paul. It was obvious that Paul was happy to see him. He saw him nodding as Epaphras explained his presence. Paul placed his hand on Epaphras's shoulder while speaking earnestly to him. They both left the rooftop and appeared to Antipas a few minutes later.

Epaphras introduced Antipas to Paul as they set off for Mordicai's. Paul spoke quickly and intensely to Epaphras as they hurried through the town. Antipas was disappointed but tried not to show it. This was not how he had imagined meeting Paul, but the sensible part of him knew that reaching Mordicai was the main thing right now.

He would have to wait until later. Paul had no time for him today.

Eighteen

When they reached the house, Rufus was waiting for them. Paul told Epaphras that he needed to see Mordicai alone and that he might be with him for several hours. He suggested that Epaphras take Antipas around Ephesus to show him the famous sights.

Epaphras wanted to protest but knew that Paul was led by the Lord and he would not interfere with his plan. The ancient led Paul to Mordicai then returned to tell them a meal had been prepared for them. They chose to have it served in the courtyard where they had been sitting earlier in the morning.

The young slave boy soon appeared with a tray containing freshly baked bread, olives soaked in oil, dates, and the now familiar sage tea. Although they were worried about Mordicai, they were both young and healthy and soon were enjoying the excellent meal. The garden was so peaceful it was hard to believe that death might be lurking within.

"Well, my friend, when Paul says several hours, that is usually what he means. I think we should follow his instructions and visit the interesting sights of Ephesus."

The two set off with heavy hearts, not knowing what they might find when they returned. But soon the sights engrossed Antipas. The architecture of the temples and public buildings reminded him so much of Pergamum, his home. Many people were entering the temples, some on their knees crying out to the gods. Antipas was shocked by the impact of this devotion to marble and stone. Now that he served the living God, this seemed so hollow and empty.

Fountains played, dogs barked, people crowded in groups, talking buzzed all around him, and over all the sun shone in its glorious splendor. It would be easy to be caught up in the rituals being played out before him if he hadn't come face-to-face with the truth. Thoughts of his grandfather ran through his mind and how Grandfather would have felt complete if only he could have found the Way. Antipas believed his grandfather was on the right track, recognizing there was so much more to life.

Epaphras broke into his reverie with a question.

"Are these scenes familiar to you?"

"Oh, yes. My childhood was steeped in such worship. I long to tell these people how wrong they are and lead them to the truth."

Antipas spoke with such passion and delight brightened Epaphras's eyes.

"I believe that God is leading you to be an evangelist like Paul."

"Oh, I could never be like Paul. He must always have been like this. I have a past that would not allow me to be like him."

Epaphras laughed softly. "One day Paul will tell you his story. You will be surprised. He will tell you that if he can be an evangelist, so can you, if God calls you to that service. Antipas, I think God is calling you. Don't be afraid to follow Him."

"I want to. I just don't know enough about being a Christian."

"That's why you have come, to study under Paul. You could not have a better teacher."

They continued their tour in silence, each lost in thought. They ended up in the open market and bought bread for their noon meal. They sat under the shade of a tree and watched the sights around them. Housewives bartered loudly with sharp merchants. A small child played with a dog close to them until the dog snarled and scampered away. Donkeys laden with wares pushed their way through the crowd, goaded on by their drivers. Braying, barking, high voices all combined in a swirl of noise. Only Antipas and Epaphras were still.

Antipas broke the silence. "Where can I stay while I study under Paul? And how do I know that Paul is even willing to let me stay and learn?"

"Paul is so in touch with God that he will recognize His calling in your life. He will have a good idea of where you can stay. Try not to be anxious about it. If it is God's will, it will all work out for the best."

As they returned, Antipas was filled with more questions than ever, but today there were no answers.

Nineteen

As they approached the house, Antipas tensed inside, wondering what they would encounter. All seemed still as they neared the entrance. Epaphras rapped quietly on the door which was opened immediately by a beaming servant.

"What's happened while we were gone?" Epaphras asked. "You look happy."

The ancient replied, "Good news, good news. Mordicai is better. Paul healed him! I was right there when it happened. Oh, I can't believe it, I really can't believe it."

Epaphras and Antipas looked at each other in astonishment. Could this be true or had the ancient one lost his mind in his grief for his old master?

"Let me take you to Mordicai," said the servant.

The two young men followed him through the house. What would greet them? They heard voices ahead in the central courtyard. As they appeared, Mordicai and Paul jumped to their feet to welcome them. Epaphras and Antipas couldn't even speak as their eyes fell on a strong-looking Mordicai.

"Please sit with us," Mordicai requested. "Paul and I have much to tell you."

Paul glanced at them and then back at Mordicai. He began speaking, his voice deep and intense as he told them all that had taken place since they left this morning. Upon entering Mordicai's room he was aware that death was hovering near. He approached the bed and laid his hand on his head.

"Mordicai, can you hear me?"

"Yes, it's time," came the faint reply.

"Time for what, Mordicai?" asked Paul.

For a few seconds there was no reply, only shallow breathing. Then a whispery, "To know the Master."

"Do you mean Jesus, the Messiah?"

"Yes, yes… I have long… known it is the truth." A lengthy pause. "I was stubborn…holding on to the old ways. And now… it may be too late."

Tears were streaming down the old man's face. Paul was moved with compassion for him. He felt the spirit of the Lord move within him. He silently prayed that God would direct him with His will for this old man's life.

Paul bent down so he could look into his eyes. "In the name of Jesus Christ of Nazareth, be healed."

Mordicai's eyes flew open as strength flowed through his aged body. Paul helped him sit up, fixing the cushions behind him.

"I'll send for food for you and then we'll talk, and oh, how we will talk."

The faithful servant was waiting on the far side of the room near the door in the event the master needed him. When he heard that Paul wanted food for him, he shuffled away to do his bidding. He couldn't believe what he had just witnessed. Mordicai was sitting up in bed!

"But it can't be real," he argued with himself, "I can tell death when I see it and it was in that room."

He quickly assembled a simple meal such as Mordicai would like and returned to the room. When he approached all was silent and he told himself he knew it couldn't be real. But upon entering the room, he was greeted by Mordicai himself.

"My faithful servant, come sit with me while I eat and listen to Paul. You have witnessed a miracle, but that wasn't the main event today. The bigger miracle is that Christ has accepted me…me who denied him daily. How could I have been so stubborn, so blind?"

"God's timing is always perfect," instructed Paul. "God has been working in your heart for a long season. He had to bring you close to death for you to finally acknowledge Him. But we waste time. We have much to discuss. Eat your meal while I tell you all that has come to pass since I first saw the light."

The old servant helped his master position the tray and then took his place some distance from Paul and Mordicai. Paul wasted no time getting started. He began at the beginning and preached Christ to Mordicai. From time to time Mordicai would ask a question or make a comment.

"Paul, how obvious it is from the Scriptures that Jesus is the Messiah. How could I have missed it?"

"Your eyes were blinded, as were mine for so long. But for the grace of God, we would both be tied to our rituals. But praise God, we have seen the Way."

This was the story Paul told to Epaphras and Antipas. They were thrilled with the outcome of Paul's visit. Mordicai motioned for them to come closer to him. He laid one hand on each of their shoulders and began to speak.

"Brothers, I have this day joined you in acknowledging Christ. I have lived a long life and have not much to offer the Savior, but what I have I gladly give to Him. You two are young and able to serve in ways I cannot. Antipas, I sense that God is calling you into service for Him. You are welcome to make my home your home for as long as you need it. Paul, my wealth is yours to build the work here in Ephesus and beyond. It would give me great delight to serve God in this way."

Antipas was overwhelmed with this generous offer. The pieces of his life were beginning to fall into place. He knelt before Mordicai, overcome with emotion, and thanked him.

Darkness descended on them. The warm night surrounded them while evening sounds could be heard beyond the courtyard. A heavenly panorama of stars stretched across the sky as they talked on. The ancient had slipped into the house earlier and now appeared with the young slave boy to serve the evening meal. When Paul prayed to bless the food it felt like heaven had come down to them.

Paul and Epaphras were deep in conversation when Antipas noticed that Mordicai was drifting into sleep. He went to him and helped him rise.

Mordicai blinked his eyes and struggled to stand. He gripped Antipas's hand as a shiver ran through his body. He looked up at Antipas. "Take me to my room, please. I want to get to know you better. I already feel you and I are going to be close. I'm hoping you will be the son I never had."

Once again Antipas felt emotion rise in his heart. God was so good. One earthly father had disowned him, but God had provided another, one who would love him for who he was.

Once Mordicai was in bed, he asked Antipas to sit with him awhile.

"Tell me about your life. I want to hear every detail. You are young to be off on your own. I sense pain in your past. I'd like to help, if I may."

So Antipas told his story while Mordicai listened intently. Sometimes there were tears in the old man's eyes. Their backgrounds were so different in many ways, and yet they both had been drawn to Christ.

When he had finished, Mordicai spoke for the first time. "My dear friend, life has not been easy for you. I am not familiar with your father's name, but I do know Claudius and have certainly heard of his relative, Horatious, and his gang. Claudius is a fine man. I sense that God led you to him for your protection during that most difficult time. It is time for you to rest now, it has been a long day. Tomorrow we will talk about arrangements for you here in this house. I welcome your presence."

When Antipas left Mordicai, he heard voices in the courtyard and realized that Paul and Epaphras were still talking. He decided to slip by quietly and let them have this time together. However, Paul heard him and called to him.

"Antipas, come and sit with us awhile. I would like to talk to you further. Here, sit beside me. We want to keep our voices low to allow Mordicai to rest well. This has been quite a day for him. I knew it would come, but it is always a surprise how God works out these things.

"You are aware that I have been praying for a student to train in the work here to carry on after I move on to the next place God calls me. I have been speaking to Epaphras about you and feel convinced that you are the answer to my prayer." Paul sprang from his seat and paced the length of the courtyard, returning to stand before Antipas. He frowned and shook his head. "I will be most blunt and tell you it will not be easy, but the eternal rewards will be great. Are you willing to embark on this journey with me?"

"I feel completely unworthy but I'm willing. I would count it a great privilege to learn from you and serve in whatever capacity you think best."

"Then let's start at first light. I have several converts to visit tomorrow and it would be a good beginning for you to meet the local Christians and see how the ministry operates here in Ephesus. I will bid you good night and expect you early.

"Epaphras, I understand you will be in the city for a few more days doing business. Will we see you at the temple later in the day?" asked Paul.

"Yes, I'll be there, you can count on it. Good night to you too, and thank you for coming so quickly. You have done an incredible work today," replied Epaphras.

"It was not me. It was the Holy Spirit working in Mordicai's life. I was just the servant doing His bidding." He strode to the door, turning at the entrance to look back at them. "I'll find my way out."

And with that he was gone.

Epaphras looked at Antipas and said, "Well, Antipas, this has been quite a day. I should say to myself, 'Oh you of little faith.' I had begun to believe that Mordicai would never acknowledge the Savior. But I think Paul realized all along that it would happen, but that it was in God's timing.

"We had better go to our rest as first light comes early." Epaphras laughed and said Antipas should get used to this as Paul wasted no time that could be used in the ministry.

"He will be a hard taskmaster, but he will not ask more of you than he is already giving himself. He is a bold one, is Paul."

"Then I'd better get some sleep, so I bid you a good night as well."

As Antipas left for his room, his mind was churning with thoughts. "What am I getting into? Will I be able to do all that Paul will demand of me?"

Twenty

Antipas was tired. The pace Paul kept wasn't even human, he decided. They had walked countless leagues since the morning three days ago when he had joined Paul at first light. Paul had such a passion for preaching the message that he didn't pay any attention to the needs of his body, only what he could accomplish for Christ.

And accomplish he did. Antipas was amazed with the number of citizens of Ephesus they had visited. Many were already calling themselves Christians and many more were eager to hear more. The church was growing.

Excitement was high as they walked along the main thoroughfare just before noon. Paul was to address the civic leaders on the steps of the temple. Some of the elders had advised against this, but Paul was adamant that he would not back down from any earthly power. He seemed without fear. Antipas was less confident, but determined to go where Paul led.

Word had spread that this meeting was to take place and many people were crowding into the spaces around the steps to hear what he had to say. Paul and Antipas pushed their way through the noisy throng and approached the steps. The civic leaders had not yet made their appearance, which gave Paul a few minutes to talk with the crowd. He fell into deep conversation with a local sandal maker who was clearly antagonistic toward Paul's message.

One of the elders of the church who had accompanied them tried to get Paul away from the man, but Paul refused to be moved and continued his talk. He ended with a promise to visit the man at his business in the morning. The man cursed violently but reluctantly agreed to listen if Paul arrived.

A hush fell over the crowd as the civic leaders made their appearance from the front doors of the temple. They took their places on the steps, arrayed in white robes with blue sashes. Deep blue turbans were wound tightly around their heads which they held high with an air of superiority. It appeared obvious they were prepared to defeat Paul verbally in front of the people.

Paul was not daunted and strode up the steep steps with confidence. His appearance was in contrast to the leaders as he was dressed as a common man and rather shabbily at that. But from within him came a light that was noticeable in the expression of his face. The leaders observed his progress with stony silence. This was not going to be a pleasant meeting.

Antipas took his place in the crowd with Gad and Joseph, two fine men who were involved with Paul in the church. They were humble men, a part of the vast working public of Ephesus. Both were staunch, faithful followers of Christ, though neither was a leader. They had welcomed Antipas warmly and with joy. They, too, had been praying for a disciple for Paul to train.

Antipas's attention was now fully focused on the steps where Paul was ready to speak.

"Men of Ephesus, listen to what the God of the Jews has to say to you."

There were gasps in the crowd. Men shuffled and whispered to each other.

"How dare he mention the Jews." A merchant spit in disgust.

"Everyone knows what they are; money-grabbing thieves."

"How dare he mention them on the steps to the temple of Artemis."

Paul was continuing so the crowd quieted. Heads were bobbing, each man trying to see around others.

"You need to hear the message He has for you, people of Ephesus." Paul's voice rose as he warmed to his subject. He swung his arms as he talked, pacing back and forth on the steps. He had the attention of the leaders as well as the crowd as he presented the message of Christ to them.

There was a commotion not far from Antipas. A woman was trying to get through the crowd, crying that she needed to reach Paul. She was young but wasted away. Her body was bent, but she continued to push her way through. Paul became aware of her and stopped his address. He waited for her to reach the steps. The crowd was so quiet now you could hear everything that was being said.

"Woman, what do you want with me?" Paul's voice was brusque as he faced her.

"I want to be healed." She fell at his feet, bending her head to the ground "I know you have power from God."

"Do you believe that God has the power not only to heal, but also to forgive sins?" He was gentle now.

There were more gasps, now from the civic leaders. They whispered among themselves.

"What should we do? If we interfere, the crowd may turn on us."

"I think you're right. The people want to see if he can heal her."

"Let's wait, we can intervene if things get out of control."

The woman had partially sat up and was now on her knees before Paul.

"I believe, I believe. I know God can forgive sins. I know He can heal."

The crowd waited in expectation as this spectacle played itself out before them. Antipas held his breath. This was a dangerous situation for Paul, as well as for the infant church. Much could be lost or gained in the next few moments.

"Because you believe, God has already forgiven your sins. Stand up and walk, you are healed." Paul's declaration rang out across the steps and over the heads of all the people.

The woman slowly straightened her body and stood. She gave a great cry of victory and turning to the crowd, she declared, "This man is indeed from God. I've been sick for many years and yet this man this day has returned my health to me. Praise God."

The crowd was in turmoil. Many were pushing their way up to Paul, pleading for healing. Others were weeping openly and declaring their belief in the God of the Jews.

Others were crying out, "Drive him out of town. He's a sorcerer."

The restlessness was like the waves of the sea, tossed by the wind. Arguments broke out between those trying to reach Paul and others wanting to harm him.

As Antipas watched, he became aware that the civic leaders had disappeared into the temple. He could only imagine what they were saying to each other. It boded ill for the Christians, he was sure.

Joseph tapped Antipas on the shoulder.

"We're going to move closer to Paul in case he needs to get away quickly. Come with us. We must stay together to help Paul all we can."

Antipas moved off with Joseph and Gad. Other Christians that he had met over the last few days materialized and joined ranks with them. The crowd was starting to disperse, judging that the show was over for the day. Paul was talking quietly to many who had come forward. He healed some and gave all of them instructions of where to meet him later today.

Finally, they were left alone and Paul descended the steps to greet the brothers.

"The Lord was truly at work here today. Many people saw the truth and will join our gathering."

Antipas was amazed at Paul's calm. He seemed either unaware of the danger, or it simply did not deter him from the cause of Christ. The four men moved off to join the others for discussion and a meal together. The events of the day were related to the group.

"What do you think the outcome will be from Paul's message on the temple steps?" Gad looked concerned as he glanced around the table at the others.

"I'm not worried about the common people." Joseph held his flatbread in one hand while he gestured with the other. "They will either believe and come, or they'll go back to their homes and forget about it by next week." He paused to swallow a piece of bread and take a sip of his drink. "The danger comes from the civic leaders."

"That's true." Gad turned to Paul, who was conversing with one of the others but turned his attention to him. "You didn't even get a chance to speak privately with any of them. The mere fact that they disappeared so quickly portends ill for all of us." There being nothing more to say, they continued eating.

When the meal was finished, Paul thanked his hostess.

Turning to Antipas he reached out to detain him. "I'd like you to accompany me. I'm writing a letter to some believers in Jerusalem and I need you to scribe for me."

Antipas knew his eyes had been bothering him lately. He was thrilled to be able to assist Paul in any way, so they proceeded to Paul's lodging.

"How can I ever be as bold as you in talking to people about Christ?" They were walking along one of the side streets toward Paul's residence.

"Boldness comes from doing and believing. You're on the right path. You must be so filled with Christ that there is no room left for fear of what people can do to you." Paul's answer was emphatic. His hands moved restlessly as he spoke.

Paul was always patient with his questions, giving passionate answers. Antipas's dream was to become bold for Christ like Paul. Would he ever feel the passion he witnessed each day with him? He asked Paul about it.

"If you desire to serve the living God, He will give you the passion you need to be His servant. Right now you are overcome with all you have been experiencing. But I sense God's hand is on your life. God has revealed to me that He has big plans for you. You just need to be willing to follow wherever He leads." A light seemed to gleam from Paul's eyes as he answered Antipas.

"Oh, I am willing. I just need to know more. I need more confidence to believe I can do this." Antipas realized he was clasping his hands together. He held them at his sides in an effort to control them.

"You don't need confidence in yourself. Your confidence is in Christ. He can do all things. You just need to be willing to make yourself available to Him."

As they walked and talked, Antipas felt his confidence in Christ grow. He had never before felt so fulfilled. This was what he had been looking for since he was twelve. This was what his grandfather sensed all those years ago. Paul would only be with them for a few more weeks before he moved on to the next city. Antipas determined in his heart to learn everything Paul was willing to teach him. He would not waste a minute in idleness. There was so much to do and so little time.

Twenty-One

The days that followed would always be a blur in Antipas's mind, but the things he learned would always stand out with stark clarity. He absorbed Paul's teaching and grew in his understanding of what Christ had done for him and what He wanted to do for all of mankind.

Many hours were spent sitting at Paul's feet listening, asking questions, and listening to the questions of others. After the day on the temple steps, scores of people had sought out Paul, many to commit their lives to Christ. The Ephesus church was growing.

As yet there had been no repercussions from the civic leaders, but no one was naive enough to believe the danger was over. These leaders had long memories and would bide their time until they were sure they could eradicate what they considered a problem.

The first direct attack came from the silversmiths. Antipas had heard rumors that the makers of the silver idols were furious because their business was suffering as more people turned away from idol worship. The rumors claimed they blamed Paul for their loss of business, and riots were possible. On a busy market morning, the protestors appeared on the steps of the temple, the same steps where Paul had preached Christ only days before.

The silversmith Demetrius led the group. He ascended the steps, flourishing a stout stick in the air before him. At the top he swung around. "Great is Artemis of the Ephesians. Great is Artemis of the Ephesians." His cries rang out across the sea of people. The mob took up the rallying cry. "Great is Artemis of the Ephesians."

The priests of Artemis glided out of the temple. They smiled gleefully as they became aware of the cause of the disturbance. They had long been discussing what to do about the problem. Maybe the people themselves would solve the situation without their interference. So much better if it came from them.

Word soon spread to the civic leaders and to Paul and his followers. Paul was ready to go to the temple and speak to the crowd. Calmer heads prevailed and he was persuaded to stay away and await word from the two they decided should go to investigate. Gaius and Aristarchus had quickly volunteered.

While they were gone, Paul gathered the others around him and led a prolonged session of prayer. They raised their voices to heaven asking for God's will in their city, for the protection of the infant church in Ephesus, and for peace for each of them as they anticipated a time of persecution.

When Gaius and Aristarchus arrived at the scene, a full-scale riot was in progress. Roiling bodies, screaming, chanting, and stones flying through the air greeted their view. Rich reds and deep purples mixed with the browns of the common people. Animal odors mingled with cooking smells from the street vendors, adding pungency to the astonishing scene. Turbans of every known color could be seen bobbing on the heads of the rioters. White robes caught the glint of the sun. Thick rods were waving from uplifted hands while knives flashed in others.

Demetrius and the group with him came down the steps of the temple and mingled with the crowd. The angry rioters surged toward the theater. Someone spied Gaius and Aristarchus and recognized them as having been with Paul. They started shouting, "Grab them, grab them. It's some of Paul's followers."

Two burly fellows seized them and the crowd rushed into the theater, pushing the two Christians before them. Gaius and Aristarchus became separated and could no longer see each other. Gaius closely watched the men holding him. He had seen one of them in the market earlier in the week. He had stopped Paul to ask questions. Gaius had thought the man was interested in pursuing the Way. He tried to make eye contact with him. Speech would be impossible in this din. He would love to talk to him and tell him more about Jesus.

The civic leaders made their appearance, trying to calm the people. No one was listening to anyone. For two hours the people chanted, "Great is Artemis of the Ephesians."

Over and over the words echoed around the theater. Scuffles broke out here and there but there was no way to stop them. The crowd was out of control. The priests joined the civic leaders. Worried frowns furrowed their faces as they watched the mob.

The chief priest of Artemis beckoned the other priests and the civic leaders to follow him out through the back archway. He led them down a quiet corridor into a little side room. There were twelve of them crowded together, five civic leaders and seven priests. The priests in their white robes were a contrast to the civic leaders in bright blue.

"We have to come up with a plan to get this stopped," the chief priest, Ahmed, spoke. "There is great danger here. Our reputation is at stake. We are the guardians of the temple of Artemis. It is our duty to protect her reputation. If this becomes known throughout the country, or worse still, in Rome, we could be discharged from our duties. That would bring disgrace on us and on Ephesus. Between us, we should be able to get this stopped before any serious offense occurs."

"I agree with you completely," the city clerk spoke next. He was the most important of the city officials and well versed in dealing with the Romans. "All our reputations are in danger. Rome will not put up with rioting. They would be ready to take over the city, but I have an idea."

He quickly outlined his thoughts. They discussed options and expressed their opinions. They finally agreed upon a plan. It was so simple it almost seemed ludicrous to try it, but they were running out of alternatives and time.

When they were ready, they headed back into the theater, where the shouting and chanting was still going on. The city clerk approached the front of the theater and ascended the stairs to the dais. He walked with great confidence, a look of arrogance on his face.

Men in front saw him and stopped chanting. A hush gradually fell over the crowd. They well knew the power he had. He could confiscate their businesses on a whim. He had done so with little cause and so they feared him.

"Men of Ephesus"—the disdain was evident in his voice—"we all know that Ephesus is the center of worship of Artemis. We all know that her temple is under our protection. We know the truth. If we have some in our midst who believe in a false god, why should we be disturbed about that? We are the keepers of the truth, the truth that Artemis is worthy of our worship." He lifted both arms high in the air. As he brought them down, he shook his hand at the mob. "Men, men, men, you are in danger of bringing disgrace on our fair city. What charge do you have against these two men? Have they robbed the temple or harmed the image of Artemis in any way? No, you know they have not. If anyone has anything against these men, let him bring it to the courts and settle it legally." He folded his arms over his chest then pointed to the door. "It's time for you to leave the theater and go back to your businesses. Much time has been wasted here today. Let me not be the one to find you lingering here. The consequences will not be pleasant. I bid you good day."

With that he descended the steps with his back stiff and straight. He walked slowly as only one with authority can walk. The men at the back turned, heading for the door leading to the street. In a few minutes, all was quiet once again in the theater and in the streets of the city. Gaius and Aristarchus were left looking at one another with great relief. They, too, turned and left the theater.

As they walked through the streets, no one even glanced their way. They returned to Paul and the group praying without further molestation. They entered the house to warm greetings and much praising of God.

It took a long time for them to tell their story. Those in the house who had been praying praised God for their deliverance. They talked quietly far into the night, knowing this was just the beginning. Paul had warned them persecution was coming.

"You may have escaped today, but there is more to come, much more. We need to bathe you in prayer, not so you will avoid persecution, but so you will be strong and not turn from the Way. Christ didn't promise an easy life, but He did promise never to leave you alone." Paul began to pace as he warmed to his subject. "You must prepare for the coming days. You need to make decisions as to how you will face life here in Ephesus. Will you go into hiding, will you move to another place, will you stay?" He stabbed his finger at each of them as he threw out his questions. "Among your group you may do all three. You need to ask God to direct you in the way He wants you to go. It will not be the same for everyone. Only one thing is sure at the moment: you cannot go on as before. Today has changed everything." He looked at their sober faces. "You should be rejoicing that God has allowed this to come into your lives. Oh, I know that sounds strange to your ears. But as you grow in your Christian life, you will learn to embrace adversity as it comes to make you strong."

The small group sat in silence for some minutes, each man searching his heart as Paul's words sank in.

Antipas wondered if he would be strong enough to face the coming troubles. He wanted to be, he really wanted to be. He had never felt such a desire before. It was as though he had been waiting for this, and had been born for just this reason. He watched Paul bow his head and begin praying for the group. Every head bowed as he prayed.

When he had finished, a strange thing occurred. To Antipas it felt like someone had poured warm, fragrant oil over his head that ran down over his body, removing all fear and doubt as it cleansed him. The others expressed that they had experienced similar things. An excitement broke out in the house as they began to praise God and sing songs to Him.

"You are now ready for whatever God has allowed to come into your lives." Paul frowned as he stared at each one. "I will not be here with you, as God has called me to move on with His message. I hereby proclaim Antipas as your leader. He will serve you well."

Many of those present embraced Antipas and expressed their support of his leadership. Antipas was overwhelmed with Paul's gesture but knew within himself that this was from God. He had no idea what lay ahead, but knew that God was leading and in control.

Slowly the converts began to leave for their own homes. They bid Paul a tearful good-bye, knowing they might never see him again in this life. Paul encouraged them to pray for him and for those who would accompany him, and to pray for each other and Antipas. They promised they would be faithful in prayer and to the leading of Antipas.

At last it was only Paul and Antipas left.

"My son, you have indeed a heavy burden to carry, but you have God's blessing on you. He has shown me that you will be a faithful servant. Continue in your studies of the Scriptures and in daily prayer. Seek God's leading with all your heart. I'll write to you from the next city I visit. Read the letters to the disciples here and pass them on to other churches."

Paul reached out and placed his hand on Antipas's head.

"May God bless you and keep you, may He make His face shine upon you and give you peace." And then he was gone.

Twenty-Two

Antipas paced back and forth in his room for hours. His hands were clasped behind his back, his head bowed. Paul's words kept drumming through his head. He was now in charge of the Ephesus church. How could that be? Paul must be mad to appoint him.

But he knew in his inner being that Paul was attuned to God's will, and he knew in himself that God had called him to this mission, here, at this time. Fear, hope, excitement, anticipation, dread—all these emotions swirled through his mind. One thing he knew for sure: if God had called him, God would not abandon him.

Morning was dawning before he was able to lie down. Tiredness overcame him at last and he slept. His first waking image was of the ancient one bending over him, speaking softly but insistently.

"There's a group of men here to see you. They say it's important, even urgent. You must get up and greet them."

Memory flooded in as his eyes focused on the servant.

"Tell them I'll join them in the courtyard in ten minutes."

The servant left to relay his message as Antipas struggled out of his bed. He took a short time to refresh himself with the warm water the servant had brought with him and to send up a plea for wisdom and guidance as he met with these men.

He approached the courtyard cautiously, not knowing whether these were men from the council or Christians from the infant church. As he neared them he recognized Gaius. A great relief flooded over him. He hadn't really felt ready to take on the council yet. That would come, he knew.

Gaius turned at the sound of Antipas's arrival and greeted him. With him were Aristarchus, Joseph, Gad, and another man Antipas had not met. Gaius introduced him as Petros, a local merchant.

"Antipas, we need your wisdom." Gaius pushed Petros toward Antipas. "Petros is familiar with the city rulers and has heard disturbing news. He came to my house early this morning to apprise me of the situation. We met with the others and then came directly to you. Petros, tell Antipas what you heard last night."

"Greetings, Antipas." He inclined his head in a bow. "My story is simple. I gave my heart to Christ a few months ago but have not yet told any of my fellow merchants. That's why they speak so freely in front of me." He lowered his eyes, seeming to gather his thoughts. "The civic leaders and religious priests met far into the night after the riot was over yesterday. They have issued a decree to secretly arrest Paul and anyone known to have been with him." He looked directly into Antipas's eyes. "They said there would be false witnesses and trumped-up charges to put away the group for a long, long time. They decided there would not be an execution as they're afraid that would stir up the people. There was a guard on all the city gates this morning watching for Paul and any of his followers." Fear radiated from Petros as he finished his tale. He looked at the others with a shrug of his shoulders.

Antipas smiled at them. Reaching out his arms, he included the whole group. "Friends, don't be afraid. Paul left the city late last night. God is watching over him and will keep him safe to carry on his work in other areas. Our concern now needs to be with our local group and how best to protect them." He was relaxed and confident as he assured them. "I have a plan." He beckoned them to gather closer to him. He could see the anxiety easing on their faces as he talked. "I need to talk to Mordicai and bring him here to listen to our discussion. While I'm doing that, a servant will bring food for you. You may speak freely in front of him as he, too, is a follower."

He slipped into the coolness of the house, gave instructions to the ancient one, and proceeded to Mordicai's room. The old man was awake, sitting up in bed drinking his morning tea.

"Antipas, I've been expecting you. God is good. He has told me about your troubles and has prepared me for your request. Go ahead, speak, I'm listening."

He stopped inside the door, his mouth open in astonishment, then he grinned at Mordicai. "I shouldn't be surprised to hear your words. I can't believe how quickly you have become so close to our Savior." He pulled a stool close to the bed and sat facing him, his eyebrows raised in expectation.

Mordicai patted the blanket and closed his eyes. "When you are my age, son, you don't have any time to waste. Besides, I had known the Way for a long time and was just too stubborn to admit it. So, carry on with your request."

"Stubborn, is it? I didn't think you would admit to that." Antipas grinned at him as he leaned closer, shifting on the stool. He outlined his plan to Mordicai with many hand gestures. At one point he leaped from the stool to take a turn around the room. The morning sunshine gleamed in his eyes as he shared his idea.

Mordicai sat up straighter in his bed. He nodded his head at every idea Antipas presented.

"Yes, yes, I agree. When can we start?" His eyes were snapping with excitement.

"Do you feel well enough to accompany me to the courtyard?" Before Antipas finished speaking, Mordicai's feet were already over the side of the bed. He wrapped his robe about his bony frame, accepted Antipas's arm, and together they passed through the house.

The men jumped from their places when Antipas approached with Mordicai. Bowing low, they greeted him with respect.

"Thank you for joining us." Gaius acted as spokesman for the group, bowing a second time.

"Believe me, it's my pleasure. Welcome to my home." He returned their bow, bending as low as his frail body would allow. He lifted his hand in greeting. "Friends of Epaphras, Paul, and Antipas are friends of mine. Please sit and we'll talk."

Antipas sat beside him and waited while the others resumed their seats. "As I told you earlier, I have a plan. Mordicai agrees with me and we'd like your opinions." The men were sitting on the edges of their seats, leaning forward, heads cocked, listening. "I've been awake most of the night and in communion with God. I sense His leading with this plan. It has become obvious that we need a place where we can meet without the eyes of the civic and religious leaders watching our every move." He paused to glance at Mordicai. He was nodding his head, a smile lighting up his aging face. "Mordicai has agreed that his home is the ideal place."

There were gasps from the men. Gaius rose, eyes wide in disbelief. "We can't accept this idea. This is too grand a place for humble people like us." He looked to the others, who were nodding their heads in agreement. "Some of our group are even slaves. No, we couldn't possibly meet here." He sat down quickly, taking deep breaths.

Antipas quieted them and nodded for Mordicai to take up the explanation.

"Friends, you don't know what you're saying. I owe a great debt to God for all my stubborn years of denying His Son, the Lord Jesus. He has laid on my heart how I can begin to make up for those lost years." Teardrops were hanging on his eyelashes. He lowered his head, shaking it slowly. "I have offered all I have to Him, to use as He sees fit. He has made it plain to me that His infant church must meet in my house." He straightened in his chair, pushing his shoulders back. His thin voice was filled with emotion. "I count it a great privilege to offer my home in this way. You would offend me terribly if you refuse to use what God has provided. I beg you to reconsider."

Gaius rose again, this time smiling. "Mordicai, we thank you from the bottom of our hearts. We would be remiss if we did not accept your kind and generous offer." He indicated his acceptance with a slight bow. "Paul has told me of your miraculous conversion and your desire to spend every minute left to you in worship of God and obedience to Him."

Antipas leaned forward, his browed furrowed in serious thought. "I think it would be wise to do more than meet here. I feel you should bring your families here for the time being, at least until the present danger has passed. There is plenty of room here for many families." Gaius jerked his head up to stare at Antipas. He motioned for him to relax. "Mordicai and I have spoken of this and have made plans to accommodate all of you." The men looked at each other, eyes wide, mouths open. "You will need to gather the rest of the followers and we'll present our plan. Once that's done, you'll need to go home to your wives and children and prepare to come."

"You're serious, aren't you, Antipas?" Gaius's face portrayed amazement with raised eyebrows. Antipas smiled but didn't respond.

"Only bring what is absolutely necessary. We want it to look like you are still living in your homes. Food will be provided here. You will need to come by different routes and at different times. There are several entrances, so it will not look like a big crowd is arriving. I would like to hear your opinions and concerns."

By now, the surprised looks on the men's faces had faded. A thoughtfulness and acceptance was seen in the nods of the head and the glances at each other and at Antipas.

"We can only say a simple thank-you." Gaius caressed his beard. "We'll do as you suggest. It's the best thing for our families. Thank you, Mordicai. Thank you, Antipas."

They discussed how this could be arranged; the distribution of jobs once they were all in, how the men would continue with their work in the city, how the children would be taught and a multitude of other questions. They agreed to meet again at dusk with the other men and finalize their plans.

"In order for this to work, there must be total secrecy. I would suggest you do not tell your children of the plans until you have arrived here with your family." Antipas was on his feet now, gripping each man's shoulder as they prepared to leave. "Farewell for now. I'll see you at dusk."

∼ ∼ ∼

Mordicai and Antipas gathered the staff together and shared their plans. Nothing surprised the servants, as things had been so different since Mordicai turned his life over to Christ. They quickly caught on to the plan and began to make the necessary arrangements.

"Even though this is such a serious situation, I have to say, I have never had so much fun in my life." Mordicai leaned on a table for support and beamed at Antipas.

"Don't get too excited and end up in bed. We'll need your wisdom when we meet tonight and in the days ahead. There is real danger here, and we need to know how best to protect the women and children. I need to leave for a tour of the city to find out what's being said in the marketplace. I'll return in a couple of hours. Perhaps you should rest until then."

"You're right, Antipas. I will at least be quiet until you return." An impish look crossed his face. Antipas wondered if he would even go to his room. He had never seen him so happy.

Antipas left through a small entrance on the east side of the property. He took a path that eventually led to the main road into the city. There were several people on the road, but all seemed focused on their own business and paid no attention to him.

It was a glorious day, blue sky with banks of fluffy clouds in the west. The air was dry with a hint of olives. The harvest season was upon them. He never failed to be fascinated with the harvest. Nets were spread on the ground under several olive trees, and men with robes tied up were beating the branches. Showers of ripe olives were spreading over the nets. It looked like a good crop this year.

He reached the gates in good time and entered the city. The busyness always reminded him of home. Pergamum. Would he ever see it again? Would he ever see his mother and brothers? He was sure his father would never see him again, but he always hoped that someday he would see the others. It was a secret dream that he allowed into his conscious mind only on rare occasions. It was too painful to dwell on it.

Shouts up ahead brought him back to reality and he moved with the crowd to see what was happening. He arrived in time to see guards struggling with a man in the market street. Some women were trying to help the man escape, but one of the guards clipped them with the handle of his sword and drove them off. He thought he recognized one of the women and pushed his way to her side. He was right; it was Dorcas, the wife of Aristarchus.

"Was that Aristarchus the guards arrested?" Antipas helped her pick up her basket and the things that had fallen from it in the altercation with the guards.

Dorcas was weeping as she placed damaged items in the basket. The grapes had been stepped on in the scuffle and were crushed. Broken eggs spattered the fresh bread. She sniffed and wiped her eyes with the back of her hand. "Yes, oh yes. We were walking to the market when they grabbed him. One of them said, 'You got away last time, but this time we've got you for good.' What will I do? How can I go on without him?" She gave a sharp cry, almost falling. He steadied her with his arm. "Oh, poor Aristarchus. He didn't fear them. He always told me not to fear those who could hurt only your body, but I'm not as strong as he is. I can't do this." She broke into wrenching wails. Antipas held her steady as he watched the guards disappear from view, dragging Aristarchus between them.

There was another woman with them. She looked familiar to him but he couldn't place her. She was supporting Dorcas on one side while he supported the other.

"We'll need to go to your home and get your children and a few things you'll need, then I'll take you to Mordicai's house, which is where Aristarchus would have brought you in another day or so."

She stopped weeping and looked at him through tear-filled eyes. She shook her head in agreement. Taking a deep breath, she started walking with them. By the time they arrived at her house, Dorcas was getting her emotions under control.

"I must be strong for my children. They'll be fearful enough without seeing their mother fall apart. Thank you, Antipas, for your help, and you too, Eunice. I don't know what I would have done without you two."

Eunice? Eunice? Could this be the young girl he had met on the way here with Epaphras? She had her head covering on and seemed to be avoiding his eyes. He finally spoke to her.

"We've met before." Antipas paused, unsure what to say next.

Eunice kept her eyes lowered, answering with a quiet yes.

"She's my niece, Antipas, and is visiting for a few weeks. She'll come with me to Mordicai's." Dorcas was now all business. She bustled around her home, gathering the things they would need. She talked with her children, explaining what had happened to their father. When she was ready, they set out with the four children.

Antipas took them through the little used byways of the city and out through a small gate a distance from the main gate. There were still many people about, so they were able to mix with the crowd and exit the city unnoticed.

Their way took them through a wooded path redolent with the fragrance of woodland flowers and trees. They arrived at the estate by traveling through a field of barley. The children were tired by this time but obeyed all the instructions.

Antipas halted them at the edge of the field, asking them to remain where they were until he gave them the signal to come to the house. He went on ahead to make sure everything was safe.

One of the servants was coming out of the house and gave him a report of the morning's activities. Everything seemed normal, so he beckoned them to come in.

He couldn't believe what he saw when he entered the house. The servants had been busy rearranging the rooms to accommodate the families they were expecting. The larger rooms had been divided with long curtains, and beds had been moved into each section. One of the servants offered to lead the women and children to a room where they could begin to settle in. Mordicai himself was in one of the rooms, happily giving instructions to his staff.

He greeted Antipas then stopped as he saw the look of concern on his face.

"What's wrong, my friend?" Mordicai asked.

"Aristarchus has been taken by the guards. I've brought his family with me."

"That is indeed sad news. I have some influence with the captain of the guards. I'll see what can be done. Introduce me to the family, and I will assure them of my help."

When Mordicai and Antipas found the women in their assigned quarters, Antipas was surprised at the composure on the faces of Aristarchus's wife and Eunice. Dorcas spoke before he had a chance.

"Antipas, I owe you an apology for my lack of control when Aristarchus was taken. I have been reminded how that showed a lack of faith in our Savior. I know that my husband is in His hands and that I need not worry. Whatever God has planned for Aristarchus will be done, and God will provide for me." Her chin was held high as she delivered her words.

Antipas murmured a reply, almost speechless in the face of such a strong faith. It was humbling to witness this when his own faith had been wavering.

"Thank you, Dorcas. You have encouraged my heart this day. Let me introduce Mordicai to you and Eunice. He is most anxious to help you."

Dorcas fell to her knees in front of Mordicai, face to the ground. Mordicai quickly reached out his hand and helped her to her feet.

"I'm not worthy of such homage. I am simply a humble believer like you. God has provided me with wealth to do His will. I am honored that you were willing to come to my home for refuge." He still held her hand in his. "You are most welcome here. It appears your husband has run into some trouble. I may be able to help. Tell me everything that happened so I will have the facts straight when I make my inquiries."

So Dorcas told the whole story once again. Mordicai asked questions here and there and nodded now and then. When she had finished there was silence for a moment. Mordicai released her hand and straightened his back.

"I will leave quickly to go into the city. Antipas, I would like you to accompany me. Eunice, if you would be so good as to find one of my servants to help you and Dorcas get settled, we will be on our way."

They left the women and moved through the house, Mordicai giving orders as they went. By the time they reached the main door, the chariot was already in place ready for their journey into the city.

"Mordicai, I don't think you should be going at such a pace. You have recently been ill and this is not good for you." Antipas held him back and spoke earnestly to him.

Mordicai laughed. "Antipas, Antipas, don't you realize that I'm on borrowed time? I have been given more time solely to do His will. He has given me an energy I have not had for years, and I plan to use every bit of it for His service. It is my great pleasure to serve Christ." He stepped into the chariot unassisted by the servant or Antipas. Once he was seated, he stuck his head out the door. "Are you coming?"

Antipas leaped in beside him, chuckling to himself. He marveled at the saving grace of Jesus. He took hardened and stubborn hearts and turned them into beautiful things. As the countryside flew by, he meditated on what Christ meant to him and what the future would hold. He knew it was not going to be easy. Satan was already raising his ugly head against the church of Jesus Christ. He prayed he would be strong enough to withstand the fiery darts of the enemy.

Twenty-Three

The prison at Ephesus was cold and damp. Aristarchus huddled in his cell trying to get warm. His body was chilled and full of pain outside, but his heart was warm. From the first moment the guards approached, he felt peace. It was almost like he had been waiting for just this moment in time.

He knew the dangers they all faced every day and wondered if he would be strong enough to endure the trials when they came. He had prided himself on his physical strength. He now knew in and of himself he was not strong, but the presence of the Lord gave him the courage to face the present trial.

He had been flogged when they reached the prison. The pain had been excruciating, but he kept remembering that Christ, too, had been beaten. He counted it a privilege to partake in His suffering. His main worry was for his family. What would Dorcas and the children do without his presence and support? What had happened to her after he was taken? Was she safe? He prayed for his family, not realizing he was talking aloud until there was banging on his door.

"Stop that noise in there, you're disturbing us." He could hear their laughter through the wall. He shifted his position, wincing from the sharp jab of pain in his back. He moaned and moved his shoulder cautiously. He closed his eyes, shutting out the dirt and grime of years.

"Lord, I pray for the guards that You will shine Your light upon them and draw them to You." He didn't care if they heard him. He hoped they would.

A face appeared at the opening in his cell door.

"You're wasting your breath praying for us. We worship Artemis, who will destroy your god one day soon. Great is Artemis of the Ephesians." Laughter again filtered in through the door.

Others took up the chant, "Great is Artemis of the Ephesians."

This went on for some time while Aristarchus drifted off into a fitful sleep. When he awoke, he realized all was quiet. Too quiet. What was happening? He gently eased his stiff frame from the pallet and staggered to the door. The opening was too high for him to see but he listened intently and could hear nothing. That was strange. Usually there was talk and laughter among the guards.

He lowered himself onto his pallet again. When no sounds broke the silence, he worked his way back to the door. Still nothing. Almost without thinking, he pulled on the door. It slid open silently. He stood there stunned, leaning against the frame. He peered into the hall but could see no one around. He slid the door closed. He stood inside the door, panting from the effort, and tried to make sense of the silence.

He was tempted to venture outside his cell but knew it would be bad for him if someone saw him. Maybe it was a trick the guards were playing on him to see if he would come out. He went back and huddled on the pallet. Back to the door again to listen. Still silent. *Maybe God is making a way for me to escape, and I'm still standing here.*

"Lord, I want to do Your will. I want to be brave under persecution, I want You to be pleased with me. What do You want me to do now?"

No answer swirled around his cell. He slid the door open again and slipped into the hall. There was no sign of anyone. He cautiously stole his way toward the guards' station. All quiet. He shuffled past the empty post, past other cells; all quiet and deserted. He finally reached a back entrance and pushed on the door. It, too, opened at his touch. He stepped out into brilliant sunshine. The light exploded against his eyes, forcing him to squint. He hung on to the side of the building until his eyes adjusted.

He knew the plan had been to meet at Mordicai's home at dusk. The best idea would be to head for there. Some of the others would have approached Dorcas if she had managed to get home and would have taken her there.

He inched his way into the busy morning bustle of the main thoroughfare. No one seemed to notice his presence. He was excited yet alert. At any moment a guard could appear and apprehend him. He knew he could be facing execution if he was arrested again.

Out through the marketplace he went, ever watchful. He decided to stick to the main routes as one person was less visible in a crowd than walking all alone in a byway. Once he reached the gates, he waited until there was a group going through and mingled with the crowd. Soon he was on the road heading into the country.

There was still a press of people and chariots going to and from the city. One chariot was approaching at a brisk pace. He moved as fast as his hurting body could manage to avoid a collision with it. The occupants glanced his way. Their eyes widened. The chariot was stopped a short distance away and Antipas jumped down and ran to him.

"Aristarchus, is it really you? Quick, get into the chariot, we'll talk later."

By this time the servant had the chariot turned around. Antipas helped him in, and the chariot took off at a breakneck pace. He leaned against the seat and drew a sigh of relief.

〜 〜 〜

"Maybe we'd better slow down. We don't want to draw attention to ourselves." Antipas looked at Mordicai as he made the suggestion.

Mordicai agreed and spoke to the servant. A much more reasonable pace ensued.

"You're shivering and in pain." Antipas grabbed a blanket from the opposite seat and put it over Aristarchus. "Tell us what happened. I can't believe it's really you."

"The pain's not as bad as it was." He sat up straighter and hugged the blanket. "I'll tell you everything." He told them the story, his voice growing stronger with each sentence. When he came to the part about the open doors, Antipas jumped for joy and nearly upset the chariot.

"Aristarchus, that was a miracle. God opened the doors, made the guards depart, and let you out of the prison. You have been released by the holy hand of God. Wow, I never imagined that would happen."

Aristarchus just stared at him. "Do you really think that's what happened?"

"But what else could it be? Have you ever heard of anyone escaping from the civic prison before?"

"Nooo. But why would God do that for me? I'm nothing. I'm not worthy of His attention."

Antipas leaned closer to Aristarchus. "Of course you aren't worthy. No one is. That just shows us how much God loves us anyway. It was a miracle, there's no other explanation."

"You're right. There isn't anything else to explain it." Aristarchus broke out in a big grin. Then all three began to praise God for this great deliverance.

"God must have something really special for you to do. He wanted you out of there for a reason. We must pray and search the heart of God for what He wants to do with your life." Antipas's eyes were dancing with excitement.

"I know you're right." Aristarchus clenched his hands together. "But it scares me all the same. What could a humble man like me do for God?"

"Don't worry, He'll show you in His time. Right now let's just rejoice in your deliverance and focus on the meeting we'll be having in a few hours to decide the next step for the Christians of Ephesus. The civic leaders won't be happy when they discover you've escaped. Some guards' heads will roll tonight."

Mordicai had remained quiet all through the conversation, but as they looked at him now, tears were running unchecked down his weathered face. Amidst the tears, he smiled broadly and chanted, "Praise be to the God of the heavens, for He is great and greatly to be praised. Blessed be the name of the Lord. I am honored to have been a part of this great deliverance."

They remained silent for the remainder of the journey. The chariot rolled into the avenue in front of the house while Antipas contemplated the dark days of persecution awaiting the Church of Ephesus.

Twenty-Four

As dusk fell, families began to gather in the common room of Mordicai's house. The reunion of Dorcas and Aristarchus was tender yet quiet. Dorcas had not been prone to emotional outbursts after the first violent weeping when Aristarchus was arrested. She had since made her peace with the Lord and was ready to accept whatever He had in store for them. She accepted his release with the same quiet trust in her Savior that she'd shown when she accepted his imprisonment. Both knew the days ahead would not be easy, perhaps including further arrests.

There was an atmosphere of calm acceptance among all who gathered together. Gaius counted one hundred seven souls, including children and servants. A hush fell over the group as Antipas rose to speak.

❧ ❧ ❧

"Friends, we face dark days." He searched their faces; hands at his sides, shoulders back, deep sigh. "There is coming a time of persecution for the church of Ephesus. God has given me an assurance that He will be right here with us through everything that happens. We need to prepare carefully not only to protect ourselves and our children, but to do only what honors our Lord." He paused to gather his thoughts. The room was silent. Only the rustle of a robe as a mother adjusted her sleeping child, and a father coughing quietly could be heard. "We have a sanctuary here in the home of Mordicai for the present time. Those of you who stay hidden here should be safe. Many of us will still venture out into the city, as the Word of the Lord still needs to be given to the lost people of Ephesus. Each of you will need to make your own decision as to whether you stay or go." He gestured with his hands. "Men, you will need to decide through prayer and fasting whether you should return to your places of employment."

A baby began to cry. His mother placed him over her shoulder and patted his back.

Antipas closed his eyes, rubbing his forehead. *I need to say this without offending them, but they need to be challenged.* Thoughts circled his mind. He opened his eyes again and sought the eyes of each man in the group. "May I suggest we not do anything that would appear to be cowardly on our parts? Being absent from regular workplaces may bring retribution sooner than we expect. Also, at some point it will be discovered that we are all here in one place. That in itself will create a danger."

A woman near the back lowered her head and could be heard weeping. The girl beside her slipped her arm around her neck and whispered to her. Antipas watched. He could see fear in the solemn faces spread out before him. Most of the women had lowered their eyes from his direct gaze.

"For the present we are safe here. No decisions need be made tonight. First we need to arrange sleeping, eating, and all the other mundane things of everyday living."

The group came alive with the discussion of the logistics of one hundred seven people living together in one house. There seemed to be comfort in organizing everyday living arrangements. Together they devised an excellent plan to make things flow as smoothly as possible. Gaius was chosen as the overseer of all things domestic, and others were appointed as his assistants. Soon everyone was comfortable with the arrangements and were ready to put the plan in place.

The tension broke once they began to implement their plan. Mothers lifted children in their arms, smiling once again. Antipas moved among them, offering advice and helping where he could. The rich and the poor, the old and the young, the hearty and the weak mingled in a surge of activity. Food-preparation volunteers were sent with their leader to be given instructions by the servants to begin the evening meal. Another group was assigned to look after making sure everyone had a bed for the night. Still others would take turns being on guard at the entrances and around the property.

Antipas would be their spiritual leader, and his duties would include entering the city on a regular basis to carry on the work Paul had started among the Ephesians. He would meet with Gaius and the other overseers when necessary as well as teach all of them from God's word each evening. As he observed the activity around him, he smiled thoughtfully. *They're going to make it.* He retied his robe and stretched his back before joining the group heading out to check the property.

≈ ≈ ≈

The next few days went by quickly as everyone settled into the routine of living so closely together. There wasn't much privacy, but the Christians were grateful to have a safe place to stay. The children had wonderful times romping on the lawns surrounding the courtyard.

During the evenings, Antipas taught the people much as Paul had done when he had been with them. Contentment reigned in their midst even though Antipas warned them that the peace could be short-lived. No one wanted to believe that these halcyon days could ever end. There were places to rest weary heads, places to play, plenty of good food, and much enjoyable company.

∾ ∾ ∾

Antipas rose from a restless night. He'd had a dream that lingered as he leaned on his window ledge watching the sky lighten in the east. The raucous call of kites in flight interrupted his reverie as they soared beyond the garden. He watched them until they vanished from sight. His thoughts turned inward again, seeing faces from his past, faces on the streets of Ephesus, faces looking for the Way. He shook his head to clear his thoughts as he stepped back from the window. One thing was clear, he had to respond to this clear call to seek out these faces and tell them about Christ.

Rufus had left warm water, which he now used to refresh himself. He knew a meal would be ready within the hour. He would need to talk to a few of the men to advise them of the plan that was forming in his mind. He would take one other person with him if anyone should volunteer. He was not about to ask, because what he had planned was just plain insane.

Once he was dressed, he decided to walk the path through the orchard down to the river that ran along the back of the property. It was a glorious morning. The air was warm with the scent of ripening fruit. He began to relax and to pray as he sauntered along the cleared path. He knew there was an arbor up ahead with a stone bench. It was toward the bench that he made his way.

As he neared the place he could hear a melodic voice singing in the arbor. He could make out the form of a woman but could not yet see which one was there. As he neared, she turned. Antipas was pleased to see it was Eunice sitting in the arbor.

"Good morning to you, Eunice." His voice felt dry as chalk as he bowed his head to her.

"A good morning to you, also." A pink flush rose in her cheeks.

"I'm sorry to disturb you. I was just walking for some fresh air before the meal is ready."

"I don't mind." Her face had an eager, but shy, look. "I wanted to talk to you and thank you for all your assistance the day Aristarchus was arrested and for the way you have helped us all settle in."

"You are most welcome." Antipas clasped his hands behind his back, shifting on his sandals. There was silence for a time, and he looked anywhere rather than at Eunice.

Eunice finally broke the uneasy quiet. "I wanted to tell you also that I pray for you every day."

"Thank you, Eunice. Please don't stop, as I'm going to need all the help I can get over the next while."

Her dark eyes looked into his. Her hands were folded in her lap. Antipas observed the stillness in her. "You're going back into Ephesus, aren't you?"

His eyebrows shot up. "Yes, how did you guess?"

"I've sensed that you aren't content to sit in safety when there is work to be done."

Antipas was surprised to hear her say what had been on his mind all night. He looked more closely at her and was pleased with what he saw. Lovely dark eyes rimmed with beautiful lashes, clear skin, with the hint of a dimple when she smiled. Strands of dusky hair escaped her scarf; but he could not express any interest. He wanted to, but his life would not be his own. He had no right to even think about marriage. He would be like Paul and just be married to his Lord.

The insistent clang of a bell announced the meal. "Shall we walk back toward the house together?" Antipas reached out his hand to help her rise.

"Yes, I would like that."

He offered her his arm. Her touch was light like the feel of a feather.

"I'm glad we met out here this morning, Eunice. It has been pleasant talking to you. Are you planning to return home soon?" They strolled along the path lit by the rising sun.

"Epaphras should soon be returning to Ephesus, and when he does, I will return with him."

Somehow this news made him sad.

≈ ≈ ≈

He spent the day praying and working on his plans for the next day. Toward late afternoon he spent time with Mordicai, outlining his thoughts for Ephesus. Mordicai was supportive but cautioned him to take care as his plans had an element of danger to them. By the time the evening meal was announced, he knew what he had to do.

Supper was a tumultuous affair with an abundance of laughter and smiling faces. The families had begun to relax and feel safe once again. Only a few faces were sober, including Antipas's. During the meal, Gad, another church leader, made his way over to Antipas.

"Are you all right, brother?" Gad leaned over and whispered in his ear. "You look pensive. I've been watching you and can see something is troubling your mind."

Antipas turned toward him, a frown shading his face. "I can't share the same feeling of relief I see mirrored on the faces before us. I fear this time is only an oasis and there is a difficult road ahead of us. I'm glad they can relax, but I hope they don't become complacent. We're all going to need our wits about us if we're going to promote the message throughout our land."

Gad nodded his head. He furrowed his brow, nodded once again, and leaned in to whisper.

"I think you're right, Antipas. I for one have been cautious in thinking we're safe. What are you planning? I can tell you have not been idle in your thinking."

"Tomorrow I head for the city. I need to find out what has happened to the homes of the people, and I need to get a feel for how the civic and religious leaders have reacted to our departure. I suspect they have not been pleased." He shivered with the thought.

"Let me come with you. I know my way around the city better than you do and could help us move as inconspicuously as possible." Gad spoke earnestly, his face close to Antipas's.

"I've been praying that someone would be willing to commit to a mission like this. If there are others, let's meet in the courtyard at midnight. I want to make sure everyone is sleeping, as I want our plans to remain secret. The fewer people who know of our movements, the better." Antipas kept his voice low so as not to alarm others around them.

"I'll return to my table now. I'll ask a few discreet questions and see if anyone else would like to go. I'll see you at midnight." Gad slipped back to his place on the other side of the room.

Antipas tried his best to enter into the spirit of the meal, but dark thoughts continued throughout the evening, the midnight meeting, and long into the night.

Twenty-Five

The midnight meeting had gone well with several men attending. The decision was made that only two should make the initial journey to assess the situation in Ephesus, as a larger group would be more noticeable. Gad had begged the group to be the one to accompany Antipas. He and Antipas had agreed to meet along the road where the crossroads connected the trade routes. It would be safer for the families if they were not observed leaving the house together.

Antipas arrived first and busied himself rearranging his pack and fixing a thong on his sandal. When he straightened, Gad was in sight and they moved off together without greeting. Once they were certain they were alone on the road, Antipas turned his head to Gad.

"Are you sure you want to do this?" Antipas shifted his pack and let his eyes roam over the road.

"You know I do." Gad kept looking straight ahead. "We need to check on each home and evaluate the safety of gathering belongings from the houses. I know the city, so we can move through easily."

The road became busier as they neared the city gates. Travelers leading laden donkeys shouted to each other as they jostled with those on foot. Donkeys brayed as people crossed their path. One donkey stopped mid-road and refused to move. Several men ran to help the driver, grunting and shouting as they pushed on its side. The poor animal bellowed while shaking his head. He gave one last yelp and took off running, chased by the laughing men and the angry owner. A young shepherd boy chose that unfortunate moment to arrive with his flock. Fuzzy white bodies scattered to both sides of the road, bleating furiously. Antipas and Gad laughed with the rest of them and helped gather the sheep.

They arrived mid-morning and entered the city without further ado. The market was busy as usual. Throngs of potential customers packed the market paths, disputing loudly with the vendors. Antipas caught a whiff of freshly baked bread that made his mouth water. It was tempting, but they did not stop. They passed unnoticed through the noisy side alleys of the market. Their disguises were simple; farmers' attire consisting of rough gray hooded robes over short brown tunics. It helped them blend in with the crowd.

The sounds and smells of the market faded as Gad led them to the street where Aristarchus lived. They slackened their pace as they entered the laneway, sauntering along in front of the houses in deep shock. The house they sought had been ransacked, and a civic guard stood before the house. The front door had been torn off and discarded in the street. Clothing and household items lay scattered nearby. They passed by, deep in conversation, without glancing at the house or the guard.

At the end of the block Gad turned into the open gate of a midsize house. As they entered, the owner of the house met them in the front courtyard.

"Is there something you desire, friend, that you enter my house uninvited?"

Gad slightly raised the hood of his robe and looked directly into the eyes of the owner. He at once recognized him and quickly led them into the coolness of the interior.

"What are you doing here? You must be crazy to come into the city. Don't you know there is a price on your head and on the heads of all of you who escaped?" The owner paced before them. He shook his fist in Gad's face. "I've been questioned so many times that I almost believe the story I tell. If you're caught, it will be prison and death for the lot of you."

"My friend, you shock me with your news." Gad spoke calmly, reaching out his hand to place on the owner's shoulder. It was quickly pushed away. "We're so sorry we've put you and your family in danger. Tell us the rest of the news quickly, and we'll be on our way. We don't wish to compromise you in any way. Are all the homes guarded and destroyed like Aristarchus's?"

"Some are even worse and have been burned to the ground. There have been riots and protests, much unrest in the city. You're to be made examples of if any of you are caught." By now he had stopped pacing and pierced them with his frantic eyes. "They have no idea where all of you have gone. The city has been searched high and low." He put out his hands. "Please don't tell me where you're staying. I don't want to know. Leave quickly and may your god go with you." He turned away from them, his back rigid.

"Thank you, my friend. You will not see us again. I will make sure the others get the message and stay hidden. I'll also continue to pray that you, too, will come to know this Lord whom we serve."

He swung around, face scrunched. "Ha! Why would I want to bring such danger and disgrace on me and my family? Go."

Gad and Antipas left the courtyard at the same slow pace. They didn't want to draw the attention of the guard. They continued their quiet conversation and retraced their steps back through the market. They had almost reached the gates when a cry rang out.

"Halt."

Antipas looked over his shoulder to see a guard running in their direction.

"Run, Gad." Antipas gave him a push as he set off down one of the paths through the stalls. He could hear activity behind him but didn't stop to see what was happening.

"Halt, I say," the guard roared as he pounded the dirt behind him.

Without slowing his pace, Antipas raced in and out of the market lanes. He had completely lost his sense of direction and the muscles in his legs were tightening. Sweat was gathering on his face and body.

With an oath, the guard stumbled on a bench in front of one of the stalls. Antipas ran on until he could see the gates. Without pausing, he raced ahead through the gates and collapsed on the grassy area to the side of the road. An ancient tree blocked him from view of the gate. He lay there panting, praying the guard wouldn't find him. The minutes droned on until he eased himself into a sitting position. Cautiously he peered around the tree. No sign of the guard. He reluctantly got to his feet. He had to go back. He had to find Gad.

He pulled his robe around him and furtively slid through the gates again. There was no sign of the guard or Gad. He moved from stall to stall, looking down each opening. Finally he located Gad.

"Are you all right?" Antipas was still panting from his run.

"Yes, I guess there was only one guard and he followed you. I ran down a few lanes then realized that I wasn't being followed. I've been looking for you ever since."

"Your friend was right. It's not safe in here. We need to leave and take our report to the families."

≋ ≋ ≋

When they entered the house, some of the men were waiting for them. Antipas greeted them solemnly. "Men, I need to talk to all of you together. Gather the others and we'll meet in the library."

When they were all assembled, Antipas spoke slowly, revealing all they had seen and done that day. His heart was heavy with the burden of the news. He recognized they were all fugitives from their homes and businesses.

In the silence that followed, Antipas gazed at them, seeing the look of dismay in face after face. Aristarchus was the first to speak.

"Brother Antipas, what are we to do? What are your plans? I know you've been praying for a sign from God. Did anything today show you the sign?"

"How spiritually mature you are becoming, Aristarchus. Yes, I do feel today was a sign from God. Whatever His reasons are, the work in Ephesus must go into hiding for the present time. You must stay hidden here for now and use your time wisely." Moans could be heard as the words found their mark. "This is the time for deep meditation on the Scriptures and the time for much prayer. You'll need strength to return and pick up your lives." His face relaxed. "Look at this time as a gift from God to gird yourselves for the spreading of the gospel in the city. These are exciting times, my friends." Antipas now spoke confidently. He was standing straight and tall before them, the picture of one who knew his mind. An inner fire was reflected on his face.

Gad looked at him and stood, arms folded over his farmer's tunic. "Antipas, I'm getting to know you well, and I recognize you have not told us all that has been revealed to you. Nowhere in your words do I hear what you plan to do."

Antipas smiled at his friend. "You, too, are growing in spiritual matters, Gad. You're right; I have not told you all. I am turning the discipling of this group of believers over to the elders of the church of Ephesus. I head for Pergamum."

There was a gasp from the group. They all knew Antipas's story, and this was the last thing they would ever have expected to hear from his lips. There was danger for him in Pergamum. It would be distressing going back when his father had disowned him, but now that he was a part of the Way, his life would be in grave danger.

Gaius spoke into the quiet. "Antipas, I sense there are reasons you must return. I would that you stay with us, but I cannot go against what God has clearly spoken to you. I speak for the whole church here when I say that our prayers will go with you daily as you step out in faith following our Savior and Lord. No matter what the danger, there is no safer or sweeter place to go. Go with our blessing, Brother Antipas."

The others began to speak, some to question, others to reiterate what Gaius had spoken. At times they all seemed to be speaking at once. Antipas soon brought them to quiet, as he wished to discuss some critical things with them.

"The first thing we must do is choose who will lead the church in my absence. You must have a leader, as there will be urgent decisions to make. It must be someone who is trusted by all of you, someone who is growing in his walk with the

Lord. I ask that you suggest a few names, then we will cast lots and decide who will lead." He now stood with his hands behind his back, surveying them.

Several names were mentioned. Antipas asked each man if he would be willing to serve if chosen. It was finally narrowed down to three names; Aristarchus, Gaius, and Gad.

"You have chosen well, brothers. I have great faith in all three of these men. God will make the final decision as He moves in your hearts to express your choice."

The lot fell to Gaius. He paled when his name was given, but rose to face the brothers.

"You have chosen a weak vessel, but one who loves the Lord and will do His bidding in the days ahead. There is much to be done in preparation for our return, and I will need your help mightily."

Each man present spoke before the group and pledged his help and support. When they had all spoken, Gaius asked Antipas when he would be leaving for Pergamum.

"I hope to leave in two days' time. We have had word that Epaphras should be arriving on the morrow. I have a matter I wish to discuss with him before I take my leave of all of you. Now, it is late and your families are waiting for word of our meeting. We need to spend time in prayer, and then you must return to your families."

The men present bowed before the Lord, and heartfelt prayers ascended. Each man prayed fervently for God's will in his life, and courage to follow His leading. Antipas was touched as they prayed for him and his coming journey into the unknown. When the last man had prayed, they embraced each other then quietly left to join their families.

Antipas slipped away to Mordicai's room, where he knew the old man would be still awake awaiting a report on the trip into the city and on the meeting. He made no sounds as he carefully moved through the house, skirting the rooms where the families were preparing for the night's rest.

As he had anticipated, Mordicai was reclining in his bed, but his eyes were bright as he watched Antipas approach.

"Well, my friend, I discern that you have much news for me."

"You are correct." Antipas slipped easily into the chair placed by the bed for nighttime talks. He watched his friend for a moment before he began.

He related all the events of the day and the evening. Mordicai asked many questions, shaking his head in agreement through most of the telling. When Antipas had finished, Mordicai lay back in his bed with his eyes closed. Antipas knew he wasn't sleeping but pondering all he had heard. At last he sat up in bed, a look of excitement on his face.

"I would not have missed these days for anything." His gleaming eyes lit up his lined face. "The power of the Holy Spirit is strong in this place, and God is going to do a mighty work here in Ephesus. And to think that I almost missed it. How could I have been so blind?" He closed his eyes as his face fell. "I have some power in the city. I will once again attempt the trip and see if an old man can still make a difference. I beg you, don't let the others know of my plan. I don't want to appear to take leadership away from them. I just want to be a background person, helping in the only way I can."

Antipas understood the wisdom of this and wholeheartedly agreed.

Mordicai stretched out a thin arm and pointed directly at Antipas.

"And about what, my friend, do you wish to confer with Epaphras?"

Antipas felt the heat rise up his neck and face, try as he might to stop it. He failed in his attempt to speak and just looked at Mordicai.

"I knew it. You're wanting to speak to him about Eunice, aren't you? I knew it." Mordicai was almost bouncing in the bed, snapping eyes and pursed lips gloating at Antipas.

Antipas still could not speak. How had Mordicai guessed his secret?

"It's quite all right, Antipas. You couldn't do better than seek the hand of Eunice. Epaphras has told me all about her family and the simple faith they have in the Lord. I'm sorry if I embarrassed you." Mordicai grinned. "But I'm still not so old that I can't appreciate the young."

Antipas finally found his speech. "You're right, Mordicai, but I don't know how you guessed." His face was still burning, but he grinned back. "I want to talk with Epaphras tomorrow. Without the advice of a father, I'm not sure of the proper procedure, but Epaphras will know how to approach her family."

"Just be prepared, son, she may already be promised to another." He fixed his gaze on Antipas. "That can be changed if you go about it the right way. I think Epaphras and I need to confer. When he arrives, bring him to me and we'll work out the details."

Antipas, getting past his embarrassment, agreed.

Long after their talk, one phrase remained in his mind. "She may already be promised to another."

Twenty-Six

A soft knock sounded on his door early in the morning. He called a sleepy "Come in," and Epaphras appeared.

"Am I ever glad to see you." Antipas jumped out of bed, a wide grin stretching across his face.

They greeted each other heartily and decided to meet in the courtyard as soon as Antipas was ready. He was soon dressed and anxious to talk. Epaphras was waiting for him near the center fountain.

"Let's walk through the vineyard so we can talk without interruption. Mordicai indicated this morning that you had news and questions."

Antipas smiled at that. "He doesn't miss much, does he." He laughed as they entered the path to the vineyard. The grass was heavy with morning dew, wetting the edges of their robes, but refreshing the air.

"He's astute for his age. I'm always amazed at his youthful spirit, especially since he has come to the Way." Epaphras pushed aside a branch hanging over the walkway. "Take your time, but tell me everything that has happened since I was last here, and ask your questions and I'll reply if I know the answers."

Antipas brought his friend up-to-date on the happenings of the last several weeks.

"Friend, I'm impressed with the leadership you're showing and by how much you've grown spiritually since I was last here." He slapped Antipas on the back. "I agree with all your decisions. Keep following the leading of the Spirit." He stopped in the path and faced Antipas. "Now, ask me your questions, friend. If they are spiritually too deep for me, I'll direct you on to Paul."

Antipas felt the color rise in his face once more. He wasn't sure how to say what was on his mind.

"Is something troubling you?" Epaphras frowned at him, laying his hand on his arm.

"Well, there is just one question and it really doesn't have anything to do with the church." Antipas kept his eyes from making contact with Epaphras's.

"Just ask me, friend. You can trust me. I see it troubles you greatly."

"Well, it's just that…well, I would like to make Eunice my wife." He was stammering awkwardly, acutely embarrassed.

Epaphras shouted with glee and slapped him on the back again. "Oh, such good news, Antipas. You've changed your mind about not marrying. I hoped you would."

Antipas faced him, clenching his hands at his sides. "Yes, yes. But how can it be good news if I don't know how to proceed, and I don't know if she'll even have me, and I don't know if her father would accept me, and I don't know if she is promised to another, and I…"

"Wait a minute. Just one thing at a time." Epaphras laughed at him. "I've often spoken with her father about her future." He kept shaking Antipas's shoulder as he talked. "He's never made plans because he wanted to keep her to himself. I actually talked to him on the way here about her. He sees that it would be selfish to try to keep her but refused to be moved." Epaphras shook his head. "Apparently she is promised to a distant relative, but Abdulla doesn't like him as he is old and according to Abdulla, has a cruel streak. But for Abdulla, a business deal is a business deal. He may see your desire as a good thing, a way to get out of this other commitment."

"Oh, this is not good news."

"But it is good news. Don't you see, Antipas? Eunice would be wasted on this unsavory relative. You can rescue her." Epaphras gave one final shake of Antipas's shoulder and stood back.

"It doesn't sound like there's much chance of that." Antipas was aware of the dejection in his voice.

"I have long been concerned for Eunice," Epaphras spoke seriously. "She deserves a family of her own. Her life has been one of service to her father and brothers. She's certainly appreciated by her father, but her brothers see her as a servant for them. This bothers me. I would be pleased and relieved to see a union between you and her."

Antipas opened his arms in a gesture of confusion. "So, what do I do now?"

"Mordicai and I will talk." They had resumed their walking and strolled side by side. "There are ways to break marriage promises. I'm sure Mordicai will do everything in his power to sway Abdulla. Some things just can't be refused. Abdulla is human, you know."

"But what can I do?" He stopped again, distress showing on his face and in the slump of his shoulders.

"Nothing. You proceed with your plans and leave the rest to me. Set out for

Pergamum as planned, and I'll meet you there before the month is out." Epaphras urged him to walk again. "I have a friend in business there. I'll give you his name and a letter of introduction from me. Make contact with him when you arrive. He'll find a place for you to stay and will be our contact. Make sure he knows where you will be so I can find you quickly." They had now reached the vineyard and the smell of ripening grapes permeated the air. "If for any reason I cannot come, I'll write you in care of his business. Relax, my friend, I feel this is right and that God is in it." He indicated they turn around. "Come, let's go break our fast with the others, then I'm sure you have much to do to be ready to leave at sunup tomorrow."

ɔ ɔ ɔ

The remainder of the day was a blur of activity. Antipas spent several hours with the elders to pray with them and assure himself that the work would go on as planned. They had spoken to all the others so everyone knew what lay ahead. He was not able to talk to Mordicai until late that evening, as the old Jew had disappeared early.

Eunice remained invisible for the day. Antipas wasn't sure if Epaphras had spoken to her. He longed to see her but at the same time wasn't sure how to handle it if he did. Did everyone anticipating taking a wife have such turmoil inside him? Surely not. People did this every day. It must be him. That thought didn't really make him feel any better.

ɔ ɔ ɔ

The meeting with Mordicai was a tender one as both men realized that they might not see each other on Earth again. Nothing was said, but what was left unsaid was poignant. Antipas now considered Mordicai as a father and knew the feeling was mutual. There was much to say, yet little to say, as they talked about Mordicai's trip into the city.

"Many people were surprised to see me." He gave a gleeful laugh and rubbed his hands together. "Some thought I must have died years ago, others thought I had moved away." He put his hand up beside his mouth. "I think some of them wished I had gone away. But I managed to answer all their questions and finally arrived in the chief magistrate's office." Mordicai shifted his body in his chair. His face glowed while he talked. "The young clerk wasn't going to let me in to see him, but I set up such a fuss that he gave in and took my name to him. It was such a delight to see that I still have power even after all these years." He slapped his thigh and roared with laugher.

"The chief magistrate must have been surprised to see you." Antipas joined in the laughter, enjoying this new side of Mordicai.

"He was incredibly surprised, but glad as well. We had been close at one time. I started telling him my story, and of course, I can't not talk about Jesus. I wish you could have seen his face." Mordicai pulled his brows together, imitating the magistrate. "He tried to get me to quiet down. I guess he was afraid others would hear us and think he was part of the Way as well." His hands raised, he chuckled again. "But I just kept on going. I had decided if I was going to make the effort to travel to the city, I was not going to waste the time. The name of Jesus would be on my lips." He nodded his head at Antipas, who was grinning as he listened to his story.

"Go on, Mordicai. I'm enjoying the tale."

"Coming from me, that was a great surprise for him, because he knows how strong a Jew I've always been. I told him I would pray for him. I think I may have offended him at that point. However, we go back a long way so he was willing to listen to me." Mordicai rose slowly, needing help from Antipas. He shuffled to the window to look out over the evening garden.

"I pleaded the plight of the Christians and outlined the hardships they've been subjected to. He has promised to see what he can do as a favor to an old friend. He made it quite clear that he would not have done this for anyone else." He put his back to the window before he continued. "He has great influence in the city, so I think you can leave with the assurance that things will improve, at least for a time. It may never be completely safe, but the pressure should soon lift." He wandered slowly back to his chair and sat heavily. "Now, tell me about your day and your talk with Epaphras."

Antipas talked for several minutes and then could see that the old man was tiring. "I must get some sleep if I am to be away at sunup. I'll be in touch through Epaphras and hope to be back someday soon."

He leaned forward and kissed the leathery cheek of the old man, noticing that his face was wet with tears. Antipas whispered, "Good-bye," and slipped from the room, his own face wet too.

Twenty-Seven

The gates of the city loomed over his head as Antipas prepared to enter Pergamum. The rush of memories and long-buried feelings surfaced with startling rapidity. His heart beat faster as he thought of his father and the terrible pronouncement he had made to him. Even the air had a familiar smell to him, the smell of home. What fate would await him here in the land of his birth?

The familiar sights and smells greeted him as he entered the city behind a large caravan. He struggled to see the leader of the wagons but was sure it wasn't Claudius. There had been no talk of heading this way when he was traveling with him. But a caravan always opened up another set of memories.

With tangled feelings he began to thread his way among the peasants and merchants. The noise was intense as vendors shouted their enticements to buy their products. He was feeling pangs of hunger but knew it would not be safe to pause for any length of time. He didn't want to be recognized just yet. It was not likely, since he left as a boy and was returning as a man, but he chose not to risk it.

He sought out the address given to him by Epaphras, wandering along several side streets before he found the right one. Soon he spied the sign of Mattias the iron merchant. This was his destination.

He approached slowly, not sure he should actually stop. However, this was his best option and Epaphras would be expecting him to be here. The door to the shop was open, and inside he could see the light from the fire as a huge man leaned over the flame with tongs in his hand.

He hesitated in the doorway, not wanting to disturb him at his work. The man must be Mattias, as Epaphras had not mentioned any other person working with him. When Mattias stepped back from the flame and plunged the tongs in a trough of water, Antipas stepped into the open area and cleared his throat. He was shaking inside with the emotion of the return and the anticipation of the future.

Mattias turned and looked in his direction. "What can I do for you?"

"I have a letter I would like you to read." He patted his pack where the letter lay.

With a deep laugh, Mattias said, "Now why would I want to waste my time reading a letter? I have enough to do to keep up with my work and provide for my family."

"This letter is from a friend of yours, Epaphras."

"Epaphras, are you sure that's the name? What makes you think I'm the person you seek?"

Antipas dug the letter from his pack and held it out to Mattias. "Please, just read the letter. If you're not the right person, you'll know once you've read the contents, and I will be on my way."

"Let me see it." Mattias held out his enormous hand to accept the letter. He moved back into the room where there was an old desk.

As he began to read, his expression changed. There was a softening around his eyes and a relaxation of his back and neck muscles. Antipas thought he detected tears sliding down his darkened cheeks. Finally, Mattias turned his back on Antipas, and he was sure he was wiping his eyes.

He turned again to face Antipas. "Excuse me, stranger, but I had to be sure it was really my friend Epaphras. There has been some trouble in the city and the people of the Way are suspect. However, this is indeed from my friend. He has instructed me to treat you like a son and accept you into my household until plans can be made for your next move. Please follow me." He turned abruptly and proceeded deeper into the shop.

Antipas hurried to keep up, breathing heavily as the reality of his situation hit him. Here he was in his hometown, a fugitive, disowned by his family and friends, in danger from the people who had educated and mentored him.

By this time, Mattias had passed through a curtain at the back of the shop. Antipas approached the curtain, ducked his head, and plunged through. He found himself in a dark hallway with rough steps leading up to another level. Mattias was already on the steps and approaching a door recessed in the unfinished wall.

As Antipas reached him, he threw open the door and preceded Antipas into a warm room. A frail old lady was sitting hunched over by the fire. She did not even raise her head as the two men entered the room.

"Grandmother Lois," the ironworker roared in his loud voice. At that she slowly turned her body and looked up at the man. She seemed unmoved by the sight of the two of them.

"Grandmother, this young man has come to stay with us for a time. Can you make him a hot drink?"

She looked closely at Antipas, smiled in a crooked sort of way, and nodded her head. She pushed the pot of water farther into the fire and slowly rose to retrieve a cup for him.

Antipas began to protest, but Mattias silenced him. "This is all she's able to do now. Don't take away what she considers her only usefulness."

Antipas understood and moved to thank the old woman. Mattias indicated he needed to return to work and would talk with Antipas later.

As he sank down before the fire, he knew beyond the shadow of a doubt that he was in the right place. He was afraid, but sensed he was where God wanted him to be. The old lady studied him closely and he could see intelligence in her watery eyes. When the drink was ready, she poured a cupful for him and one for herself.

"Welcome to Pergamum, young man." At last she spoke in a whispery voice. "I think you are of the Way, you have the look about you." She seated herself stiffly in her former place by the fire.

Antipas leaned in close to her and replied in a raised voice. She raised her hand to stop him.

"You don't need to raise your voice. I'm not as deaf as they think I am. I can read lips quite well, so if you face my direction and speak slowly, I can follow what you say."

With that established, they began a rather lengthy conversation. He was amazed with her knowledge and her faith in Christ. She had heard about the Way herself a few years ago and embraced the teachings. Her heart was full of love for her Savior.

"The family thinks I have lost my faculties because they don't take the time to spend with an old lady. You are the first person to really talk to me for many days. I have enjoyed our conversation. An old woman still has a lot to offer if she is given a chance. I'll look forward to having more conversations with you while you remain in this house." She struggled to rise again. "Now I must show you where you will sleep tonight and begin preparations for the evening meal. The family will soon be arriving home and there will be no more time to talk. Thank you for listening. You have made an old woman happy."

With Antipas's help she was now standing. She crept across the floor, balancing herself on walls and furniture and indicated he was to follow. She led him down a dark hallway to the back of the house. Through an archway there were steep steps that led to an upper room. This would be his home for the present. She left him at the foot of the steps, explaining that her back would not allow her to ascend to the room.

"It's always kept ready for guests, so you should find everything you need. Come back in an hour for the evening meal."

Antipas quickly climbed the steps and was surprised to see the neatness of the room. Guests were obviously important to this family. A small hearth was laid with the makings of a fire. He lit the fire, pushed the pot of water over the flames, and soon had water for washing.

Clean towels were readily available as well as handmade soap. He soon felt refreshed from his journey. He unpacked his bag, which didn't take long as he had traveled light. His needs were few.

He lay on the cot for a few minutes to relax his muscles after his journey. He fell asleep immediately and was visited once more with a dream. This one took him back to his home, where his father threatened to contact the civic leaders calling for his arrest if he didn't leave Pergamum at once.

"You are the enemy now. I have heard rumors about you. You are not my son; I established that by law several years ago. I consider you a danger to my family and will leave nothing undone to lead to your imprisonment. I give you one chance to leave because of my wife, who has the foolish notion that you are still her son."

Antipas sat bolt upright in bed, the sweat pouring from his body. He was shaking as he carefully approached the window to get some air. Darkness was falling and a cool breeze ruffled the curtains.

He sat and stared out into the garden at the back of the house. As he sat, the dream replayed itself in his mind. Finally, only one thought remained. "My mother still considers me her son. I want to see her. I will find a way to see her. I think this dream was sent, not to scare me, but to assure me of my mother's love."

He thanked God for this wonderful revelation. He would have to be careful and work out a plan whereby he could see her without the knowledge of his father. A thought hit him. Maybe the old woman knew her, or maybe knew someone who knew her. He would have to be careful, but he determined he would find a way to see her. With that happy thought, he prepared himself to join the family for the evening meal.

As he descended the steep, narrow steps, he could hear voices in the central area of the house. Mattias's voice was easily distinguishable above the others. A mellow female voice caught his attention as well as the sound of happy children. The noise ceased as he entered the room. Mattias turned to greet him as the others watched and waited for introductions.

"Antipas, meet my family. This is Larium, my wife; my oldest son, Saul; my little daughter, Tabitha; and my second son, Aaron."

The family made him feel welcome as they settled in to a plain but hearty meal. A thick stew of vegetables and lamb with fresh bread made an excellent meal. The talk around the table centered on the activities of the family during the day. Larium had been selling her handmade products in the market. She reported that business had been brisk, as there were many visitors in the city.

"There is a delegation from Rome in the city, and it seems they've brought all their servants and families with them. The women were looking for unusual things to take back to their homes. I sold everything I had." Larium's face lit up as she recounted the day's activities. "There was talk of the meetings taking place between the Roman officials and our local leaders. Apparently they're still trying to eradicate the teachings of Jesus. They claim His teachings are false and a menace to our way of life. I just listened as many merchants engaged in conversation." She used her hands continually while she was talking, adding texture to her words.

"There will come a time when we must speak up and declare ourselves, but the time is not yet. Our people are still too ungrounded to face the trials ahead." Mattias spoke behind a mouthful of stew, punching the air with his spoon. He turned to Antipas and shook the spoon in his direction. "That is why I'm so glad you've come. Epaphras indicated in his letter that you are just the person we need at this time. He said you would help teach the people and give leadership to our growing group."

Antipas leaned back as stew threatened to spill from the spoon. "I want to be where God wants me to be, doing what He wants me to do. I had a strong urge to return to the city of my birth and I'm willing to serve you in any way I can." Mattias had retuned to eating so Antipas leaned back over his plate again. "I know there will be danger, but I want to be where God can use me."

"You were born here?" Larium raised her eyebrows.

"Yes, I'd like to tell you my story sometime soon. I also have some questions for you."

As they finished the meal, the children left the adults to join friends, and soon only Mattias, Larium, and Lois were left with Antipas.

"Would you feel comfortable sharing with the three of us? I can assure you of our trustworthiness. Anything you say will not be repeated beyond this room." Mattias wiped his hands on the towel Larium had passed him.

"I feel comfortable with all of you and know that my story is safe with you. You may even be able to help me with something I feel I need to do." He relaxed back on his chair, pulling his thoughts together before he began. He leaned forward to be able to see each of them as he spoke, pouring out his entire story to attentive listeners. Occasionally one of the women would make a sound of agreement or of sympathy, but otherwise, they were silent. He sat back and relaxed. It always felt like he had shed a burden when his story was shared. The group sat quietly when he had finished.

"Antipas, I want to ask you a few questions." Larium was the first to speak.

"Of course, anything you want."

"Did I guess correctly that you would like to try to make contact with your mother?" Larium narrowed her eyes and brushed some crumbs from the table in front of her.

Antipas rested his elbows on the edge of the table and looked at her intently. "If I could do that without putting her in any danger; that would be the desire of my heart."

"It may be possible," continued Larium, "because I know your mother."

The quiet was shattered by a cry from Antipas. The others gasped at the news.

"Wife, how would you know a woman of her rank and you just an ironworker's wife?" Mattias was looking at her with a grimace on his face.

"I know it seems strange, but I do know her. She stops by my stall at the market to buy goods from me for her house. She has often spoken to me. You have a wonderful mother, Antipas." She looked from her husband to Antipas. "I know it's her because your father has risen in the ranks of the city leaders and has become well known. She likes to still do some things for herself even though she no longer needs to be involved. I've heard the others talk about her, about how her heart broke when she lost her son and how the father has legally disowned him." She wiped tears from her eyes with the corner of her apron. "She has a soft heart, and although she has always been obedient to her husband, there have been rumors that she has made inquiries into the whereabouts of her son."

Antipas was on his feet, almost knocking over his chair in his haste. "How could we do this? Would I not be putting her in grave danger to attempt to see her? I would not do anything to harm her." He sat down again abruptly. "Is there a way?"

"I think I know how it might be done." Larium nodded her head. "I'll speak to her next market day, indicating I might have news she would be happy to hear. I'll suggest a meeting place, a place where she would not be recognized or put in any danger."

Antipas was smiling with expectation by now. His hands moved restlessly on the tabletop. "Do you know of a place that might work?"

"There's a graveyard just outside the small gate used as a service entrance to the city. The paupers are buried there, and wealthy people sometimes come there to make a show of caring for the graves of the poor. It's mostly for show, but I think it will serve our purposes well. There are trees and walkways that lend themselves to privacy, and you would be able to meet and talk undisturbed."

Antipas felt a lump in his throat and swallowed quickly.

"Thank you, Larium." His voice broke as he spoke. "I can't imagine what it would be like to see her again. It is my greatest desire to meet with her."

Twenty-Eight

A knock sounded on his door. "Come in, please." Little Tabitha entered, balancing a tray containing a pitcher of warm water and a clean towel.

"My mother says the meal will be served as soon as you can be ready. You're to come quickly, as my father has plans for you today."

"Plans? What plans are those?" Antipas leaned down to Tabitha's level.

"I don't know what my father plans, only that my mother says you will not want to be late."

"Then I'll hurry, my little Tabitha." He patted her head and grinned at her.

A huge smile spread over her young face. "I think we'll be great friends, Antipas."

"I think so, too."

She scuffed one toe of her sandal on the floor. "My brothers don't have time for me, they just tell me to run away and do girl things. I get upset but my mother tells me that is the life of a woman."

Antipas raised his eyebrows at this sage remark. There was obviously more behind these words. He determined to get to know the little girl better and try to show her that not all men were like that.

A warning call from her mother sent her scurrying from the room with the admonition to hurry. Antipas hurried, too, not wanting to miss anything that Mattias had planned. In record time he was ready and on his way down the now-familiar back stairs.

The smell of grain cooking tantalized his nostrils as he entered the main room. Grandmother was bending over the cooking pot, looking warm and already tired. The family took her presence for granted, and although she spent much time sitting by the fire, the little cooking that she did was far too much for her. He also was aware that she would not appreciate the family's knowing of her weakness. She was proud to be able to do this little bit to help. He would never steal this last shred of dignity.

"What are you cooking, Grandmother Lois?" He peered into the pot and sniffed.

She looked up at him and gave him a toothless grin. "It's an old family recipe. My family enjoys the mix of grains ground together and boiled. It warms the body and fills the stomach. There is no better food than that."

"I agree. If it tastes even half as good as it smells, I will declare it the best food I've ever eaten."

"Ah, you tease an old woman." But she stood a little straighter and showed her gums in a smile.

How he longed for the members of his own family. He had forgotten how comforting it was to feel that sense of belonging. His reverie did not last long, as Mattias's shape soon filled the doorway. Everything about the man was big, especially his voice.

"A good morning to you, young man. I trust you were able to sleep in our humble dwelling."

He didn't pause long enough for Antipas to answer.

"I've great plans for us today, Antipas. I've already spoken to some of the followers of the Way this morning, and they are anxious to meet you and to question you on a new doctrine they've heard. Once we finish the meal, we'll head out through the city to our meeting place."

The children arrived just then, and the family sat down to break their fast together. Larium had already gone to her market stall. This was expected to be another big day with all the visitors to the city.

Mattias and Antipas were soon walking through the bright morning sunshine. Pergamum gleamed just the way Antipas remembered. The memories were so poignant this morning that his chest felt compressed with the load. He engaged Mattias in conversation to take his mind off the memories and also off Larium at the market. Would she see his mother today? That was too painful a thought.

Mattias took back ways around turns and angles Antipas never knew existed. They saw many people on the trek through the poorer section of the city, but all seemed friendly and many knew Mattias by name. He was greeted by a number of people, but no one stopped them to talk. He seemed to be a well-known visitor to these parts, and as such, Antipas was accepted as his companion.

Antipas was surprised when they neared an obscure city gate. It was a small one used only for trade and local traffic. "Mattias, I remember this gate. My grandfather brought me through here many years ago. I remember it because of the unusual carving on the wooden gate." He stopped and ran his fingers over the scene. "Grandfather told me a skilled workman wanted to leave a permanent gift to the city and carved this elaborate scene. It's always stayed with me."

"I've never really stopped and looked at it before. It's just always been there." Mattias, too, felt the carving. The wood had weathered with time, turning smooth and gray.

They joined a number of others as they moved through the gate, including a cart loaded with a family obviously moving into the country. Several children sat on top, singing while they giggled and teased each other. It was a joyful scene. Antipas wondered if he would ever experience a family of his own. He wondered how Epaphras was progressing with his plea to Eunice's father. Would the answer be yes? Or would they just laugh at his proposal? It was hard to be a young man on his own without a father to negotiate such things.

Once beyond the city gate, they began to relax and chat about the day ahead.

"You'll enjoy the men we'll meet today. They come from all different backgrounds, but are all committed to Christ." Mattias picked up their speed once they were through the gate.

They left the main road a distance from the gate and proceeded along a pleasant lane overhung with tree branches. It was like walking through a beautiful arbor. The lane was cool after the heat of the city.

They took a few more turns until they were walking across a farmer's field. The crop of vegetables was abundant and promised a good harvest.

"The farmer of these fields is a member of the Way. We're headed to an isolated stable at the back of his property." At the end of the field, they once more entered a wooded area and moved along a narrow path. They soon spotted the structure and approached quietly.

Mattias tapped gently on the doors before slipping through the open space. It was dark inside and they waited a few seconds to let their eyes adjust. Once they could see again, Mattias strode to the far corner and entered another room. This one smelled strongly of old leather, but Antipas quickly forgot that as he looked into the eyes of a dozen men.

Some were quite young, but others had seen many years. Most were dressed in peasant robes and appeared to be workingmen. Weather-lined faces and gnarled hands spoke of their occupations. Others appeared to be merchants and businessmen, but what was most striking was the warmth Antipas noticed radiating from their faces.

The greetings were warm, and the welcome extended to Antipas was one of deep respect. Mattias made the introductions then asked one of the men to speak on behalf of the rest.

"You are not only welcome here, but your coming is in direct answer to the prayers of many of us. We have heard about how you have been leading the church at Ephesus. We desire what news you have of the brethren there and then want to know your plans for your stay in Pergamum." The speaker stood with his feet apart, hands at his sides. "I will be bold and tell you we are hoping you will lead our fledgling group of believers here. You know the culture and what we face and could make a huge difference in our little church. This is a long speech for me, so I will stop and let you bring us your news."

The speaker, Emin, sat down quickly and wiped his face on his robe. It was obvious that he was not accustomed to speaking in such a setting. Antipas then began to present his news about the church at Ephesus. He spoke for several minutes, occasionally being interrupted as someone would ask a question for clarification or would ask about a specific person.

The time went quickly. Antipas felt an overwhelming love for these people. He sensed that this was where God had been calling him; he sensed his destiny in this group of farmers and merchants who wanted to follow Christ and build a work for Him in Pergamum. He forgot the danger, his personal problems, and all else as the vision of the work ahead took shape in his mind.

The others seemed to feel the same thing as he spoke. They made plans for him to speak to the whole group on the third day from now. The location would be made known to Mattias, and the families would be there.

After the men had drifted away one by one, Mattias and Antipas left. There did not seem to be anyone about as they exited the stable into the warm, bright day. They retraced their steps back through the woods, across the field, along the lane, and onto the main thoroughfare leading into the city.

Twenty-Nine

When they neared the house, Antipas tensed in anticipation of Larium's return from market. Would she have word from his mother? Just thinking about it gave him a warm, but terrified feeling. Before he reached the door, he could hear the voices of both women so he knew Larium was back. His knees felt weak as he pushed open the door and slipped into the room. Larium looked up as he entered and greeted him warmly.

"Come, sit by the fire. I have much news for you."

Antipas quickly complied and looked expectantly at her.

"I saw your mother today."

Antipas was surprised at the tears suddenly coming to his eyes.

"I approached her carefully, as she was with another woman. I asked if I could speak to her privately. She looked surprised and frightened but quickly agreed. My face was certainly familiar to her, as she visits my booth often, but I had never spoken to her before except for what was needed to complete a purchase." Larium pulled a chair to the other side of the fire and sat facing Antipas. "We moved to the side of the booth and I spoke to her of her son. At first she thought I was talking about one of your brothers, but she gradually came to understand that I was talking about you. I thought she would faint on me. She went pale and began to shake, but quickly got herself under control and started demanding information about you. 'Tell me everything you know,' she said to me. I told her what I could then asked if she would like to meet you."

"I can hardly believe you actually talked to my mother. Go on, tell me more."

"She looked around furtively as if she expected someone to be listening. 'It would be the greatest desire of my life. If I could only see him one more time I think I would be content. My heart has been broken because of this separation.'"

Antipas coughed into his arm, trying to hide his emotion. He gestured for Larium to continue.

"We spent the next few minutes making plans as to where you could meet in safety. We decided the cemetery was too open a place, but quickly agreed upon another location. Tomorrow at noon she'll be there. It's in a remote section of the city where there's a safe house. It belongs to a member of the Way and is also known to your mother."

Antipas could hardly take in the news. All the agonies of the past few years washed over him, and his desire to be reunited with his mother overwhelmed him. He choked back his emotions as Larium ceased speaking.

"There's so little I can say to express my thanks to you. You have given me back my youth and my life. To know that my mother wants to see me is more than my mind can handle, but to actually see her, to feel her touch again, is the thing my dreams are made of."

The rest of the day crawled by in an agony of memories. Antipas tried to focus his mind on other things, but the face of his mother was constantly before his eyes. The questions flowed through his mind. Would he be able to see her often, or would this once have to suffice for the rest of his life? He wasn't sure he could cope with this being the last time. Somehow, it had to be a beginning, not an ending.

He worried about his mother as well. She was risking so much to see him. If his father should ever find out, it could mean her life. He finally fell to his knees in prayer to his Savior.

"Lord, this is too heavy a burden for me to bear. I need You on so many levels in my life. Please keep my mother safe. Keep this information from my father. O Lord, may this be the beginning of many times of being together with my mother. Most of all, I need peace, the peace that only You can give. Amen."

He was able to sleep through the night, wrapped in the thoughts of his meeting with his mother. The morning was fresh and clear, promising a good day. Mattias was to lead him to the house where he would meet his mother. Late morning they set off through the city. Once again, Mattias led them through side streets into the section of the city where the house was located.

"This is the street." Mattias leaned close to Antipas and spoke in a low voice. They were reluctant to speak any louder for fear someone would overhear and become suspicious.

"It's the third house from the end of the street. I will leave you at the next alleyway so you can proceed alone. Don't knock on the door, just go right in. The owners will not be there, so you will be able to visit in private. Don't worry, it's safe. We have taken all the precautions necessary to protect your mother."

Before Antipas realized what was happening, Mattias disappeared down the side alley. Antipas kept walking slowly toward the third house. Would his mother be there already? Or had his father found out and kept her from coming? Would soldiers be waiting for him instead?

The door was slightly ajar as he approached. He took a deep breath, sent up a quick prayer, then pushed open the door. He heard a gasp then felt familiar arms surrounding him. He soon realized both he and his mother were crying unashamedly. They stayed in this embrace for several minutes. He didn't want to let her go.

"Oh, my son, my son! I thought I would never see your dear face again. I have grieved for you for so long. I can hardly believe you're here. Let me look at you."

She gazed tenderly at her son, caressing his face as she spoke softly to him.

"Mother, I have dreamed about seeing you again every day since the day my father sent me away. Are you sure you aren't in danger meeting like this?"

"Oh, I'm sure that I am. Your father has not changed at all in the last few years. In fact, he's more rigid than ever. We would both be in desperate trouble if he found out about this meeting. We've all been forbidden even to speak your name. But one look at you is worth any risk. I will risk it again and again, if I can only just see you." Antipas held her hand as they talked. "It's as safe as we can make it. If you're willing to take the risk, I am more than willing."

"Then it is settled. We'll meet whenever we can."

They embraced once again, then sat down together to get caught up on each other's lives since they had parted. Many tears flowed as Antipas recounted his experiences and he found out what had been happening in the family. Both of his brothers took the same hard stand as his father. They no longer treated their mother with respect. She was more a slave in the household than a wife and mother.

"So, we are in danger from your brothers as well. But I have nothing else to live for except to see you. You have given me a reason to live again."

The talk moved on to Antipas's relationship with Christ. His mother listened intently, asking questions and making comments.

"Your grandfather believed in God, I am sure. I would like to hear more. You have a calmness about you that makes me want to have what you have."

"Oh, my mother, nothing would give me greater pleasure than to lead you to my Savior. We'll have many talks when we meet. Accepting Christ is life-changing."

Soon there was a soft knock on the back door. Antipas turned quickly. This was not part of the plan. The face of Mattias appeared, then his whole body slipped into the room.

He slid up beside Antipas. "There's someone watching the front of the house. I saw him first and was able to turn into an alleyway beside a house farther down. We're in extreme danger."

"Is there a way out?"

"The only way I can see is out through the back. It's rough through the field behind here, but we can't go out the front."

"But my mother, how can we keep her safe?"

"I'll keep her with me if we have to split up."

Banging started on the front door.

"Open up," commanded a loud, strident voice.

Mattias quickly shoved Antipas and his mother out through the door. As he closed the back door they could hear splintering from the front. They slipped behind an outbuilding, waiting to see which way the intruders would go.

"There's no one here. I told you it was just a rumor. He wouldn't be brave enough to show his face in daylight."

Military steps thumped out the front door and faded into the distance. The three slipped from behind the outbuilding and began their trek across the field. All three now realized the danger was greater than they had feared.

Thirty

Now the real work of the church began. Antipas met with the same group of men on several occasions to discuss their vision for Pergamum. They spent many long hours in prayer for God's wisdom. It was never safe, but safety was not their concern. The message of Christ had to be spread to the city no matter the cost. They felt compelled to push forward.

Antipas found the men willing, but they had little teaching. He began a series of teaching sessions with them to help ground them in their beliefs. The hours he'd spent with Paul in Ephesus were paying off as he passed on to these brothers the teachings of Paul. They spent many happy hours discussing, sometimes even arguing about, the things they were hearing.

"This whole idea of forgiveness is hard." Emin stroked his beard as he spoke. "Some of our lives are in danger because of our beliefs. How can we forgive the people who have disowned us and threaten to kill us if we don't turn back?"

"Paul says that Jesus said we are to forgive not just family members and friends, but enemies as well, even up to seventy times seven."

"Do you think the people of Pergamum will be able to accept this teaching? If seems as though holding a grudge is the accepted practice." David wore a puzzled look on his face.

At this point, Antipas realized it was time to share his own story with them. As he talked, he knew he needed to change his attitude to his own father. "I know now that I am not responsible for the actions of my father. It would be wrong of me to hold a grudge against him, or to hate him in my heart. What he has done is the weight he has to carry. I don't have to carry it. I only have to give it over to Christ and He will carry it for me."

As he spoke, he was aware of a great weight lifting off him. He hadn't realized how it had been pulling him down the whole time Christ was lifting him up. He knew now he would be able to forgive his father if he was ever asked to do so.

The talk moved to other things as the men continued to ask questions. Plans were made for a missionary journey into Pergamum early the next week. They would talk to their families and friends to swell the numbers ready to approach the city.

The plan was to converge on the marketplace early in the day. They would talk with people they knew; friends, neighbors, fellow workers, anyone who would listen. All would be invited to attend a gathering planned for the following day outside the eastern gates. This was a bold move, but they decided they needed to be bold for Christ. Their lives were now totally committed to Him and no risk was too great.

"I think we need to pray through the night hours, seeking God's direction." Mattias looked to Antipas. He agreed and three other men decided to join them. They prayed for hearts to be softened to the words they would be hearing. They prayed far into the night, only ending when they felt the Holy Spirit prompting them. They still had a few hours before dawn and fell into a deep sleep for the remaining time.

Before the sun was fully up, they were on their way into the city. They had decided to go individually and in small groups; this would draw less attention to them and make them more effective as they spoke to people.

"There is always the chance that someone in the city may recognize me," Antipas mentioned to Mattias as they walked.

"If that happens, we need to leave the area as quickly as possible." It wasn't a matter of fear anymore, but a matter of keeping Antipas safe to be able to carry on the teaching ministry he had started with the young church. Antipas knew they really needed him at the present time. God would protect him, but he also knew that God expected him to be prepared and aware of what was going on around him.

Before they reached the marketplace they could hear the vendors hawking their wares, the voices of children laughing and playing, the inevitable barking of the city dogs, as well the mingled noises of animals connected with all market-places. The familiar smells brought a nostalgia to him as he remembered the many times he had visited this same marketplace with his mother. He also remembered the last time he had seen it, the day his father had disowned him.

He put all those thoughts aside as they moved among the stalls. He was here for a different purpose today. The last time he was here he was a defeated teenager. Today he was a victorious Christian. What a difference in his outlook. Then he had no hope and had no idea what the future would hold for him. He now had a hope and a future.

He turned his attention back to the present in time to see Mattias approach a middle-aged man. He was selling produce from his farm but was not occupied at the moment.

"Lucian, my friend, I have not talked with you in some time."

"I haven't seen you around the market for several weeks." Lucian glanced around at the vendors close by, then stared intently at Mattias. "Have you been ill?"

"No, I've been out of the city for much of that time. I've discovered good news that I'd like to share with you."

"I hope you haven't become involved in that new cult I've heard about." He kept his head lowered but continued glancing from side to side, moving only his eyes.

"What cult is that?" Mattias moved closer to him.

"Some new god people are talking about. A Jewish god at that. I've never heard anything so crazy in my life." Lucian spit on the ground beside his stall.

"Would you like to hear about the one true God?" Mattias spoke in his normal tone.

"Can you actually say there is only one god?"

"I can and I do." This was proclaimed boldly in a loud voice.

"Not a chance. You know there are many gods. You are part of that new cult, aren't you?" Lucian's lips curled in a sneer.

"I assure you, I'm not part of a cult. I've found the true meaning of life."

"Life doesn't have much meaning where I come from."

Just then some women arrived to haggle over prices for the produce. Mattias and Antipas stepped aside until the transaction was finished. Once the women had moved on to the next stall, Mattias stepped up again. He softly told Lucian about the meeting to be held tomorrow outside the eastern gate.

"Sounds sinister to me." He kicked the ground, sending little showers of dirt into the air.

"Lucian, we've been friends for a long time. Have you ever known me to be involved in anything offensive?" Mattias leaned closer again.

"Well, no. But this seems suspicious." Lucian shrugged in his robe, drawing it tighter around him. His eyes continued to shift from side to side.

"Why not come and find out for yourself?"

"I might come." He threw his head back and looked up at the sky.

They had to be satisfied with that as more customers came. The two men moved off to find others known to Mattias.

By noon Mattias had invited several people, some who agreed to come. They sauntered out of the marketplace, as noon was the time agreed upon to stop the contacts for the day. As they walked back to the house, they were quiet for the first part of the way.

"We did it! We spoke boldly in the marketplace. Our prayers for boldness and for softened hearts were answered. We'll need to pray long again tonight in preparation for the meeting tomorrow." Mattias's robe swung at an angle as he jumped into the air.

Antipas, too, felt the excitement. They had made a beginning. Where it would end he didn't know, but the end was not his business, that belonged to God.

Thirty-One

A gray, dull morning crept over the horizon, but Antipas's spirit could not be influenced by the weather today. This was a big day; meeting day. Today the fledgling church was putting it all on the line for Christ; willingly, joyfully, prayerfully.

Nothing else mattered anymore. The men were filled with the Holy Spirit in much the same way the disciples were said to have been at Pentecost. His power flowed through them as they proceeded to the appointed place outside the eastern gate.

Antipas wanted to arrive long before the others and had left the house before dawn. He was now on his knees on the spot where later in the morning he hoped to present Christ to a large crowd of unbelievers. He offered himself once more to Christ, asking for his Lord to be seen through him that day.

"O Lord, it is not I who am important, it is You. Let the people see You, not me. Father God, let Your will be done today, both in my life and in the lives of those who hear about You for the first time. Give me the words to say and the power to say them. Amen."

As he rose from his knees, the first of the converts were arriving, accompanied by their wives and children. There was an atmosphere of hope and excitement as the numbers swelled. Antipas recognized that many people were not of their little group. His heart grasped the anticipation of the crowd.

The believers moved among them, welcoming those they had invited yesterday. Many of the guests had also brought their families as well as friends and neighbors. God had truly opened hearts with a curiosity and a longing to hear what this was all about.

Antipas guessed there were several hundred people present by the time he rose to speak. There was much talking and movement until he bowed his head once more. A hush fell.

"I am here today to tell you about the one true God." His voice rang out over the crowd. "The God who created the heavens and the earth. Look around you and see His marvelous works. Recognize that only a superior creator could have designed what you see." He pointed with his hands to the trees ringing the field, the colorful display of wildflowers, the sky. He lifted one arm high over his head. "Consider the heavens, the sun and the moon, the stars that you see each night. You look at the night sky and name the stars and the patterns they present to your eyes. Only God could create and maintain a universe like ours." He could see people were watching him, listening attentively.

"But this God is far more than a creator. This God came to earth because of His great love for you." His arm now swept the crowd. "Yes, people of Pergamum, even though you don't know Him, He knows and loves each one of you. He knows what is in your hearts. He even knows the number of hairs on your head. He knows these things because He designed and made each one of you. Because He made you, He loves you. He wants you to know Him and love Him. Because of this, He came into our world."

Antipas told of the birth of Jesus, His life, His miracles, His death, His resurrection. He told them of changed hearts, of forgiveness of sins. He talked for over an hour and still the crowd listened.

As he spoke, God was working in their hearts, softening them to the words being spoken, convicting them of the sin in their lives. Antipas's words were falling on open, hungry hearts. Even the children sat quietly as their elders listened.

Finally Antipas stopped. He prayed aloud this time and asked God to bring unto Him as many as He desired today. When he opened his eyes, he spoke to the crowd again. "You have heard the truth, my friends, the truth about the only God. He wants you to come to Him. Come, my friends, don't say no to God."

As he spoke, people began to fall to their knees, imploring God to save them, to accept them into His kingdom. They acknowledged that He was the one and only God and turned their hearts to Him.

Antipas and the other Christians talked and prayed with the many who wanted to give their hearts to Christ. They shared their own experiences of how Christ had changed their lives. As people opened their hearts to God, his Holy Spirit was poured out on them as it had been on the others. It was evidence that they truly believed and were now children of God.

Antipas rose to speak once more. "Friends and now brothers and sisters in Christ, evening approaches and you need to return to your homes. We will be here tomorrow at the same time, and we'll begin to teach you more about Christ. You have witnessed an outpouring of the Holy Spirit. You are about to embark on a journey such as you have never taken before. Go now to your homes and come tomorrow if you are able."

As the crowd began to disperse in small groups, the weary but ecstatic believers gathered around Antipas. They all began talking at once, their voices filled with excitement.

"Fellow believers, you, too, need to take your families and go home to rest and eat. We all need to be here before noon tomorrow. After the meeting we will need to make plans for future meetings and discuss how we can effectively teach so many people. What an awesome problem to have. But now we all need rest and refreshment. Go, my friends." He shooed them away, pointing in the direction of the path.

At last only Mattias and Antipas remained.

Mattias clapped his hand on Antipas's shoulder. "Now you need to take your own advice and head for home with me."

"You are so right. I have never experienced a day like today. But tomorrow will be a big day as well, so let's go."

Evening shadows were lengthening as the two set out. The sun rested on the horizon before it slid out of sight to begin its nightly journey toward tomorrow. Some cults believed that this was a dangerous time of day when evil was abroad. Antipas had no such worries as he knew evil was abroad at all times, but he was convinced that Paul was correct when he said, "Greater is He that is in me, than He that is in the world." It was so releasing to put your trust in the living God. Antipas believed that nothing could come into his life that wasn't sanctioned by his heavenly Father.

The men were silent as they walked, filled with the events of the day. Antipas was amazed with the outpouring of God's Holy Spirit on the group.

"Mattias, I've never experienced anything like what we witnessed today. I feel humbled that God could use even someone like me. I was an outcast, but He took me in. Can you believe it?"

"I surely can. I'm nobody and He accepted me. We're on the brink of something more wonderful than we can imagine. It also scares me, as we know that the evil one will be at work extra hard tonight as these new believers return to their homes. Many of their homes are filled with idols that have been dedicated to the gods." Mattias shook his head sadly. "Will they be able to resist the influence of them while we try to teach them and ground them as Christians? We need to pray the night through again, my brother."

"Mattias, you are sounding like Paul."

"No, that will never happen, but I have talked more than I usually do. I'm just so excited about the events of the day that God has loosened my tongue." They laughed together.

As they neared home they could see the lamp burning through the window. The family had left before them to prepare the evening meal. They were suddenly hungry and increased their pace. As they entered they heard voices in animated conversation. Antipas stopped and listened. He was sure he could hear the voice of Epaphras talking with the family. Mattias heard it too and put his arm around his shoulder.

"Get moving, Antipas. There may well be good news waiting for you."

He entered the room, his heart racing.

Thirty-Two

A ntipas, greetings." Epaphras bounded across the room and gripped him in a hug.

"Epaphras, you're here. We have much to tell you. You won't believe what has been happening here in Pergamum." Antipas slipped out of his outer robe, folding it carefully before placing it on a table.

The words tumbled out as Antipas tried to cover his excitement at seeing Epaphras and his anxiety regarding what Epaphras would have to tell. He wanted to blurt out his questions but knew it would not be proper to ask in front of the whole family.

"The women have the meal ready." Mattias gestured toward the readied table. "We can talk as we eat."

Antipas sighed within and looked to Epaphras. Epaphras graciously accepted Mattias's suggestion, forcing Antipas to contain his anxiety awhile longer. Soon the family was gathered around the table as the food was placed before them. A prayer of thanks was offered to the God who provided, then they began to serve and enjoy the savory dishes.

Talk soon turned to the events of the day. Epaphras was delighted to hear of the amazing things taking place. He offered suggestions on how to teach so many people the message of the gospel. Once the meal was over, the men continued their conversation. The three talked and prayed well into the night.

"Friends, we need to rest for a few hours before we meet again with the crowds for teaching." Mattias stood, stretching and yawning.

Epaphras was spending the night on a mat in Antipas's room, so the two climbed the stairs together. Once they were safely inside their room, Antipas could wait no longer.

"Tell me quickly, what did her father say? I've tried not to let my hopes rise, as I know that I'm not worthy of her, that I have nothing to offer. Why did I ever think he might say yes? Why—"

"Antipas, will you stop talking long enough for me to speak?" Epaphras laughed at his friend. Antipas looked at his smiling face, and hope began to rise again in him.

"Everything is arranged, Antipas. Her father did indeed say yes. We negotiated for several hours before we came to an agreement, but I expected that. I think he is delighted with your offer." Epaphras clapped him on the back.

"My offer? What offer is that? I have nothing." He crossed his hands over his chest, his mouth hanging open.

"That's true, but you have friends in high places who took great pleasure in making it worthwhile for Abdullah to accept your offer. I suspect from previous conversations he would have accepted you anyway, but it gave Mordicai such pleasure to offer a bride price. He says you are the son he never had."

Emotions welled up in Antipas as he considered the old man and the incredible news Epaphras had just given him regarding Eunice. He looked at Epaphras, who put a hand on his shoulder and grinned at him.

"Your cup is full, Antipas. What more could you ask for in life? You have been successful in your attempts to reach the people of Pergamum, and the desire of your heart has been fulfilled in Eunice." He squeezed his shoulder.

"I'm dazed. I'm happy. I'm thrilled beyond everything. God has enriched my life far beyond my dreams. And I know nothing about how to proceed with a wedding." Antipas was moving restlessly around the small room.

"Relax. Abdullah insists the wedding will be in his village and he will make all the plans. You only need to show up when he tells you to. He said to give him six months from the day we reached an agreement, and that will be the wedding day."

Antipas collapsed on his bed. "But what of Eunice? Has she been asked? Maybe she won't want to marry me."

Epaphras pushed his shoulder. "You're worse than an old woman. She's been in love with you since the day we first arrived at her home. It's been obvious to those of us who know her well. She will make you a wonderful wife. An obedient wife is a good thing. An obedient wife who also loves you is beyond compare. You will not have cause to regret this decision."

"But what if I'm not worthy of her?"

"I'm going to sleep now. You talk and worry too much. Good night, Antipas."

With that, Epaphras blew out the candle and settled down on his mat. There was nothing left for Antipas to do but lie down in his bed, too. Epaphras was soon asleep, having traveled all day and talked most of the night. Antipas was too keyed up to sleep. What a day.

❦ ❦ ❦

Antipas awoke with a gasp. His body was gripped in a cold sweat. He shook his head to clear his thoughts. Another dream. The remnant of it sent shivers down his spine. Would he ever get past these terrors in the night?

Slowly his heart returned to a normal rhythm as he recounted the events of the dream. As usual, his father played a big part. Tonight he taunted him with the happiness Antipas had felt wrapped around his spirit. His father warned him that for someone like him, happiness was only an illusion.

"Revenge," his father spat at him. "I will have revenge for what you did to me. No son denies his father's wishes the way you denied mine and lives. You will experience my wrath in ways you can't imagine. You think you can find love with this common girl? You disgust me. I have no son named Antipas. No son... no son... no son..."

That was when Antipas awoke with the shouts of his father ringing in his ears.

Now as he lay quietly in the dark of the night, he wondered if his father was right. Maybe he shouldn't get married, maybe it wasn't fair to Eunice to be tied to one such as he. His father was wrong about one thing; Eunice was not a common girl. It was his family who was not worthy of her.

"O Lord, make me worthy of her. Help me to love her the way You have declared a wife should be loved. And Lord, give me peace. Help me to know that this is the right thing for Eunice and for me."

The warmth of the night stole over him as he prayed. He drifted into a deep, dreamless sleep and was awakened by the birds in the garden singing their good morning melody. He stretched leisurely, feeling well rested. The events of the previous day gradually crept into his awakening awareness, bringing joy to his heart as he thought about the new converts and about his impending marriage.

When he opened his eyes, he realized he was alone in the room and the sun was up farther than it should have been if he was going to be prepared for the teaching sessions awaiting him at noon.

He quickly jumped from his bed, dressed, and refreshed himself with the basin of cool water left for him on the side table. He hurried down the stairs and into the bright sunshine of the main room. The smell of breakfast lingered in the air, but there was no one around. As he wondered where the family had gone, Epaphras and Mattias appeared in the doorway.

"Good morning, Antipas, you sleepyhead." Epaphras grinned at him, coming into the room. "It's well past the hour you should have arisen, but we decided you needed sleep more than anything else this morning after all the excitement of yesterday. Mattias and I have made all the preparations for the sessions at noon today."

"I can't believe I slept late. I'm ready now, I can eat on the way."

"No, no." Mattias gestured to the table. "My wife has prepared a meal for you, and you must eat before we begin the walk to the meeting place. You're going to need all your strength today. From what I hear in the village, we can expect even more people today. Apparently we are being discussed in the marketplace."

"What are they saying? Is it good or bad?" Antipas was now seated and attacking the meal of fresh bread and fruit.

"Some say we're crazy, and we can live with that. Others are saying we've got evil spirits in us and that we'll destroy Pergamum. But there are many who believe and want to know more. All of them plan to come today to see what will happen." Mattias reclined on the couch across from him.

When Antipas finished, he suggested they pray together before they set out. They bowed on their knees in a circle together and asked for the Lord's guidance for the day. Paul had told them often enough not to worry about what they were going to say, that the Holy Spirit would give them the appropriate words when they needed them.

The three friends set off before the sun had reached its noon position. They were silent as they walked, drinking in the beauty of the morning. Soil had been turned over in a nearby field, delivering an earthy smell on the sleepy breeze. The early mist still had not completely dissipated and it clung to grasses in low-lying areas. When the sun touched it, the resultant brightness turned the whole area into a sea of sparkling gems.

The promised warmth was already making the men feel warm, but this they ignored as they pondered the significance of the day. Antipas expressed the excitement they were all feeling when he said, "The Church of Pergamum has been born. I feel like a new parent, excited but scared as well. How will we look after this baby church?"

There was no reply to his query. There were no answers as of yet.

They heard the voices even before they could see the open field where they were to meet. As they breasted the hill, the field stretched out before them, already crowded with men, women, and children. Dogs were running here and there among the people, hoping for morsels from lunches that might fall to the ground. Antipas guessed there must be three or four thousand people awaiting them. He breathed a quick prayer. "God, You are awesome. My human mind can't comprehend Your greatness. These people before me are here at Your command. I am simply Your servant, here to do Your work. Give me the courage and stamina to feed this flock."

And then they were spotted. A great cheer arose, although the men could also hear jeers among the sounds rising to meet them. They quickly climbed to the highest part of the field. Antipas took charge, feeling strength from the Lord course through his body.

"I am here today to introduce you to Jesus Christ, who died to rescue you from your sins." Antipas had to raise his voice to a shout to be able to be heard over the noise in the field. Once he started, quiet descended over the throng and they gazed at him with rapt attention.

For the next hour he told them about Christ, the God who lives, not like the idols they worshipped in the temple each day. He told them about the love the Father had for them and how He willingly sent His only Son, Jesus, to die for them. They seemed amazed that Jesus came to earth and that He willingly gave His life. This was such a new idea. All the gods they knew demanded things from them like money and the sacrifice of not only animals, but sometimes humans as well. That there was a God who became the sacrifice for them was incomprehensible.

When Antipas finished speaking, he told the people to come again the next day when plans would be in place for further teaching. The crowd slowly began to disperse. Many seemed reluctant to leave and talked quietly in small groups. The believers crowded around Antipas again and an earnest conversation followed.

Antipas had been giving much thought as to how they could best teach all these people. "I suggest we form groups that will meet in your homes and each head of the household will be the leader of the church that meets there."

At first there was some resistance to the plan. "How can we do that? We're not trained."

"What Antipas is proposing is similar to what happens in the Jerusalem church." Mattias spoke earnestly to the group. "I think we need to consider his suggestion."

"I don't feel I can accept that responsibility." Heads began to shake. Lines of worry were visible on several faces.

"God will give you whatever you need to become a leader and teacher." Antipas studied their faces, watching for their reactions. At last they began to sense that this was from God and that He would bless what they were doing.

Before they left, ten men had agreed to host such gatherings. Antipas promised that he would visit each group in turn and teach them and that he would teach the leaders as often as they could meet together. He would be available to them at all times. Excitement began to build as they thought of the possibilities.

Soon the field was empty, even the dogs having left with the larger group earlier. Antipas, along with Mattias and Epaphras, knelt in prayer on the grass at their feet. They could feel the Holy Spirit present with them.

As they began their walk home, Antipas knew that things would never again be the same for them. A new era was being born, and he didn't want to miss anything that God had in store for them.

Thirty-Three

ntipas's days were filled with plans as the ten new house churches began to take shape. People returned to the field the next day; the leaders were ready and divided the families into groups according to their location in the city. There would be some adjusting to this plan as the days went by, but it was a great beginning.

The role Antipas would now play would be overseer of all the churches. It was decided that he would visit a different one each Sunday and teach the people what God put on his heart. Several times during the week he would meet with the church leaders for teaching purposes to help them feed their hungry spiritual flock. He would also continue to make contacts in the city and funnel any new converts into the various house churches.

Mattias agreed to act as his assistant, as there were many duties to perform and many people in need of ministration. Mattias also needed to continue his iron work to feed his family and help the more destitute of the new converts.

Epaphras helped for as long as he could stay and promised to pray unceasingly for the work in Pergamum. He would be visiting other churches on his journeys and would bring tidings from the church in Pergamum. All of these established churches would be in prayer for them as well.

On the last evening before Epaphras had to leave, he asked Antipas to walk with him a distance into the country. It would give them a good opportunity to talk over plans for the wedding. As they set out, the full moon was just rising, throwing a silver sheen over the countryside. The evening was warm but pleasant, and the two men walked at a comfortable pace.

Epaphras slapped Antipas on the back. "It was the night of the last full moon when Abdullah and I made the agreement for your wedding, brother. So, four full moons from now will be your wedding day. It's said by the old wives that it's lucky to be wed at the full moon."

"I don't believe in luck, or in the tales of the old wives. But I will be overjoyed to marry Eunice under any sky. Are you sure, brother? Only four full moons?" He breathed the night air, filling his lungs with the freshness. "I can't believe it's really going to happen."

"Spoken like a true bridegroom. I will plan my next business trip to Pergamum a month before the wedding and accompany you back to Ephesus. Mordicai will be more than happy to see you again. He misses you and will want to talk to you before you wed." A cloud passed over the moon, obscuring the path for a moment. They ceased their conversation and slowed their pace until the moon once again made its appearance. "Mordicai has business regarding the bridal settlement he wants to discuss with you, as well as other matters related to the support of the church here in Pergamum. What a difference in a man. He has always been an incredible person, but once he surrendered to Christ, it's like he's really living for the first time. I've never seen him so happy and fulfilled."

"I, too, long to see him. That and leaving Eunice were the two things hardest for me when I came here." Antipas gazed at the trees swaying gently in the evening air. The outline of a few sheep appeared on the rocky hillside to their left. The soft tones of a shepherd singing drifted to them.

"I think he will also ask you and Eunice to stay with him for a time after the wedding. A man should have some time without responsibilities to enjoy his newly married state." Epaphras punched him playfully on the arm. "The church in Ephesus would be thrilled to have you spend a few weeks with them. Mattias can take over for you here for a little while."

"It sounds selfish but wonderful. I'll spend time in prayer about it before I commit to any delay in returning to Pergamum. I've also been thinking that I need to visit my mother again. She will want to know all the plans that are being formed." He shook his head sadly. "I've been afraid for her safety and have seen her but once. However, I think it might be prudent to try to see her again. My father is just as powerful, but she is no longer afraid of him. She knows he can have her put away, or even killed, but he has already broken her spirit and she no longer fears what he can do." He gritted his teeth when he spoke of his father. "I feel the same way. I know that I will encounter him again and that it will not be pleasant, but God is in control and I also no longer fear him."

"It's amazing how God can remove our fears. You are rapidly growing spiritually. Every time I see you, the change is astounding. What a great God we serve."

They at last turned their walk back toward the city. It was getting late and Epaphras wanted to have an early start next morning.

≈ ≈ ≈

Once Epaphras departed, Antipas sought out Larium to inquire about the possibility of meeting his mother again. Bread was baking, filling the house with its fragrance. He heard Larium's voice in the kitchen and approached quietly. She looked up as he entered the room.

"Good morning, Antipas. Did Epaphras get away as early as he had hoped?" She was stirring the pot by the fire in preparation for the first meal of the day.

"Yes. I've just returned from walking him to the stable. I wondered if I could speak with you privately for a minute."

"Of course, just let me take the bread from the oven, and I'll meet you in the garden."

Antipas sat on the stone bench by the arbor until Larium appeared. He nervously watched her approach. He knew that what he was about to ask was dangerous for her and for his mother, but he felt compelled to ask. He must see her again before his marriage. She must be informed of her son's imminent wedding.

∾ ∾ ∾

Larium studied the young man in front of her as she approached the bench where he was sitting. Her handsome young guest was troubled, she could see as she quietly sat down beside him.

"Why are you so troubled, Antipas? I would have thought this would be the happiest time in your life as you await your big day."

"I am happy, Larium. It's just that I need to see my mother again. I want so much for her to be a part of all that is changing in my life. She would be so happy with Eunice for a daughter-in-law. I know they would be comfortable with each other. I know they could love each other, and yet they may never meet. It's a sad thought." He lapsed into silence and for a time all that could be heard were the many birds with their morning calls vying for space at the feeding stations Larium so faithfully provided for their pleasure. It was a wonderful garden, but Antipas seemed barely aware of his surroundings this morning.

Larium broke the silence. "Antipas, I still see your mother regularly at my market stall. She looks at me longingly, but doesn't say anything. I could easily set up another meeting for you."

"Do you think it's wise? I worry about her safety and about yours. We had promised each other that we'd meet often, but that was before the guards searched the house where we were meeting." His hands were clenched in fists in his lap.

"Antipas, I have long since stopped worrying about safety. If God wants you to see your mother before your marriage, then He'll look after the protection. We can't live in fear anymore." She smiled softly at him.

"Yes, you're right. Please see what you can do. I know my mother wants to see me, too." He sniffed and turned his head. "We'll just have to take the risks and leave it up to God."

⊗ ⊗ ⊗

Larium left shortly after their talk, and Antipas spent the day teaching the home church leaders at the stable where he had first been introduced to them. He was humbled by their support of him as their teacher. He was still a young Christian himself, but had grown so much under Paul's teaching that these Pergamum Christians looked up to him.

He answered their many questions and asked them many of his own. They discussed their answers back and forth, arriving at common decisions. They spent time sharing what was happening at each home church and the needs of the people. Already some of the home churches had divided and formed new churches to accommodate all the people wanting to attend. They prayed earnestly for the new converts and for wisdom to teach them.

After the session, Antipas hurried home to see if Larium had seen his mother. As he neared the house he could hear hysterical weeping. He rushed into the house to find that Tabitha had taken sick during the day and was unconscious. Lois and Larium were beside themselves trying to revive her. Mattias had gone to get help.

Antipas entered her room and approached the couch were she lay. Her forehead was damp and cold to his touch. He could see that she was still breathing, but lightly. Her skin was exceedingly pale. Mattias arrived at this moment with the local man who called himself doctor. He used the name casually, but did have some experience dealing with sick people.

"Doctor, I encountered something similar to this while traveling with the caravan. If you would allow me to help, I would be grateful for the opportunity." Antipas had stepped back from Tabitha to allow the doctor to minister to her.

"Thank you. I could certainly use your help. What do you think we should do first?" The doctor straightened after feeling her forehead.

They talked together as how best to help her and how to handle the family, especially the women. Antipas said he would look after the women and then return to assist the "doctor."

"Mattias, you need to help me lead Larium and Lois into the other room." Antipas gently laid a hand on his shoulder.

"Yes, yes. That would be best. Allow the doctor to work." His eyes were glazed, and Antipas could see that he was trembling. They escorted the women to places by the fire. The earlier weeping had eased to a sniffle or two. Antipas knelt before the two women.

"Larium and Lois, I need your help. We will try our best to revive Tabitha, and so I need you to do a few things for me. Lois, would you please heat water and make the soothing drink you have given me on occasion when I have been weary."

"Oh yes, I can do that much." She immediately began to gather what she needed, seeming to be happy to do something to help.

"Larium, I need you to gather blankets and heat them by the fire. Also, put a couple of bricks in the fire to heat and then wrap them in several layers of soft cloth."

"Thank you, Antipas. I can do those things," Larium whispered as she rose to get the blankets.

"When both things are ready, Larium, please come to the door and let me know." He raised his eyes to his friend's worry-creased face. "Mattias, I need you to get on your knees and implore the Lord to heal your daughter. Please also pray that the Lord will give us wisdom to know the right things to do for her."

"I'll go to the back garden and pray as I have never prayed before." Mattias was already heading for the door. With all three of them busy with their tasks, Antipas returned to the sickroom.

Tabitha still lay as she had before. The doctor was bending over her but seemed puzzled as to what to do.

"Doctor, I have a plan if you will allow me to present it to you."

"Please do, I really have no idea what to do for her. I have never seen such cold dampness before. I'm used to dealing with fevers and sores, but this has me puzzled." The doctor stepped back to stand beside Antipas.

Antipas explained his plan and the two men set to work. The window was opened to make way for some fresh air to flow through the room. Antipas removed the damp bedding from around Tabitha and dried her face as much as possible. By this time Larium had arrived with the bricks and the heated blankets. Antipas put the wrapped bricks on the bed then wrapped Tabitha in the warmed blankets. He arranged the bricks around her and then stepped back.

"Doctor, that is all we can do for her at the moment. The rest is up to God. You may go and check in later if you wish. If we arrive at a crisis, I'll send for you again."

Surprisingly, the doctor took the orders from Antipas and quietly slipped out, saying he would return before sunset. Antipas knelt before her bed and poured out his heart to God.

"Awesome God, I thank You for the guidance You gave me concerning treatment for Tabitha. I have done all I can think to do and now the rest is in Your hands. I beseech You to heal her in the name of Jesus. Please restore her to her family. Father, You healed many people while You walked the paths of our Earth; please heal this little girl. This prayer is offered in the powerful name of Jesus, the ruler of the universe, the great healer and Savior of men. Amen."

A sense of calm stole over him. He sat back, ready to await what the Lord would do in Tabitha's life. Mattias had slipped into the room and was kneeling at the end of her bed. He was still praying quietly but calmly. Larium and Lois joined them, much more under control now.

The hours blended into each other as they kept their vigil. The doctor looked in on them and saw there was no change but that everyone was handling the situation well. He went out, asking them to send for him if he was needed. The boys had come home earlier, and Larium directed them to go to Simeon's house close by.

The endless night dragged on with little change. From time to time, Antipas would check her, ask Larium to get more bricks or blankets, and the process was repeated. Lois kept water heated for whatever time it might be needed.

Toward morning, Tabitha stirred in her bed. The adults gathered around her as she opened her eyes. She seemed startled to see them gathered around her.

"What's wrong?" she whispered in a small voice.

Her mother moved in beside her, explaining to her that she had been sick.

"I'm tired," she moaned, "and thirsty."

"Lois, would you get her the drink you have ready?" Antipas helped Lois to rise.

Lois moved off slowly, her shoulders bent and her feet shuffling, but there was a huge smile on her lined face.

When the drink arrived, Mattias helped his daughter to a sitting position, and her mother let her have a few sips of the fragrant drink. Antipas touched Tabitha's forehead. Her skin felt normal and her color had returned. She settled back in her bed with a huge sigh and said, "I need to sleep."

The adults slipped out to the fire to give thanks to their heavenly Father, who had just healed their child. There was quiet rejoicing as they knelt together. Tears were streaming down their faces.

"Antipas, we would never have been able to do this without you." Mattias hugged him tightly. "I see that God is truly in charge of your life. I was amazed at your calmness and how you seemed to know exactly what to do."

Larium and Lois joined him in their praise for Antipas. Antipas began to feel uncomfortable with all the attention.

"Brothers and sisters, the praise and glory belong to God. I only did what I felt He was instructing me to do."

"Nevertheless, we owe you a debt of gratitude, even if we embarrass you." Larium now stood beside him, taking his hand in hers.

There was quiet laughter after her remark. Larium told the others that she would sit with Tabitha for the rest of the night and that they needed to get some sleep. She promised to call them if there was a change in Tabitha and she needed help.

~ ~ ~

Antipas paced in his room, anticipation high as he considered the budding church of Pergamum and his role as overseer. "Lord, make me equal to this task," he prayed. "This is Your church, and I feel it is on the brink of great things."

The future was bright, but the pall of persecution hung over the church and over him personally.

Thirty-Four

Antipas, I want to hug you." The sleepy form of Tabitha stirred on her bed, arms stretched out to embrace him.

Antipas leaned over and gently put his arms around her. She gave him a kiss on the cheek and laid her head on his chest. He held her gently, rubbing his hand over her hair. He was overcome with emotion as he looked at her.

"Thank you, thank you." She snuggled closer to him, whispering into his shoulder. "I wouldn't be alive if you hadn't been here."

"I'm so glad you're okay. God is the one who deserves the thank-you. I only did what He led me to do."

"I know, but you did do what He said, and you were the one here to do it, so I will thank you." Shiny eyes and a big smile grinned up at him.

He released her and eased her back down on her bed, sitting beside her where he could look at her and assure himself that she was back to normal.

She closed her eyes again as she relaxed against her pillow. Her eyes flew open and the grin returned. "So, tell me about Eunice. I hear you're going to marry her. I thought you would wait for me, but oh well." She sighed. "I guess I can let her have you."

"So, how did you know about Eunice?" Antipas flicked the end of her nose, grinning back at her.

"I listen when people think I'm not around. I hear lots and lots of things." She struggled to sit up, poking him in the ribs. "So come on, tell me about her."

"I guess you're not going to rest until I tell you." He cocked his head sideways at her. She pouted in return, and he relented. "Well, she's the most wonderful girl in the world, I think."

The pout deepened. "What about me?"

"You're the most wonderful girl your age, and she's the most wonderful girl her age."

"I can live with that, I guess." The mischievous grin was back.

"I think you and she will become best friends. You'll meet her soon." This seemed to satisfy her for now. Antipas stood and leaned over her again.

"I'm going to let you rest now, but I'll be back later to see how you're doing. Go back to sleep."

"I am getting sleepy again. I'll see you later." Her eyes were already closed when he stepped back from her bed.

He returned to the room where the others were breaking their fast. They were all talking about Tabitha and the amazing miracle God had performed in their midst. Mattias made room for Antipas on the wooden bench, and they passed an enjoyable meal together.

The ladies cleared away the food while the two men talked. Mattias wanted an update on how Antipas's meeting had gone yesterday. Antipas gave him a summary, mentioning that he hoped to meet with them again tomorrow.

"They have their own businesses so they can't meet every day. If I can meet with them individually or in a group, three or four times a week, that is about all they have time for. In between, I want to visit the new converts, answer questions, or even just encourage them. It's tough to be a new convert in Pergamum." He frowned as he thought about the implications, complications, and dangers there were in following Christ. "The evil one is active here and aware of the work of Christ in our area. We need to get the converts grounded in Christ so they know Christ is real." He pounded on the table in an uncharacteristic gesture.

"It seems the more converts we get, the more Satan is active." Mattias shook his head thoughtfully. "I know some of the families are afraid, but they are being so courageous. They refuse to give up on their newfound freedom in Christ. It's so exciting to hear them and watch them grow." He jumped from the table, rattling the bowl of dates in the center. "God go with you, Antipas. I have to get to my shop; I hear the bell ringing."

Antipas strolled out into the garden where he knew Larium was working. He found her weeding in the vegetable patch.

"Hello, Antipas." She wiped her hands on the towel lying by her side and stood as he approached. "Come, let's sit on the bench in the arbor." They sat together in silence. The heady perfume of the flowers drifted in the morning air. Antipas watched as a small lizard scurried under a tree branch, chasing a bug that quickly disappeared into the tree.

Larium spoke first. "I did see your mother yesterday. There was so much going on last night that there was no opportunity to tell you."

Antipas smiled at her and nodded for her to continue. He gripped his hands together and felt the tension pull on his shoulders.

"She was so excited to hear about your engagement to Eunice. She asked me question after question. I couldn't answer all of them. Before I even had a chance to mention another meeting with you, she asked me if I could arrange one for her. Of course I said yes and told her that you wanted to meet with her as well."

Excitement shivered through his body. "Go on, Larium."

"We've come up with a different plan for this meeting. She suspects the other house is being watched and wouldn't be safe for you. She suggested the solution. One of her friends has become a Christian and attends one of the house churches. If you can arrange to be at that church on Sunday, she will be there also. You can meet in another room while the others are having a meal. Your father will be away and so will not know she has been out."

"But is it safe for her?" Antipas swung around to face her.

"It's as safe as anywhere else. Besides, she no longer cares about safety. She just wants to see you. I'm to take a message to her tomorrow."

"Tell her yes. I will make the necessary arrangements to be at that home. Tell her I love her and can't wait to see her." He rubbed his face with both hands. "I can't thank you enough for doing this for us."

"Oh, Antipas. I can't thank you enough for everything you've done for our family and for the church here. Don't talk to me about thanks. I count it a privilege to do this for you."

He walked her back to her garden, gave her a quick smile of thanks, and returned to his room to prepare for the walk into the country to visit with converts.

Thirty-Five

Antipas left the house shortly after his conversation with Larium. He thought of his mother, how brave she was, how special in his life. The thought of her was like a warm flame burning steadily in his heart. He had the love of two precious women, his mother and Eunice. How he longed for them to know and love each other as mother and daughter. Would it ever be possible?

As he walked his thoughts turned to the day before him. Today he would travel around the area, visiting the homes of families who had given their hearts to the Lord. He hoped to be an encouragement to them. It was not an easy thing to be a Christ-follower in Pergamum at this time. Even his own father had a reputation for seeking Christians and bringing them to "justice." He knew that it was only a matter of time until his father found out that not only was he back in Pergamum, but that he belonged to the hated sect of the imposter, as Christ was called.

His first visit took place in a little hamlet that had grown up in. It consisted of shepherds and their families just outside the city gates, where they were free to come and go from their homes to their flocks even at night.

The shepherd Petros was at home with his wife, Tulia, and their five daughters. Mattias had told him that Petros was a disappointed man, as a shepherd hopes to have many sons to help with the sheep and to carry on the business. He had been angry and every month had made offerings to Zeus, pleading for a son. Alas, his petition had never been answered. The coming of Christ into his life had changed him, but he still carried resentment in his heart.

Antipas found Petros emerging from the stable at the back of his property. He hailed him and identified himself.

"Welcome, welcome, my friend," Petros boomed at him, waving his pitchfork in the air. "Mattias mentioned that you would be dropping in today. You are most welcome in my humble home."

"Thank you." Antipas laughed as Petros lumbered toward him, still wielding the pitchfork. "I hope to be able to speak with you and with your family."

"They have been waiting for you by the hearth. I wouldn't be able to keep them away from your visit even if I wanted to, they're so excited." A deep laugh started low and spilled out over his lips.

Antipas fell in step beside the shepherd as they walked around his house. They entered through a rough-hewn door at the back. It was a small house, barely more than one room, but Antipas was greeted with a wealth of smiles from the ladies and warmth from the fire.

He was met with six identical pairs of dark brown, sparkling eyes. Mother and daughters all rose to greet him. The round faces of the daughters were scrubbed clean and were ruddy from their exposure to the elements on the hills where they helped care for the sheep.

They gathered around the fire and insisted he take one of the two chairs the house boasted. Petros took the other one while his wife sat on the sturdy wooden bench surrounded by her daughters, some on her lap, some on the bench, and two on the floor. The speech and surroundings were rough and poor, but the faces radiated a joy he encountered so often among the converts.

"We have some questions for you." Petros opened the conversation after a slight pause. "We believe in Jesus, but we don't understand why He would want us poor people and why he would do what he did."

With that opening, Antipas was able to present Christ as the Shepherd, and the family as the sheep. The family nodded from time to time and laughed uproariously when Antipas talked about us needing the guidance of a shepherd.

"Jus' like our silly sheep." The smallest girl giggled, showing a gap where two front teeth were missing. "If we didn't make them go where they're supposed to, they'd be all over the place." All the little girls laughed at this comment.

"That's right." Petros slapped his knee while his shoulders shook with laughter. "I understand now why Jesus looks after us. I have to look after our sheep or I wouldn't have any left. And because I look after them, I'd do just about anything to protect them." He peered at Antipas from deep-set eyes under heavy brows. "I've risked my life a number of times for them. They certainly are obstinate, and I guess we are, too."

Tulia smiled while her daughters and husband made comments. She hugged the little girls closer to her, smoothing back dark hair from chubby faces.

After more illustrations from Antipas, Petros asked him to stay for the midday meal. Even though Antipas knew they didn't have food to spare, he had learned that it is best to share what people do have. It made them feel they were participating in the work of Christ, and that was important.

Had fresh bread, cheese, and tea ever tasted so good? Antipas had answered many of their questions and encouraged them in their faith, but he had a sneaking suspicion that he received even more encouragement than he gave. He meditated on this thought as he traveled to the next village, where he would visit a larger household where some of the family had given their hearts to Christ but others were hostile to the gospel. It would be a most interesting call.

Alas, the call was not to take place today. On the outskirts of the village a young lad raced toward him. He skidded to a stop in front of Antipas, roiling the dust with his bare feet. His tunic was short and streaked with dirt. He stood panting, feet apart, hands on hips, in the middle of the road.

Antipas stopped when the boy put up his hand in front of him. He couldn't help smiling at the picture the boy made. "Did you wish to speak to me?"

"Are you Amphas?' The boy squinted one eye up at him, twisting his mouth around the word.

"I'm Antipas. Is that who you're looking for?" Antipas pursed his lips to keep them from tilting upward with merriment.

"That's it. I got a message for you." He pointed a grimy finger at him. "Joanna, you know Joanna?" He scrunched up his face against the glare of the sun in his eyes.

"Yes, I'm on my way to visit her." Antipas went down on one knee to be on eye level with the lad.

"Not today. She says you can't come today. Her master's home. Not come today." He shook his hand at Antipas, tramping both feet in the dirt around him.

"Thank you for bringing me the message. You're a good boy." Antipas rested his hand on his head before he turned away to return to the city. The boy ran off doing twirls down the road on his way back to the village.

Antipas thought about Joanna as he walked. The life of a Christ-follower was not easy. He prayed for the family, asking God to soften the heart of the master and that he would join with his family members in following Christ. He prayed for extra strength and faith for the converted family members and for their protection. He also asked for boldness for them to not hide their faith but to share it with the master.

He enjoyed his walk along the farm fields. A lazy breeze ruffled the heads of the ripened wheat, making the field look like the waves of the sea. Men with brown turbans, tunics tied up above their knees, labored among the harvest. Some backs were bent over scythes, cutting long swatches while others gathered the stalks and tied them into upright sheaves to dry. Faces were shiny with sweat from their labor. He was hot and thirsty but drank in the homey view of honest labor.

There was still time in his day, so he decided to visit one of the home churches.

As he neared the city, the foot traffic increased. He attached himself to a group of people entering the city and slipped through the gate where Mattias had taken him when he first arrived in Pergamum. Someday he would take the time to study the carvings on the gate, but it was not wise to linger today. It was safer not to stand out from the crowd. He could ill afford to be recognized.

As he mingled with the crowd on the busy street, he was lost in thought. He became aware of horses making their way down the narrow street, and of riders calling, "Make way, make way." He jumped to the side as he knew the whip would be used to good advantage by the riders. As they passed he glanced at the men on horseback and was startled to see a familiar face. It was his younger brother, Paulus. Even though several years had passed since he had last seen him, he would have known him anywhere.

Antipas slipped into the shade of a building and adjusted the hood on his robe. He didn't want to be recognized. Just when he thought he would be safe, he glanced up into the staring eyes of his brother.

He and Paulus had been good friends as boys growing up, but he knew from his mother that Paulus was now like his father and older brother. Antipas had known it was inevitable that he would meet one of them at some point in time, but he had wanted to delay the encounter as long as possible.

Recognition passed between the brothers. Paulus made no outward sign. The riders moved off down the street.

Antipas was left feeling vulnerable and exposed. Would this be the end for him in Pergamum? Would Paulus go straight to their father with the tale?

Thirty-Six

Sunday finally arrived. Antipas was up and out early to spend time with the house church family before the other converts arrived for the teaching session. He barely noticed the glorious morning with its intense blue sky and a smattering of small puffy clouds.

So many things to think about; the training of the church leaders, the feeding of the people, the sick and the poor, his mother, and the nearing date for his marriage to Eunice. His mind was swirling as he walked. His feet beat out a rhythm to match his thoughts.

The approaching meeting with his mother was foremost on his mind. He knew the plan exactly, but it wouldn't be easy to follow. She would arrive with her friend and attend the service. He must not even glance her way or acknowledge that he knew her. There had been rumors of spies in their churches. He wouldn't put it past his father to have his mother watched and followed, especially when he was out of town.

There was much activity in the home when he arrived. Emin, the owner of the house, greeted him and led him to the atrium. Young men were setting up wooden benches there, jostling each other and talking together. Women were gathering on the benches to one side, heads together, whispering while holding wiggling children on their laps.

Emin and his family occupied this large house on the outskirts of Pergamum. He owned several vineyards and an olive grove. He'd started out as a small farmer and soon prospered due to his quick mind and willingness to give everything he had to work his business. Although the results of his efforts gave him a comfortable lifestyle, he and his family were simple people with a heart for others.

His wife and young daughters had all embraced the Way and were excited to open their home to other Christians. Emin was learning to teach the group each week but always rejoiced when Antipas or another came to teach. It would never be his strength, but he was willing to share what he knew to further the kingdom of his Lord.

Antipas glanced around the room with pleasure. "Emin, you are doing a good work here. I'm thankful for your willingness to hold services."

Emin's wife, Clea, quietly entered the room to greet Antipas. She was dressed simply, but Antipas recognized the quality of the fabric of her clothing. She smiled at Antipas as she bowed her head toward him. "I have a meal prepared for you. I was sure you wouldn't take the time to eat this morning. You and Emin can talk while you eat. Come this way, please." She turned without waiting for a response, the fine garment swishing as she moved to exit the room.

"We might as well do as she asks." Emin nudged Antipas with a grin. "She doesn't give up easily. We can certainly talk at the table. It will be just the two of us, as the others have eaten. Come, my friend, I can see that you didn't break your fast yet."

"You and your wife are right, I didn't take time to eat." They followed her out through a simple curtain. Antipas knew they could well afford silk, but chose to use a more economical material rather than spend money frivolously. He knew they gave away vast amounts of money each year to feed and house many of the poor in Pergamum. When asked, Emin always said, "How can I enjoy having things that my Lord did not have while on earth? No, my mission is to follow His example. He has blessed me with riches to use them for His glory, and that's what I intend to do."

Clea had laid out fresh bread with oil and fruit. The warm bread was fragrant and delicious. Dates were his favorite, and his eyes lit up when he saw a large pottery bowl holding an array of them laden with honey. Antipas was soon deeply immersed in good food and good conversation. He was always thrilled to talk with Emin and see the spiritual growth developing in him.

Emin paused in his eating to dip his fingers in the water bowl, wiping them carelessly on a soft white towel.

"Antipas, I have a situation to discuss with you. It's delicate but I'll give you the details as I know them." He laid the towel down beside his plate and frowned at the table. He nodded his head before he looked toward Antipas. "One of the women converts is married to a merchant who does business with me. The husband has discovered his wife's new "religion," as he calls it, and is threatening to take his business elsewhere." He sighed and drummed his fingers on the table. "Antipas, I need counsel and prayer for wisdom. I hope this might be an opportunity to tell him about Christ. His wife is, of course, worried and doesn't want to be the cause of lost business for me."

"This is a sensitive situation. What have you done so far?" Antipas leaned his elbows on the table while they talked. A servant had slipped into the room and was quietly removing dishes from the table. Emin waited until he was finished before he took up the threads of his story.

"I've tried to convince her that the business is the least of my concerns, but nevertheless, she's worried. I'm afraid she'll renounce her Christian beliefs." The pain of the situation was evident from the slump of his shoulders and furrowed brows.

Antipas asked more questions then volunteered to visit the man at his business and his wife at home. A new voice might be able to convince both of them not to do anything foolish.

"Friend, would you really do this?" Emin brightened at the suggestion.

"Of course I will. Why don't we pray about it and for this morning?"

Voices could be heard in the other room as people began to arrive for the service. Antipas and Emin entered the room to find it already crowded and many conversations taking place. People were quickly getting seats as no one wanted to miss anything that might be said this morning. The word had gone out that Antipas would be speaking.

Careful not to draw attention to any one person by his actions, Antipas glanced around the room. Near the back he saw his mother with her friend. It took great self-control not to stare, or even worse, to go to her and wrap his arms around her. He said a quick prayer asking for restraint and then rose to speak. God was with him and his teaching was plain and urgent. People were responding with tears and nods.

At the close of the time together, many came to Antipas and Emin to ask more questions and to tell them about problems they had encountered during the week. The two men prayed with many of them and encouraged all of them. By the time they finished talking, the room had cleared and some of the young men were lifting the benches and storing them for the next meeting.

Emin laid his hand on Antipas's shoulder and spoke in a low voice. "It's time, my friend. When you go through the curtain, walk straight ahead until you come to the last room on the left. Enter there and spend as much time as you wish. Go, my brother."

Antipas casually drifted in the direction of the little room and entered quietly. His mother was sitting in the middle of the room watching the entrance. She rose when he entered and they met in a tight embrace. They wiped each others tears and she tenderly stroked his face.

"Oh, my son. I'm so happy that we could have another meeting. You look wonderful." She smiled at him through her tears, a coy look crossing her face. "I think you must be in love."

He looked at her with wonder in his eyes. "How can you be so happy and serene when you live under such awful circumstances?" He searched her eyes, looking for the truth of her life.

"Because I have found your Savior and He is now mine as well." She removed a square of cloth from the folds of her robe. It was small help in stemming the tide of tears.

Antipas was overcome with joy. "Now we are complete." He pulled her to him, comforting her with low words. "You and I are in perfect harmony. If only we could be together more often. I so want you to meet Eunice."

"I think that will be possible." She drew back from him and touched his cheek. "I will be coming to this gathering as often as I can get away. Once you have married Eunice and return to Pergamum, we will meet often. I feel safe here and I know that Jesus is in control of my life. He will allow us to meet, I feel sure." She kissed his face again.

"You are a brave lady, my mother. I am proud of you." His voice quavered as he looked at her happy face.

"I have something for you to give to Eunice from me. It has been in the family for many years and once belonged to my mother."

She handed him a tiny package, which he took with trembling hands. There would be a family gift after all for Eunice. He had longed for this but had consoled himself that it wasn't possible. He opened the package carefully and withdrew a beautiful gold ring engraved with delicate flowers.

"It's just perfect. Eunice will wear it with pride. It will bring a special tie between you and her. Thank you for thinking of this. I'll be able to go to the marriage knowing a part of you is with me."

Thirty-Seven

The noise of merrymaking in the village increased their excitement as Antipas and Epaphras approached Selçuk. The journey had been pleasant as the two friends chatted amiably about everything. The journey was now coming to a close, and Antipas's stomach was in knots.

Scouts were watching for them and when they were spotted a mighty cheer went up. The men and boys of the village swarmed around them to escort the groom into the village center, where shelters were set up for the guests. Antipas was greeted by Abdulla and Eunice's brothers as well as some of the elders of the village.

"Greetings, Antipas." The burly shepherd barked at him. "I trust you are prepared to treat my daughter well. It's not too late for me to change my mind, you know." He winked at the others around him, clapping them on the back and roaring with laughter.

Antipas wasn't sure how to take this remark. He glanced at Epaphras, who grinned at him.

"Don't worry, Antipas, he's only joking. He has no intention of giving up the generous bride price. Besides, he knows that you'll treat Eunice with the greatest of respect. Abdulla, leave the nervous groom alone." Epaphras joined in the laughter, shoving Abdulla's solid shoulder. Much laughter greeted these words. Abdulla looked innocent but then broke into loud guffaws, slapping his leg in his mirth.

"Don't take me seriously, Antipas." He managed to get out the words around his chortling laughter. "Eunice would never forgive me if I went back on my word."

A group of ladies descended upon them, and all foolish talk stopped as the ladies greeted Antipas by wrapping a brilliant cloak around him. A tall, dignified lady stepped in front of him, bowing low to the ground. "Follow me, please."

He fell in behind her with trembling knees. He looked to Epaphras, who took up his place beside him.

"You can do this," whispered Epaphras.

"Where is Eunice?" Antipas asked in a shaky voice, scanning the area for her.

"Oh, you won't see her until the actual marriage ceremony. She's greeting guests in another part of the village. You'll greet guests here and the party will go on all around you. Just smile and say thank you. That should be all you need to worry about. The ladies will make sure you're where you're supposed to be at the right time."

"I would feel so much better if I could just catch a glimpse of her."

"It's considered bad luck, so it's not going to happen, brother."

By this time the tall lady had led him under a beautiful embroidered canopy where a comfortable chair was placed. He was seated on the chair and offered a cool drink. He readily accepted and began looking around to take in the sights and sounds as he anticipated his union with his beloved Eunice.

Music and talk swirled around him. Brilliant costumes lent a festive air to the occasion. The children thronged around him laughing and singing. Groups of people as well as individuals began approaching his chair, greeting him and wishing him well in his marriage.

The savory scent of roasting meat bombarded his nostrils, as well as the aromas of hot tea and baking bread. He couldn't believe all the festivities were in honor of Eunice and him. He felt humbled to be the center of so much attention.

From the center of the activities, the local rabbi detached himself and approached him. Tiny bells tinkled along the hem of his ceremonial robe as he walked. His gold headpiece glowed in the sunshine. He was a dazzling sight in white, blue, and scarlet. Antipas was awed in his presence.

"Greetings from the temple." He extended his arms over Antipas and closed his eyes while intoning his blessing. "The blessing of Jehovah be upon you. May He watch over you and keep you."

Antipas was speechless before his splendor but listened carefully as he was given instructions for the actual ceremony. As he walked away, he couldn't help thinking that a Jewish wedding was a wonder to behold. Waves of colors, sounds, and smells permeated the air. A young boy brought him a plate laden with food. He didn't think he could eat, but courtesy dictated he take the offered plate. He thanked the boy and was surprised to discover he really was hungry. He quickly finished the portion on the plate. The food was delicious and he wondered if there was more he could have.

One of the ladies spotted him looking around still holding an empty plate. She approached him, holding out her hand for the plate.

"Would you like more?"

"Yes, that would be wonderful." She took his plate and quickly returned with a generous portion. That, too, disappeared rapidly.

He was beginning to enjoy the party. Names and faces blurred as he met the villagers. Jewish music and energetic dances piqued his excitement as he watched the dancers whirling and twisting, displaying an array of colorful costumes. He had been learning the bridal dance so he could perform it with Eunice after the ceremony. He didn't wish to embarrass her.

Antipas became aware of one of Eunice's brothers approaching. He was dark and hairy, with his face twisted in an ugly glare. He looked around furtively.

"If I had my way, this marriage wouldn't be taking place," he snarled at Antipas.

Antipas just stared at him at a loss for words. His mouth opened in disbelief.

"She should be marrying someone from her own village where she belongs, not some foreigner." He spat at his feet, arm raised in a threat.

"We have your father's permission." Antipas met the glare of anger coming from his soon to be brother-in-law.

"Bah, my father's old and lost his senses years ago." He cursed and spit again.

"That's no way to talk…"

"Just watch your back. I know people. I've heard about you." He turned on his heel and marched off through the crowd. Antipas watched him go, hoping that he didn't talk to Eunice and upset her before the wedding.

≈ ≈ ≈

The moon was already high in the sky when Epaphras came to collect Antipas to spend the night with friends of Abdulla's. It would not be appropriate for Antipas to stay with Abdulla during the pre-wedding festival. He was so tired by this time he didn't even ask where they were going.

The head of the household greeted them and led Antipas to the guestroom as the honored guest. He thanked his host and gratefully fell into bed. He had no idea where Epaphras would spend the night, and he was too weary to care. He fell asleep immediately.

His father was standing at the foot of his couch staring at him. He shrieked and sat up quickly as his father's menacing face neared his own. He was startled by the depth of hate he saw there.

"So you think you're going to be allowed happiness, do you? Let me warn you that I know all about you and am biding my time. You, your common wife, and your inept mother will all feel the force of my hand in the future. You'll never know when or where I'll strike."

Antipas could feel his father's hot breath on his face, he was so close. He shook violently and closed his eyes. When he opened them again, the sun was streaming in through an opening in the roof and he could hear the voice of Epaphras approaching the house. He shook his head, wondering if the dream was an omen, or even if it was real and his father was here in Selçuk. He might never know.

He shook off the dream, sending a quick prayer to heaven to protect his mother and Eunice. He no longer feared for his own life as in the brightness of daylight, logic told him that he would die only when God determined the time. His father was powerless to act unless God granted.

Today was a day for rejoicing, not for gloomy thoughts of his father. Today was his wedding day! Today he would see Eunice and be united with her forever. He splashed cold water on his face to chase away the last vestiges of the dream. He was dressed and ready for the first meal of the day when Epaphras appeared in his room bearing the marriage robe and a grin larger than life.

"Good morning, *chatan*." Epaphras filled the room with his excitement and his hearty voice as he made Antipas feel included in the family by using the Jewish name for grooms. "This is your big day. Come; let's break our fast with your host. By then, the relatives will be here to help you with the dressing ceremony. Don't forget you asked me to be your parents' representative today. I'll expect you to behave like a good Jewish boy," Epaphras teased.

"I'm sure you'll keep me in line." Antipas pretended to groan and sulk, pouting at him. "I'm actually hungry this morning, so let's eat."

The host had outdone himself with the morning meal. It was truly a meal fit for a groom. The best dishes had been dusted off for this momentous occasion. It wasn't every day there was a groom at your table. Although Antipas was nervous and excited, he ate well, complimenting his host on the delicious meal.

The host's wife was nowhere to be seen, as the ladies of the village had met at dawn to begin the preparations for the day. Tables were set, decorations put in place, food readied, and children amused. The entire village was involved in one way or another.

When Antipas had finished dining, the parade of village men arrived to assist in preparing the groom. Jokes were told and there was heartwarming laughter as Antipas was readied for the ceremony. The ceremonial robe was a work of art with its intricate needlework on fine-quality material. A woman of the village who was renowned for her work had lovingly prepared the robe, having known Eunice since she was a child.

As it was draped over his shoulders, the men placed their hands on his head and began reciting Scripture over him.

"Praise the Lord.

"Blessed is the man who fears the LORD,

"Who finds great delight in his commands.

"His children will be mighty in the land;

"The generation of the upright will be blessed.

"Wealth and riches are in his house,

"And his righteousness endures forever."

As the Scriptures poured over him from the lips of these Jewish men, he felt such an outpouring of love for these people. He knew they did not yet know the one they called Messiah, the one they were waiting for. They did not yet know that this Messiah was Jesus. He knew in his heart that he and Eunice would need to come back to this village sometime in the near future and share the message of the gospel with these men and their families.

As his thoughts continued, many more Scripture passages were said over his head, psalms and proverbs predominating. It was a beautiful experience to be covered by the words of the Lord.

When they had finished with the dressing ritual, they prepared to escort him through the village to where the *chuppah*, or canopy, was set up for the ceremony. Epaphras took the lead as the representative of his parents. The other men gathered around and behind him as the procession began. The chanting continued as they wended their way through the village. There was still no sign of Eunice, which worried him a little, but no one else seemed to be concerned so he decided he was just a nervous bridegroom.

When they reached the center of the village, the chuppah was before them with its sides open, the white top gleaming in the morning sun. The others fell back as Epaphras led him beneath the bright beauty of the canopy. He turned him around to face in the direction from which the bride would come.

He quietly whispered to him, "I'm going to stand over there with the other men to watch the ceremony. You'll do fine."

Antipas didn't have time to answer as Epaphras quickly slipped out from under the chuppah. He lifted his eyes to watch the narrow village street and was rewarded with a vision of loveliness.

Eunice, led by the rabbi and followed by her father and brothers as well as the village women, was walking slowly toward him. He couldn't see her face beneath the veil, but her dress was simple and stunning and she shimmered in white in the blazing sun. The world lit up once she was in his vision, all his nervousness gone. He had eyes for only her.

The rabbi was dressed in his ceremonial robes and seemed to flow along the roadway rather than walk. He, too, was chanting Scripture as he led the procession. As they neared the chuppah, Abdulla and Eunice left the others and approached the canopy. Her father led her beneath the white roof and presented her to her groom.

He knew to stand still as she, the *kallah*, began slowly walking around him. She circled him seven times as he knew she would. Seven is the God number and symbolizes the union that was to take place. When she completed the seventh circle, she stood at his right side.

The rabbi then stepped forward and the ceremony began. The villagers became quiet as they watched the proceedings. Even the children ceased their play and stood by their parents to watch and listen. A light breeze was blowing through the trees, and the fragrance of blossoms wafted through the air.

The betrothal blessing was given, the ceremonial wine sipped, and the ancient prayers offered as the wedding ceremony progressed. Antipas was thrilled that the name of the Lord was upheld and honored in every part of the day so far.

Epaphras had instructed him to have the ring that his mother had given him ready for Eunice. The rabbi chanted a final blessing and indicated to Antipas that it was time for the ring. He felt it in his hand and turning to Eunice, proclaimed the time honored words of the ceremony according to the Law of Moses and Israel. Then he placed the ring on her finger, signifying they were now officially husband and wife.

The veil was lifted and he gazed with wonder into her eyes. She smiled at him and all the tension left him. Only she was in his focus for the remainder of the ceremony. More blessings were said, more wine was tasted, cheers went up from the guests, but he saw only her. The culmination of all those anxious weeks and months was now fulfilled in this beautiful ceremony.

She had to lead him to the seats placed for them at the wedding feast. The festivities began with much noise, music, laughter, dancing, and food. It was a joyous occasion. Children ran wild after staying so quiet during the ceremony. Even the village dogs caught on and added their voices to the merriment. Antipas began to relax and enjoy himself.

People gathered around them with congratulations and good cheer. He couldn't get a chance to talk with Eunice, but knew he had a lifetime to spend at her side. Darkness began to descend but still the party continued. Lamps were lit all around the area as various entertainments were presented.

At long last, people began to wind down and say their good nights. Epaphras approached Antipas to let him know it was now permissible for him to lead Eunice to her father's house. Her father and brothers were going to a relative's house to allow them to have the place to themselves.

"Brother, I hate to mention that we need to leave early in the morning. We have a long journey tomorrow and must have an early start. I'll come around by sunup to collect you."

"That sounds good. We knew from the beginning that we would need to leave right away. I understand the parties will continue even though we aren't here." He kept Eunice pressed close to his side as he talked with Epaphras.

"That's so. You can't spoil a good week of festivities just because the chatan and kallah aren't here," Epaphras quipped before leaving them alone.

Antipas leaned toward Eunice. "Are you ready, my dear?"

"Yes, my husband, I am ready." He took her by the hand and they began the walk to her father's house. Cheers and blessings followed them.

At long last they were alone. The shyness he had dreaded slipped away with the night and he claimed her for his own.

Thirty-Eight

Long before the sun appeared, Eunice was up preparing a meal to break their fast and one to take with them on the road. Antipas entered the room and slipped in behind her. He wrapped his arms around her, and she leaned back into his embrace.

"My husband." She turned her face to his. "I can finally call you husband."

"Yes, my beautiful wife, you may indeed."

Epaphras arrived just as the sun was slanting its rays over the village. He apologized again for having to disturb them so early, but they assured him that they were anxious to get on the road as well.

Eunice had said a tearful good-bye to her father and brothers last night before they left to spend the night at relatives. She knew they would have already left for the pastures with the flocks. She had no idea when she would see her father again, but she was at peace and incredibly happy to be traveling to Ephesus and then to Pergamum with Antipas. As long as she was with Antipas, she didn't care where she was. God was so good to her to have brought him into her life when she thought she would always be the housekeeper for her father.

The horses were prancing in the courtyard as they loaded their bags and mounted. With a shake of the head and a soft whinny, the three began their journey. The blanket's rough texture grated under Eunice, and the stable smell clung to everything. She adjusted her position to accommodate the sway of the beast. It was cool as they left the village behind. The decorations were still up along the village thoroughfare. It was strange to be leaving, knowing the guests would still be celebrating today.

There was little talk, as all three were still tired from the festivities yesterday. The sun touched the olive trees and the pastures, making a splendid picture. The wind gently stirred the leaves, sending warm scents their way. The view was stunning as the low sun-drenched hills came into view. Flocks of sheep and goats were swarming the grasses below where rocky outcroppings jutted above the grass. The strains of a song came on the breeze from a shepherd boy perched on a rock.

At noon they found a shallow brook tumbling over a rocky bed beneath some trees. They dismounted and unloaded the lunch Eunice had packed. Fresh bread, fine cheese, and olives with oil for dipping made a tasty lunch. A handful of dates completed the meal, washed down with cool water from the brook. They filled their water skins with fresh water before they set out again.

"Mordicai will be counting the hours until we arrive, I'm sure," Epaphras commented to his companions as they left the brook.

"I can hardly wait to see him again." Eunice spoke with excitement, a sparkle in her eyes as she shielded them from the sun. "He became special to me while we stayed in his house. I was thrilled that he asked me to come to his room on several occasions to discuss everything from our walk with God, to good recipes, to my ideas about marriage." She laughed as she told them the story. "I was so embarrassed the first time he asked me questions, but I soon came to think of him as a second father or grandfather and was comfortable with him. I know now, he was testing me to see if I measured up to his standards of a wife for Antipas."

"I guess you must have pleased him, because he speaks so highly of you." Antipas took her hand as they climbed the incline to where they had tethered the horses. They exchanged a secret smile that spoke volumes.

"You two are crazy, crazy in love." Epaphras laughed and shook his head.

"What do you mean?" Antipas raised his eyebrows at him with a look of innocence.

"Figure it out for yourself." Epaphras punched him lightly on the shoulder, laughing at him. They all joined in the laughter as they mounted then jogged along in a comfortable silence.

"Just wait." Antipas was the first to break the silence. "I've seen Helene looking at you when she thought no one was watching. You'll be the next."

"Oh, funny man that you are." Epaphras wrinkled his nose. "I'm a confirmed bachelor. How could I keep a wife and run a household with all the traveling I do?"

"Oh, one of these days you'll catch Helene looking at you and you'll fall face first. I just hope I'm there to see the fall," Antipas goaded him.

"That'll be the day."

≈ ≈ ≈

Silence settled again while the afternoon wore on. By now Eunice was becoming tired but would not mention it. She knew the men wanted to make good time today, as they still had a long journey ahead of them. Her thoughts went back to yesterday. Had there ever been such a beautiful wedding? She couldn't remember one as beautiful or as joyful as hers had been.

This led her to think of the one person missing from the celebration: her mother. What would it have been like to be raised by a loving mother? She had no complaints about how her father had raised her and she knew he loved her, but surely it was different with a mother. Her mother would have held a place of honor yesterday. She remembered when her cousin was married last year, and all the plans her aunt had made and how she had shone on the day of the marriage.

But that was not to be, and she gave thanks to God for the upbringing she had and asked a blessing on her father. She determined in her heart that if she and Antipas were blessed with children, she would do everything in her power to be the best mother ever.

Her thoughts were interrupted by Antipas whispering to Epaphras and the horses slowing. She instantly became alert and quietly asked what was wrong.

"Up ahead there's dust hovering over the road. Someone moves there. It's probably only a traveler like us, but it pays to be cautious in this barren stretch of land." Antipas moved his horse closer to hers, his eyes never leaving the dust ahead.

They moved along guardedly for awhile, on the alert. Whatever or whoever was making the dust had slowed as well.

Epaphras gradually slowed his mount and signaled for the others to do the same. He motioned for them to follow him as he moved off the trail and onto a little-used track. They wound their way up through a narrow canyon and up into a treed area. He stopped and indicated they should dismount.

"Get down over behind that rock," he whispered. "I'm going to keep watch from here."

Silence hovered over the site as they crouched in their positions. Eunice could hardly breathe and realized she had her eyes shut tightly. She slowly opened them and reached for Antipas's hand. He smiled encouragement at her as he squeezed her hand.

All they could hear was a lone bird calling to its mate. The heat beat down on them even through the trees. It seemed like forever before they heard the distinctive clop of a horse approaching at an unhurried pace. Fear washed over Eunice as she held her breath. They stayed in position for another space of time before Epaphras appeared behind the rock.

"I think it's safe to move on now. I think he was looking for someone, with ill intent in his mind, but he's disappeared back the way we came. Let's move out quickly before he decides to come back."

They picked up their gait, talking only when necessary. Epaphras made periodic forays back along the trail, but saw no one. By the time they reached their overnight stopping place, they were still on alert. While Eunice spent time refreshing herself and laying out the meal, Antipas and Epaphras went apart to discuss the happenings of the day.

Antipas stretched his back after the long ride. "I don't want to alarm you, but I caught a quick glimpse of our stalker and I'm sure it was Horatious from the caravan. I imagine he still blames me for his departure from it, and has certainly vowed revenge on me. It would have been easy enough for him to hear about the wedding and our plans to travel."

"I had thought about that as well. At the next village, I'll ask discreetly to see if I can gather any information." Epaphras was gathering sticks for a fire while they talked.

"There's something I haven't told you. At the wedding, one of Eunice's brothers made some threatening remarks to me. He indicated I should watch my back and that he knew people. I wonder if it was Horatious he was referring to."

"That's possible. Horatious gets around."

They returned to where Eunice was setting out the food and gratefully sank down on the saddle blankets to eat their meal. Epaphras thanked God for their deliverance today. They talked long over their meal in sweet fellowship. They discussed the work in both Ephesus and Pergamum. Antipas raised the possibility of a missionary effort in Selçuk.

"I agree more work needs to be done there, but I'm not sure you're the person to do it. The people there see you as a young groom and would not give you the respect and attention needed for reaching them. I've been working with one of the shepherds who has given his life to the Lord. He's considering starting a home church there."

"Who is that?" Eunice had been quietly listening to their conversation.

"Ahmed, the shepherd. You know him, of course."

Eunice lowered her eyes. A characteristic redness crept up her neck and face.

"Did I say something wrong, Eunice?"

"No. Only he sought to marry me before I met Antipas. I refused him, but I am so glad to hear he has come to know Jesus."

Epaphras turned to address Antipas. "This may be a little bit awkward, as I was going to ask you if you would consider teaching him anytime you are in the village."

"I would have no problem doing that, unless it would bother you, Eunice?"

"I would be delighted to see a work started in Selçuk. It won't bother me. That was a long time ago."

"Excellent. Then may I tell him when I am on my way back through?"

"Certainly, only we don't know when we'll be back again."

"He's a patient man and will study on his own for the time being. I'll get him started on some things when I pass through. Maybe you would consider sending him some letters? Paul does this quite effectively, so why not you?"

"That's a fine idea. I think we could do that. I can probably get one ready for you to take back with you."

"I could write some, too, if you both think that would be acceptable." Eunice looked eagerly from one to the other.

"Why not?" Epaphras spoke enthusiastically. "You've listened to your father and I discuss many things over the years. You could write a letter, Eunice, and you could read it, Antipas, so you wouldn't both write the same things. This could be exciting and get the work going much faster in Selçuk. Ahmed could have the letters read during the home church sessions so the people could discuss the material."

Antipas let his thoughts travel over the possibilities. It was amazing what could be created when everyone pooled ideas. He could envision the gospel spreading across boundaries to areas never yet visited.

Unfortunately, thoughts of Horatious kept interfering with more pleasant thoughts for Antipas. He prayed silently while they sat by the fire. He didn't want Eunice to know he was worried and he didn't want her to have to encounter the man. Horatious would not be above harming her as a way to get back at Antipas.

It was still dark but dawn was fast approaching as they broke their fast and prepared to leave their campsite. The early birds were welcoming the day. Eunice was deep in thought as the morning advanced. She was happier than she'd ever believed she could be. She'd thought she would be trapped in her village, in her father's house for all of her life, and here she was off on an adventure with an incredible husband by her side. How she longed to begin her ministry to the people of Pergamum. She and Antipas had talked about how she could minister to the families. He felt she could make an impact on lives.

Her thoughts wandered to arriving in Ephesus. Mordicai had promised her he would make sure she and Antipas had a chance to spend time alone when they arrived at his house.

A bride and groom need time alone to get to know each other and start to build a strong relationship. I know these preacher men, they sometimes can't think about anything else except the job at hand. I'll talk some sense into this one for you. Mordicai had winked at her as he made his promise. She could hardly wait. She loved Epaphras like a brother, but a girl didn't need a third party along when she had just been married!

Thirty-Nine

At noon they stopped at a small village, seeking to purchase bread and replenish their water supply. Epaphras engaged some of the villagers in conversation. Antipas kept Eunice occupied as he knew Epaphras would be inquiring about Horatious. He didn't want to alarm Eunice unless it was necessary.

Before they left, Epaphras called Antipas aside.

"Were you able to learn anything about Horatious?" Antipas asked anxiously as he stepped aside with Epaphras.

"Oh, yes. He's been here. The men recognized him right away. He asked many questions but received few answers. The locals are quite astute in reading character and pegged him for an unsavory person."

Antipas glanced over his shoulder. The women of the village were helping Eunice store the supplies they were able to purchase. He brought his eyes back to Epaphras.

"They figured out he was looking for someone with revenge on his mind. Apparently he's on his way to Colosse, so he's going in the wrong direction." Epaphras gripped his arm.

"Do you think he might inquire in Selçuk?" Antipas folded his arms over his robe.

"I think it's unlikely after the reception he received here. Also, most people in Selçuk are unaware of where we're headed. I felt it was safer not to disclose too much information. For sure, he won't get any information from Abdulla. I think we need to stay on the alert. It won't take him long to figure out that we've gone in the other direction."

As the leagues added up, there was still no sign of Horatious. Antipas became more confident that they had avoided him. He was still alert, and he could see that Epaphras was as well, but the edginess had mellowed. Once they reached Ephesus, he felt sure Horatious wouldn't be able to find them. His confidence was shattered with the sound of pounding hooves. As he turned to look, dust was rising like smoke from a fire.

"Take shelter!" Epaphras bellowed, yanking on the reins and turning his mount to the left.

But there was nowhere to hide. The horses were upon them before they had time to react. Horatious jumped down from his steed first, his blade gleaming in his clenched fist.

"Stand and fight." Rage twisted his face into a snarl. He took his stance, feet apart, sword gripped tightly in his hand. One of his partners was small but lithe, dancing on his feet, brandishing a long, narrow knife. The other two were big with bulging muscles. They circled Horatious like bodyguards.

Antipas and Epaphras jumped off their horses, ready to fight.

"Eunice, get back as far as you can." Antipas gave her a push as he yelled at her.

The fight was on. The opponents came together with a clanging of metal against metal. Bodies were intertwined in hand to hand combat. Groans, shrieks, curses split the air.

"Take that, you filthy beast." Sweat gleamed on Horatious's wild-eyed face as he lunged at Antipas. His blade pricked the skin on Antipas's arm. Antipas ignored the cut, taking a wild swing with his sword.

Eunice sank to the ground. "Mighty God," she screamed aloud, her hands clasped and eyes toward heaven, "You are more powerful than man. Please fight this battle for us." She slumped against a rock, unable to take her eyes off the men locked in combat.

With four against two, the advantage was all on Horatious's side. As the fight continued, moans joined the clanging of swords and battle cries. Blood sprayed, mingling with the dust. Someone was badly hurt but Eunice wasn't able to tell who. She kept praying.

At last Horatious stood over Antipas. He slammed his foot on his back, panting, face flushed, sweat dripping from his forehead. An angry scowl distorted his face. His turban had come off, and dirty black hair hung limp down his back. He wiped at the sweat while watching his victim. Antipas did not move. Eunice clasped her hands over her mouth and whimpered.

Horatious looked around, his gaze encountering her. His protruding lips stretched in an evil smile as he gripped his sword with both hands, lifted it, and pointed it down at Antipas's back.

Forty

In the sudden silence, broken only by ragged breathing, the sound of hooves pounding the earth could be heard. Horatious lifted his head. "On your horses. Someone's coming. Let's go."

As quickly as they'd come, they were gone. Eunice ran to Antipas, bending over him and weeping openly. Epaphras staggered over to her.

"Can you turn him over?" He bent over at the waist, dripping sweat from his face on the ground around him. "Easy. He's badly hurt."

As she tried to turn him, he groaned softly.

She let go, jumping back from him. "He's alive. I thought he was dead." She covered her mouth with her hands and looked down at him.

"Just keep turning. We need to see how bad it is."

She put her hands under him again but could not turn him by herself. Epaphras leaned over and helped as much as he could. He was bleeding from a gash on his shoulder. Working together, they finally had Antipas on his back.

Eunice gasped for breath. "His face. Oh his poor face." She covered her eyes again and rocked back and forth, moaning his name.

His eyes were swollen and already turning dark blue. Blood seeped from several cuts. Epaphras knelt beside him, using a cloth from his pack to wipe the blood.

"He took quite a beating. I caught glimpses of Horatious using his fists on him as well as his blade." Epaphras eased the tunic away from his shoulders and chest where more gashes were visible.

"Eunice, can you get me some water from your pack?"

"Yes, of course." She jumped up, quickly retrieving the water. When she returned her tears were dried and she knelt beside Epaphras, helping him.

"They said someone was coming just before they left. I don't see anyone." Eunice scanned the horizon in all directions, pushing the hair back from her face where it had fallen when she was leaning over Antipas.

Epaphras looked up from his work to follow her gaze. "They must have headed in another direction. I don't see any sign of anyone either."

Eunice again knelt beside Epaphras and together they washed the wounds, putting strips of cloth around them, all the while talking softly to Antipas. His open eyes were glazed and his face was ashen. His moans were mere sighs.

"Antipas, can you hear me?" Epaphras asked, softly touching his face.

"Yes, yes." His voice was a whisper. He blinked his eyes and turned his head slightly.

"We're going to try to put you on your horse. Do you think you can sit up?" Epaphras put his hand under his back on one side while Eunice did the same on the other. Antipas nodded his head in response. Together, they got him to his feet. His face was deathlike but he made no sound.

✿ ✿ ✿

It was a slow journey with many stops, but the gates of Ephesus finally came into view. By the third day, Antipas was able to sit on his horse for longer periods of time, and his wounds were beginning to heal. Epaphras led the way through the city gates.

Antipas never failed to be moved by the sight of the city. The cries of urchins flocking around them looking for handouts were so familiar. The fabled dogs were barking stridently, running in and around the brown, bare legs of the little boys. Cooking smells were emanating from the stalls of the marketplace.

"I hadn't realized I was hungry until I smelled freshly baked bread." Eunice's laugh broke out as she looked at her two companions.

"Mordicai will have a feast prepared for us, you can be sure." Epaphras grinned sideways at her, not taking his eyes off the way before him. The road was crowded with foot traffic as well as the usual assortment of carts, donkeys, and horses. A Roman chariot hurtled by, grazing a cart in its haste. Loud protests went unheeded as the chariot swept on.

Antipas said nothing. It was still too much of an effort for him to speak if it wasn't necessary.

Their road led off to the right through a maze of vendors crying their wares. The horses picked their way, tails swatting at the inevitable flies. It was with joy and relief they turned toward the home of Mordicai.

"Tonight: soft beds and real food." Eunice's eyes expressed her excitement.

The yard was quiet when they entered. A young stable hand hurried to greet them. He bowed his head to them. "Mordicai is expecting you. I'll stable your mounts for you and bring your bags to your rooms."

"Thank you. We appreciate your help." Epaphras helped Eunice first and then

Antipas from their horses. The stable hand took the horses and ambled off toward the stables leading the three mounts.

Antipas looked toward the front entrance just as Rufus appeared to welcome them. He shuffled toward them, his robe bunched up in his gnarled hands. "Epaphras, Antipas, Eunice, I can't believe you're finally here." He greeted each one with a kiss on the cheek. "My master will be so pleased. He awaits your arrival. I'm to bring you to him immediately." His thin frame was bent with age, but the curve of his lips over straight teeth belied the years. He turned, beckoning them to follow, and led them to the front entrance.

They followed Rufus into the cool interior of the house. He walked before them to the room where Mordicai awaited them. Mordicai's lined face creased in smiles as he saw them enter. He struggled to rise to his feet, but Epaphras stopped him.

"We'll come to you with our greetings. Stay, Mordicai." The greetings were warm and intimate. He hugged Eunice tightly when it was her turn. He looked into her shining eyes.

"I can now call you daughter." He lifted his hand to her face, whispering to her in his frail voice. "I call Antipas my son, so that makes you my daughter." He smiled at her tenderly.

"I can think of no greater compliment than to be called your daughter." Eunice kissed his cheek again as she whispered back to him.

When Eunice straightened, he turned to Antipas again. "What's wrong, my son, you don't look well. What's happened? Have you had an accident?"

"More like an attack. We'll tell you all about it."

Antipas and the others pulled seats close to Mordicai. He had to hear all about the attack, the wedding, and the trip here. During the recital of the attack, his brows drew together and the lips that had been smiling turned down at the corners. He clenched his thin hands as the tale continued.

"It's disturbing to think he's still looking for you." Mordicai shifted in his chair, his shoulders tight. "I think I'll have someone look into this to see if we can locate him and settle this once for all."

"I don't want you doing anything to upset yourself." Antipas looked alarmed at the thought of Mordicai's getting involved.

"Don't worry about me. I've got lots of contacts. Let's put him out of our minds for tonight. Tomorrow will be soon enough to deal with him."

As the friends talked, Rufus brought food and drink to them. He set up small tables for each of them and laid out a simple meal.

"The evening meal will be served later, but I know you need to eat after your journey." Mordicai indicated the food Rufus had brought.

"Thank you, Mordicai." Eunice sipped the tea, sighing with pleasure. "I'm especially grateful for the hot beverage. We weren't always able to have it on the road, and I missed it.

Antipas yawned behind his hand several times and his eyelids were drooping.

"Antipas, you look tired. Rufus will rub a salve on your wounds that will bring you quick relief. Eunice, take him to bed." He lifted a small brass bell from the table beside him and shook it wildly. Rufus appeared immediately. "Lead Antipas and Eunice to their room and use some of the good salve on Antipas." Eunice and Antipas bade the two good night while Epaphras stayed to continue the conversation.

❦ ❦ ❦

"Excuse me, master." Rufus appeared in the doorway, bowing as far as his back would allow. "The groom has just reported that he has seen someone at the back of the property."

"Horatious, do you think?" Epaphras jumped up from his seat, eyes wide and alert.

"Rufus, rouse the other servants and do a thorough check of the property," Mordicai instructed.

"I'll come, too." Epaphras hurried from the room behind Rufus.

A search of the property proved fruitless. Whoever had been there was gone. Epaphras knew in his heart that it was Horatious. Even here in the house of Mordicai they were not safe.

Forty-One

I n the morning Mordicai sent for his friend, a centurion in charge of a centuria in Ephesus. Promises were made to pursue Horatious, who was known to the centurion. There was nothing else they could do at present.

"I refuse to be intimidated by him. He's not in charge of my life. Whether I live or die depends on God, not Horatious." Antipas spoke firmly, jutting out his jaw in defiance of Horatious.

"I agree," Mordicai nodded. "But you must be careful. You have a wife to look after now."

"We both agree that fear of Horatious won't run our lives." Eunice, though with a serious look clouding her lovely face, spoke confidently.

"I know you're right, but I still feel uneasy, especially as I need to leave tomorrow." Epaphras looked from Antipas to Eunice.

"I'll make sure we don't head into danger unnecessarily." Antipas was not sure he could do this, but was not going to be intimidated.

⮑ ⮑ ⮑

The days passed quickly in a haze of pleasure. Each morning Antipas and Eunice walked in the garden and made plans for their future. The afternoons were spent visiting the church families in Ephesus, renewing acquaintances and meeting needs where they could.

Although Antipas was enjoying his time here in Ephesus, he was getting restless, wanting to get back to the work in Pergamum where he felt he had been called. Mordicai kept insisting they stay longer, but finally one night Antipas shared his heart with Eunice and his urgent longing to get back.

She quickly agreed with him. "I'll go wherever you want to go. It's enough for me just to be with you." She reached for him and laid her head on his chest, arms around his neck. "I, too, am anxious to begin our life together in Pergamum and to meet all the people you've told me about."

"Let's get some sleep now. I'll need to talk to Mordicai of our decision in the morning."

⋙ ⋙ ⋙

As Antipas entered his room with a determined look on his face, Mordicai looked up, lips pursed and nodding his head.

"You're ready to head for Pergamum." At Antipas's startled took he smiled. "I understand, my friend. Excuse an old man for wanting to keep you to himself for longer. I know I'm being selfish and that you need to move on to Pergamum. Don't look so surprised. I've seen this coming for days. I can read your face like a book." Mordicai shook his finger at him laughingly.

"You make this much easier for me, Mordicai." Antipas pulled the familiar chair closer to the bed and eased himself down beside Mordicai. "I was really worried about telling you, thinking you would think I was ungrateful for your offer to stay longer."

"I'm just an old man, but I know the yearning of a young man's heart. You will go with my blessing." He placed his trembling hand on Antipas's head.

Antipas bowed his head. A warmth crept into his heart, and he was humbled by the blessing of this dear friend. "I will miss you. I can't even begin to express what you mean to me. Your support and love have been outstanding. How can I ever thank you?"

"Just do the work God has called you to do, and that will be all the thanks I need." He relaxed back on the pillows. "Will you bring Eunice to me later this morning?"

⋙ ⋙ ⋙

Eunice and Mordicai spent an hour together.

"Hand me that box on the table." Mordicai indicated a small box sitting among the combs and lotions on the table. When he received the box, he opened it to reveal many precious jewels. "These are for you, Eunice. There will be times in Pergamum when you or people around you will have needs. You'll be the heart of the ministry to people in need. These will give you funds of your own to help without having to trouble Antipas."

Eunice stared at the jewels. Warmth spread up her neck and face. Placing her hand over her heart, she looked into Mordicai's smiling face.

"Just say you'll take them and use them as you see a need." He held out the box to her.

"Mordicai, I love you like a father. Thank you. I'll never forget your kindness or your generous gifts." She rose from her chair and wrapped her arms around the old man's neck. "You are an incredible man."

"You embarrass me, Eunice." But he was smiling as he spoke.

When she emerged from his room, she was smiling through her tears.

Forty-Two

Now, for the first time since their wedding, Antipas and Eunice were truly alone. As they traveled along the dusty roads heading for Pergamum, they enjoyed a quiet companionship. They talked when they were so inclined, and were silent when they wished. Often they would glance at each other and a smile would pass between them that said many things.

Antipas couldn't have been happier with his bride. Eunice was proving to be everything he believed she was and everything he had heard from others. Her gentle spirit complemented his passionate outlook on life. She would be a support to him in the days ahead. He knew that living in Pergamum would not be easy for either of them, but he firmly believed that God had called him to that city, the seat of Satan. He also realized that their lives were in danger as well as the lives of fellow believers. But the leading of the Holy Spirit could not be refused. He must go on.

He planned to take Eunice to Mattias's home until they could move into a place of their own. He knew some of the church leaders were hoping to have a place ready for them, but until they knew, they would stay with Mattias and Larium.

As they approached the gates of Pergamum, Antipas glanced her way and saw worry in her eyes. He brought his horse closer to hers and reached out his hand. They slowly moved along in the flow of people, hand in hand. The guards on the gate were questioning a group just ahead of them. Voices were raised as the guards shouted orders and threats. A few people began to move around the commotion. Antipas and Eunice were so closely packed in the group that they, too, began to move around the group. Just when Antipas thought they would pass through unde-tected, one of the guards turned in their direction.

"Halt, you in the brown turban."

Antipas stopped, still holding Eunice's hand.

"Move off to the side and be quick about it," the guard barked brusquely.

They eased their way through the press of people to the side of the road. Antipas could feel Eunice's hand tremble in his. The guard, tall with broad shoul-ders, approached them. His arm muscles bulged under his tunic. Dark, heavy eye-brows were drawn in a deep frown.

"Where do you come from?" He flung the words at them.

"We're traveling from Ephesus."

"Ephesus, you say? How do I know you're telling the truth?" He spit on the ground then twisted his face to look up at Antipas.

"You have only the word of an honest man," Antipas replied with a calmness that didn't extend to his heart.

"What is your business in Pergamum?"

"We're journeying to the home of Mattias, the worker in iron."

The guard turned from them and consulted with two other guards. They could be seen gesturing in argument. Only some of their words could be overheard.

"How can we be sure…his word…suspicious…"

"Antipas, what are they doing?" Eunice grabbed his arm. Her fingers held tightly to the sleeve of his robe. Her eyes never left the guards.

"I'm not sure. They must be looking for someone and maybe think I'm him." He patted her hand, hoping to reassure her.

The first guard returned, bringing one of the other guards with him. "Dismount." Antipas slid off his horse and assisted Eunice.

"Open your saddlebags."

This was quickly accomplished. Nothing of interest turned up in Antipas's bag. Eunice's things were dumped on the dusty ground. She gasped softly as they began to scrutinize each item, handling them carelessly.

The second guard jumped to his feet, a look of glee on his face.

"Look what I found," he shouted to the first guard. Together they gaped at the opened box of jewels, Mordicai's gift to Eunice.

"We'll just relieve you of this little package." The smirk on his face was cruel.

"That was a gift to my wife from a friend," Antipas protested, trying to reach for the box.

The sun glinted off the jewels as the guard held them up out of his reach. The two guards looked at each other, laughter playing in their eyes.

"That's a quaint story." The first guard laughed as he slapped the other guard. "You stole them. That's obvious."

"That's not true." Antipas reached again to retrieve the box.

A fast kick to the knee made him cry out in pain.

"I'll decide what's true and what's not." The laughter turned to a snarl. The guard's eyes darkened with anger, and a ruthless curl twisted his lip. "Be on your way and be grateful we aren't throwing you in prison. Maybe we will if you aren't out of our sight when we look again."

He smashed the cover back on the box and deposited it inside his robe. The two marched away in military precision.

"Quickly, Eunice, back on the horse. We need to move with all speed." Antipas gave her a boost up to her horse, mounted his quickly, grabbed the reins, making sure she was with him, then mingled with the flow through the gate.

Once inside they hastened down a market laneway and out of sight of the guards.

"Eunice, I'm so sorry." Antipas slowed the horses, stopping along the side of the road.

"It wasn't your fault, Antipas. It's made me realize what we'll be confronting here."

"But you needed those jewels to help people."

"But God doesn't need them, Antipas. Let's just put them out of our minds for now and enjoy our arrival in Pergamum."

He was touched by her acceptance. "It will be as you say. I don't want the others to know yet that we've been singled out by the guards."

As they moved along the hard-packed streets and alleys of the marketplace, Antipas assured her they were quite close to their destination. They reached the house safely and dismounted. Tired and sore from the journey, they found it a great relief to arrive.

Antipas entered the shop and stopped just inside the door. Mattias looked up. Recognition blossomed on his face, and he bellowed a greeting. They laughingly embraced each other, and Antipas presented Eunice to him. He greeted her warmly and welcomed her.

"You won't believe how excited my womenfolk are that you're coming. Tabitha has been talking about nothing else for days. You look exhausted and I can assure you there is a room ready for you. Come on, let's go meet the family. Look who's here. Larium, Tabitha, Grandmother, you'll never guess."

They looked up to see Antipas and Eunice enter the room. Tabitha almost knocked Antipas over as she bounded to him. Larium came with more grace and hugged Eunice.

"We've been anticipating your arrival for ever so long. Welcome, my dear. I see Antipas has done well in a wife."

Eunice returned her hug with many thanks for making her feel so welcome.

"You're part of the family now, dear. Antipas is just like a son to us."

He now greeted Grandmother Lois and brought Eunice over to her side. She smiled and reached out her hand to Eunice.

"Welcome from an old woman who is still not too old to appreciate young love."

Eunice blushed as she leaned over to kiss the wrinkled cheek. "Thank you, Lois. Antipas has told me so much about you."

Larium already had water boiling for tea and was bustling around preparing a meal to refresh them after their journey.

"Come eat. I know you must be tired after all your travels. Eat first, and then you can rest as long as you like in the room prepared for you."

Tabitha insisted on sitting beside Eunice. She leaned her head on her shoulder. "I know we're going to be great friends. Antipas said I could have you for a friend."

"Of course you can. Antipas has told me about you, and I could hardly wait to meet you. We'll have lots of time now to get acquainted."

As the conversation swirled around her, Eunice could feel her eyes threatening to close.

"Eunice." Larium reached over and patted her arm. "I'm going to take you to your room. This family will keep talking to you, asking questions, but I can see the fatigue on your face."

"Thank you, Larium." Eunice smiled at her gratefully. "I am tired."

Larium led the way to the room where Antipas had spent so many days.

❦ ❦ ❦

Antipas and Mattias left soon after the meal to visit some of the house leaders who were anxious for Antipas's return. On the way, Mattias informed him that a small apartment had been found for them in the home of one of the newest converts, Augustus and his wife Salome. It had its own entrance from a private courtyard where they could sit undisturbed in the evenings.

Antipas was thrilled with the prospect, as he wanted to get settled as soon as possible.

"The ladies have been getting the place ready as a labor of love for you and Eunice. You shouldn't need for anything for some time. I know, because I've carted half the stuff over there for you." He gave a loud guffaw, cuffing Antipas.

"That's incredible." Antipas stopped and stared at him. "We weren't able to bring much with us from either the village or Ephesus. I feel so humbled by all this attention."

"We'll stop and see the place and find out when you can move in." He resumed walking, chatting easily to Antipas.

It proved to be everything a newlywed couple could want. Later that week Antipas and Eunice moved into their first home. There were enough supplies and food to last them a long time. The Christ-followers of Pergamum had opened their hearts and homes to the couple. Antipas was already well respected and loved. Eunice was taken into their warm embraces and welcomed as one of the family of believers.

Once they were settled and Antipas had taken up his duties again as head of the church in Pergamum, he longed to bring his mother and Eunice together. He knew she came to the gathering in Emin's house whenever she could, but that wasn't often as his father was having her watched. Emin had told him she was growing in her faith. Antipas was thrilled with the news and rejoiced. He wanted to share everything with her, but knew he couldn't put her at risk often.

He talked to Emin about setting up a meeting with his mother. He said he would be happy to but didn't know how soon he would see her again. They had to leave it at that as Antipas was not content to involve Larium again; his father in all likelihood had spies in the marketplace. He knew it was just a matter of time before he encountered his father or one of his brothers. He was not afraid, just felt an urgency to build the church in Pergamum before he might be stopped forever.

Forty-Three

Antipas stirred in his sleep as demons writhed around his head. "Get them away from me. No, no, no. Go away. Leave me alone. You can't...no, no..." Arms grabbed him as he shrieked and struggled. They would never take him alive. He gagged as the smell of sulfur nearly choked him.

"Antipas, wake up! You're having a bad dream."

Antipas heard the voice in the distance. He peered through the haze to see who called his name. The voices of the demons began to fade as consciousness returned and he was once again in his own bed with his wife shaking his shoulder.

"Talk to me, Antipas. You're scaring me." Eunice was up on her knees, bending over him, still shaking his shoulder. He sat up and turned to gather her in his arms, burying his face in the soft fragrance of her skin.

"I'm so sorry to scare you, Eunice. I haven't had one of these for a while. I thought they were gone."

She hugged him as she rested her head on his shoulder. "I was so scared, but I'm okay now." She sat up in bed, her head in her hands. "Do you know what I think? I think Satan is afraid of what you're doing here in Pergamum where he's had full control for so long. He doesn't want you doing what you're doing so he's trying to turn you aside. That tells me you're where God wants you to be."

"Yes, I'm sure this is where I should be. I can live with the dreams, but I'm so sorry you have to as well." He sat up beside her, circling her with his arms.

"That's part of what being a wife is, to support your husband. We can make the dreams shorter, because I can wake you sooner than you would on your own."

"You are indeed a treasure, my love." He kissed her soft cheek.

"Let's pray about it before we go back to sleep and ask God to give you peace for the remainder of the night."

And so they lifted up hearts bound together in love to the One who loved them more than they could ever grasp, and who had power over the evil one who sent troubling dreams. They slowly drifted back to sleep and the dreams did not recur that night.

There were no more dreams for the next few weeks, and the work in Pergamum proceeded as Antipas had hoped and prayed. He was humbled by the outpouring of love from the converts and the growth he could see happening every day in those who had been walking in the light for some time.

More places needed to be found for gatherings, and a plan was put in place for a citywide meeting. Antipas and the church leaders met to decide on the location.

"There could be no better place than the field where we had the meetings when you first came, Antipas." David, one of the early leaders, folded his arms over his chest and nodded to him.

Agreement came from the others, including Antipas. They set a date for the coming week then decided on a plan of how to spread the news. As usual, the individual approach seemed the best idea. They would announce this on Sunday at the home gatherings and begin approaching people the next day.

There was excitement once the plan was announced, and many promised to talk to family members, neighbors, business associates, customers and anyone else who might be interested in coming.

Antipas spent many hours in preparation and in prayer. He was so thankful for Eunice's support of him. "Thank you for listening to my ideas," he told her often. "You've had some good ones of your own, too. It's so nice to have someone to pray with me."

He met with Mattias, Emin, David, and several of the others to sharpen the plans. The night before the gathering they decided to hold an all-night vigil of prayer. Antipas would only participate in the first part of the night, as he needed sleep in order to be at his best the next day.

As the Christians began to talk to people, there was a sense of urgency about their approach. No one was naive enough to think that this wasn't risky. The peace was fragile; the city was deeply religious in its worship of Zeus and the emperor. Most civic and religious leaders considered the Christians a cult that should be eradicated. Approaching so many people increased the risk that word would reach the wrong ears. But the church was brave and the members courageously carried on with their mission of inviting everyone they knew.

The night was far advanced when Antipas joined Eunice in bed. He was almost too tired to sleep, but he knew the group praying was lifting him up before their Father and requesting rest for him. He fell into a deep, refreshing sleep. The sun was just topping the horizon when he opened his eyes.

Eunice was already busy preparing a lunch to take. They would eat after the meeting in the field. It would give the families time to visit with each other and any new converts time to talk and pray with the leaders and meet some of the Christ-followers.

"I'm so excited, Antipas." Eunice was almost skipping as they walked from their home to the meeting place. "I've never been to a large meeting like this."

"It's exciting to be together. The hunger of the citizens of Pergamum really humbles me. I'm so glad God led me here, right back where I grew up."

Soon other families joined them walking along the road as they left the city. There was an air of celebration, with people shouting greetings to each other and children running in and around the crowd.

When they approached the field, Antipas was overwhelmed by the number of people already in attendance. "There must be five thousand or more." He quickened his pace in his excitement. "God, give me the right words to convey your message."

People quickly found their places on the grass. Antipas was well into the teaching when he saw a horse and rider approach off to one side. The man's helmet caught the rays of the sun reflecting the light over the field; he must be a temple guard. His face was angry and belligerent. The elevated tilt to his chin spoke of scorn. He stopped and watched Antipas as he spoke.

Antipas wasn't sure what the guard might do, but he continued his message. The horse and rider skirted the crowd on one side of the field, stopping again at the back.

"Focus on the sheep who need your words," Antipas whispered to himself as he knew he was being distracted.

The guard worked his way down the other side. He stopped where he had a good view of Antipas. He listened for a few minutes then yanked on the reins and rode off the way he had come.

Antipas was deeply moved by the number who came after the message to hear more and to pray with the leaders. Some were in tears, some just looked confused. A few were even argumentative. But Antipas and the other leaders talked to all and answered questions to the best of their ability.

When Antipas finally joined the group where Eunice was eating with friends, the talk was all about the incredible response to the gospel. Families were sharing lunch with those who had accompanied them and continued to answer their questions.

Finally someone asked, "What was Marcus the temple guard doing here?"

Marcus! He should have known. He hadn't known Marcus was a temple guard, but it made sense. He had always liked to play the part of the oppressor. It didn't bode well for Antipas, nor for the converts. One thing was clear: Marcus knew he was in Pergamum.

Forty-Four

Marcus arrived at Julian's place of business.

"Father, I need to talk to you right now." His voice was strident in the quiet of his father's office, and Julian frowned as he looked up into the face of his eldest son.

"What troubles you?" He looked back at the work on the table in front of him, picking up his quill.

"We need to talk privately and it's urgent." Marcus put his hand on the table over Julian's work.

"Fine." Julian closed the scroll in front of him, slamming in down with the others. He covered the ink pot, setting it back in place. He glared at Marcus, wiping the quill carefully.

"Go to the back and make certain no one else is in there. I'll be right there." In slow motion he laid the quill with the others on the table.

Marcus snorted, flipped his hair back over his shoulder, and stormed off in the direction of the room indicated. The room was empty so he sat down to await his father. Thoughts and plans churned through his head as he waited. He stood up and began to pace the room. Measured, military steps. He heard his father's footfall in the outer passage.

"What's this all about, Marcus? What's so important it couldn't wait until this evening?" His father strode into the room, deep anger lines on his brow.

Marcus swung around to face him. "Father, I saw Antipas today."

His father turned pale and quickly sat down. He immediately jumped up and said harshly, "You know you're not permitted to speak that name in my presence."

"Father, he was speaking at a gathering of that new religious cult. I think he's their leader."

"What?" Julian roared as he began to pace, rubbing his hand over his face. "Is this really true?" His face flushed once more, and his hands shook.

"Oh yes, Father. You remember me telling you that a large group would be meeting in that field outside the gate? Remember you asked me to keep an eye on them as you think they're subversive?"

"Yes, yes, I know all about them. You're sure it was him?"

"Absolutely. I'd know him anywhere."

"I knew I should have had him killed." He flung the words at Marcus like an accusation.

Julian continued his pacing. He appeared to be pondering. Sweat was beginning to form on his forehead. He wiped it away with a quick jerk.

"Think, think. What will we do about this? Your mother can't be told. She's a fool and would only try to see him. She must never know he's back in Pergamum."

"Don't worry, Father. I would never tell her. There never was any love lost between me and him. But what about Paulus?"

"Don't tell him anything yet. We need a plan. This may well work in our favor. We may be able to take him down and the whole traitorous movement with him. Yes, it may be to our advantage." Julian vigorously rubbed his hands together while he paced. "For now, keep him in sight until we work out a plan. See if you can find out where he lives and what he does with his days. Also find out the names of people close to him. This could be good." Julian stopped and stared at his son. "Leave me now and begin your watch. Report to me every day."

Marcus bowed to his father and left his presence. He had a job to do, not an easy one, but one that would bring him pleasure.

Forty-Five

ntipas mulled over the encounter with Marcus. He wondered what it would mean for the Christ-followers. He would need to be on guard and careful for Eunice and the church leaders. Marcus could be cruel and probably had gone straight to their father.

It wouldn't be safe now to introduce Eunice to his mother. The father-and-son duo would be watching her carefully to make sure she didn't find out he was back in Pergamum. She already knew, but they didn't know that, at least he hoped they didn't. He wondered about his other brother, Paulus, if he was as hardened against him as Marcus and their father. He had heard that Paulus was in thick with them, but he remembered a softer Paulus.

He was sitting in their tiny courtyard as he did his pondering, waiting for Eunice to join him with tea. They tried to sit out here together as often as his schedule allowed. It was a special place for them, a place where they could be just themselves, together. Antipas relaxed as he saw his wife approaching. She smiled at him as she set the tea on a little wooden table. She sat at his side with a big sigh.

"What is it, my love?" Antipas looked at her closely. She wasn't in the habit of sighing.

She smiled again and took his hand in hers.

"Eunice, what are you not telling me?"

She smiled again and waited.

He squinted his eyes at her, a frown drawing his face down. "Eunice, that's enough. You must tell me what has you smiling like you have some secret."

"Actually, I do have a secret."

"Eunice…" He couldn't help the smile that twitched at the corners of his mouth.

"Oh, Antipas, I'm so excited!" She clapped her hands, mischief dancing in her eyes.

"Eunice, maybe I'd like to be excited, too. Now tell me what this is all about." He tried to be stern, but couldn't quite manage.

"Antipas, I think you'll make a wonderful father." She folded her hands in a prayer pose and sighed again.

"What?" He came off the chair and knelt in front of her grabbing her hands.

"Haven't you guessed yet?"

"Are you sure?" He squeezed her hands, the frown returning to his face.

"Yes, I'm sure." The secret smile reappeared and the sigh returned.

Antipas jumped up and stood in front of her. "Shouldn't you be resting? Is there something I can do, something I can get for you?"

"Just relax, Antipas. I don't need to rest and there's nothing I need right now except for my foolish husband to sit down and talk to me."

Antipas broke out in a big grin as he sat at her side again. "You have made me happy beyond words. What a wonderful wife you are."

"Thank you. Just keep thinking that."

They talked about the coming birth of their first child and made big plans for "him" and dreamed big dreams. As they talked and sipped their tea, the sun headed for the west ready for its journey toward daybreak tomorrow. Red and orange streaked the sky as clouds scudded across the sunset. As the evening dew began to settle around them, they softly entered the house and prepared for the night. As always, they ended their day talking to their Savior.

When they were settled in for the night, Eunice broke the silence.

"Antipas, are you still awake?" She shifted her position in the bed to snuggle closer to him.

"Yes, my mind won't stop going around in circles." He turned to her, hugging her tightly.

"Do you think our baby will be in danger?" In the darkness he could hear the fear in her voice.

"I didn't want to say anything to break our peaceful mood, but yes, that's why I can't get to sleep."

"I know. I'm so excited, but on the other hand I'm worried about our baby."

"I'll be honest with you, Eunice, I don't know what my father would do if he were to find out." He felt her stiffen in his arms.

"But this baby is his grandchild." Her tears fell on his chest. He dried her cheeks with his fingers.

"He won't see it that way. If I'm no longer his son, then this baby would be a threat to him because it would bear his name. This little one also becomes a target, a way to further hurt me."

"Then he'll just have to be God's child." She relaxed against him.

"For sure, he's already that. We'll have to be careful after he's born."

"We'll keep the news from your family as long as possible. They don't know who I am yet."

"That's true. His future is in God's hands the same as ours is. We've already committed him to the Lord. Go to sleep now, my love."

∽ ∽ ∽

The days passed quickly as the work in Pergamum grew. Many came to know Christ in the days following their talk in the garden. Eunice had an easy pregnancy, delighting in the development of her baby in the womb. The baby became active and sometimes kept a steady rhythm inside her as little hands and feet pushed against her.

One of the women in Emin's house church, Susanna, was a midwife. She agreed to come when the baby was due and came to visit Eunice several times.

"Everything is looking good, Eunice. The baby seems to be developing normally." She stepped back from Eunice and allowed her to sit up. "It's a boy for sure. No girl would be guilty of so much activity."

"It doesn't matter to me if the baby is a boy or a girl, as long as he or she is healthy." She smiled as Susanna shook her head.

Emin's wife, Clea, had become good friends with Eunice and was now sewing several outfits for the baby. This baby would be a well-dressed little "man." Eunice, too, was sewing for the baby. Word had reached them that Antipas's mother had been told about the baby by her friend who still attended Emin's church. She was unable to attend herself, as things had heated up at home with her husband not allowing her any free movement in the city.

∽ ∽ ∽

One night Antipas awoke and realized that Eunice was not in bed with him. He grabbed his robe and went into the other room. Eunice was sitting by the dying fire with a shawl wrapped around her. She seemed to be dozing. Antipas touched her shoulder lightly and she opened her eyes.

"What are you doing out here?" He stooped over her and lifted her chin.

"I couldn't sleep so decided to sit out here awhile and let you get your sleep." She put her hand over his.

"Are you feeling okay?"

"Well…I have had some…"

She doubled over with the next contraction.

"I'm going for the midwife. I'll get Salome to sit with you before I leave. Will you be all right?" Antipas pulled his robe tighter and tried to keep the panic from his voice.

"I think so. I thought I was going to be so brave, but I'm scared." She was trembling as she rocked back and forth on the stool.

"It'll work out just fine. We'll soon have a beautiful baby, a fine son." He wrapped his arms around her and held her close. "I really need to go so Susanna can get here and I can be back by your side. I'll get Salome."

Antipas rapped heavily on the door to the house. There was silence for a space then he heard feet shuffling inside. Augustus opened the door, took one look at the panic on Antipas's face and called for Salome. She was already putting on her robe and was soon beside her husband. Antipas explained that he was going for the midwife, and Salome said she would go right in to Eunice.

"Don't you worry about a thing, Antipas. You've got plenty of time. First babies take their time coming. Go now, and I'll take good care of Eunice."

"Thank you so much." He turned away and fled through the night. Susanna had been expecting the summons soon and so had a bag packed ready to go. She quickly rose when she heard Antipas coming and left with him. He carried her bag and tried not to walk too fast for her.

When they arrived back at their home, Salome had done wonders. Eunice was in a clean robe, sitting up in their bed, which had been remade ready for the birth. She had made an herbal tea for Eunice, who was sipping it quietly. Antipas couldn't believe his eyes. Gone was the frazzled woman Antipas had left an hour ago. Salome also had stirred up the fire and had two large kettles of water boiling on the hearth.

Eunice greeted them warmly and assured Antipas she was doing fine. It had also been decided that Antipas would go into the main house with Augustus and try to get some rest. The women promised they would call him when the birth was close or if Eunice needed him before that. They let the young couple have a few minutes to themselves before ushering Antipas out the door.

Antipas paced around the room Augustus had taken him to until he finally collapsed on the only chair. He began to relax and talk with his heavenly Father.

"Father, I know I shouldn't be fretting and worrying so, but I've never been a father before. Please keep Eunice and the baby safe and spare Eunice too much pain."

He felt more relaxed as he rose from the chair and lay down on the bed. It was a few hours later when Salome was shaking his shoulder telling him the birth time was near. With great excitement, he got up and entered his home. Salome instructed him to sit by the fire and not be too alarmed if he heard Eunice cry out. That was quite normal, she assured him, and would mean that the baby would soon be here.

Just when he thought the child would never be born, he heard a baby's cry. He started up from his seat, his heart pounding in his ears. Salome stuck her head out the door and beckoned him to enter. As he came through the door opening, he saw Eunice holding the baby close to her heart. She looked up at him. "Come see our son."

The women faded into the background as he approached the bed, drinking in the sight of his wife and son. Eunice handed him the baby. He took in every detail, the little hands and feet, the shock of dark hair, the tiny dark eyes looking back at him.

He looked at Eunice and whispered, "He's perfect."

She closed her tired eyes. "He sure is. He's just like his father."

"We need to give our little blessing his name. Are you ready for this?"

"Yes. I know you will have picked out a strong name for him. I can't wait to hear it." She was struggling to stay awake but didn't want to miss this most important part.

"His name will be Simon Mordicai Abdulla son of Antipas." He kissed the head of his son then passed him to his mother to hold.

She looked lovingly into his little face. "That's a perfect name. Thank you for choosing my father's name as well as my 'adopted' father's name. What a fortunate boy to carry such powerful names."

Her eyes really closed this time. The midwife reached for the baby to swaddle him. He, too, closed his tiny eyes in sleep. Peace reigned in the expanded household of Antipas. He sat by the fire and closed his eyes, praying his thanksgiving to his heavenly Father and for safety for his new son.

Forty-Six

Life took on a new rhythm with feedings and broken sleep. It was an idyllic time in their lives, and they determined to enjoy every moment. The baby had a lusty pair of lungs and let them know in no uncertain terms when he had needs. They loved it and rejoiced in his strong personality. He continued to grow and develop in a satisfactory way.

Eunice had asked Antipas to share with her everything about Marcus's appearance and all about his younger days at home.

"Oh Antipas, I feel moved by your story." She slipped her arm through his and snuggled her head on his chest. "We've both seen hardships in our early lives, but we've also seen the power of the Holy Spirit change everything for us."

He patted her hand, basking in her nearness.

"Please don't hide anything from me. I want to share everything with you." She looked up at him, smiling her sweet smile.

Wrapping his arms around her, he drew her closer. "I promise. I want you to be a deep part of my life and I also want you to be prepared for whatever might happen."

They spent many hours in prayer together.

~ ~ ~

"I had a dream that was so vivid it's still with me this morning." Eunice put her elbows on the table where they were breaking their fast and looked at her husband, a worried frown breaking the peace of her face. "I feel God is telling me that we need to pray specifically for your family, for their salvation."

Antipas reached over and gripped her hands. "I have been praying for them, but you're right, we need to do it specifically and together." He moved around and sat beside her. "Let's start right now." He realized he had always prayed for his mother, but had only prayed against his father and brothers.

Paulus became a particular matter of prayer, as Antipas felt there still might be some feelings of things past in him. Marcus and his father were hard and set in their ways and Paulus might well be, too. His mother seemed to think he was no better, but they could always hope.

God began moving in his heart in a way he wasn't expecting. He felt an urgent desire to contact Paulus. If he was deeply in league with Marcus and his father, Antipas could well be putting his life on the line, but if the Holy Spirit was prompting him, then shouldn't he do it?

It became such a burden on his heart that he knew he needed to share it with someone. He discussed it with Eunice and decided he should talk with Mattias, who had become such a dear friend and brother in the Lord. Eunice would accompany him and have a visit with Lois and Larium. They were always ready to welcome them and have time to play with Simon.

He spent an hour in prayer with Eunice in the evening, determining that early the next morning they would set out to visit Mattias. If he was busy in his shop they might have to wait, but it would be worth it to have his input. He spent a restless night but as morning light filtered into their room, they were in agreement that this next step should be taken.

Eunice fed Simon while Antipas prepared a simple meal for them. In his home growing up, men never dealt with food other than to eat what was set before them. Antipas, however, had learned much while with the caravan and then traveling with Epaphras so was able to help Eunice. Some of the brothers teased him, but he pointed out that in Christ we are all equal, so why shouldn't he help his wife?

It was still early when they left their home to walk the distance to Mattias's. It was a cheerful morning filled with the sound of birds calling to each other in the still air. The fragrance of blossoming flowers permeated the morning, creating a delightful ambience for their walk. Antipas carried Simon proudly. He still couldn't believe his good fortune to have Eunice and Simon. God was certainly good to him.

Mattias was outside his shop talking with a customer. He finished his conversation with the man just as Antipas and Eunice moved in beside him. His face broke into a huge grin as he greeted them. He grabbed Simon, covering his head with kisses.

"You are indeed a welcome sight this morning." Mattias passed the baby back to Antipas. "Larium is off today and will be so pleased to see all three of you, but especially Simon. It's been a long time since there was a baby around here. He's almost like a grandson to us."

"Can we talk while the women visit?" Antipas grabbed his shoulder.

"Of course. I just finished with a customer and there's no one else in sight right at the moment. Let's get Eunice into the house and we'll talk here in the shop."

Larium came running out of the house. "I thought I heard your voices. Welcome, welcome. Come right in, Eunice." She, too, gathered the baby in her arms and began to talk to him. He smiled at her and gurgled in his baby way.

"Look, he knows me and wants to tell me a story." She kissed his dark curls, cuddling him to her.

By this time they had reached the inside of the house, where Grandmother Lois was in her usual place by the fire. She was getting frail but her spirit was strong. She reached her arms out to Eunice, who knelt beside her to greet her.

"Grandmother Lois, would you like to hold Simon?"

"Oh, yes, please." Her hands were shaking but a beautiful smile ringed her face.

Larium carefully laid the little bundle in her arms. Lois looked at him, lovingly taking in each tiny feature.

"He's beautiful. I think he looks like his father." She gently caressed his little head.

"Yes, that's what everyone says. It makes Antipas happy when someone says that. He's a proud father." Eunice smiled at Lois and Simon.

The ladies talked as Larium made tea for them. The men had stayed in the shop to have their conversation. No customers came, so Antipas had Mattias's undivided attention.

"That could be suicide, Antipas. You know your mother believes he is as bad as your father and Marcus. What makes you think differently?" Mattias shook his finger at Antipas.

Antipas related all that had led him to this conversation. He told Mattias about the prompting of the Holy Spirit in both of their hearts.

"I can't agree, Antipas. This is just too risky. You have no way of knowing whether he is any different from the others." He jumped off his stool and took a turn around the shop. He stopped in front of Antipas, arms folded. "You need to think about the church members, too. This could mean trouble for them as well."

"I know that. I've given this careful thought and have spent many hours in prayer. Would you at least pray about it, too?" Antipas laid his hand on his arm.

"I see this means a great deal to you. Of course I'll pray." He sat on his stool again, leaning toward Antipas. "Let me think for a moment. We need to have a careful plan to even consider this." Mattias rubbed his beard. "I do have an idea that may help us." His face lit up as he spoke.

"Please, I'm open to any suggestions. I knew I had to talk to you about it. You're such a true friend and brother in the Lord. What's your idea?" Antipas now stood and rested an elbow on the workbench.

"Voss, one of the new converts in David's home church, is a government official. He's not a high official, but he may know your father and brothers." Mattias shook his head in thought. "His conversion has been spectacular, and he's suffering persecution at the hands of some he works with. I think we can trust him fully and should talk to him before we make further plans. Would you agree to a meeting with him?" He stood with Antipas, lightly touching his shoulder.

Antipas stared at the tools on the table. He turned to face Mattias. "Let's pray about it for a few days before we move on this. It feels right but I would like to have God's peace for this next step."

"That's the best idea. Why don't we meet again in three days, and by then you'll know how God is leading you." Mattias clapped him on the back. Antipas flinched as the mighty hand made contact.

"Thank you, my friend." Antipas straightened his back, still feeling the weight of his hand. "You are indeed a good friend."

Antipas spent a few minutes with Lois and Larium before they left for home. Once they were beyond the house, Eunice asked him how the meeting went with Mattias. He told her everything they had talked about and she agreed fully. That night they began to earnestly seek God's leading in the matter.

≈ ≈ ≈

At the end of the three days, Eunice and Antipas felt they should go ahead with the plan. Antipas said he would see Mattias in the morning so they could set up a meeting with the government official to ask him what he knew about Paulus.

Mattias was happy to set the plan in motion as he, too, had been praying and reached the same conclusion. Mattias and Antipas agreed to visit David that evening after Mattias had closed his shop. They wanted his opinion and help with the plan.

Antipas told him about Paulus, how they had been close as children and how God seemed to be prompting both him and Eunice to contact Paulus.

"I've heard your story before, Antipas, and can't believe you came back to Pergamum knowing your life would be in danger. But I see the hand of the Lord in all of this." David was seated with Antipas and Mattias in the courtyard at the back of his house. The evening air was pleasant. The flickering lamplight cast a glow on the low shrubs and flowers bordering the courtyard.

David leaned forward. "Why don't I approach Voss then set up a time to meet as a group. If he doesn't know your family, the three of us can meet again to decide on another approach."

❧ ❧ ❧

David came to Antipas's house the next afternoon saying a meeting would take place in his house that night. Voss did indeed know the family and would be happy to talk with Antipas. David was on his way then to give the message to Mattias.

As Antipas approached David's home that evening, his stomach felt like it was on fire. He was nervous, yet excited. Could it be possible that it was safe to see Paulus? To have contact with another member of his family?

Voss, a small wiry man with graying beard, had information for him. "I know your family. You know your father has risen high in the political and business world of Pergamum." Antipas nodded his head. He had heard. "Your father has a reputation as a bitter and cruel man. There is no room for mercy in his life. Before I came to Christ, one of my colleagues was a Christian. Your father found out and had him beheaded. I was told that he watched the whole thing himself."

Antipas shook his head, nausea welling up in his throat. "It appalls me to hear it but I don't doubt your word or your story."

Voss had not heard the story of Antipas's life, having come to Pergamum recently. Antipas briefly told him the events surrounding his father's dismissal of him.

"That doesn't surprise me, knowing what I do about your father. I know Marcus as well. He is even crueler than your father." Voss's eyes seemed to flash as he talked about Marcus. "It seems like he doesn't have a heart at all. As a temple guard, he instills fear in everyone. I've seen him slash beggars in the street because they didn't move fast enough. He even kicks children out of his way when he walks through the marketplace."

Antipas felt sick just thinking about what his father and brother had become. "What about Paulus?" He swallowed his distaste, bowing his head in grief.

"The word is that Paulus is not of the same caliber as either his father or his brother but that he toes the line because of his fear of them." He smiled for the first time. "I think you're right that there's still a soft spot in Paulus. I have met him on more than one occasion and have seen a spark of humanness in him that is lacking in the other two." He was nodding his head vigorously by now. "Instead of kicking children I've seen him give them coins and speak kindly to them when he hasn't been with Marcus."

"Then how should we go about this?" Antipas asked Voss with anticipation growing in his heart.

"You know this is extremely dangerous, don't you?" Voss stared into Antipas's eyes.

"Yes, but I've felt the Lord pushing me to do it." He wiped his forehead, where drops of sweat were beginning to form.

"If your father or your older brother ever hears about it, both you and your mother could be imprisoned or even killed." Voss's brows lowered and fine lines appeared on his forehead as he said these words.

"Yes, I know, and that's one thing that has kept me from pursuing it, not fear for myself, but for my mother. But I do know that if there is any possibility of reaching Paulus, she would not care for her own safety." He rose from his seat and stood at the edge of the courtyard, gazing into the night. He turned back to face the three men. "I believe I have to try to reach him."

"Why don't I approach Paulus, as I know him slightly. I'll watch for a good opportunity. We need to protect as many people as possible." Voss glanced around at the others.

The four men prayed together, asking for God's leading. "I feel that God is saying go ahead and that we shouldn't worry about what Voss will say or how he will say it." Antipas drew back his tense shoulders, stretching his muscles. "I believe God will give him the right words." He turned to Voss, resting his arm on his shoulder. "Go, my brother. I know I speak for the others when I say we will all be covering you in prayer as you make the approach."

"That's how I feel as well." Mattias shifted his bulk on the garden chair. "When do you think you'll have the opportunity to approach him?"

"Sometimes I see him in the marketplace or at places of business. I'll look for a time when he is alone and let God lead me from there."

"Are you absolutely certain you are comfortable doing this?" Antipas asked quietly.

"Absolutely. I've been asking God to use me in His work and as yet haven't felt His leading. Now I do. I know this is what I've asked for."

The men said good night to each other then left one by one. They took every precaution not to cause suspicion. As Antipas walked through the streets, his mind was on his brother and the strange twist his life was taking. It was like he was deliberately putting his life on the line.

Forty-Seven

Voss watched for Paulus during the following days. He saw Marcus on several occasions but managed to avoid him. Julian, Antipas's father, was also visible once or twice. He had such an arrogant air about him. It chilled Voss just to see him and to hear him speak to those he considered beneath him. He ranted and raved at an old woman selling her wares at the market just because she called to him to buy her produce. He was a ruthless man.

One morning while doing business with one of the merchants in the city, he saw Paulus walking toward the marketplace. He quickly finished his business and headed after him. He could see him working his way through the vendors, obviously with some destination in mind.

Voss caught up to him and touched him on the shoulder. "Paulus, I wish to speak with you."

Paulus turned and looked questioningly at him, his brow furrowed in a frown. "It's Voss, isn't it? What did you wish to say? I'm in a bit of a hurry." His tone was sharp and impatient as he looked at Voss.

"I won't detain you, but wondered if we could meet somewhere at your convenience." Voss bowed stiffly to Paulus.

"What is it you want to speak about? I'm not in the habit of meeting with lower government officials." He looked down his nose at Voss.

Voss was beginning to wonder if Paulus was as hard as his brother and father. He took a deep breath and sent up a plea before he replied. "I have information that will interest you."

"I can't imagine that you have any information that could even remotely interest me." Paulus started to move away.

"It concerns a long-lost relative."

Paulus stopped in his tracks and turned back to look at Voss.

"I don't have any long-lost relatives."

"I believe you had another brother."

"I have no other brother, good day." And with that he swung around and disappeared through the market toward the open area on the other side.

Voss stood where he was, squinting his eyes as he watched Paulus's back disappear. He slowly turned and headed back through the market. What should he do now? Antipas would be so disappointed. And would he now be in greater danger?

He prayed as he walked, finding comfort as he talked to God. As he reached his place of business, two men were waiting for him and he soon became caught up in his own affairs. He had a quick lunch then got back to work. Things were starting to settle down as the afternoon wore on. He finally put away the last of his work and left the building.

He was alone in the evening; his wife and children were visiting her parents in the country and wouldn't be back until tomorrow. He prepared a meal and sat beside the fire in deep concentration. He heard a soft knock on his door. He looked up as it came again. Voss wondered who could be wanting to see him so late and opened the door inquisitively.

A man with a hood pulled down over his face asked entry regarding an important matter. He stepped back and let the man enter. Once he had closed the door, the man pulled back the hood to reveal the face of Paulus.

"Paulus!" Voss exclaimed.

"Please hear me out. I'm sorry I was so rude to you today, but there are spies everywhere." Paulus hung his head while he pleaded. "Please tell me what you know of Antipas."

"Come sit by the fire and I'll tell you all I know." Voss took his cloak and hung it by the door.

Once they were seated, Voss began his explanation. He told Paulus that Antipas had long wished to contact him, but hadn't known if it was safe to do so, and that lately he had felt compelled to make the attempt. He explained why he was the messenger.

Paulus's eyes never left Voss's face. His shoulders slumped as he listened.

"Antipas is right, it's not safe, that's why I've come by night in disguise." He was restless, drumming his fingers on his knees. "I, too, would desire to contact him." He spoke softly then looked up at Voss. "Do you know where he is?"

"Surely you know he is in the city again? Marcus has seen him." Voss lifted his chair closer to Paulus.

"Yes, I did know. I encountered him one day in the street but didn't speak to him." He paused, his eyes closed for a moment. He opened them again leaning forward in his seat. "Marcus tells me nothing. I do everything asked of me, but neither Father nor Marcus confide in me. I'm glad they don't. I don't wish to be as they are." He sat back, shaking his head sideways.

"Would you be willing to meet with Antipas? I know he would prefer to tell you his story himself."

"Let me see what can be worked out. I don't want to put him in danger or myself either. It'll take careful strategy to work this out, but I'll do it," he said, jumping from his seat. "Give me one week and I'll come to your house again. It'll be late. Is that convenient?"

"I'll be waiting for you," Voss promised as he followed him to the door, handing him his cloak. And with that, Paulus was gone.

Voss slept sporadically, his encounter with Paulus rushing through his mind. He would need to contact David as soon as possible to take word to Antipas.

∾ ∾ ∾

To Antipas it felt like the week would never end until Voss would meet again with Paulus. Would this bring danger to the church or an opportunity for Paulus to hear the gospel and be reconciled to Antipas?

∾ ∾ ∾

Voss was ready when the night arrived. He told his wife he was going to sit by the fire awhile and would come to bed sometime later. She put the children to bed and then retired for the night. The house was soon quiet. About midnight the soft knock came on the door again. This time Voss was there before the second knock. He opened the door and Paulus rushed in.

"Thank you, Voss. I've barely slept since I last saw you." He shrugged out of his cloak for Voss to take it. "Antipas and I were close as children. When he was sent away, I cried myself to sleep for weeks and vowed I would someday find him." He talked and gestured with his hands as they moved in beside the cozy fire. "I guess I grew up and the vow faded in my mind." He paused, chin in hands, and shrugged his shoulders. He finally lifted up his head. "I have a plan I think will work."

They discussed the details. The meeting would take place three nights from now. Antipas would have to come alone to ensure safety. One of the difficulties would be that Antipas would have to trust Paulus. The other would be the possibility of encountering the spies that were afoot in the city.

"I know he has no reason to trust me, but I can't see any other way to meet. I'm watched by my father's cohorts. During the day would be too risky for both of us."

Forty-Eight

There were no stars visible in the sky as Antipas slipped from his home close to midnight for his reunion with Paulus. A stiff breeze caused him to clutch his cloak tightly around him. He had taken every precaution possible and had worked out the safest route to the rendezvous. Few houses showed any light; most city folk had long since retired for the night. The roadways were silent except for an occasional dog barking and the scurrying of some night animal.

Antipas chose the back alleys and side roads to avoid being seen alone. Twice someone shuffled toward him, but he kept his head down and no one spoke to him or stopped him. He knew he was getting close to his destination when he passed the silversmith's shop. Next left, then two houses down, he reminded himself.

The dwelling was dark, as he expected. He slid into the laneway beside the home and worked his way around to the back. He pushed the door open and glided into the room. All was still until he heard soft breathing.

"Paulus, is that you?" He paused, ears attuned for the slightest sound.

A rustle startled him as a small lamp was lit and placed on a table close by.

"Please sit down close to the light so I can identify you." A disembodied voice whispered the words.

Antipas did as instructed all the while praying that God would help him stop shaking. Now that he was here, it was all so mysterious and frightening. He heard a sigh of relief. "Yes, I can see it's you, Antipas." Paulus moved into the light of the small flame.

Antipas started to rise, but Paulus put his hand on his shoulder. "Stay seated, Brother, we need to be as still as possible. I may have been followed here."

"Paulus…"

"Brother, tell me what has happened to you since I last saw you." Paulus sat across from him, letting his eyes roam over his face.

Antipas leaned toward him with tears in his eyes. "Do you truly want to hear my story, Paulus?"

"Please speak. I don't know what the future holds for either of us, but I need to hear what you have to say." His face looked distorted in the swaying light of the small lamp.

Antipas began at the beginning, the day he went to his father and was disowned by him. He told him about the caravan and meeting Epaphras. He related how he had come to know Christ and that his whole life was now centered in Christ. He told him about Eunice and Simon, the loves of his life. When he had finished, he looked into the eyes of his brother and was surprised to see him wiping tears from his face. This time Antipas did get up and wrap his arms around him.

Paulus returned the embrace. "I missed you so much when you left. I didn't understand why you left or why we could no longer even mention your name. In my heart I never let you go." He stood as well. "I vowed I would find you when I grew up. But as the years went on, I thought about you less and less until I became tied in with Marcus and our father." He leaned back and searched Antipas's eyes. "You know you aren't safe? You know Father has threatened to have you killed if you ever show your face again?"

"Yes, I know that. I also know that Marcus knows I'm here in Pergamum. I saw him at an open air meeting." Antipas had stopped shaking but was overcome with emotion at this reunion. The brothers sat again, this time gripping each other's hands.

"It puzzles and scares me that they didn't tell me about Marcus seeing you. It tells me they have something evil planned for you." Paulus tightened his grip. "You must be careful. You should leave Pergamum while there's still time."

"No, Paulus, I won't leave Pergamum. God has called me here, and I'll stay until He calls me elsewhere, or until Father has his wish." He gave Paulus a small smile. "I won't run away. I'm not afraid. But I am afraid for you, Brother. You're not like them. You need to become a Christ-follower and leave them."

Paulus stiffened. "You know I can't do that. I wouldn't live until morning. I know too much, too many things that they've done."

"But Paulus, Christ can protect you if—"

"Brother, I'm glad you've found peace, and doubly glad that we could meet, but that's as far as I can go. I can never embrace your religion; it would be my death sentence."

"Paulus, know that I will be praying for you, that you will change your mind and that the power of the living God will illuminate your heart. What man can do to you is brutal, but what God can do is eternal." Antipas patted his arm in a brotherly gesture.

"Our time is up, Brother." Paulus stood with Antipas.

The brothers embraced again and Antipas could feel Paulus's body shaking. Paulus blew out the light and cautioned Antipas to keep close watch on himself.

"Don't leave until you're sure I'm out of sight. You will never know what this meeting has meant to me. If I see you on the street someday, I will go by you as though I don't know you, but know in your heart that I am embracing you."

When Antipas left the building, there was no one in sight. He made his way back to his home with a heavy but thankful heart. He knew that this one brother still considered him a part of the family and still loved him. He also knew that the message of the gospel had been given that night. God would have to work out the next step. Antipas could do no more except pray, but that was a big exception.

❧ ❧ ❧

The following day he took the news to Mattias of his meeting with Paulus. Mattias agreed that prayer was the only thing left for them to do. He would pass on the report to David, who would talk to Voss and thank him for his part. All told, it was a better outcome than they had even dared to hope for. Paulus was certainly soft inside, and the seeds of the gospel had been planted.

❧ ❧ ❧

During the following weeks rumors began surfacing in the streets of the city. Something was up. Zeus worshippers in the marketplace began to be vocal against the Christ-followers. Restlessness embraced the city. A measure of verbal abuse became commonplace for the converts. Even some of their businesses began to suffer.

As one of the local Zeus festivals drew near, Christians began to worry about what might take place. One report said that Christ-followers would be rounded up and sacrificed to Zeus. The newest, least grounded of the converts began to miss Sunday morning meetings out of fear for themselves and their families.

Things came to a head one morning in the marketplace. A customer accused a Christian vendor of trying to cheat him. He began shouting that all Christians were cheaters and liars and should be put in prison. Someone started throwing vegetables, and the riot was on. More and more people joined the ugly fray. The noise was deafening as tables were overturned and wares came crashing to the ground. Fistfights broke out, and the red of blood added a frightening dimension to the scene.

"Here come the temple guards!" The shout rang out over the noise and confusion.

Marcus led a contingent of guards into the midst of the fracas. He and the other guards used their whips on any who were in their path. They soon had the riot under control. Tempers seethed as people began to slink away out of reach of the terrible whips.

"Who's responsible for this?" An erect Marcus thundered the words from his mount.

The man who had begun the riot stepped forward and pointed at the terrified vendor. "He tried to cheat me." His voice reached screaming proportions. "He's just like all the other Christians, cheaters, all of them."

Marcus motioned to one of his guards to arrest the vendor. He was grabbed roughly, put into chains, and taken away. Marcus then cleared the area in front of his stall. He took one last look around before riding out. Business slowly commenced again and the marketplace returned to normal, except for the stall of the arrested vendor.

A pale, frightened face appeared from the back of the stall. It was a young boy. He cautiously ventured into the stall. Broken and trampled vegetables were strewn over the ground. He started picking up the tables, then the vegetables, setting them gingerly on the uprighted tables. Arranging the vegetables in somewhat the same order as before proved impossible. Many of them were no longer saleable.

An old man approached. He leaned in close to the boy and whispered to him. The boy looked frightened but nodded his head in understanding. The old man shuffled in behind the tables and began to wait on a customer who had just arrived. The boy ducked out from under the canvas at the back and disappeared from sight.

The boy, Martin, ran as quickly as his feet would carry him, away from the market, away from the sight now etched in his mind. He sped to his home and rushed through the door, startling his mother, who was making bread for their evening meal.

"Martin, whatever is the matter? You look positively white." She wiped her floured hands on her apron.

"Mother, oh Mother. They've taken Father… I don't know where…awful… whips cutting the air…"

"Martin, slow down, I can't follow what you're saying." She drew him to her, hugging his body in her warm embrace.

Gradually he was able to tell his story. His mother's face turned pale as she fell into a chair. She held her head in her hands and tried to think.

"If the temple guards have him, they'll have taken him to the prison. We'll have to go to David's house and raise the alarm. There's probably not much we can do for Father, but we may be able to warn the others. Oh, my poor Peter. I think it's started." She rocked back and forth on the chair, moaning softly.

"What's started, Mother? I don't know what you mean." Martin's eyes were wide with fright.

"The persecution we've heard rumors about. It's not safe to be a Christ-follower anymore." She looked at her son trembling before her. "But how could we deny our Lord who's done so much for us? It's going to be hard. Only a miracle will bring my Peter back." She stood slowly, beckoning to her son. "Come, Martin, I'll need you with me. Let me get my cloak and we'll go to David's. He'll know what to do. He may already have heard about your father."

They left their home, ever watchful, keeping to back streets and alleys.

"What did you do with the stall and the produce?" she asked him.

"An old man came to the stall and whispered that I should go home and tell you the news. He started waiting on the customers and I ran to you."

"I wonder who that could have been." She wrinkled her brow in thought.

David was not at home when they arrived, but a servant led them into an inner room and suggested they wait there as he was expected home soon. He brought them a cool drink, but neither of them could focus on anything other than the arrest of Peter.

"Do you think they'll let him go? He hasn't done anything wrong. He didn't cheat that man. Father doesn't cheat anyone." Martin couldn't sit still. He walked in front of his mother.

"The guards aren't interested in the truth, Son, they're only interested in removing any opposition to Zeus. They know the Christians don't believe in him, therefore they see us as a threat. I don't know why, we're only humble people."

The scuff of sandals on tile alerted Maria, and she looked up as David entered the room and greeted both of them. The sight of David's calm face undid Maria, who fell to the floor in front of him, crying out for help. David lifted her up and asked her what had so upset her. She poured out her story with Martin filling in the gaps. When they had finished, David called for his servant, gave a few quick orders, then told Maria and Martin to stay where they were as it might not be safe for them to return home.

"I'll go out and see what I can learn. This doesn't sound good, but don't give up hope. We have God on our side. I'll send Miriam in to sit with you." He quickly left the room.

David mounted his horse and headed into the main part of the city. Everything seemed quiet at the moment. He rode through the marketplace and was surprised to see Peter's stall set back to order and closed for the day. There was no sign of the old man Martin had mentioned.

He visited some of his contacts in the city, guards who were sympathetic to the Christians, and found out that things were worse than he'd feared. He was advised that the Christ-followers should flee for their lives; the governor was ready to sweep the city and arrest as many as he could find. With this admonition ringing in his ears, he decided he needed to contact Emin and make plans for the next few days, at least until tempers calmed down.

Marcus had gone directly to his father to report what had taken place.

"I know Antipas is behind all this 'Christian' activity. I say let's arrest him and be done with it." Marcus's hands were flying through the air as he punctuated each sentence with a fist punched in front of him.

"Take it easy," Julian advised, a troubled look on his face. "We want to do this right. When we take him, I want to make sure I have my revenge for his disgracing the family name." Julian's face was twisted with hate. "We have to make plans. I think it's time we talked to the governor."

Governor Justus Anthony was a sadistic and brutal man. He had earned the post of governor because he tolerated no subversion in his realm. The report that Marcus and Julian would give him would incite him to action. Once he knew the situation, Julian believed, nothing would stop him.

When they arrived at the palace, they were shown into the great room. Justus Anthony was dining with several women when the two men entered. The servant announced their arrival.

"Governor, two men to see you." The servant bowed stiffly before Justus Anthony. His brilliant tunic of red and purple was topped with an ornate turban of gold. Matching gold sandals with straps extending to his knees completed his attire. His hooded eyes gave nothing away.

Julian and Marcus looked at the scene before them. The women were taking turns feeding grapes to Justus Anthony. He laughed at their antics as each one leaned over him. When the men's arrival was announced, he looked up, frowning.

"I cannot and will not be disturbed until I've finished my meal." He turned his attention to the ladies again, licking at a grape dangling close to his lips. "Tell them they can wait in the anteroom if they so desire. It matters not to me." One of the women slid onto his lap, and he laughed heartily. He pushed her off and laughed again as she landed on the floor with a squeal of pain.

Julian decided to wait, even though it galled him to do so. He was an important man, and to be treated in such a cavalier way greatly disturbed him. However, the arrest and subsequent punishment of Antipas was enough to keep him there.

The father-and-son duo paced the anteroom while they waited. There was little talk. Julian fumed, eager to rid himself of Antipas, the thorn in his side that must be removed.

≈ ≈ ≈

As a child, Marcus had always known Antipas was his mother's favorite, and he was glad when the favored child was dismissed from the house and the family. His training as a temple guard had deepened his loyalty to Zeus, making Antipas's defection to another cause, as he considered it, seem even worse. Antipas was a traitor. He deserved the punishment that was coming to him.

"I loathe him and all he stands for." Marcus's lips curled as he thought about all the shame Antipas had caused the family.

Governor Justus Anthony sent for them three hours later. By this time, Marcus was beyond rage. He could barely tolerate the thought that he and his father needed Justus Anthony if they were to fulfill their desires.

≈ ≈ ≈

"Well, you decided to await my pleasure, did you?" Justus Anthony sneered at them as they entered his presence. He had no patience with the pair who thought themselves better than the Romans. Mere provincials.

Julian's jaw and throat worked as he swallowed and breathed deeply, lips pressed tightly. He bowed before Justus Anthony as was the custom, visibly gritting his teeth as he did so. He told the governor the news he had learned this day.

Marcus remained silent, as he should; a temple guard was beneath the notice of one as great as Justus Anthony.

Justus Anthony listened inattentively, breaking in now and then with a scathing comment about the people of Pergamum. He stared intently at Julian when he had finished his speech.

"So, what is it you expect me to do?" He slouched in his chair, legs crossed at the knee, studying his fingernails. The news had turned out not to be as petty as he'd initially thought. He sat up abruptly, glaring at Julian. "Do you want me to wipe them off the map? Nothing would give me greater pleasure, the disgusting vermin."

"Sir, I know you have the power to destroy this sect and in particular the leader. We await your pleasure in this tense situation." Julian bowed again, his face devoid of expression.

≈ ≈ ≈

It nearly killed Julian to grovel at the governor's feet. He knew what the governor thought of him and the other leaders of Pergamum, but he needed the authority of the governor to accomplish his desire.

"I heard a rumor about the leader, what's his name? Alibis, Antimius, something strange." Justus Anthony had gone back to studying his nails.

"Antipas, my lord." Julian almost choked on the name.

"Yes, yes, Antipas. I heard he is related to you, maybe even your son." His eyes never moved from his nails, but the words rained down like liquid fire.

"My Lord, please dispel these rumors. I have no son named Antipas." Julian's eyes widened and his mouth opened. He straightened his shoulders, back stiff.

"I think you protest too vehemently. There must be some truth to what I heard." He now lifted a small file to apply to his nails. "It did come from a reliable source. But you provincials have strange practices, so play your game, I don't care who he is. But I'll keep it in mind; the information might be useful someday." He put the file down and shifted his legs impatiently.

Julian heard the threat in his statement and trembled inside. It steeled his resolve to have Antipas receive his just reward for all the hurt he had caused.

"What will you do about the Christians?" he spoke through clenched teeth.

"I've already put a plan in motion. They'll be sorry they ever heard the name of that Christ fellow. They'll be crawling back to ask Zeus's and the emperor's forgiveness." He leaned forward, eyes snapping. "When I'm done with them, there may not be any of them left to extend forgiveness to." He laughed, the sound curling around and striking cold in Julian's heart.

Amid his laughter, he bid Julian and Marcus be on their way. "If I need your help, I'll send for you." He waved them off, accompanied by more frightening laughter. "And don't forget the rumors. How do I know you aren't in cahoots with them? Better go while I'm still in a good mood. The thoughts of you and this cult are enough to give a man indigestion. Go!"

They fled from his presence, faces burning with shame and fear.

"Antipas will pay for this, oh how he will pay." Julian yanked his cloak around his shoulders, spitting out the words as they left the presence of the powerful Justus Anthony.

Forty-Nine

Help, run for your lives, the guards are coming." The cry rang out through the marketplace. People scattered as the horses galloped through the narrow lanes of the market. The leader pulled on the reins and his horse reared and screamed, adding to the melee.

"We're looking for people disillusioned by the Jewish scoundrel." The guard boomed out his message over the cowering crowd. "Step forth, we know some of you are here."

The crowd yelled and jostled each other. Names were shouted, but no one stepped forward. The vendors and market goers began to look around, but there was no sign of any Christ-follower.

People continued to shout names and offer information. The guards dismounted and started questioning anyone willing to talk. A number of names were given, but little else of any value was gleaned. Wrists twitched and arcing whips fractured the air. The crowd fell back as the lashes made contact with skin. Finding nothing more to be gained, the guards swung up on their horses and thundered away.

Fear ground through the crowd in their wake. Pilfering broke out in the empty stalls of the Christians until there was not a vegetable, egg, or piece of meat left. Some looked on in horror, guilt pricking their consciences, but the lack of interference by the guards in stopping the looting quickly made them feel justified in their act.

The Christians had fled at the first sight of the guards. Many had run through the alleyways and out of the marketplace. A few had hidden and were now afraid to make an appearance for fear someone would contact the guards. They would have to stay put until the market closed and the other vendors had gone home.

The ones who escaped eventually arrived at David's house. Those with family members still at home had quickly gathered them together. This was the plan put in place in the past few weeks when trouble was looming. David would be able to protect them for now, but a safer location needed to be found. Returning home was not an option, as many of them would be watched.

David's servants busied themselves preparing a simple meal, digging out blankets for the night, and securing the property. David and his wife, Miriam, ministered to the people. Many needed words of encouragement to calm their fears. Once the meal was over, David organized a time of prayer. He had earlier sent word to Antipas, who arrived shortly after they finished their meal.

Antipas knew he was partly to blame for the renewed interest of the guards. He had been soul-searching as he walked the distance to David's home. Was he putting the Christians at risk by his presence? Was all of this a smoke screen to mask the real reason the guards were out, namely to arrest and destroy him? Was his father involved? He couldn't help but think he was, after seeing Marcus at the meeting.

Should he take his family and return to Ephesus? He knew he would be welcome there. He wasn't afraid for himself; whatever God had planned for his life, that was what he wanted. It was the people, the frightened innocents. They hadn't bargained for this when they joined the cause of Christ.

No matter which way he looked at it, and no matter how many times he prayed about it, he still felt God's calling for him to be in Pergamum. He would talk to the leaders and the people and if they wanted him to go, he would go. Otherwise, he would stay and see this persecution through to the end.

As he entered David's house, all seemed quiet. He was surprised; he'd expected to hear weeping and lamenting. He was ushered into the room where David was praying with the people. He quietly fit himself between two of the local market vendors and joined his heart in prayer with theirs.

When the time of prayer was over, they gathered around him, looking for direction.

"Friends, my heart weeps for you. You are in a circumstance not of your choosing." He watched their faces. "I fear it may be worse for you because of my presence in Pergamum." Heads started shaking and audible cries, "No, no," reached his ears. "It is my thought…"

"How could we blame you for the evil that is rampant in this city? You didn't bring the evil; you brought the good news of salvation to us." Martha stood from where she had been sitting, cradling her youngest son. "For that we won't ever be able to thank you enough. You put your life on the line to bring us this news. We'll be grateful forever. You risked your life for us; we'll be happy to risk ours for you and for the sake of the gospel." She sat abruptly, lowering her eyes, her face red.

"Well said, Martha. I think all of us agree that we need Antipas among us. If any feel otherwise, we'll hear your concerns." Mattias looked around; many heads nodded in agreement.

Then from the back a new convert jumped up. "I think we need to look at this with clearer heads. You have put us in danger. I, for one, would like to see you leave the city." He promptly sat.

There were murmurs of accord from others at the back.

"It's hard enough trying to live this life without this new danger. You weren't there to see the guards pounding through the marketplace. It was frightening." One of the vendors spoke hotly, thrusting his arms in the air.

A debate broke out between the two sides. Antipas looked to David, who moved over beside him. "Let them talk it out," David advised, patting his shoulder. "They need to be certain of their thoughts before we can make any progress with them."

Finally David rose to speak to them. He began to talk to them about bearing the hardships that were coming. He had some of Paul's writings with him, in which Paul had written about the hardships he had endured for the gospel and how Christ had been faithful to him in every trial. Gradually calm returned to the room. They finally agreed that it would be better for Antipas to stay with them. They needed his leadership.

Antipas rose to address them. "We know God will be faithful to us as well. We serve the same God as Paul."

"Amen, brother." Mattias jumped from his seat, arms in the air.

Antipas smiled at his friend. "We'll trust Him for the outcome and make plans for the present. We need places for you to stay with your families and a way to provide food. It won't be safe for you to return home at present. The governor, along with his cohorts, wants to wipe out all the Christ-followers. They see us as a threat to their religion, and praise God, we are."

Several were on their feet now, their amens ringing through the room.

"Once people have heard the gospel of Jesus Christ and have seen that this is not a mere religion, but a loving relationship with the Lord Jesus Christ, they can begin to see the hollowness and fear of being a worshipper of Zeus or the emperor. I say we keep preaching the gospel boldly."

"Yes! Yes!" The converts were shouting their agreement and their praises to God.

"We'll do all we can to protect the women and children, but I want men who are willing to put their lives on the line along with me. You will need to talk this over with your families, and then we'll come up with a plan. For tonight, you will stay here with David. By morning, we'll have places for you to hide for now. Yes, this is a frightening time, but it is also a time of rejoicing. Rejoicing that our God is so powerful that He puts fear in the hearts of even the governor and his highest officials." The group was sitting again, listening.

"Rest now, my friends. I will meet with David, and we'll have plans for you in the morning."

Antipas left the room, greeting most of the people on the way out. They promised to be praying for him and David. A calm and an acceptance had come over the converts as David had prayed and then Antipas had spoken to them. He bid them all a good night and followed David into the solarium.

⧳ ⧳ ⧳

"Were you able to find out anything about Peter?" Antipas wiped his forehead on the tail of his turban.

"They're holding him in the prison behind the temple. I wasn't able to see him, but my friend the prison guard warned me that it doesn't look good for him. He says the governor wants to make an example of him. I've spoken to Maria and Martin, and they're sad; they realize they may never see Peter alive again." David walked over to the open door, breathing in the night air. "Maria says she and Peter have talked about something like this happening and have been praying for God's strength and peace if it should ever come about. She says she trusts God whatever the outcome."

"She is a precious example of what the grace of God can do in our lives." Antipas joined him in the doorway. "I fear many may lose their lives before this is over. I long ago offered my life to Christ and will not turn back, no matter what the pain." Antipas leaned on the door frame and turned his head to David.

"I, too, though not as strong as you in the faith, want to be faithful to our Lord." David stepped back into the room, followed by Antipas. The two men sat on a low wooden bench.

"Then let's make some plans for these followers and pray that God will have His way in their lives, whatever it takes. The apostles all have suffered persecution, and we're going to be no exception. David slapped his fist into his other hand.

"I've been thinking of places for the women and children to hide." Antipas rubbed his jaw. "We could get them to Herra's place in the country. It's close to the city, secluded, and large enough to house a good number." Antipas bent to flick a bug from his tunic.

"That is exactly what I had been thinking." David gripped Antipas's arm. "I think God is placing ideas in our heads. We'll need to send a messenger to Herra as soon as the gates are opened in the morning." His eyes had fire in them as he warmed to his idea. "I suggest we ask Martin to go. I think he'd be happy doing something. He feels he didn't support his father when he was taken, even though I explained to him that wouldn't have helped his father, only would have gotten him arrested, too." David shook his head, a solemn look on his face as he mentioned Martin and Peter.

"It's decided, then." Antipas jumped up. "We'll need to get word to the other home church leaders so they can make arrangements for their groups. Everyone won't be able to go to Herra's. I'll go see Emin in the morning and get his input as well. Let's meet as leaders back here at noon. We need to decide how we'll proceed with our evangelization of Pergamum." Antipas moved toward the door as he spoke. He put his arm on David's shoulder. "I appreciate your strong support. You've grown so much spiritually in the last few months. I know God will honor your commitment." He stepped into the darkness. "Good night, my friend. There are dangerous days ahead, and I have a feeling life will never be the same for either of us."

Fifty

Antipas left the house before the others were up. It was crucial that he talk to Emin before the events of the day crowded in on him. Emin greeted him with questioning eyes.

"Come in, brother. What brings you here so early? I can see it's not good news." Emin stepped back to allow his guest to enter.

"No, it's not good news, but God is good." Antipas slipped past him, entering the room Emin indicated. He then proceeded to tell him the whole story.

Emin sat with his head in his hands. He looked up finally and smiled. "We knew this was coming. We'll just have to trust God and not worry about our lives, which belong to God anyway. I'm with you. We preach the gospel!" He raised his fist with a shout.

Emin agreed to spread the word to the other church leaders and to the Christians in his home church. They bid farewell to each other, agreeing to meet at noon at David's to plan their next move.

When Antipas reached David's house, the converts were ready to leave for Herra's. The children were excited at the prospect of a journey, not understanding the seriousness of the situation. David and Antipas prayed with them before two of David's servants left with the families in the wagons. Antipas was certain that Herra would welcome them into his home. Martin had left at dawn to carry a message to Herra asking for shelter for the group.

〜 〜 〜

Eunice greeted him with a worried frown. "What's wrong? You've been gone for hours."

"I know, love, but it's been necessary. I want you to pack a few things. I'm going to take you and Simon to Mattias's for awhile." Antipas held her in his arms while she continued to look at him, her eyes asking questions. "I know you'll be safe there and Mattias will look after you."

"The persecution has started, hasn't it?" Her face was twisted with pain as she probed his eyes.

"Yes. We don't know how bad it will be, but we want to protect the women and children as much as possible." He hugged her closer. "Peter has been taken, and we fear this may be only the beginning. We're moving some of the women and children to Herra's."

She leaned back in his arms. "What about the men? What about you? You're not going into hiding, are you? I know you; you'll be right on the front line. Oh, Antipas, I know you need to do this and I agree it's the right thing to do, but I'm afraid." She put her head on his shoulder while he hugged her to him and patted her back.

"I must speak for my Savior. I know He led me here and I can't run away at the first sign of trouble. God will look after you and will help you bear whatever He brings into our lives. Keep praying and loving our son and I'll join you as often as possible." He released her, still holding her hands in his.

"I'm okay now, I'll just put you in God's hands and try to be brave." Tears were escaping, but she smiled.

❧ ❧ ❧

His heart was heavy in contrast to the glorious day in Pergamum. Although the sun was blazing, a refreshing breeze was blowing in from the sea. He paid little attention to his surroundings as he walked the distance to David's. He was almost there when he saw David's gardener running toward him.

"Oh, master, something terrible has happened. David's been arrested. Just after you left this morning, the guards arrived. They searched the house looking for the Christians and were so enraged when they couldn't find them, they shackled David and dragged him off to prison. Please go in quickly. The family is distraught." The servant was panting and wringing his hands.

Antipas passed through the familiar rooms and approached the weeping family. He embraced them and spent time praying with them. They were numb with grief. They wanted to stay in their own home in case there was something they could do for David, or he was able to get some word out to them. It was decided that if the guards had wanted to take them that day, they could easily have done so. It appeared that it was the leaders they were after. Antipas agreed with this and asked if they would allow him to stay as well.

"But will you be safe here?" David's wife, Miriam, searched his face with haunted eyes. She rubbed the tears away from her cheeks.

"I'll not be safe anywhere, but I have taken Eunice and Simon to stay with Mattias and would like to stay and help you here. It's also a good place to work from, as we plan to continue our evangelism in Pergamum."

It was settled, and the family seemed to draw a sigh of relief that he would be there with them.

≈ ≈ ≈

Emin rubbed his eyes as he listened to the story Antipas had to tell him about David. "It's really happening, isn't it? When Peter was taken, we knew things were heating up, but now that they have David, it's real." He paced the floor, hands clasped before him. "They're after the leaders. If they can remove the leaders, they think it'll squash the movement."

Antipas watched him pace. "They don't realize we have the power of Almighty God behind us. Remove the leaders and God will raise up more and stronger leaders to replace them."

Emin stopped where he was and stared at Antipas. "I hadn't thought about it that way. All I've been thinking is that my turn will come, and will I be able to bear the burden and be true to my Lord." He ran his hand over his beard. "But you're right, Christ will be right there with me. What a glorious thought, to suffer for Christ." His eyes seemed to shine.

Antipas nodded his head as his lips curved up in a smile. "Paul has reiterated that over and over. What a blessed privilege it is to be one of Christ's followers." Antipas stood beside him, his hand on his shoulder. "We do need to face the fact that not all of our converts will be able to bear this. Some are still living in fear and will deny us and deny Christ. We need to be in much prayer for the brethren, that they will be strong and throw themselves upon Christ." Antipas threw his arms wide open.

"What's our next move?" Emin raised his eyebrows in question.

"I believe we need to be seen on the streets of Pergamum this day so the common people will know that what we preach, we also live. We can't retreat and hide ourselves, or our message will become lifeless." Antipas was getting excited as he talked. He gestured freely as he gave his opinion. "We'll take every precaution to protect our women and children, but as men we must be strong in the Lord." He swung around to face Emin. "Are you ready to join me on a tour of the city?"

"Yes, I'm ready. I'm still a little shaky inside, but I don't ever want to deny my

Lord." Emin lifted his chin as though in defiance of the ones who would wipe out the Christ-followers.

The two men left the house together and began to walk energetically through the busy streets, heading for the center of the city where the temple of Zeus was located. They were bent on challenging Satan where he resided.

As they approached the steps, many people were moving in and out of the temple. It was the day of one of the celebrations to Zeus, so crowds of people were milling around the entrance. Antipas and Emin boldly mounted the steps of the temple. When they reached the first landing, they turned and faced the crowd.

"People of Pergamum." Antipas raised his arms to the heavens. "Listen to me. You are deluded with the worship of Zeus. I bring you news of the one true God, who loves you and wants to welcome you into His kingdom." He walked from side to side on the steps, watching the crowd from every angle.

Many in the crowd stopped on the steps and in the street to listen to the words. Some ignored him, proceeding into and out of the temple, but the ones who stopped were looking at him with curiosity. Antipas took advantage of this and continued his message.

"Zeus is not a living creature who can help you when you have troubles. Our God is alive and once walked among us. He died that you might receive His eternal life. Just think about that, people of Pergamum, eternal life!" He punctuated his words with a finger pointing at the people then at the sky.

Murmurs began to rise from the knots of people. Calls of "Heretics" were heard. "Call the temple guards" floated over the other noises. But some faces were registering a hunger for the message. Antipas could feel the fear and the longing in the crowd.

Two temple guards, mounted on restless horses, helmets shining, waited at the fringes of the crowd. But no attempt was made to arrest Antipas and Emin. Antipas caught a glimpse of Marcus. Their eyes met, and he read hate and anger there.

Antipas sensed trouble was coming faster than anticipated. His time to speak for Christ might be short. He continued to talk, then he and Emin spoke with several people quietly. Some agreed to come to a home meeting on Sunday. The crowd dispersed; some continuing into the temple with their sacrifices, others to haggle in the marketplace. When it appeared they had said all they could for today and had spoken to all who wanted to talk and ask questions, Antipas and Emin descended the steps and left the temple area.

Antipas was in a state of high excitement. He and Emin had done what they felt God was leading them to do, and God had protected them. What great things would they see as a result of today?

"I can't believe it was that easy." Emin strode beside him, a huge smile on his face.

Antipas put his hand on Emin's arm, stopped him, and looked at him closely. "Don't get your hopes up; the guards are biding their time. I'm not sure what they're waiting for, but you can be sure they will strike."

Fifty-One

Emin and Antipas approached David's house.

"Come quickly, Antipas; Peter and David are back!" a servant called to them. They gathered up their robes and ran the rest of the distance. When they entered the house, they were surprised to hear weeping from the women. "What's wrong? I thought the men were back." Antipas's eyebrows drew together.

"Oh, Antipas," sobbed Miriam, "they're back but in such bad shape. They've been beaten badly." Her tears flowed down her cheeks. "I think David's going to die." She buried her face in her hands as she wailed.

"Take me to him."

He followed her through the house to the sleeping area. Deep moans stirred the air as he entered the room. The window shades were closed to block out the light. Antipas waited until his eyes adjusted to see the form writhing in pain on the bed. David was unrecognizable.

Antipas leaned close to him. The parched lips opened. "Antipas, keep preaching… they can… only…"

"Don't try to talk, David. Just rest for now, and when you're feeling better, we'll talk."

"No…need to talk…now…"

"David, I'll stay right here with you. Sleep first," Antipas pleaded.

"Must talk… keep preaching… they can… only hurt…"

There was a long pause. Antipas pulled up a stool and sat by the bed, watching his lips. He could see that David was determined to say what was on his heart.

"The body…" Another long pause. "Can't touch…the soul."

David appeared to doze but then his eyes opened again. "God…will give strength…and peace…to bear…all."

This time David did fall asleep. Antipas watched his friend for a few minutes, then left him with the servant who would watch over him.

He sought out Emin to report David's message. Emin had been sitting with Peter, who was not as badly beaten as David.

"Peter is waiting to see you," Emin told Antipas as they met in the hallway outside the sleeping rooms.

"I'll go right away." He entered Peter's room as quietly as possible. One of the servants was sitting with him. He jumped up when Antipas appeared.

"Sit here please. Peter has been awaiting your arrival."

He nodded his thanks to the servant and sat down next to the bed.

"Peter, it's so good to see you awake." The sight of his battered face made Antipas's chest ache.

"I'm just so glad to be here." His voice was weak, but he managed a smile.

"Do you feel up to telling me what happened?"

"I want to do that. It may help some of the others avoid arrest." He sighed and shifted slightly in the bed.

"Just take your time." Antipas sat forward to listen.

Peter took a ragged breath. "The day I was arrested, I was taken to the prison, thrown into a small underground cell with no window, no light, no other prisoners." He paused as though reliving the details. His hands were restless on his blanket, picking at the material.

"Someone brought me bread and a small cup of water once a day. Even this was pushed under the door so there was no contact with anyone." He looked up at Antipas, his eyes heavy lidded. "I think I minded that the most, no one to talk to, complete isolation. That or the smell. If you can imagine unwashed bodies, rotting food, filth, putrid air, and dampness all mixed together, you wouldn't even be halfway to describing the stench." He wrinkled his face as though smelling it again. "My only company was a couple of rats who were happy to share my crust of bread."

He closed his eyes. Antipas wondered if he had drifted off to sleep.

After a pause, Peter's eyes opened again. "I had no idea whether it was night or day or how long I had been there." He shook his head. "A few hours ago I was awakened by one of the guards banging on the cell door and shouting. He slammed open the door and grabbed me, yanking me to my feet and shaking me." Pain rippled across his face. "I couldn't believe how angry he was. Two others joined him, and they dragged me out into the courtyard." He gave a gasp, then swallowed. "They roped me to a pole in the center and that famous Roman whip appeared. I finally passed out, and when I opened my eyes, I was in an alley a league from the prison." A shudder wrenched his body.

"Don't go on if it's too painful." Antipas touched the hand that was still kneading the blanket.

"No, no. I want to finish." He raised his hand to push Antipas's away. "I managed to get to my feet and crept here to David's house. One of the servants saw me at the back of the house and carried me inside."

He closed his eyes and this time didn't open them. Antipas watched him for a few minutes then called the servant back to sit with him. Antipas sought out Emin.

"It's hard to rejoice when we hear of such suffering." Antipas shook his head sadly as he and Emin sat together in the solarium. "I would far rather it had been me."

"Your turn will come soon enough." Emin pointed at him. "Until that time we have work to do."

Antipas checked on David once more. He was still asleep, albeit restlessly. He moaned and tossed in his bed. The servant caring for him had to watch him constantly lest he roll from the bed. Antipas went from there to talk with the family. Miriam had herself under control by now and was holding up well, trusting David's life to her Savior.

"We knew this might happen." She was sitting quietly in the atrium when Antipas found her. "We now have to be brave and let the Lord work in our lives. David is prepared to meet Jesus." She wiped her eyes with a damp cloth.

"Let's pray he has more years with us still. I'm so proud of you. Your attitude is Christlike. God will supply all our needs. If you are settled for now, I would like to go to Mattias's house and visit with Eunice and Simon. I'll be back in a couple of hours." Antipas stood, ready to leave.

"Of course, go. Eunice needs to know you're safe for now. She'll have heard some of the news. When you get back, please come to my room even if it's late. I would like you to pray with me before I retire for the night. For now, I'll sit with David. It's comforting just to be near him." Miriam also rose, using the damp cloth again.

~ ~ ~

The streets were quiet as Antipas glided through them. He kept to little-used ways, hoping to avoid the guards on their sweeps through the city. The sound of laughter and shouting floated to him from the next street. It sounded like someone was celebrating this night. He pulled his cloak closer around him to keep out the chill of the wind. It seemed symbolic of the position of the converts this night, the cold wind of persecution.

He reached Mattias's house before the household had retired. He was welcomed with urgency, as the family craved news of the day's events. After greeting Eunice warmly, he sat with the family and Eunice and related the story.

"Will David live?" Mattias questioned him with a worried frown.

"That's in God's hands. Everything humanly possible is being done for him. He's weak and broken but his spirit remains strong. He encouraged me—no, commanded me—to keep preaching, as they can hurt only the body, not the soul. It was touching coming from someone beaten so badly by the enemy." He clenched his hands in his lap.

"What about Peter?" Tears welled in Eunice's eyes.

"He'll be sore for a few days, but he wasn't beaten as badly as David. I think you'll see Peter out on the streets defying all the threats they made to him. It has strengthened his resolve to stand firm for his Lord."

The talk had gone on for some time when Larium announced her family needed to go to bed and let Antipas and Eunice have some time together before Antipas had to return to David's house. Each family member gave Antipas a warm embrace before leaving the room.

When the two were finally alone, they talked quietly by the fire. Antipas held the sleeping Simon, marveling at his mass of dark curls and the clear skin of his face.

"He's such a beautiful baby, Eunice, or do you think I'm just prejudiced?" He planted kiss after kiss on the dark curls.

"I'm sure you're prejudiced." She moved closer, linking her arm in his. "But he is beautiful and special." She smoothed the hair back from his tiny face. "I can't ever imagine life without him. He's such a comfort to me when you're away." She reached up and kissed Antipas. "Oh, I wish things could be different. I don't like being without you."

"I know, but we can't deny our Lord. We must preach about Him to these lost people." He laid his head against hers. "Eunice, I've been so burdened with the chains these people wear as prisoners of Zeus worship. I see fear in their eyes and a hunger for the message that we're bringing to them." He shifted Simon in his arms. "No matter what happens, I know we're doing the right thing." He reached one arm around her while still hugging Simon.

"Yes, I know that, too." She buried her face in his robe. "I just wish it wasn't so hard. I'm so afraid I'm going to lose Simon or you." She sat up suddenly. "But you're right, we can't deny our Lord. I'm content to stay here with Mattias and Larium— it's like a second home to me—and let you do what the Lord has laid on your heart to do." She smiled bravely at him.

At last Antipas stood up and said he must go. Eunice stood, too, and he wrapped her in his embrace. They stood for a long while, gathering strength from each other. In his heart Antipas knew Eunice was right. There was a good chance she would lose one of them. Finally, with one last kiss to both Eunice and Simon, Antipas slipped out into the night.

Fifty-Two

The days following the release of the two prisoners were tense. Many of the converts wanted to turn their backs on God and embrace the worship of Zeus again, but fear of reprisals kept them in hiding. Antipas knew it was time for him to meet with as many of the Christians as possible to encourage them in the faith.

He traveled to Herra's estate as well as to others where the converts were hiding. They listened to Antipas and heard news of what was going on in the city and heard the stories of bravery shown by the leaders of the church. Some of them took heart and surrendered their lives to the Lord again. But many were angry and ready to return to pagan worship. They were terrified of what might happen to them and their families. He met with strong opposition from some of the men. In the days ahead, he would need to visit often to try to win those ones back.

On returning to Pergamum, Antipas knew it was only a matter of time before he would be taken. He and Emin plus some of the other brethren stood daily on the temple steps, proclaiming Jesus Christ to the people. As always, there were temple guards on the fringes of the crowd. Rumors were circulating about what might happen. Some of them certainly were true.

One quiet evening, just before dusk, Antipas was walking through the deserted marketplace on his way back to David's house. Rough arms jerked him and hands grabbed his cloak. A rancid odor bit his senses as his assailant's robe brushed his face.

A cold, cutting voice informed him, "You're under arrest."

A hood was yanked over his head, cutting off the light of early evening. Dust from the hood clogged his nose, and he gasped for breath. His arms were bound to his sides with a rough rope, so tightly that his wrists ached. A swift kick behind his knees knocked him to the ground, and his feet were tied together. He struggled in the bonds, but they had been tied securely.

Someone grabbed his feet and dragged him over the uneven ground. Dust filled his lungs until he could hardly take a breath. Grunts and curses filled the air as he was pulled along.

"You got him?"

"Yes, yes, I got him. What'd you think?"

"Hold on, you fool."

The bouncing stopped for a minute. He heard heavy breathing before he was lifted up and unceremoniously thrown onto a hard wooden surface and covered with rough cloth. Jarring movement told him he was in a cart. It rattled noisily through what Antipas believed were the side alleys of the market.

The captors had been clumsy and rough; not temple guards, then. They would have been more professional in their approach. No doubt he would learn who had taken him soon enough.

The journey was jolting as the cart bumped over the uneven surface of the alleys. He tried to follow turns to figure out where he was being taken, but there were too many twists in the way. He could be almost anywhere by now. His mind kept going over and over the details, trying to decide who had captured him and why. He had almost no feeling in his hands, and his wrists felt raw from the chafing of the rope. If only the dust would stop. It kept sifting in through the hood, choking him.

The cart came to an abrupt halt and he was dumped to the ground in a heap. Strong hands gripped his clothing, dragging him into a building. The rough texture of the floor scraped his back. He was deposited in the center of what appeared to be a large chamber, judging by the echoes. A few brutal kicks to his ribs, a stomping away of boots, then silence.

He wasn't sure how long he had lain there when he heard footsteps. Two sets of steps. He sensed someone bending over him, then a voice he'd thought he would never hear again: his father's.

"Take off the hood." The voice was cold and the order brusque.

He felt hands moving behind his head. The cloth fell off and he was looking into the angry eyes of his father. Julian's face was dark, his mouth writhing in a snarl. He paced, not speaking, for several minutes. In that time, Antipas saw all the hatred of the last few years culminate in the icy eyes looking into his own.

His father worked his lips, grinding his teeth. "I told you never to show your face in Pergamum again." Spittle flew, landing on Antipas's face. "Why was my order not obeyed?"

Antipas chose his words carefully. He had to represent his heavenly Father in an appropriate way. With emotion nearly leaving him speechless, he whispered, "You, my earthly father, disowned me, but I now have a heavenly Father whom I obey. He directed me to Pergamum."

Fire flashed from Julian's eyes. "How dare you speak to me in such a way? You mock my authority." He shook his fist and this time spit deliberately.

Antipas was unable to wipe his face but he kept his eyes focused on his father's eyes. "My intent is not to mock you, but to tell you my reason for being here."

"You must leave at once. This whole sect would crumble if you left it." He brought his fist close to Antipas's face. "They're nothing but the lowest rabble in Pergamum; weak willed, outcasts of society, dull farmers and peasants. You're a fool for leading them." Julian's face had turned dark red. He glared from below tightened brows. His body was visibly shaking.

The second man in the room came closer. Antipas was not surprised to see Marcus. Disdain curled his lips. He saw no anger, just loathing.

"Father, you are overexerting yourself. He's not worth this much anger. You'll do yourself harm." He touched Julian's arm.

"If I do, I will blame him." He shrugged off Marcus's hand. "He's to blame for everything I suffer. He's ruined my life with his rebellious attitude, and now this bizarre cult." He walked away from Antipas, muttering to himself. "I should have killed him, not sent him away. I should have known he would come back to haunt me." He raised both hands in the air, punctuating each word with a jab of a fist.

"Father, control yourself. We're accomplishing nothing while you rant and rave. The question is what are we going to do with him?" Marcus stayed beside Antipas, watching his father.

Julian walked back over and looked down at Antipas with a hatred so strong in his face that Antipas feared for his father's life. Somewhere deep in his heart, he harbored a love for his father and a desire to see him come to know his Savior.

"Father." Antipas kept eye contact with Julian.

"Don't call me that. I am not your father. I have no son named Antipas." He shouted as he threw his hands in the air in a desperate gesture. He stormed around the room several times, shouting his denial.

"I should never have allowed you to live. You have brought me nothing but trouble. I should—"

Marcus stood up to his full height and faced his father. "Father, have you forgotten what Justus Anthony said?"

Julian stared at Marcus, panting, letting his arms fall to his sides. "You're right. I haven't forgotten. We must do what we must do."

His father leaned over him once more, leering. He spit again in Antipas's face then straightened. "You have disgraced and humiliated me repeatedly, but no more. I'll not have it happen again." Julian was breathing heavily. "You will stay tied up here in this warehouse until someone comes to claim you." He gathered his face in a twisted snarl. "They've been paid well to remove you from the city and take you far away." He flung his arms in the air. "Once you're gone," he roared, "the cult will fall apart and I'll be left in peace."

Antipas remained silent, watching his father. He could see the sweat beading on his forehead. He felt such pity for him. He was surprised at the strong emotions struggling in him at seeing his father again. He would submit to the will of his heavenly Father. If He wanted to rescue him, then good; if not, then so be it. Antipas closed his eyes.

Marcus drew back his foot and connected with flesh and bones. Antipas felt the crunch and then the hood was yanked back over his head. Father and son walked out of the area together, their feet echoing on the floor. Antipas heard the bar falling into place on the door. He was truly alone.

As he lay there, swells of nausea crept over his body. Again the dust filled his lungs as he struggled to breathe. He determined he would not give in to the physical pain but spend the time just talking to his heavenly Father. This was not the time for panic or remorse.

"Lord, I willingly submit to Your plan for my life. If this is the end, then I will soon be with You in heaven. But if You have more for me to do on this earth, then I am ready to do that. Keep the church strong here in Pergamum. This is the seat of Satan. He can't be allowed to claim this city any longer. Help the Christians keep the vision alive."

He heard steps outside the warehouse. Subdued voices came through the walls. The bar was lifted and heavy footsteps approached him. Another vicious kick was administered, and he gritted his teeth, determined not to cry out.

"Get up, you worthless bit of humanity, we've got to get going." He could hear breathing but could not see through the hood.

Antipas tried to get up, but the ropes binding him prevented him from doing so. One of the men picked him up and flung him over his back. Once outside, he was dumped into what felt to be the same cart and the rough journey began again.

As Antipas lay in the cart he felt the nudging of the Holy Spirit. The words formed in his mind. *Roll off the cart.*

Antipas dismissed the thought. How would it help to roll off the cart? The thugs would only see him, stop, and probably give him a beating for his efforts. And if that didn't happen, what could he do bound the way he was? He would just die by the side of the road.

Roll off the cart.

"This isn't making any sense." Antipas tried to shift his position but even that was difficult.

Roll off the cart.

"Okay, Lord, I believe You're speaking. I'm totally in Your hands."

Antipas began to shuffle his body to the back of the cart. It was a slow process as he was tightly bound. He could hear the two men talking to each other. Neither commented on the activity in the cart.

Inch by torturous inch, he worked his way back. An agony of pain gripped him as he moved. A short rest, then another inch. At last his feet felt the edge. Fortunately the cart was open backed. One last slide and he was falling to the ground. He landed with a thump he thought could be heard by the men. But the cart kept going.

He lay in a huddle on the ground, bruised and dizzy. The sounds of the wheels slowly died away, leaving him helpless on the road.

Fifty-Three

His body hurt from the fall and from the abuse he had suffered from his brother's foot. He lay still, focusing on breathing. His brain refused to function, until the thought of being run over by the next cart going by helped him to start thinking. He struggled to move, moaning with each try, but it was useless with his feet tied together. He gritted his teeth as the ropes rubbed on bruised skin.

As he struggled he sensed a person nearby. He called out, hoping it was someone who could help him.

"What happened, mister?" The voice was soft and sounded gentle.

"I rolled off a cart a few minutes ago. Would you help me with the hood and the ropes?" Antipas struggled to move.

Even as he spoke, the hood was removed and the rope binding his hands was cut. An old man dressed in ragged clothes, with a long, shaggy white beard, was working on him.

"There, that should do it." The man cut the last rope and straightened his back.

"I owe you my life." Antipas gingerly sat up.

"Let's get you on your feet. We need to get you moving and out of the way of any other carts." The old man helped him to his feet. Every part of his body felt weak after being tied up.

"Lean on me, and I'll help you walk."

The two began their journey. Antipas had no idea where he was, but the old man seemed to know what he was doing, so Antipas just focused on walking, not concerned with where they were going.

The city soon appeared and they slipped through the gate. Antipas realized he was close to Mattias's house. In fact, they went in that direction. Soon he could see the house. He told the man he would stop there as he had friends. He turned to thank the man, but he was already turning to leave. He dismissed his thanks with a wave of the hand. Antipas stood for another moment, watching him go.

He shook his head to clear his thoughts and entered Mattias's house. The lamp was already lit and he could smell the wonderful odors of a meal cooking. He realized he was hungry and anxious to see Eunice and Simon as well as Mattias and his family.

When he entered the room, Eunice jumped up with a small cry of joy.

"Antipas, we didn't expect you tonight. I'm so glad to see you." She ran toward him only to stop and put her hand over her mouth. "What happened to you?"

He moved toward her and held her gently; anything else would have been too painful. He realized that she might have been receiving different news tonight had it not been for the old man who'd helped him. He related the story to the family amid their exclamations of shock and relief. He was ready to die for Christ, but he was grateful for more time with his family.

∽ ∽ ∽

David continued to improve, Peter healed quickly, and Antipas was more determined than ever to continue his previous activities. What his father and Marcus knew, he didn't know. He heard nothing from them in the weeks following his capture and subsequent dismissal from Pergamum. He spoke daily on the temple steps and was undisturbed except for a few hecklers.

The people of Pergamum seemed anxious to hear and respond to his message. Daily converts were added to their number. It was with great joy that Antipas watched these tender new believers grow in their walk with the Lord.

But tensions were high. Rumors continued to circulate through the city, frightening some of the women. They were trusting in God, but knew the lives of their husbands, fathers, and sons were at stake. It became real when the body of one of the newest converts was found in a field outside the main gate. Nothing could be proved, but it appeared obvious that it was the work of a temple guard.

The Christians began to move in groups when it was necessary to travel. They were nervous and furtively watched for temple guards. Antipas understood their fears and tried to encourage them to remain steadfast in their faith.

∽ ∽ ∽

It was a great day when David felt well enough to mount the temple steps once again. On that day Antipas, David, Peter, and Emin approached the first landing and turned to face the gathering people.

Up to this point, Antipas had simply preached to them the crucified Christ. But lately in his personal time with the Lord, he had felt God prompting him to expand his ministry approach. He had spent time in prayer struggling with the nudging he was feeling. It was one thing to preach—that was easy for him—but it was quite another to reach out a healing hand to those in need. He had left it with the Lord to bring an opportunity if indeed this was what God wanted.

On this already special day, the four of them had no sooner got themselves situated when they were approached by a young mother carrying her baby. She was weeping quietly as she clutched her child. When she reached them she fell on her knees in front of Antipas.

"Please, sir, my baby is dying. Is there anything your God can do for us? I've listened to you speak for many days, and today I must speak. My baby does not have much time." She lifted her baby to Antipas. "Feel his forehead; he's burning with fever. He has seizures on a regular basis. The doctors say his heart won't take much more." She brought him close to her, holding him tightly. "Please, sir, I beg you, do something for him." She bowed her head to the ground.

Antipas knew it was time. This was the sign he had been praying for. "Woman, stand up. Please let me hold your baby."

She rose and passed the baby to Antipas. He lifted his eyes to heaven and prayed to his heavenly Father. "Father, You are the Creator of all things, the Creator of this tiny baby. I know You desire life for him."

He faced the people, holding up the baby for all to see. "In the name of Jesus Christ of Nazareth, be healed." He lifted his eyes to heaven, arms stretched out, holding the baby.

He handed him back to his mother, who was overjoyed to feel his cool body and see his clear eyes. The baby smiled and gurgled at his mother. "He's healed." She twirled around to face the crowd, her face wide with a smile. "He's healed. Rejoice with me, my baby is healed!"

She kissed the hands of Antipas, and holding her baby closely, descended the temple steps and worked her way through the crowd, continuing to cry in a loud voice, "He's healed."

The crowd went wild. There was shouting and praising the name of God. The press of people was almost smothering. The four men tried to calm them, but the shouting became even louder.

At the back of the crowd, the ever-present temple guards watched with drawn swords, but even they were wise enough not to try to quell the people. Antipas suggested to the others that they not speak publicly today, but just talk to people individually. This they did, and they were able to spread more good news about Christ.

The crowds began to demand Antipas every morning. As they approached the temple area, they could hear the chanting.

"Antipas, Antipas, we want Antipas."

Things in the city were working up to fever pitch. The Christians were highly charged with adrenaline, and more and more of them appeared each day with Antipas, David, Peter, and Emin. The families were gradually moving back into their homes, against the wishes of Antipas and the other leaders.

One of the men said to them, "The guards can do nothing now that the people are behind us. They wouldn't dare rile the people. We're safe."

Antipas didn't share their optimism. He knew the tide would soon turn against them. People were fickle; as long as they were getting a good show, and healing as well, they were for it. But just let one small event displease the crowd, and they would turn against them. Once that happened, it would be a short trip from the temple steps to prison and death.

Antipas continued with his preaching and healing ministry because he knew it was still the will of the Father that he do so. The temple steps leading to the great altar became the scene of many healings. They were taking place right under the nose of the altar to Zeus. This was Satan's territory. It was heady stuff for the new converts. The whole city was awake to the gospel.

A young boy was brought to Antipas who had been injured two years before and had not been able to walk since that time. His parents were anxious, as it would mean he would not be able to work and thus would be a burden on his family for the rest of his life.

The father carried the boy and laid him at Antipas's feet.

Antipas looked at the father with compassion in his eyes. "What would you like me to do for him?" Antipas kept his hands at his side while watching the father.

"Please master, I know you can heal. I saw the baby healed and others, and now I've brought my son to you. Please make him walk again." There were tears running down the father's face as he made his plea to Antipas.

Antipas leaned over and touched the boy's shoulder. "Do you want to walk again?"

"Yes, yes. I can't play with my friends anymore." His hands fluttered in front of him as he met Antipas's gaze.

"Do you believe God can heal you? You know it's not me who heals, but God." Antipas pointed to heaven.

"Yes, master, I believe." The boy nodded his head vigorously.

He reached out his hand and laid it on the boy's head. "Then in the name of Jesus Christ of Nazareth, stand up and walk." His voice thundered across the crowd. The people were silent as they watched the drama unfold before their eyes. Each head was straining to see what was taking place.

A great cheer went up as the little boy slowly stood on his once-useless feet and took two steps away from his father. Both of his parents were unashamedly crying. The boy continued to take steps, laughing as he did so. He turned back to Antipas, walked to him, and threw his arms around him.

"Oh, thank you, thank you. I'm just like other boys now."

His parents approached Antipas and tried to hand him a bag of money.

"No. I won't accept your money. I heal in the name of Jesus. It is God who heals, not me. I cannot accept your money."

"But we feel we need to pay you for what you've done for our family today. Please take the money." The father held out the small bag to him.

"There are many poor people in Pergamum. Give it to them. God cannot be purchased."

The parents finally turned away and moved through the crowd, which parted for them. Many people reached out and touched them, exclaiming over the healing. Temple guards watched it all with impassive faces, swords glinting in the sunshine. The parents were overcome with gratitude for what had taken place in the life of their son. The father went into the marketplace, and it was reported that he found beggars and divided up the money among them. And so the miracle continued and was passed on.

≈ ≈ ≈

Antipas was left standing alone once the crowd had dispersed. The others with him were ministering to smaller groups along the street. He looked around at the people and the ever-present guards then slowly descended the steps from the altar. Two of the guards withdrew from the others and moved in beside him. He calmly surveyed them as they glared down at him.

"Come with us." The guard on his right reined in his horse and beckoned with his head.

Antipas glanced around for the others. He was unable to see them and sighed with relief. Keeping his eyes lowered, he turned and followed.

They led him to a quiet side street to the west of the temple. He could see a man leaning on a stone wall. As he moved forward, the man stood, arms folded, turban pulled low over his forehead. Even at this distance, Antipas recognized Marcus.

The riders quickly rode away, leaving the brothers facing each other. Marcus stood, feet apart, arms folded over his chest.

"So, you didn't leave town as you were told." The words slid like oil from his mouth as his lip curled mockingly. His shoulders shook with laughter.

"I take orders from my heavenly Father and it's His will that I stay." Antipas paused a stone's throw from Marcus and looked deeply into his eyes. "There is still work to be done."

"I would think you would obey your earthly Father, seeing as you're so perfect." The last word was drawn out with a sneer as Marcus took a step toward Antipas.

"According to you and our father, I am no longer his son." Antipas felt sweat forming on his palms. He clenched his fingers together in tight fists to keep from wiping his hands on his robe.

"This discussion is getting us nowhere." Marcus closed the distance between them. "You listen to me, Antipas…"

"We meet again, O noble Antipas," a man said behind him. He turned to see who it was. A low bow accompanied the words.

When the man stood, a ripple of recognition and fear leaped through Antipas.

Marcus glanced from one to the other as he drew his sword. "Who is this, Antipas?"

"This, my brother, is Horatious, a long-time acquaintance." A muscle twitched in his jaw as he stepped back beside Marcus.

"Brother?" Horatious's gaze darted between them.

Antipas nodded. Marcus kept his own counsel.

"No time to talk, Antipas, only time to die—for both of you." Horatious spit at his feet as his scimitar sprang from under his cloak. He lunged at Antipas.

Marcus surged forward, cutting him off with his sword.

"So, you wish to die also." Sword and scimitar clashed, splitting the quiet air. Antipas withdrew the small knife he carried as now brother and brother fought a common enemy. Marcus was more skillful in hand-to-hand combat and lighter on his feet. He danced around Horatious, thrusting his sword successfully.

"Ahhhhh, I'll kill you both." Horatious crouched lower. Marcus knocked the scimitar from his hand. It skidded away from him, scraping the ground. With a howl of rage, Horatious pulled his knife and drove it downward at Antipas. Antipas swung away from him, and the blade pierced his cloak.

The three men were breathing heavily, sweat pouring from Antipas's body. Horatious snarled and attacked again. This time Marcus was ready. His sword pierced him. Horatious clutched his side. A look of horror slackened his face. He staggered, then collapsed on his back. He stared up at the brothers.

Marcus leaned over him, shoulders heaving, breath coming in gasps. "I will not die today, nor will Antipas. You will die, Horatious. I have plans for Antipas and I will not have you disrupting them." He pulled the sword from Horatious's side, wiped it on the grass, and sheathed it. He turned to face Antipas.

From the temple a clamor arose. Temple guards' swords flashed. Marcus looked over his shoulder, then back at Antipas. His eyes narrowed.

"This changes nothing. Watch your back. Your days are numbered." He turned on his heel and moved off down the street to disappear around the first corner.

Antipas watched him go, took one last look at Horatious, then walked off in the other direction. He was left with the realization that his time was short.

Fifty-Four

ate one afternoon as Antipas and his partners were leaving the temple area, a noisy group of young men crowded the walkway in front of them. Antipas stepped aside so as not to bump into them. As he did so, another smaller group approached him on the other side. He again stepped aside and found himself heading down a darkening alley. He tried to regain the main thoroughfare, but found he was blocked on all fronts. Having no alternative, he turned to walk the alley to gain access to the street again at another location.

He had been separated from his friends and wondered if they were trying to locate him. He thought he heard them shouting for him, but there was so much noise and confusion that he couldn't be certain.

The alley stank of rotting garbage. He cautiously felt his way in the fading light of late afternoon. He thought he detected a shape leaning against the wall farther along, but he couldn't be sure. He began to suspect he had been caught in a trap. His heart beat rapidly. As he neared the shape by the wall, the figure stepped out in front of him. Marcus.

Antipas stopped a few feet from him. "Marcus, I didn't expect to see you here."

"No, I'm sure you didn't." The sneer curled around Marcus's face, giving him a sinister look. "How long did you think you could get away with your tricks and propaganda?"

"No tricks, Brother. Faith in Christ is real. More real than anything you have ever encountered in your life, Marcus." Antipas reached out his arm, palm up.

"Be quiet. Do you want me to kill you right here? And don't call me 'Brother.' I have no brother other than Paulus." Marcus smashed his fist into the wall beside him. "You are under arrest for treason, among a whole lot of other things." The thin veneer of civility fell off as Marcus shouted at him, moving in closer.

Antipas folded his hands together. "Do whatever you need to do, Brother. And know that I will ask God to forgive you."

That got him a crack on the side of the head. He reeled from the blow, staggered, but did not fall. He refused to let his brother see how much it hurt. Marcus pushed him.

"No more talking. You've done enough of that to last you a lifetime." The pushing continued down the length of the alley.

At the end of it they emerged into an unlit back street. Two shapes glided from the darkening night. Temple guards. Antipas's throat tightened. They grabbed him from the custody of Marcus and shoved him along until they reached a corner. At the corner they turned right and proceeded along the thoroughfare.

It was deserted now; the throng, having spent its energy, was heading in the opposite direction. As he watched the sun disappear below the horizon, Antipas could see the outline of the prison ahead of them. It loomed through the darkness, a gloomy, foreboding place, a place of cruelty, evil, and despair. Antipas didn't want to enter there but had no choice. He determined that above all else, he would enter without fear, trusting in his Savior whatever the outcome.

He glanced around to see if Marcus was still with them, but he, too, had disappeared. He was likely reporting to their father, who undoubtedly was behind this arrest. They had now reached the entrance to the prison. The guards at the gate held a whispered consultation with his captors before the gates were inched open to allow them to enter. The first thing that registered with Antipas was the smell; the smell of death, the smell of filth, the smell of sickness, the overwhelming smell of defeat and human suffering.

With his head held high, back straight, Antipas entered the prison. His captors had no need to drag him along, but they did anyway. They passed through the inner gate and into the courtyard where a fire was smoldering in the center. Several of the guards were gathered around it, warming their hands against the coolness of the approaching evening. One guard separated himself from the group and approached them.

"Who have we here?" He looked the prisoner up and down, pursing his lips.

One of his captors stepped forward, saluting the guard. "We have Antipas son of Julian, Captain."

"Well, well, well. Interesting." He fingered his beard as he continued to stare at Antipas. "Bring him along and we'll find nice accommodations for him." The captain nodded at them, a smirk overtaking his face.

Antipas was yanked along behind the captain. He recognized the man as a friend of his father's. He didn't seem surprised to see him. No doubt his father had told the captain that he would be receiving Antipas at some point.

They advanced into the building. The narrow hall was damp and dingy, the prison smell intensifying as they entered. The walls echoed low moans, terrifying shrieks, as well as loud voices raised in protest against their imprisonment.

Chains rattled and clanked against cell doors.

The captain led them past these cells with their remnants of humanity trying to gain the attention of anyone who would listen. At the end of this hallway they passed through a barred entrance and began to work their way down a ramp. A rancid odor greeted them as the dampness deepened. Down, down they went. Antipas began to wonder if there was an end to the descent. Weak calls reached out from the depths of cells as they passed in the darkness.

As the light behind them receded, the captain took a torch from an alcove in the wall. Except for the torch's flickering light, all was darkness. The guards no longer spoke, seeming to be suppressed by the atmosphere of the place. Antipas sensed they would be glad to deliver their prisoner and escape back into the city. He heard one of the guards mutter something about evil being in this place. The other guard hushed him.

Antipas tried to remember what he knew about the captain. He remembered one instance in particular when he was a child. His father had taken him to work with him for some reason that day. He was playing in the passages of his father's workplace when he heard raised voices. He wandered down the hallway until he was just outside the office. His father was speaking with a stern-looking man in a uniform. They appeared to be in a heated discussion, but at the end they shook hands, and his father stated he would look into it and get back to him.

The scene had soon left Antipas's mind, but he remembered another day when his father took him to a meeting at the captain's house. Again they talked in low voices while Antipas played close by. Someone had been disloyal to the worship of Zeus. To his father and the captain, this seemed close to treason and reason enough to imprison the man. Again, Antipas did not retain the information, but it came back now as he followed the captain on the same journey plotted for the disloyal man so many years ago.

When they could go no deeper in the earth, the narrow hallway turned. A short distance brought them to a low, small door embedded in the wall. This was yanked open, and Antipas was unceremoniously thrown in. The door clanged behind him and he heard the bolts being lowered in place and footsteps receding, then all was darkness and silence. Panic rose in his chest and his body began to tremble. He got a grip on himself and knew the first thing he needed to do was pray.

"Father God, Lord of heaven, I know You are in this place."

Peace. He felt as though warm oil had been poured out over his entire body. There was a presence in the room with him, the presence of Christ.

"Thank You, Lord. This is what I needed to know, that You are with me here, and anywhere I am taken, through anything devised for me. Your strength, O Lord, that's all I need."

Antipas sank down on the hard-packed earth floor. It was damp and slimy, but nothing seemed to matter just now except the presence of God.

When Antipas finished praying he stood again. The cell ceiling was low, so low he could not stand erect but had to bend his neck to avoid contact with the hard-packed mud and stone overhead. He reached out his hands and slowly made his way around the tiny room. All too soon he was back at the door. The space was small; hardly room enough to lie down. There didn't seem to be anything else in the chamber; no bed, no table, no chair, no blanket, no pillow, no light, nothing. Just Antipas. And God.

He prayed for all those outside who would soon be hearing of his arrest. He prayed that they would remain strong and bold, that they would not lose heart now that they had lost their leader. And finally he prayed for Eunice and Simon. It was such an intimate prayer, it was almost like holding them in his arms.

"Jesus, You will have to be everything for Eunice; her husband, the father of her child, her comforter, her provider. Father, I'm so glad You are all the things that she needs."

He slumped down on the floor once more. He had to have a plan. He couldn't just rot away in here. He had to keep his mind focused. Scripture, that's it, he would recite Scripture. Could anyone hear him? Were any other prisoners nearby? It was possible, so he would recite aloud. He knew it would help him even if no one else could hear.

His mind went first to Psalm 145. He knew David had written it. David had many troubles in his life, so this was a good place to start.

"I will exalt you, my God and King; I will praise your name for ever and ever." His heart constricted as the Word of the Lord washed over him. "O Lord, it is my desire to exalt You. You are my God and You are my King. Imagine the King of heaven is right here in my cell. I'm praising your name, oh yes, I'm praising your name.

"Every day I will praise you and extol your name for ever and ever." This verse, too, warmed his heart and brought words to his lips. "Lord, I don't know how many days I have left, but I will praise You on each one of them."

With each word he uttered, he could feel strength coursing through his body.

"Great is the Lord and most worthy of praise; his greatness no one can fathom."

"Is anyone listening?" Antipas shouted to the blank wall of his cell. "If you are, know this, God is great. You need Him in your life."

Antipas continued reciting the psalm and shouting his responses to each line. He knew that God could hear even if no mortal was close by. After a while his energy was spent and once again he lowered himself to the ground. He leaned his head against the door and closed his eyes. He was drifting off to sleep when he thought he detected a noise. He sat up quickly, listening intently.

There it was again. A faint knocking. He was sure it was. Someone was trying to make contact with him. He shouted a few times, trying to make contact in return, but other than the slight tapping sound, the cell remained quiet. He decided that someone could hear him, but for some reason was not able to reply.

He thanked God for this opportunity and began again with his Scripture recitation. This time he chose Isaiah 53:5–6.

> But he was pierced for our transgressions,
> he was crushed for our iniquities;
> the punishment that brought us peace was upon him
> and by his wounds we are healed.
> We all like sheep, have gone astray,
> each of us has turned to his own way;
> and the Lord has laid on him
> the iniquity of us all.

"That's what Christ has done for you and me. He was crucified, He bore our sin for us, and because of His wounds we can have eternal life. Do you understand the message? God died for you and all you have to do is confess your sins and accept Him as your Savior."

The knocking was louder now. The knocker was agitated or excited, Antipas couldn't tell which. Whichever was true, Antipas rejoiced. It was contact with the outside world, and it was also a chance to speak up for Jesus.

The noise stopped suddenly. Antipas sat and listened for several minutes, but the sound did not resume. What could it mean? His every sense seemed to be heightened in this narrow cell. He had a feeling of floating through time, as though he were somewhere other than the cell.

"Lord, what is it You want me to do?" He raised his eyes to the ceiling.

Again he felt the presence of God with him. Into his mind came the thought that he needed to continue his preaching here in the prison. Who knew who might be able to hear him? Even the guards might be near. They, too, needed the Savior.

"Lord, I want to be Your vessel wherever I am, in whatever circumstances."

He settled down on the floor in the most comfortable position he could manage in such a place. The silence was total. Not even rats or mice could enter this tomb. His last thought as he drifted off to sleep was how privileged he was to be able to suffer for the Savior.

The howling woke him. Wave after wave of unearthly howls. The sound penetrated his mind and he sat up, rubbing his head. What could make such sinister noises?

The howling subsided, and he lay back down. It started again, closer this time. Grotesque creatures circled the ceiling of his cell. They created just enough light that he could see their outlines.

"It can't be real." He rubbed his eyes, trying to clear the images. Then the dream came crashing in on him; scene after scene played out its fury.

The demons raged at him as they circled his head, shrieking out their venom on him. "You're finished, Antipas," they howled at him in their grating voices.

"You're defeated. Your God can't save you now. You're done, you're dead. You've failed."

Then his father's face appeared on one of the demons' heads. "I told you not to disgrace me, but would you listen? No, you had to go your own way. Now it's over. I've won. You'll never torment me again." His mouth opened, revealing an ugly blackness inside.

Marcus appeared, shouting at him in a high-pitched scream. The wailing and howling drenched the room. Antipas knew he couldn't breathe much longer in this atmosphere. Then over in the corner, he could see a tiny pinprick of light, just glowing there, peaceful and undisturbed. He knew it was the presence of God and took comfort from this assurance.

When the howling reached its peak, it stopped as suddenly as it began. Antipas slowly opened his eyes. All was darkness and dampness. Even the light in the corner was gone. His body was trembling and sweat clung to him. Another dream. He'd thought he was finished with them.

As he lay there trembling, he remembered the light. "Yes, the light. I remember the light." He tried to see it again in the corner. Nothing changed. But he could remember the glow.

Somehow he managed to sleep again. When he awoke, he had no idea if morning had arrived or if it was still night. It made no difference in this place.

Eventually he heard footsteps outside his door. The bolts were drawn back and the door flung open. Light from the torch pained his eyes, but before he could cover them, brawny arms grabbed him and pulled him from the cell.

"Get on your feet. You have an appointment."

Antipas asked about the appointment, but a sharp crack from the whip discouraged any more talk. They returned the same way they had come several hours earlier. When they burst into the courtyard, the light from the morning sun blinded him after the intense darkness of the last few hours. The guards continued out of the courtyard and around to the steps leading up to the altar and temple.

How many times he had stood on these steps in different circumstances. They almost framed the parameters of his life. As a small child he was brought here by his parents to offer homage to Zeus, as a child just reaching puberty he was brought here to offer his first manhood rights to Zeus, as an adult he preached Jesus here in Satan's territory, and now he was being yanked up the stairs in an undignified way by cruel, inhumane guards. His destiny was here. He felt it this morning and he was ready.

There were many spectators on the steps. He glanced to one side and thought he saw a familiar face, then more and more. It finally dawned on him that the temple steps were lined with converts. They reached toward him but didn't try to touch him. He recognized the gestures, gestures of love and support.

Near the top a young woman was standing with her small child in her arms. He became aware that this was Eunice. Oh, how he longed to reach out and gather her in his arms, but to do so would be to risk her life. So their eyes met and had to communicate the whole message each of them wanted to send to the other. Simon was smiling and gurgling at his father. Eunice pulled the hood closer around her face as she smiled bravely through her tears.

Antipas saw David standing with a stick for support, Emin with a strong determined look on his face, Peter with Maria and Martin, tears running down their faces, Mattias looking like he would be happy to tackle the guards if Antipas would just say the word. The silent tableau played out before his eyes. By the time they reached the top step, his heart was singing with encouragement and the love he felt for these people was swelling in his heart.

All too soon they reached the great doors of the temple. These were swiftly thrown open and Antipas was ushered in. The dim interior was heavy with the fragrance of incense, a cloying smell submerging all others. The guards marched him through the common area of the temple into a separate chamber at the back. He was pulled down into a kneeling position and left there.

He prayed quietly while awaiting the next event. He knew his fate would be decided here. He looked around him and recognized the room where he had gathered with so many of his friends when they were twelve years old and about to go through the manhood rights. He could almost hear the high, whispery voice of the chief priest.

Steps approached, the steps of many feet. A group of men entered, their robes swishing on the tile floors. They ranged themselves in front of him.

The governor, Justus Anthony, stood in their center, flanked by Antipas's father and several of the priests and city officials. He was unable to see Marcus but felt certain he was there somewhere.

"Let's sit down, gentlemen." Justus Anthony indicated seats with the small scroll he carried.

Each one quickly found a seat and waited for Justus Anthony to speak again.

"Arise, prisoner."

Antipas struggled in his shackles to a standing position.

"You are present to hear the charges against you." Justus Anthony watched him with hooded eyes, betraying nothing in his glance. He paused to look around the room, searching the faces of those present. "Let's first establish who you are. You are Antipas, son of Julian—"

"I have no son named Antipas," Julian spluttered, lurching to his feet, face red and angry.

"You will keep your counsel or be removed from the chamber." Justus Anthony sent a hard glare his way.

Julian sat down. Antipas was afraid his father would have an attack. His skin was turning dark. Rage was threatening to explode from him. The official beside him put his hand on his shoulder and spoke quietly in his ear. He gradually calmed down and continued to listen to Justus Anthony.

"Let me begin again." He frowned at Julian, almost daring him to interfere again. "Without interruption this time, I hope."

He addressed Antipas. "You are Antipas, son of Julian, merchant of Pergamum. Is that correct?" He unrolled and consulted the scroll.

"Yes, that is correct." He stole a glance at his father.

Julian rose from his seat, lifting his arm, his hand in a fist. No sound came from his mouth. The same official grabbed his arm and pulled him down. Antipas could see the man whispering agitatedly to his father.

"You were born in this great city of Pergamum." Justus Anthony walked around Antipas.

"Yes." He kept his head up and answered in a clear voice.

"Besides your father, you have two brothers, Marcus the temple guard, and Paulus."

"That, too, is correct."

"You made your first sacrifice to Zeus when you were twelve right here in this temple."

"Also correct."

"You were then educated here by the temple priests." Justus Anthony seated himself in front of Antipas, intent on the scroll before him.

"Yes." Antipas nodded with each answer.

"After the age of eighteen we neither hear from you nor see you again until you appear in a changed form."

"As you say, my lord." He gave a slight bow of his head.

Justus Anthony lifted his eyes to Antipas, a scowl on his face. "Be careful how you speak to me; your fate is in my hands." Justus Anthony snapped his fingers in Antipas's face.

"With all due respect, sir, my fate lies in the hands of God." Head held high, he kept his eyes on the governor.

The governor's face swelled with rage. "We'll see what your god will do for you." He seemed to grow in stature as he bellowed. "Zeus reigns here. Your god is ineffective." With that he strode around the room for the second time.

"Hear, hear," came from the back benches. "We've heard enough," others echoed.

Justus Anthony stopped in front of them. He slowly eyed each one before he snapped his fingers at them. "Enough. I make the decisions here." He swung around to face Antipas again. "Why did you come back? My understanding was that you had been told by your father never to come near this place again." He crossed his arms as he waited for the answer.

"With respect, Governor, what my heavenly Father tells me takes precedence over what my earthly father says." Antipas looked at him directly.

"Blasphemy, blasphemy." The priests and officials were getting restless. Julian was visibly agitated.

"Just sentence him to death." Julian stood, pointing a long finger at his son. "Death to him who tries to lay claim to my family name. He is nothing, nothing, nothing." Julian was yelling now, his eyes beginning to roll back in his head.

One of the old priests beckoned to a guard. He held a whispered conversation with him, and the guard withdrew, walking back to the other guards on duty where he could be seen giving an order. Two burly fellows in uniform separated themselves from the group and approached the seats. They quickly surrounded Julian; each one grasped his robe on a side and ushered him, protesting, out of the room.

Marcus didn't even glance at them as they removed his father from the room. His eyes were glued on Antipas.

Justus Anthony continued as if Julian didn't exist.

"You haven't answered my question. Why did you come back? You could have settled anywhere in the kingdom, and yet you come back to the place where you have been told never to return on point of death. What would cause you to do such a foolhardy thing?"

"Governor Justus Anthony, nothing would give me greater pleasure than to tell you my story and give you my reasons for returning." Antipas stood tall and confident, his heart rejoicing at the opportunity.

"Carry on." The governor shifted his feet and nodded at him.

So Antipas told his story, starting with his grandfather's talks with him and moving through his subsequent dismissal by his father, his days on the caravan, his powerful meeting with God, and his strong compulsion that God was directing him to Pergamum to preach the gospel.

His speech was punctuated with gasps from the priests and cries of "blasphemy." But Justus Anthony kept his full focus on Antipas and his story. When Antipas finished he bowed his head and waited for judgment. Even the priests stopped their calls.

Finally Justus Anthony paced the length of the room for the third time. It seemed as though the audience collectively held its breath. The governor returned to his seat and sat. Antipas looked up to find Justus staring directly at him.

"An interesting story, Antipas, son of Julian. Too bad you had to run away. I could have used someone of your caliber in my inner circle. Too bad, too bad." He shook his head sadly.

Rustling of robes could be heard where the priests and officials sat. Mutterings were audible and feet shuffled.

Justus Anthony looked again at Antipas, who had not moved.

"Even now it may not be too late for you. You could renounce this new 'religion' and turn back to Zeus and your family. If you were to turn your back on these so-called followers of yours, I would consider leniency and reinstate you as a citizen of Pergamum. What do you say? Will you do it?" Justus Anthony sat forward on his seat, one finger on his chin.

Antipas felt the presence of the Lord grow strong in him. He stood to his full height and faced the governor and the others. In a loud, clear voice he declared, "I will never renounce the God who sent His son Jesus to die for my sins and yours, O noble Justus. His blood has washed me clean and given me a hope for the future and a freedom in my soul that cannot be measured or replaced by anything you can offer."

Again there were gasps and agitated movement from the audience. Justus Anthony folded his arms over his chest, a frown gathering on his forehead.

"The answer to your question, Governor, now and forever, is no." Antipas dropped his hands to his sides and waited.

An uproar broke out. The priests were on their feet shouting for death. Scrawny arms poked out of robes as hands were waved in the air, fists clenched. A few priests surged toward the prisoner.

Justus Anthony turned and faced the crowd. "Stop. I will have silence in my chamber or I'll have you removed."

An uneasy quiet ensued. Necks were stretched to catch every word and action that would take place.

"Your answer brings me sorrow, Antipas." Justus Anthony extended his hands toward him. "You and I could have done great things together. However, you leave me no alternative but to sentence you to death." The word hung in the air like a millstone around his neck.

Antipas remained standing tall, strengthened by the Spirit of Almighty God. Then the priests and officials began cheering. Justus Anthony slumped in his chair.

∽ ∽ ∽

It was later said by some that a glow could be seen around Antipas as he accepted his sentence. "It was almost like he was some heavenly being," reported one of the officials. "Quite frightening, really."

The governor called for the guards to lead Antipas away. Once he was gone, Justus Anthony rose, walked out of the room with shoulders slumped, head low, sorrow playing over the lines of his face.

Fifty-Five

A ntipas was returned to the same cell, and the guard opened the door and shoved him in. Once the door clanged shut, he knelt on the floor while images of his father's face flashed before him. All he could feel for Julian was pity.

"How could someone be so blind to the truth," he mused. "It's the power of evil. You don't have to be in Pergamum long to feel its existence here. Zeus is no one; the demons behind him are the real power."

He began praying aloud for his family; his father, mother, brothers; for the Christian converts; for his beautiful wife and son. He prayed for Pergamum, for God to break the power of evil present in the city.

While he was praying, the knocking started again. This time it was coming from more than one direction. That proved it. He could be heard. He had his mission for as long as he had life. He would preach to the prisoners. God had called him to preach—he just hadn't known he would be preaching in prison.

He raised his voice, staring at the dark wall. "If you can hear me, just knock once."

He listened intently. A single knock was heard, then another from another direction, until he had heard a number of them.

And so he started. "In the beginning God created the heavens and the earth." He continued with the covenant God, God the provider, God the protector, God the Savior.

His voice finally gave out, and he assured his listeners that he would begin again after he had rested awhile.

Antipas drifted into an uneasy sleep in his damp prison, curled up in a cramped position on the cold dirt floor. His dreams were disturbing but not frightening as so many had been in the past. The face of Justus Anthony was continually before him, the face of regret. In one dream Justus Anthony was crying and begging Antipas to turn from his wicked ways.

He slowly regained consciousness to experience an oppression surrounding him. Evil was certainly present in his cell. Although it was dark and he could not see, he was quite aware of demonic power. He could hear what he thought was the swish of wings and deep voices raised in anger.

In the midst of this, he could see the tiny pinpoint of light high up on his wall again. He watched as it slowly descended from the ceiling, down the back wall and along the floor. As the light moved around, the oppression lifted with a great whirr of activity. The pinprick of light rose again toward the roof of the cell and gradually faded into the ceiling.

Once it was gone, Antipas lay there considering what he had seen.

"Father, I have seen Your presence with me in that tiny light. Just a small point of Your light can dispel the forces of evil. Thank You, God, for who You are and for Your incredible power. Thank You for that reassurance that You are with me. Paul told me that You have promised to never leave Your children or forsake them. Lord, I believe."

He sank down to try to sleep again but within moments he heard steps approaching. The *clomp, clomp* of heavy feet and the clanging of prison doors preceded the opening of his cell door. He wondered if they had come to lead him to his death.

The door opened on rusty hinges. A massive guard threw it back against the wall. Antipas had not seen this guard before. In the light of his torch, he could see that he was tall with broad shoulders. Muscles on his chest and arms gleamed in the torchlight. But it was his face that was arresting. Antipas had never seen a face with so much hatred glaring from cold eyes.

"Get up, you scum. Brutus is going to give you something you won't forget for a while." He slapped the crop of his whip against his hand as he stood, feet apart, head thrown back.

He reached into the cell and grabbed Antipas by the hair and heaved him out. He didn't wait for Antipas to get his footing but started dragging him behind him. They went down the passage beyond the cell in a direction new to Antipas. He watched the doors of other cells go by as he was yanked past them. Although in pain and distress, Antipas wondered if these cells housed the men who had been listening to him preach. He prayed aloud for each person as the cells went by in a blur. His eyes were watering from his hair being pulled so hard. He finally was not able to distinguish whether they were still passing cells. Where were they going, he wondered?

At last they emerged from the passageway into a dimly lit room. Antipas was dropped on the floor as Brutus began arranging things. Antipas was finally able to wipe his eyes. What he saw made him want to close then and never open them again.

Ropes hung from the damp walls, and cruel racks were lined up along one side. Long instruments with spiked ends hung in rows. Short leather whips with sharp, jagged nails were grouped together on one of the tables. Dark stains marred the floor. Torture and death breathed from the walls.

Was he to be slain here, or was he destined for torture first? Somehow he felt that Brutus would want torture first. He had a sadistic look that communicated that death would not be enough to slake his thirst for violence.

When he was ready, he grabbed Antipas and moved toward the far wall. There were shackles hanging at different levels along the wall, and Brutus fixed Antipas's hands and then his feet in these. His feet just touched the floor and his arms were stretched beyond their natural limit. Pain rushed through his body. Somehow he felt this pain was nothing compared to what was coming.

Brutus left him for a few minutes, choosing his whip carefully from a number of them hanging to the right of Antipas. He could see him out of the corner of his eye and shuddered at the sight of the whips. Brutus found one that looked particularly sinister, long narrow strands embedded with sharp pieces of iron jutting from each length, and turned to approach Antipas from behind.

"Now, let's see how far your faith in this Jew-God will go," snarled Brutus.

The lash sliced into his back, tearing flesh with a sickening sound. Tears erupted from his eyes and a moan escaped from his lips. Pain snaked through his body.

"Ha, you can't take much, can you?" mocked Brutus. "Let's give that one a minute to sink in before we share another one, you and I."

Antipas sent a prayer heavenward. "Lord, You can give me the strength to bear all things. Help me to be a strong witness for You. Help me not to deny You or Your name," he whispered.

The second lash was harder and went deeper than the first. He could feel the slice of the whip. But this time Antipas was ready. Pain seared his body. "The Lord is my Shepherd, I shall not be in want."

The sound of Antipas's voice incensed Brutus. He slashed with the whip, harder and faster. Blood streamed down Antipas's back. He continued to recite the psalm, now shouting the words. The more he shouted, the more violent Brutus got.

❧ ❧ ❧

A gruesome scene met the two guards who were sent to retrieve the battered and bloody form of Antipas. As they entered the room, the smell of spilled blood was overpowering. The floor was slick with it. One gagged and turned away. The other's face contorted in horror. They had seen the results of beatings before, but this one went beyond all that was human. They were tough prison guards, but this was sickening.

They had heard Antipas preaching on the temple steps and in his cell. They knew he was an innocent, harmless man who didn't deserve this treatment. They approached the wall, expecting to see a corpse but were surprised that although still unconscious, he was alive. They released his shackles, lifted him from the wall, and carried him back to his cell.

They wondered how much they could do for him without getting themselves in trouble. A glance between them assured each other that they planned to do whatever was in their power. The fact that he was still alive was a miracle.

One guard went for water and soft cloths while the other one gently laid him on the packed earth. They carefully washed his back, soaking the cloths with blood several times before the flow was stemmed. Ointment was applied liberally and then his wounds were covered with clean linen. Having done all they could, they left him alone and locked the cell door.

Fifty-Six

Eunice was sitting by the fire talking to Lois and holding a sleeping Simon when Mattias entered the room. "How are you this morning? Are you standing up all right under the strain?" He spoke quietly to Eunice so as not to disturb Simon.

"I can't believe how much peace God has given me. I know that I may never see Antipas alive again, but God has promised to be everything I need. I'm clinging to that." Eunice smiled at him, cuddling Simon closer to her.

"We just heard a report from Antipas's appearance before Justus Anthony early this morning. His father was present and had to be taken from the room by the guards because he was in such a rage." Mattias shook his head and sighed. "Marcus was there as well. There was apparently no sign of Paulus. It appears that Justus Anthony was willing to let Antipas go if he would renounce Christ." He threw his hands in the air as he looked at the women with eyebrows touching and brow furrowed in a frown.

"Of course, he wouldn't, he couldn't do that." Eunice's mouth flew open and her eyes widened. "What happened then?" She sat up straighter in her chair.

"You're right, he refused. He was even able to witness to Justus Anthony. It sounds as though Justus Anthony was moved by his story, but there is much pressure on him to solve the Christian 'problem' in this city."

"I'm so proud of Antipas." Eunice wiped away her tears with one hand.

Mattias drew a chair close to Eunice and sat facing her. "Eunice, I have bad news. Please know that I wish I didn't have to tell you, but you must know, you must be prepared."

"What is it, Mattias? Tell me quickly." She shifted in her seat to see him better.

"Justus Anthony sentenced him." Mattias rubbed his hands over his thighs.

"What was the sentence?" Her voice was a whisper as she leaned forward in her seat.

"Death." The word dropped from his lips like liquid metal.

Lois gave a gasp, struggled from her seat and shuffled over to Eunice. She gathered her in a warm hug.

"I don't know why this has to be." Lois wept while she held Eunice. "Only God can make sense of such a disaster."

Eunice clung to Lois, tears flowing. "I still trust God," Eunice cried, "even when I don't understand. Antipas and I talked several times about this happening. I knew before we were even married."

Lois handed her a cloth to wipe her face. Larium arrived home and had to be told the news. She wept with them and comforted Eunice as best she could.

"I'm going to visit the others and bring several back here for a prayer meeting." Mattias stood, pressing his lips together. "God isn't finished with us yet. We'll see if we can pray Antipas out of this seemingly impossible mess."

With that he grabbed his cloak and left the house. Larium busied herself preparing food for the family and for the visitors. "We do have to eat to keep up our strength and spirits. He is still alive and as long as he is, there is still the hope that he'll be let go." Larium seemed to bang the pots harder than was necessary. Eunice snuggled the still sleeping Simon closer to her and kissed his dark curls.

~ ~ ~

When Mattias returned with a group of the converts, he met a hopeful group of women, ready and willing to let God be in charge. The group talked as they partook of the evening meal in preparation for an extended time of prayer.

Once the meal was cleared away, Mattias instructed the group to find places to kneel, and hearts were united in prayer before their heavenly Father. The presence of God was felt in that gathering. He drew near to them with His strength and comfort. Whatever the outcome, they pledged to keep on preaching His word and remaining faithful to Him who had done so much for them.

David wept as he prayed and remembered his time in prison. He knew firsthand what Antipas was facing. He also remembered how close he felt to God while he was there, even through the pain of the beating.

~ ~ ~

Antipas awoke in his cell. It was still dark and uncomfortable, but now pain was added to the misery of prison. He groaned softly as he tried to move his body. His back felt like a flaming mass of flesh. He was unable to control the moaning or the shaking in his body.

"They can break my body, but they can't break my spirit. Lord, I need your help. I want to be a strong witness for you." He tried to stay as still as possible, as each small movement brought excruciating pain. He became aware that there were bandages covering his back.

"Someone has sympathy even in this place," he marveled.

He began to pray for the giver of kindness to him. He decided it must have been one of the guards. He could remember nothing since he collapsed during the beating. It certainly wouldn't have been Brutus. He was surprised to still be alive. Brutus was well named.

The minutes stretched into hours as he drifted in and out of consciousness. At one point he was aware that someone was checking his back and new ointment and cloths were being put on, but he wasn't able to speak nor was he able to distinguish who this giver of kindness was.

When he regained consciousness the next time, he was aware of the presence of another person with him. The light of a torch illuminated the face bending over him.

"You must try to drink some water," the kind voice said.

A cup was placed at his lips and he drank gratefully.

"Who are you?" Antipas tried to see him in the darkness.

"I'm one of the junior guards."

"You know you're risking your life helping me," Antipas whispered.

"I know. Brutus nearly killed you. I've heard you preach on the temple steps and in here. I...I don't know what to believe, but I know you are an innocent man."

Antipas digested this information. "What did you think of my message?"

"I would like to hear more." The guard's voice broke, and he wiped his face with the damp cloth.

"You will. As soon as I can speak I plan to continue preaching to anyone and everyone within the sound of my voice." Antipas raised his hand slightly.

"Rest now or you'll not get your strength back. There is one other guard who will be stopping in to help you. We're both on your side."

"Thank you. Yes, I'll rest for now. I'll need my voice in the days to come." With a sigh he eased his battered body down again as the guard left the cell and closed the door.

∽ ∽ ∽

Eunice continued to pray after the others had left. She settled Simon in his cradle and crawled into her own bed. Weariness gripped her body, but her mind refused to give in to sleep.

"Father, what can I do to help Antipas? You know how much I love him, and I know he is Yours. But there must be something I can do to ease his pain." She lay still for several minutes, letting God minister to her. She felt His peace wrapping around her, and she felt the assurance that God had Antipas in His hands. As she continued to listen, a radical thought entered her mind.

"Is this from You, Lord? Am I thinking crazy thoughts or are You in this one?" She sat up in her bed and wrapped a shawl around her shoulders.

She finally became convinced that the thought had come from God, and that being the case, it would have success. She leaned over to make sure that Simon was sleeping soundly, then rose and slipped out of her room. In the dark she felt her way to Mattias and Larium's bedroom. As she approached their room, she could hear them still discussing the events of the day. She knew they would welcome her interruption.

She knocked on their door and awaited their offer to enter.

Mattias and Larium had not yet retired for the night and were sitting by their open window enjoying the night breeze. "What is it, Eunice?" Mattias asked. "You look excited."

"Oh, I am. I've been talking to God, and He has given me the most wonderful idea." She smiled as she delivered her statement.

"Well, God certainly does give us exciting ideas. What's this one of yours?" Mattias asked as he indicated a bench for her to sit on. She sank onto the bench, wrapping her arms around herself.

"I want to visit Antipas in prison. I want to go in his cell and minister to his needs."

Fifty-Seven

The jailer moved through the passage carrying a feeble torch.

"I can't believe I'm doing this."

"I can," the shrouded figure following him replied.

"You can! How would you know what I would or wouldn't do?"

"I don't. But I know someone who does."

"You do? And who would that be?" he snarled.

"God."

"God! What kind of drivel is that?"

"I prayed that you would let me."

"And this God of yours would listen to the likes of you?"

"Not just me. Many people were praying."

"Don't talk to me about it, or I may change my mind."

Eunice continued following in silence. It would be devastating to have to turn back now. Mattias had been hard to convince, but God had opened impossible doors. Much fervent prayer was sent heavenward by so many. Then someone knew someone who knew someone, and so it went, and God began to open doors.

Eunice took in the surroundings, the dark and damp passage, the unbelievable smells, the stifling air; how could anyone survive in this atmosphere? And the passageways went on and on. Would they ever get to his cell?

She pulled the hood closer and clutched the warm robe. The floor was hard-packed dirt, slick with moisture that was seeping in from some unseen source. Every so often there was a divide in the passageway with smaller paths heading off in other directions. It was like a warren down here. If the guard were to leave, the way back would be untraceable.

Moans came from unknown prisoners, and cries of agony and despair reached her ears. Horrible pictures played across her mind and she followed the jailer.

"Lord, I need your strength to minister to Antipas without letting him see the despair in my face or hear it in my voice."

The guard stopped abruptly before a small door. This was quickly opened and Eunice was ushered in. The door slammed behind her. She had no idea if she was in the right cell, for the darkness was penetrating. While she considered what to do, the door opened again and the guard thrust in a lantern and told her he would be back with more oil later.

"I don't know why I'm doing this."

"I do."

"Don't start that again. Just be glad you have light." And with that the door slammed again.

Eunice lifted the light and saw what she supposed must be her husband lying on the dirt floor. The smell was smothering. She knelt beside him and spoke his name. There was a slight movement in the form huddled in front of her.

"Antipas," she whispered.

The form moved slightly again. She was unable to believe the condition of her husband. The beating had been far worse than she had imagined. His face was blackened and puffy. She could see bruises on his arms and legs. His back was swathed in bandages.

His eyes opened and he squinted against the light. "Lord, you have sent me a vision, a beautiful vision. Thank You, it is encouraging me."

"Antipas, I'm not a vision. I'm really here."

"Eunice? Is it really you? Now I know that I'm dreaming, but I hope the dream never ends."

Eunice leaned over him and stroked his face.

"My darling, you're not dreaming. I'm really here."

He finally began to comprehend that she was there in the flesh.

"How did you get in? I can't believe this."

"It's a long story, but one of victory, of answers to prayer, of God doing the impossible. I'm here and I can stay to look after you. I don't know for how long, but we'll make good use of every moment we have together."

He sighed and reached his hand out to touch her, moaning with the effort.

"You are real. Impossible, but real."

"I've been allowed to bring in a few things. The first thing I want to do is check your injuries and put salve and new bandages on them. I'm going to help you turn now so I can work."

She helped him turn as carefully as she could, but even with her gentle hands, she could tell the pain was agonizing. When he was in a good position, she placed the lantern where it would give her the most light and began to carefully remove the bandages.

When she lifted them, waves of nausea and horror swept over her. She'd had no idea it would be this bad. The flesh on his back was shredded and showed signs of festering. How had he survived? Only by the grace of God. How could one human do this to another? This was cruel, sadistic, the work of a madman.

She was so quiet that Antipas realized what was happening.

"Eunice, it's all right. God gave me the strength to bear it and the opportunity to spread his message even in this den of Satan. You won't believe the way God has worked," he told her in an excited voice.

She was astonished by his positive attitude. God had really met him in this place.

"If I hadn't been put in prison, I wouldn't have had access to these prisoners. If I hadn't been beaten, I wouldn't have been able to witness to the two guards. Even Brutus heard more than he wanted to. Who knows how these seeds will grow? I've done my part; now God will work His way, even in here."

He was exhausted after this speech. He stayed still while Eunice finished peeling off the bandages. The salve felt wonderful as it penetrated the wounds. He silently thanked God for this miracle of Eunice.

She helped him rise to a sitting position and placed a small pillow at his back.

"A pillow. What a luxury. How did you manage to get that in here?"

"Remember I told you that the guard let me bring in a few things. You wouldn't believe how much I can pack in a small bag."

"Eunice, you are a miracle yourself. You have enriched my life in so many ways, and now this. Not many wives would willingly come into such a place as this."

She sank down beside him and circled him with her arms. "Where you are is my home, my husband. I would not wish to be anywhere else."

They spent several minutes rejoicing in their reunion. They both had thought they might never see each other again. God had been so good to them to allow this meeting. Antipas had many questions about Simon and about the Christians. Eunice answered all his questions, brought him greetings from others, and told him any news that had happened since he was arrested.

Eunice had also brought a blanket for him as well as fresh bread and other good things to eat. She fed him herself, enjoying his pleasure as he savored each bite. When he had finished, she pulled a copy of the Scriptures from her bag. His eyes were bright with tears as he held God's word once again. She then handed him a letter that had come from Paul to the church at Pergamum. She had copied it by hand so he would be able to keep the copy and read it over and over.

They talked quietly to each other until Eunice decided it was time to give him some medication she had been able to get from a doctor. It was to ease the pain and help him sleep. She mixed the powders in water and held the cup while he drank. When he was finished, she helped him down onto the blanket, slid down beside him, and covered him with her robe.

"Go to sleep now, my husband, I'll be right here to watch over you."

"You're going to stay with me still?" he asked in a listless voice.

"As long as they let me stay."

"Then this is no longer a prison, but a heavenly garden where I can walk and talk with my love."

He drifted off with his head on her shoulder. She stayed awake a long time, praying for him, for Simon, for the Christians who were suffering a deepening persecution, and for the spread of the gospel right here in the den of Satan.

Fifty-Eight

Eunice was able to stay two days with Antipas. The two guards who had retuned him to his cell stopped by a number of times and brought salve as well as a few other small things for their comfort. Each day brought some healing to Antipas, but it would be several weeks before the effects of the beating would be gone from his body.

Eunice cleaned the wounds each day, smoothing on the precious ointment and covering his back with clean bandages. But it was her presence that brought the most healing. It was giving him the will to live and the courage to continue in the prison.

On the second day she was startled when she heard knocking coming from several different directions.

"Antipas, what's that noise?" She jumped and turned to look at him.

"This is my audience, Eunice. This is the group of men I preach to whenever I can."

He raised his voice and began to teach them about Jesus' ministry here on earth. Exhausted and filled with pain as Antipas was, God gave him the strength to talk for several minutes. Eunice sat in wonder and amazement as this man of God put aside his pain and his imprisonment to preach to the unlovely, the rejected of society. Truly, God was in this place.

At last his voice could not project another word, and he sank down to the floor, exhausted but happy. Eunice was just opening her mouth to ask him a question when the door to the cell was flung open and a huge guard filled the opening, feet spread apart, fists on hips. From Antipas's description of his tormentor, she recognized him as Brutus.

"Woman, get out of here," he roared. He was breathing heavily with rage. He bellowed for two guards to escort her from the prison. God was again at work, and the two that came running were the same two who had been visiting them. They each took an arm and led her away.

Brutus grabbed the lantern and slammed the door shut. Antipas was once again plunged into darkness. The night of the soul had begun.

Antipas wept softly for several minutes. Despair threatened to overtake his soul. He tried to pray, but a weight had settled on his body, heavy and oppressive. He covered his face with his hands and bent to the floor.

The noise started quietly then built to loud swishes and hollow laughter. He felt wind on his head as something swooped around his cell; faster and faster the sounds circled.

The shriek of demon voices built to a crescendo over his head, pressing him into the dirt floor of his cell. Louder, harsher the sounds built, until the whole cell was screaming with demonic voices. They screamed his name, over and over. He was terrified and lay cowering on the floor, face pressed into the dirt. His tears dampened the floor beneath him. He could barely breathe.

He tried to pray again, but he felt his prayers being forced back down. The tumult increased in intensity. He knew he could not bear much more. He felt his consciousness slipping, terrible thoughts swirling round and round in his mind. He was going mad. He was dying. The shrieks were now his as he writhed in agony on the floor. He screamed until he had no breath left.

A jab of pain jolted his back. Something had touched him. He lifted his shoulders and faces appeared in the darkness; grotesque, ugly, twisted, leering faces. They glowered, red and angry. Each seemed to be targeting his head. He closed his eyes and put his hands over his ears, breathing with gasps, trying to force air into his lungs.

There was a short break and in the lull of sounds, a terrible voice emanated from somewhere in the prison.

"Enough! Depart! Enter the abyss!" the voice boomed with authority.

A few last whimpers, a final swish of wings, then silence and darkness.

☙ ☙ ☙

His first thought on waking was the gift of the presence of Eunice for two days in his cell. He had no idea how this had been allowed, only that it was a gift from Almighty God who knew no boundaries. No prison wall was thick enough to exclude His presence or His power. Antipas knew for certain that if the Lord decided he should be released from prison, he would be.

But somewhere in the depths of his heart he knew that God had a higher plan for him, a plan that included prison, and perhaps martyrdom. Whatever the plan, Antipas wanted to be in the will of God.

"Father, I desire Your will. I'm simply a humble sinner, saved by Your mighty power. Do what You will in my life. I give everything to You, who have given everything for mankind."

He waited in silence for several moments. The darkness was so thick he could feel it engulf him. As he waited, strangling with the oppression, he knew there was a battle going on around him, the battle of the ages; angels and demons in conflict for his soul. He remembered the turmoil in his cell a few hours ago. As the images reappeared in his mind, he began to tremble.

"Lord, I release them to You. I cannot bear these images, too awful for human comprehension." His hands were over his face as he knelt in the dirt.

At last the oppression began to lift. Up in the corner of his cell he saw the light. At first it was just a pinprick, visible because of the intense darkness. The pinprick grew until it took shape, an incredible shape, like nothing he had ever seen on earth. He knew in his heart it was a heavenly being.

The being drifted down from the ceiling to perch softly in the far corner. Wispy wings fluttered gently and settled on its shoulders. The eyes turned on Antipas and a hand lifted in greeting.

"Antipas, you have been chosen by God." The voice was no more than a whisper.

But it was like no voice Antipas had ever heard. He could not only hear the voice, but he could feel it, almost touch it, experience it in ways beyond human understanding. Antipas was speechless as he stared at the being. He could sense the voice wrapping itself around him. He cherished the sensation.

"I have been sent to you to encourage and strengthen you at the Lord's command." The gossamer wings fluttered and settled again.

Still Antipas could not speak. He decided God had sent this messenger in a dream, and he never wanted to wake up. The voice alone was healing, like balm on an open wound.

"You have been permitted to see me for a time. When that time is completed, I will still be here, even though I will not be visible to you." The being reached out toward him with a small hand.

Antipas gathered himself together and attempted to speak. Nothing happened. He tried again. "W-who are you?" His voice was a tiny croak.

"You may call me Ises. My real name would be unrecognizable on Earth."

"Are you an angel?"

"Let's just say I'm a heavenly being. I have a host with me, but you are not permitted to see them."

"Why am I permitted to see you?"

"Because you are facing a battle that will take all of us to win."

"A battle?"

"This is warfare. You have been chosen to play a part in the struggle, but you will not be alone."

Antipas peered into the darkness of the other corners of his cell, trying to see the host that Ises said was there. He could see nothing but darkness. But the darkness seemed friendlier than it had earlier.

After a lengthy pause Antipas ventured to speak again.

"What is this battle? Is it between demons and angels?"

"You might say that, but it is more than that."

Antipas thought about that for a few minutes.

"More than that? What could be more than that?"

"Antipas, you are living where Satan has his throne. And yes, it will be basically a battle between angels and demons, but the demons inhabit the gods of Pergamum. We will be fighting against Zeus and all the demons associated with him. It all comes back to Zeus." Ises paused to adjust the filmy wings again. Each time the wings fluttered, a tiny shower of light sifted from them like a sprinkle of stardust. "You once were initiated into the worship and service of Zeus. That is why you have been chosen. Satan desires to recover you into that service, but God is greater than Zeus." The small hands were now folded in front of Ises.

Antipas processed this new information. Zeus was real and wanted him back? What irony. He had never believed in Zeus to begin with. Why would Zeus want him now?

The being could apparently read his thoughts because it now responded, "Why indeed." The hands rippled before its face. "You will be visited by emissaries of Satan, both from the physical world and the supernatural. They will all try to bring you back. You must be strong. They will promise you everything, but remember their promises are hollow."

"I would never return to Zeus worship."

"Be careful what you say. The incentives will be powerful, and you will survive only by the grace of God."

"You frighten me."

"It is good to have a little fear when up against the evil one. He has power on earth, power over mortals, and he wants more. You would be a gem on his sword hilt if he could recover you. You are light. He is darkness. If he could extinguish your light, he would win a big victory."

"But I believe Jesus is greater than Zeus, and His power far exceeds the power of Satan." Antipas wrinkled his face, shaking his head.

"True, true. But remember you are mortal and subject to all the failings of fallen man. It will be only through the power of Christ that you will overcome."

"How can I be ready to face this onslaught you say is coming?"

"You will remember that I and my host will be right here in the cell with you. You have only to call on the name of the Lord, and we will fight on your behalf. But we cannot fight without your call. It all depends on that. We have been restrained except by your call."

This was far more than Antipas could take in. He closed his eyes in thought. When he opened them, Ises was gone. Had he imagined this conversation? Wait. Up close to the ceiling he could see a residue of light, so filmy it could barely be seen, but it was there. It was real.

"O Lord, all-powerful one, I'm scared. I don't know what will happen next, but I truly want to be victorious. Your grace, Lord, give me Your grace."

He could hear footsteps in the corridor outside his cell. The door swung back on its creaky hinges, and in walked his father.

His chest began to constrict. His breathing became labored. Why was Julian here?

"Antipas, it's been a long time since I saw you. I heard you were in prison and wanted to visit you." Julian's face was wreathed in a smile.

Antipas was suspicious. This must be one of Satan's emissaries Ises told him about. His father never smiled at him nor spoke to him in such pleasant tones. He would be on his guard. It was either his father coming with an ulterior motive, or a creature from the otherworld appearing in his form. Either way, it was danger.

"I have been thinking," Julian said as he moved closer to Antipas, "that I was too harsh with you when I sent you away. I should have taken into account that you were still young and impressionable. Please allow me to make amends for that." He reached out his hand to Antipas.

Antipas was unable to speak. He stared at his father and at the hand proffered.

"I apologize for our last meeting when I had you bound and taken from the city. I've spoken to Marcus; there'll be no more persecution from him.

Julian leaned over, now almost in Antipas's face. "I have talked this over with your mother, and she is most anxious to have you home again. I've made arrangements with Justus Anthony to have you released from prison so I can take you home." The smile stayed in place.

Home. Was there ever a word to compare with that? Home. *Oh, Mother, how I would love to come home.*

"We are most anxious, your mother and I, to meet your wife and our grandson."

His hand tingled as he eased it from his side, ready to reach for his father's. "The only thing you would need to do is tell Justus Anthony that this whole religious sect business was a mistake, and all would be forgiven." Julian folded his arms over his chest.

Antipas dropped his hand. The eyes, it was something in the eyes, something was not right. A coldness seemed to glint from them. Just in time he remembered Ises and the warning. Satan was clever, but not clever enough this time.

"Ises, the battle begins, fight!" He sat up, raising his eyes to the ceiling.

His father grabbed his chest as if he had just been punched and turned hate-filled eyes on Antipas.

"I told Justus Anthony this wouldn't work," he gasped. "You're no son of mine. I denounce you and hope you get what you deserve." He bent double, clutching his chest. "No punishment is too great for a traitor like you." He stumbled out of the cell amid shouts of victory from the unseen host surrounding Antipas.

As the door slammed shut, Antipas wept. He hadn't realized how much he desired to be restored to his family. This was going to be a nasty fight. He would have to be alert to all kinds of threats and promises. He didn't imagine Satan had thrown his worst at him first. There would be much more difficult things to come.

He still couldn't see Ises or the host but now knew they were still there. He had heard them. He lifted his eyes to the tiny glow in the corner and simply said, "Thank you."

He bowed in prayer and meditation. He wondered what form the next visitation would take. He didn't know what to expect, only that whatever it was, it would be unexpected. Satan was clever. He would need the host again and again, he suspected.

In the midst of his meditation he heard knocking again. He wasn't sure he had the strength to shout his message, but he had promised God he would preach the gospel for as long as he had life and breath. He gathered his strength and began a new lesson. As he talked, he gained strength. He pleaded with the hearers to turn their hearts over to the one true God.

When he finished, he slumped exhausted to the floor. Sometime later his daily portion of food was pushed through the door, and he pulled it close to himself. Lukewarm, watery, tasteless soup, but necessary for his body. The cup of water had taste, but not pleasant. He finished the meal and tried to rest.

He was startled by the face of his mother, hovering just above his head.

"My son, why won't you come home to me? I need you. I know your father invited you. Oh, won't you please come with me?" She began to weep loudly, protesting his refusal to come home. "You don't love me anymore. Your poor mother means nothing to you."

Something clicked in his mind and he realized it couldn't be his mother. Even in his wildest dreams people still acted in character. His mother would never say the things this specter was saying.

"Stop." He lifted his hand to cover the face. "I know you're not my mother. Leave me."

Hideous laughter poured from the open mouth. It grimaced and let out a howl that reverberated around the cell. He was terrified, frozen in place. He roused himself enough to call out to Ises. It was enough. The face disintegrated before his eyes and the air fell silent once more.

Sweat poured from his body. How much more of this assault could he take? His mind would bend under this type of pressure. Once again he looked to the ceiling. The small glimmer was still there.

"Am I to be allowed to see you again, Ises?"

There was no answer, but the glow seemed to intensify for a moment. That would have to suffice for now. With that little assurance, he was once again able to fall asleep, leaving all of his troubles with the Lord.

He would need the sleep to face what was coming next. Ises and his host hovered over the sleeping form huddled on the floor of the damp and dismal cell. Because of their presence, it was holy ground.

Antipas awakened to the sound of his cell door opening. The light from a lantern moved into the room, swaying in the hands of the holder. The light blinded him for a moment and he shaded his eyes trying to see his visitor. He could finally make out the shape and was astounded and thrilled to see it was Eunice.

She smiled sweetly as she set the lamp down in a safe corner. She knelt beside him and took him in her arms. They wept together, husband and wife. They wept for all the things they were missing and the things they knew they would miss in the days to come. At last she straightened up from him, caressing his face and smoothing his hair back from his forehead.

"Oh, my love," she sighed. "This can't go on much longer. I can't bear to face life without you."

"You must be strong, Eunice." He touched her face with his fingertips. "You have our son to raise, to teach him about Jesus, the only one who makes any difference. He must grow up to love and serve Him. He must one day take my place in leading the people to Christ."

Eunice sank down beside him again. "Oh, Antipas, Simon cries for you every night. I can't bear it. There must be some way to get you out of here." Her tears were flowing down her face and over his.

"I don't want to give you false hope, my love, but I may never get out of here except by death. I, too, would love to come home and lead a normal life again, to be your husband and watch my son grow. We would have more children to love and care for, but it's not to be."

"But why not? There must be a way. You don't know what's going on outside this prison, how many have proven that Zeus is the only god and that Jesus was just a good man. I know you love Him, but He deceived you. The other church leaders have seen the error of their ways and are now turning back to Zeus." As she talked she continued to caress his face and head, soothing him with her hands.

He was overcome with terror at her words. How could this be? He knew Jesus was the only way, the one true God. How could the others so quickly turn from him? How could Eunice turn from Him? She loved Him as much as he did.

As he pondered this, his eyes traveled to the upper corner of his cell. His eyes fell on the little glimmer which was now shining brighter. He could see the outline of a filmy wing palpitating back and forth. Light dawned on his soul. He knew with absolute clarity that this wasn't his Eunice. He would have to confront her. He sat up suddenly and moved away from her slightly. She looked startled.

"Depart from me. You are not Eunice. You are an emissary of Satan. You come in sheep's clothing." His body trembled as he looked her in the eye.

She gasped sharply, eyes widening, mouth open. "How can you say such a thing to me, your wife? I love you and only want what's best for you." Soft tears seeped from her eyes, and his heart constricted.

Again Antipas looked to the upper corner. The light was quite bright now. It gave him courage to continue.

"Leave me, you are no more my wife than this lamp. I recognize you for who you are. In the name of Jesus Christ of Nazareth, depart!"

When the name of Jesus reverberated through the cell, the apparition began to wail. The lovely face of Eunice began to disintegrate, being replaced by a face so twisted and evil Antipas leaned back in horror. The whole body began to shake and with one last shriek, dissolved before his eyes and turned into a heavy mist that extinguished the lantern.

Antipas shook violently, vomiting repeatedly.

Fifty-Nine

Eunice awoke from a troubled dream. She snuggled Simon to her, watching the predawn light begin to stain the sky outside her window. She couldn't remember the details of the dream, only that Antipas was in it and there was something that had frightened her.

She arose when she heard movement in the household. Simon opened his eyes and smiled at his mother. She picked him up, hugging him tightly.

"I don't know what the future holds for you and me, but I'll raise you the way your father would want me to raise you. We'll just have to trust Jesus to be husband and father to us if your father can't make it back to us."

She sighed deeply as she prepared for the day. Simon would never know his father unless a miracle took place. She certainly believed in miracles, but she knew Antipas felt the end was near for him. She must be brave. In fact, now that she thought about it, that was what he was saying to her in her dream. Funny things, dreams. They seemed so real at the time, but so unnatural when dawn broke.

Mattias and Larium were already breaking their fast when she made an appearance in the great room. They were surprised to see her up so early.

"Were you not able to sleep, my dear?" Larium put her bread down on her plate and indicated Eunice should sit.

"I did sleep but was troubled by strange dreams."

"I'll be happy to look after Simon for a while if you'd like to rest." Larium rose to slice more bread for Eunice.

"No, now that I'm up I'm ready to face the day. I need to talk to both of you, though, if you have time now." She looked from one to the other of them, her eyebrows raised in question.

"Of course." Mattias sat back from his empty plate, wiping his hands on a damp cloth. "We'd take time if we didn't have it, but I have a few minutes before I need to open the shop."

Eunice sank down next to Larium. She looked at both of them lovingly before she started to speak.

"I have a strange compulsion this morning. I can only believe it's from God, for

I don't believe I would ever have thought of it myself. I know I can't get in to see Antipas again, the guards made that clear. But I want news of him, of how he's faring, of his injuries, and whether healing is taking place, oh, just everything." She gestured with her hands as she talked.

"I can understand that, Eunice." Larium patted her hand. "What is this strange compulsion?"

"Well, I was thinking about who might be able to get in to see him, but everyone I thought of would have less chance than I would. I prayed about it, and the Lord sent a strange answer."

"Who?" Mattias drew his brows together and cocked his head.

"Paulus."

Mattias's eyes stretched open, and Larium covered her mouth with her hand. The name seemed to echo in the room. Frightening, yet maybe possible.

Mattias recovered his voice first. "Antipas did have a good meeting with him. He seemed to be of a different opinion than Marcus and their father. But he's not a Christian and we don't know if Marcus or Julian has got to him yet." He sat back in his seat, folding his arms tightly across his chest. "I say it's too risky."

"Don't be so fast, Mattias." Larium put her arm around Eunice. "If God sent the name to Eunice, then he's the only one who should go."

"I still say it's too risky. Not just for Eunice, but for all the people of the church. We need to keep a low profile until things settle down."

"Now that certainly doesn't sound like my brave, believing husband." Larium shook a finger at him.

"We've all experienced fear since Antipas was arrested. I'm sorry, Larium and Eunice; I do need to trust Christ for the right answer. I'd like to meet with David and Emin and get their opinion. Would that be okay with you ladies?"

"Thank you, Mattias." The corners of Eunice's lips slipped upward. "That sounds like the best idea to me. What do you think, Larium?"

"Excellent."

The three bowed their heads and asked God for His will and His way and for protection for the church. Once they finished, Mattias said he would open the shop, service his customers, and be off to David's at the first break in business.

Larium and Eunice played with Simon, talking over the situation while they did so. Eunice knew she would need to be the one, wanted to be the one, who approached Paulus. She knew that Mattias wouldn't like that, but somehow she would have to convince him. "After all, he is my brother-in-law."

Eunice soon took Simon in for his nap. She would need to fill the hours today so she wouldn't dwell on the answer Mattias would have for her tonight. While she waited, she decided to write a long letter to Antipas just in case it worked out that Paulus could and would go to visit him. She knew there was no light in the cell, but perhaps Paulus could leave the lantern, or let him read the letter while he was there. Either way, it was worth writing. It made her feel she was doing something to help Antipas.

The day wore on. Larium and Eunice worked on some new clothes for Simon, who was growing so fast.

At long last dusk began to gather in the eastern sky. Soon Mattias would be back for the evening meal. He had left the house shortly after the noon meal, saying he would be sure to be back by sundown, if not before.

The stew cooking over the fire gave off a fragrant aroma. Eunice felt hungry even though she wasn't sure she could eat. Larium was completing preparations for the meal when they heard Mattias's footsteps on the stairs. Eunice held her breath as he entered the room.

"You look pale, Eunice. Sit down and I'll tell you everything that was said and decided."

She sank into a chair and waited for him to continue.

"I met with David and Emin. We talked long and prayed longer. They had many questions and just as many concerns. But we finally came to the decision that we should proceed."

Eunice gasped and put her hand over her breast. Her heart pounded as she thought about the danger to Paulus and Antipas. "They've agreed?"

"They've agreed. With reservations. We decided we would only proceed if you agreed we bring Voss into the discussion and let him make the approach to Paulus." He pulled up a couch and sat, reclining back on the cushions.

"I agree Voss should be involved, but I want to be the one who talks to Paulus. I've been in the prison so know what it will be like. And besides, he's my husband and I want to be involved." Eunice watched him intently.

He sat up, knocking the pillow to the floor. "No, no. It's too dangerous."

"But I must talk to Paulus. Let Voss arrange a meeting between Paulus and myself. I'm not afraid."

"You're talking nonsense, Eunice." He stood, knocking two more pillow over. He bent to pick them up.

Larium waved her wooden spoon at them, a frown crossing her face. "Mattias, please consider letting Eunice be involved in talking to Paulus. This was her idea, and it is her husband." She reached over and adjusted the pillows. "Besides, Paulus is her brother-in-law and may have a weak spot for her."

"Well, it looks like a conspiracy in my own house." He sat down again, crushing a pillow under him.

Eunice smiled. She knew she had won her point. Mattias stood and pointed a finger at both of them.

"I'll talk to David and Emin again. I think I can get them to agree. But you must," he said, turning to Eunice, "you must follow our instructions to the letter."

"Thank you, Mattias. I promise to do whatever you men say, as long as I can talk to Paulus." She closed her eyes and lowered her head.

"Also remember, Paulus may not want to talk to you or be involved in any way." Mattias touched her shoulder.

"I know. I'll be praying that God will soften his heart," Eunice said quietly.

"Actually, I need to confess that I thought you might have something like this in mind, so I've already mentioned it to them and asked David to bring Voss here tonight. We'll talk the whole thing out and make the safest plans we can."

Eunice clapped her hands for joy.

≈ ≈ ≈

They were finishing their evening meal when a knock sounded at the door below.

"That must be David and Voss now." Mattias hurried to open the door.

When it was open, David entered followed by someone with a dark hood pulled down to his forehead. As the hood was pushed back, Eunice gave a sharp gasp and her eyes widened as she clamped her hand over her mouth.

Paulus stood before them!

Sixty

Mattias was the first to recover.

"Paulus, welcome to my humble home." He bowed low from his waist.

"Thank you, Mattias." He looked around the room, glancing at Larium and Eunice.

David took him by the arm and led him over to Eunice.

Eunice stood and stared at the man coming toward her. The family resemblance was strong. She could see several similarities in his face and bearing to remind her of Antipas. She held her breath, waiting for him to speak.

"It is my great pleasure to meet you, my sister-in-law," Paulus said in a polished tone. Even his voice reminded her of Antipas. "Antipas is indeed a lucky man to have so beautiful a wife."

He kissed her on each cheek and then released her. She looked into his eyes and liked what she saw there. She instantly felt she could trust this man, even though she would still be cautious.

David now greeted the group and introduced Paulus to Larium and Lois. "Paulus has agreed to meet with you, Eunice, with Mattias and I present. He's curious as to why you want to see him and what you hope to gain by it. I told him nothing other than you wish to speak with him."

Mattias indicated the seats. "Please sit by the fire. Larium will look after Simon and Lois. We can then talk over our plan."

Larium picked up the baby and helped Lois from the room. Eunice smiled shyly at Paulus and David. Paulus sat down with them, looking at Eunice with his eyebrows raised.

David sat down beside Paulus. "I'll not interfere in your conversation. I'm just here to listen." He directed his comment to Eunice.

"Thank you, David." Eunice nodded her head and spoke with a slight tremble in her voice. She looked at her brother-in-law, her hands clasped tightly in her lap. "You must be wondering why I wished to speak with you."

"I am curious, curious enough to cause me to come and meet with you." He watched her closely, his eyes never leaving her face.

"Then with your permission I will begin my story." She smiled shyly.

He nodded to her so she began to talk, telling him a little about herself and Simon, leading up to her reason for asking to see him. "I want to know how Antipas is faring in prison, if he's healing from his wounds, if he's in good spirits." She bowed her head in a brief prayer. "I was able to visit him once, but that door has closed. None of my friends have access to anyone who might know or who might help them gain access…"

"So you want me to try to get you into the prison, is that it?" Paulus's voice interrupted her. "Because if that is the purpose of this meeting, you have just wasted your time. I don't have that kind of power."

"No, no, that is not what this is about. I know I can't ever go back in. I want you to go, Paulus." She let her gaze linger on him.

"What? Are you crazy? I can't do that." He jumped to his feet and turned his back on her. He swung around quickly, his face twisted in a grimace. "Whatever made you think of this?"

"God told me to approach you." She didn't move in her seat, but she kept her eyes on him.

"God? Why would He want anything to do with this?" He looked down at her, a frown lodged between his eyes.

"Please, sit down again, Paulus, and I'll explain what I think He has to do with this."

He sat down, his jaw tight below the frown, and Eunice proceeded to tell him about Christ and the power He had in the world. She told him that when God speaks, you can count on what He says.

"So, because some God I don't even know tells you that I should go to the prison, you think I should just do as you ask." Paulus shifted in his seat, clenched his hands, and stared at her.

"That's right." Eunice nodded and smiled.

"You astound me." He shook his head as though to clear his thoughts. "I've never heard anything like this. I should put my life on the line, because you got a message from your God."

"But don't you see, Paulus, you wouldn't be putting your life on the line, because God has promised me that you will be safe." She bent toward him while nodding her head.

"Now you're talking nonsense. How would I even get into the prison?"

"I feel sure you must know someone who could help you gain access." She sat back and just watched him.

Paulus stood and walked to the fire. His hands were never still; rubbing his chin, running his fingers through his hair, slapping his thighs. His head jerked up and he turned to face Eunice. "Actually I do know one of the guards who owes me a favor. I had forgotten about that."

"So you see, it is possible," beamed Eunice.

Paulus stared at her before he answered, a strange look on his face.

"Okay, I'll approach him and see if such a crazy scheme is even possible." He shook his head as he said, "I can't believe I'm agreeing to this."

"It will be all right, Paulus. God has assured me that you will be safe and that you have goodness deep in your heart and a love for your brother."

He arched his eyebrows and looked at her. "I will meet with you a week from today if I have been able to arrange anything."

Sixty-One

The week finally ended and Eunice was once again sitting with Mattias awaiting Paulus's arrival. The knock on the door started her heart beating a heavy rhythm.

Paulus entered the room and quickly embraced Eunice and greeted Mattias. As he sat down he shook his head. He looked at both of them before he began to talk. Eunice sat on the edge of her seat.

"It's been an unusual week, to say the least." Paulus began, rubbing his hands together as he talked. "Leaving here last week I never would have believed how events would unfold."

He paused before continuing, taking a deep breath. "I approached the guard I know, to feel him out as to how we might be able to do as you asked. It almost seemed as though he had been waiting for me to come to him."

Paulus again shook his head in bewilderment. "He told me that Justus Anthony will be out of town for the next several days and things are quiet at the prison. Then he whispered that this would be a good time for someone to slip into the prison to visit a relative. I'm sure my jaw dropped."

Even Mattias was sitting on the edge of his seat, his full attention on Paulus.

"Tell us more, Paulus. How did you respond?" Eunice encouraged him, almost breathless, waiting for him to continue.

"I asked him if he was serious. He assured me he was. He then said if I wished to see a certain prisoner, he could make the arrangements. I said that would be desirable."

"When can you go?" Eunice was wringing her hands in her lap.

"He told me it would need to be during the night watch, just after the guards change shifts. We have set up the meeting for two nights from now."

Eunice jumped from her seat and embraced Paulus. His eyebrows shot up and he fumbled with his hand, patting her back.

"God has answered our prayers," she exclaimed. "I knew this was the right thing to do."

"It's still a risky thing to do. I could be facing imprisonment myself if Marcus or my father were to find out I am doing this. My friend and I are working on a cover story to explain my presence in the prison if such should be needed."

Eunice's eyes filled with tears. "Oh, Paulus, I am truly grateful to you for making this sacrifice. I firmly believe that you will be safe, but I understand your concerns. Would you be willing for Mattias and me to pray with you before you go?"

"I don't think that's necessary, but your God does seem to be interested in this happening."

Mattias spoke for the first time. "While you are in the prison, I will be meeting with a group of believers, and we will cover your whole visit with prayer."

Paulus frowned and looked more uncomfortable than ever, but just shook his head. He left after promising to return the night after his visit to Antipas.

Sixty-Two

Antipas lay in a spent heap on the floor. Darkness surrounded him like a shroud shutting out all thoughts from his mind. He lay panting for several minutes until his eyes adjusted to the darkness.

At last he looked to the ceiling. The light was still there. As he watched, it grew in intensity until the whole cell was filled with it. Lovely voices began singing a sweet melody. It sounded like heavenly music to him.

Ises appeared, again fluttering down to where he could see without lifting his head.

"Well done, Antipas. You have passed the test. You have been victorious. The worst is over. Satan will no longer torture you. You will experience the presence of Christ in an intimate way. It will be precious to you. Be assured, the church is strong in Pergamum."

Antipas lay basking in the light flowing from Ises. If he could always have this, life in prison would not only be tolerable, but desirable. But Ises was still talking and he didn't want to miss a word.

"You will have another visitor. This one will be who he says he is and will be speaking the truth in all he says. You will be surprised by the visit, but great good will come from it."

As the last words were spoken, the light began to dim until he could only see the outline of Ises. This, too, faded but the tiny light drifted up to the ceiling and stayed there.

◈ ◈ ◈

Antipas was restless in his cell. He tried to sleep but could find no position that didn't cause pain. Hours had gone by since he had seen Ises and listened to the beautiful words. They had been hours of tranquility, hours spent in fellowship with his God, hours of beautiful memories of Eunice and Simon. Now he was trying to sleep but sleep would not come.

One of the friendly guards had been by earlier to check his wounds and bring him a decent meal. He wasn't sure how he was able to do this, but he was appreciative of the gesture.

He finally decided that God didn't want him to sleep at this time, that he would need to be alert for whatever was next on God's agenda. He sat up, leaned against the cell wall, then sat up again as pain sliced through his shredded back. He would have liked to preach now, but didn't have the strength to do so. He also felt it was night by something the guard had said. So he sat, body rigid in agony.

He heard sounds in the hallway but dismissed them as the creaking of an old building until he heard the latch being lifted on his cell door. He was expecting it to be the guard again and looked toward the sound in the penetrating darkness.

As the door began to open, he could see that whoever was coming was carrying a lantern. The lantern light made its way into his cell, followed by a large person. As his eyes adjusted to the light, he was astounded to see Paulus.

Paulus put the light down and knelt beside Antipas. The brothers looked eye to eye and Antipas could see something there, a longing perhaps, or a memory. Whatever it was, it was encouraging.

"Antipas." Paulus touched him, searching his eyes.

"You're a welcome sight, my brother." He raised his head to take in the sight.

"I have a long story to tell you. Are you feeling up to this visit?"

"Nothing would give me greater pleasure. Please, tell your story. I will not miss a word."

∾ ∾ ∾

Paulus stifled a desire to gag. The prison smells were cloying and repugnant and even worse here in the cell with his brother. He forced himself to focus on Antipas and on what he wanted to tell him. He sat down in the dirt beside his brother, wiping his forehead with his sleeve, and began to talk.

"The night we met was a turning point in my life. I couldn't get the things you said out of my mind. I tried to put them aside and carry on, but they kept crowding in on me at the least expected times. When I would lie down to sleep at night, our entire conversation would play over and over." Paulus moved the lantern back against the wall.

"I had no idea what to do about it or if I even should do anything. Things stayed that way for quite some time until at last I started having dreams. The dreams were horrible. They frightened me more than I wanted to admit." A shudder swept over his body.

Antipas made a choking sound that caused Paulus to stop and look at him.

"Are you all right, Brother?"

"Please carry on, Paulus. I'm fine."

"In the dreams I was always dead." Paulus paused again, swallowed a few times, wiped his brow again.

"I would look around the city, and I was nowhere to be found. What was really frightening was that I didn't know what would happen to me after I died. I could see a light up ahead, but a voice kept telling me I couldn't go to the light. Then I would turn around. The sight that met my eyes was horrific, too ghastly to repeat." Sweat was beading on his forehead. He swiped at it with his sleeve. "It was at that point I would always awaken. I kept asking myself, what does it mean? I had no answers, but somehow I knew you had the answers."

Antipas kept still as Paulus told his story. His lips moved silently but fervently. Tears were streaming down his face.

"But how could I ask you when you were in prison? What made it even harder was the fact that you were in prison at the demands and the efforts of our father and brother. I was pondering night after night how I could reach you, when an unexpected thing happened."

Antipas struggled to sit up straighter, grimacing with the pain. Paulus leaned over and put his arm gently around Antipas and helped him to a more comfortable position. Paulus continued, "I was walking through the market area one morning when our mutual acquaintance, Voss, fell in beside me. He asked me if I would be willing to meet with him in private. I wondered if the meeting had anything to do with you, as he was the one who made the arrangements when we met before.

"I was reluctant to meet with him, knowing that I might be putting you in more danger. He pressed me for the meeting, and I finally agreed to meet him right away as I had no appointments just then. We met at his house as we had before.

"He told me that your wife, Eunice, desired to speak with me. The request was so unusual that I was speechless. He kept insisting that it was very important. I finally agreed to go to Mattias's house and meet Eunice."

Antipas reached out and grasped his hand in his. The brothers held tightly.

"When I went home I paced the hallways, unable to settle anywhere. I went over all the reasons why I shouldn't meet with her. I thought about her safety, your safety, my risk in seeing her. But through the whole afternoon, one thought kept coming back. I needed to talk to you. I knew I would never have peace again until

I was able to see you." He paused and drew a cloth from under his cloak. With it, he wiped the tears from his brother's face and then from his own.

"By dusk I began to think that meeting with Eunice was one step closer to you and that it would be worth the risk. She must have already known it would be dangerous and decided whatever it was she needed to say to me would be worth it. I decided that if she was brave enough to take the chance, I needed to have the courage to do likewise.

"To make a long story shorter, I met Voss, who introduced me to David, and I've met with Eunice twice since then. She asked me to come see you. I have to tell you I nearly choked when she asked me. It was the one consuming desire I had had in my heart for weeks."

Antipas smiled and squeezed his hand. "She's one special lady."

"That she is," Paulus nodded. "I, of course, protested that it would be impossible, having already gone over all the reasons I couldn't visit you myself. But then she started talking about her God and how He had told her to approach me and that I would be safe if I came here."

Antipas was grinning. "When Eunice gets something in her mind…"

"I couldn't believe what I was hearing. Here was this helpless woman showing a courage I had only dreamed of having. And she talked about her God the same way you had talked about yours. From somewhere a little voice seemed to be saying to me, go, it'll be okay."

Antipas laughed softly. "Who but Eunice would come up with a scheme like this and be convinced that everyone else should see it just the way she did?"

"I was able to make the arrangements to come here, impossible arrangements. Eunice said she would be talking to her God about them and that she was sure I would get in. And here I am."

He stopped talking abruptly and looked closely at Antipas. Tears were running down Antipas's face again. Paulus leaned closer.

"Are you okay, Brother?"

"Oh yes, Paulus, I am more than fine. I'm so excited to see you and to hear your story. I think I have the answers you're looking for. Come here, my brother."

Paulus leaned over and the brothers embraced.

"Paulus, when our father banished me from my home and family, I thought the world had come to an end for me. Then I met a friend who introduced me to Jesus. I knew right away that this was what I had been missing all my life." He told Paulus about giving his heart to Jesus, and what that had meant in his life.

Paulus drank in every word. When Antipas told him about the brutal beating and how with each bite of the lash, he had cried out and God had sustained him, Paulus covered his face with his hands and wept. His shoulders shook while tears poured down his face. Antipas reached out his hand and gripped his brother's. The two mingled their tears in the damp prison cell.

"Brother, you need to come to Jesus, too. He can take away all the sin and guilt from your life. He died for you, Paulus. He died for me." Antipas kept talking, showing him step by step how he could come into a relationship with Christ.

Paulus wiped his face with his arm. He sniffed and swallowed, then took a deep breath. "I think I'm ready to take this step. I'm afraid, but I'm more afraid not to. Please show me the way."

And there in his prison cell, Antipas led Paulus into a saving relationship with Almighty God. When they finished praying, Paulus looked up, blinking the tears from his eyes.

"I can't believe the peace that has come over me." Paulus smiled while crossing his hands over his heart.

"That's the peace that only God can give you. Zeus can't do that for a man."

"I believe, oh yes, I believe." He clasped his hands together and closed his eyes.

The brothers spent the next hour talking about what his next steps should be.

"I know you've been accepted by God and I want to send you to David for spiritual feeding."

"That is my desire. I want to know more. I sense this is only the beginning."

Then they talked about their family and all the problems there. Paulus told Antipas that the first thing he was going to do was to go to their mother with the good news. He had known for some time that their mother had embraced this new religion, but he had refrained from telling his father or Marcus. Now he was so glad he hadn't reported what he had heard. He and his mother could now fellowship together.

He gave Antipas the packet of letters he had brought from Eunice. He had also brought scrolls and ink and gave them to Antipas to write return letters. The guard who had let him in had promised to collect any messages from Antipas and deliver them to Paulus.

When he had to go, the brothers embraced again.

"You have given me pleasure beyond anything I could have imagined here in this cell." Antipas kissed his cheek.

"You have given me eternal hope." Paulus returned the gesture. "We may never meet again here on earth, but now I know I will meet you again one day in heaven.

That's what you have given me, my brother. I will learn to pray and you will be in my prayers everyday."

"Go with God, and may He bless you abundantly." Antipas raised his hand in farewell.

Sixty-Three

Paulus left the prison in high spirits. Somehow his fear had been left behind when he surrendered his life to Christ. He couldn't believe the peace and hope he had in his heart. He would no longer fear his father or Marcus or what the gods could do to him. He now served the living God, the one true God. Neither would he meet Christians at night, in secret. He would openly associate with them. He was now one of them. If he was arrested, so be it.

He hardly knew where he was going, his euphoria was so great. He found himself in the street next to Voss's house, which didn't surprise him. He approached the house, wondering what sort of a reception he would receive from Voss.

He knocked sharply on the door. Voss answered and quickly ushered him into the house.

Voss took his cloak while studying his face. "Paulus, what's wrong?"

"Nothing is wrong. In fact, everything is right." Paulus gripped his shoulder and grinned.

"Come, sit by the fire and tell me what's happened. You look like you've had an experience." Voss led him to the seats facing the smoldering fire.

"You could say that. I've just come from spending a few hours with my brother."

"But it's more than that, isn't it?"

"Oh, yes, it is. I've met God and He has accepted me into His kingdom," Paulus declared with a ring of victory in his voice.

Voss stared at him in wonder.

"I know it seems unlikely for someone such as me, but it's real, Voss. Believe me, I am now one of you. I am now a convert." Paulus couldn't sit still. His hands were in motion and his body restless. "Antipas has sent you a short note assuring you that this is true. He will send more letters later. We had time for only this short one for now." He reached inside the folds of his robe and extracted a small scroll.

He handed it to Voss, who opened it slowly. His eyes scanned the page. When he looked up, he smiled at Paulus.

"The note is definitely in Antipas's handwriting. He's stated that we are to accept you into our fellowship as you are now a new convert." He rose from his seat and put his arm on Paulus's shoulder. "Welcome into the fellowship of believers, Paulus. This is far more than we could ever have dreamed of when we approached you with this mission."

"The same goes for me. I would like to tell you my story, if you would like to hear it."

"I would be delighted to hear it. Please, tell me everything."

And Paulus did. He told him everything right from the beginning until now.

"What a beautiful example of the grace of our Lord Jesus Christ," Voss exclaimed when Paulus had finished. "We need to go to Eunice and then you need to meet the others. Come, let's not waste any time."

"I agree. Lead me where you will, I'm a willing follower." He jumped from the seat and turned toward the entrance.

And so they went. First to Eunice, who cried over him and welcomed him most warmly, then to Mattias and Larium, then David and Emin, then to others who were available. Paulus was overwhelmed with the welcome he received. For the first time in a long, long time, he felt like he belonged. He felt clean and free and wanted.

They planned a gathering to be held at David's house that evening. They would share a meal together and then spend time listening to David share truths about Christ and pray together. All this was new for Paulus and he couldn't wait to participate.

≈ ≈ ≈

The meal was sweet on Paulus's tongue. He had eaten more elaborate meals almost every day of his life, but he had never eaten one in such congenial, loving company. He couldn't believe how accepted he was by all the believers.

The talk by David was another feast for him. Where had such teaching come from? How had he missed it all these years? He realized with clarity that Antipas was the one who was successful with his life. Even while in prison his life was richer and more rewarding than that of his other family members, and until today, of Paulus's own.

When the prayer time was over, another new experience for Paulus, David asked him if he would like to say a few words. At first he panicked and wondered what he could say to this group who knew so much more than he did, but then he felt what could only be the prompting of the Holy Spirit to share what he could do for them.

"Thank you, David. I would like to say a few things." He turned to face the group, fear and wonder churning in his heart. "Thank you for accepting me. You didn't have to do that, especially knowing my background with Zeus worship and my relationship with my father and my brother Marcus, but I am truly grateful. You have all heard my story and my report on my visit with Antipas."

Heads were nodding in agreement with him. A few people said kind words to encourage him to continue.

"I've already spoken to Eunice about what I will share with you. She knows and accepts what will probably happen. I hesitate to tell you that things are not looking good for my brother Antipas. Justus Anthony, spurred on by my father, is determined to wipe out Christianity. I think he will carry out the death sentence on Antipas."

There were murmurs throughout the crowd. Some of the women wept as he spoke. He continued in a subdued voice.

"Antipas is also aware of this and accepts this as from the Lord. He is at peace about it, as is Eunice. No date has yet been set, but I am in a position to be aware of any new developments. I will keep you updated." His face was tight and his shoulders straight.

"I, too, am aware of this." David came to stand beside him. "I have felt for quite some time that it is not in God's plan to rescue Antipas, but that He has a much higher plan for him and for the church of Pergamum. This is a time of great testing for him and for us."

Silence fell on the group. Several people, including David, dropped to their knees. Someone started to pray aloud and the next several moments were filled with audible prayers before their heavenly Father.

David rose from his knees. "When this sad event occurs, we need to be prepared. I feel strongly that we need to be present and show support not only for Antipas, but for the cause of Christ. We need to gather all the believers together and stand up for Christ."

"Yes, yes," came from several places in the room.

"Paulus and I will be in constant touch and we'll let you know when we have further information."

The group broke into smaller groups, discussing what they had just heard. There was fear, but also a sense that they were following God's plan. To gather so publicly might make their persecution worse, but that was a risk they were willing to take. Slowly, families began to leave, somber yet encouraged. Paulus was the last to prepare to leave.

"David, you will never know what tonight has meant to me. I have never experienced anything like it before."

"Just remember, my friend, not so long ago many of us were where you are. It's amazing what the grace of God can do in a life. When can we meet again?" David walked to the door with him.

"I want to meet every day, but I know that isn't practical. Would the next night be suitable for you?"

"We can meet every night if you wish." David smiled at Paulus. "But the next night is agreeable to me. Come for the evening meal with my family, and then you and I can spend time discussing our walk with the Lord and in prayer."

Paulus left the house feeling more complete than he'd ever felt in his life. The road ahead would be filled with troubles and sorrow, but he now knew the One who had overcome the troubles of the world. He felt cheated that he and Antipas would have so little time together but knew that Antipas's fate was in the hands of God. He took a deep breath, pulled his cloak around him, and headed for his home, a new creature in Christ.

Sixty-Four

The church continued to multiply. Word of Antipas spread to all the converts and they doubled their efforts to bring friends and neighbors to Christ. The more Justus Anthony tried to wipe out the Christians, the stronger they grew.

Several of the men started going to the temple steps again to preach to anyone who would listen. Even before they arrived, crowds would form in anticipation of their coming. Some of the more mature believers were able to perform miracles, healing the sick and casting out demons.

With every demon cast out, there was an uproar among the priests and temple guards. They didn't dare interfere, but they were afraid they were losing ground. Justus Anthony called for a meeting with his counselors, the priests, and some of the higher ranking temple guards, as well as Julian.

Marcus moved through the throng listening to the Christians, hoping this madness would soon be over. He was convinced, as was his father, that the whole mob would settle down once Antipas was dead. Maybe today he could convince Justus Anthony that the sooner he was killed the better. He knew some of the other temple guards were with him on this.

The mob was noisy, with many people milling about. They seemed especially excited today, like something out of the ordinary had happened.

"Probably one of the fake miracles all the city is talking about," he supposed. He glanced around surreptitiously, not wanting to make eye contact with anyone.

He was almost to the top of the stairs when he thought he saw a familiar face. He stopped and glared at the crowd. Only strangers. It reminded him of Paulus, but surely he wouldn't dare show himself around this gathering. Paulus was getting soft. He'd warned his father to watch him more closely, but not even Paulus would identify himself with this bunch of fools. Nevertheless, it would be wise to be vigilant.

When he arrived at the meeting, the room was almost full. Voices were raised in debate as he entered. He saw his father but turned in the other direction as he remembered his outburst at Antipas's trial. He didn't want to be a part of any weakness. He found a seat toward the back, wanting to be as inconspicuous as possible.

Some of the temple guards had started taunting him, trying to identify him with Antipas. He had called out a couple of them and they had settled the score a week ago. He didn't think anyone else would dare cross him. The two he'd taken on would feel the results for a while.

The atmosphere in the room was tense. Things were coming to a climax in the city. The elders feared riots would soon start. The people were showing far too much interest in these cult worshippers.

～ ～ ～

Justus Anthony arrived in a flurry of swishing robes, accompanied by several of his retainers. There was a scowl on his face and a determination to settle this question once and for all. He had hoped this would all go away quietly once Antipas was in prison, but it was only getting worse. He didn't want to kill him, but he was running out of options. He hoped he could keep the meeting under control today.

He rose to his feet, and a static silence descended. He looked over the faces gathered. "We are here to seek a solution to the current problems in the city caused by this crowd of cult worshippers."

"Hear, hear," could be heard from several attendees.

"I have a proposal for how to deal with the situation, but I would like to hear your ideas first."

Several hands immediately went up.

"Clement, you may begin."

Clement rose to his feet while the group with him cheered for him.

"I think," Clement boomed, "it's high time we sacrificed this infidel on the altar of Zeus!" Cheers and cries of "Yes, Yes," greeted his speech. Several priests and most of the temple guards stood to their feet, clapping their hands and pounding their sandaled feet on the tile floor.

Justus Anthony brooded in his chair. Clement had spoken the words many of them wanted to hear from him. Somehow he could not bring himself to do it. Something in his inner being felt drawn to Antipas; he needed to settle this group.

"Silence." An uneasy quiet hovered over them. He leveled withering glances at those nearest to him. "Does anyone else wish to speak?"

Several priests spoke next, agreeing with Clement. One of them spoke forcefully, "Our power has diminished since this group has come to Pergamum. I speak frankly, friends, this is a strong God they worship. Zeus is not pleased." He gestured with his arm to include all the priests. "We, his priests, are not pleased. It's time for action. We must force this sect out of our city if we are ever to return to our former way of life. They are disrupting our lives, everything we believe." He flung his fist in the air while pivoting his body to include all those present.

He was shouting by the time he finished. The room erupted in chaos. The priests were on their feet again, and now their anger was directed at Justus Anthony. He felt the first spurt of fear pluck at his heart.

"I think your feelings are getting in the way of your good judgment—"

"Down with Justus Anthony." The cry came from somewhere in the back.

A shocked stillness chilled the room. The guards snapped to attention.

"Who spoke?" Justus Anthony was on his feet, scanning the faces watching him.

"It was Marcus," an unidentified voice shouted.

"It was not me." Marcus hotly denied it, getting red in the face. While he was protesting, another voice took up the chant.

"Down with Justus Anthony."

The guards seized several speakers and took them into custody. Marcus they left alone. When order was restored, Justus spoke once more.

"It is obvious," he said, his voice heavy with sarcasm, "that you are unable to come to any coherent agreement. This meeting is adjourned until further notice." He gathered his robe around him and swept from the room.

Alone in his quarters, he pondered what his next move should be. He had to keep the priests happy and he had to restore order in the city. He had wanted to protect Antipas, but perhaps that wouldn't be possible. But maybe it would…

A plan started to unfold in his mind. Frightening in its intensity. Massive in its destructive potential. He needed to talk to his closest advisors, the ones who didn't have a personal animosity like the priests and temple guards. Ones who put him first and held his ideas as prophetic.

Once they were gathered, he laid out his plan. He could see shock register on some of the faces to quickly be replaced by determination. They were unanimous in their agreement. Now he only needed to give the orders and it would be accomplished. The temple guards would be needed, but they, in the end, would do his bidding.

The primary group involved would be the Roman soldiers. He would need at least a legion of them. Manpower was essential. The temple guards would be needed when the plan came to fruition.

He met with the centurion posted to Pergamum and outlined his plan. The soldier, Petrius, was all business. He accepted his orders without comment and assured

Justus Anthony it would be accomplished as he had requested. They set the date for two days from now, that being the day of worship for these deceivers.

Justus Anthony could hardly wait. "I'll show these Christians just who is boss, and I'll defy the priests and guards. I know I want to protect Antipas, and I'll not be dictated to by the priests of Zeus."

∽ ∽ ∽

The first day of the week dawned bright and clear. Sunlight slanted along the streets, outlining the houses and stalls in the marketplace. A gentle breeze ruffled the flowers growing along the byways. Puffy white clouds lazily drifted along the horizon. Birdsong trilled from sturdy branches, welcoming the day.

Believers from all over Pergamum and outlying areas prepared for a day of worship. Lunches were packed, as many would not travel home until the evening, spending the day with fellow believers; worshipping, praying, and fellowshipping together.

There were many places of worship today, David's and Emin's being only two of several. The exact number of believers was estimated to be several hundred by now. They had thought the imprisonment of Antipas would affect their numbers; people turning back, and new people unwilling to associate with them, but just the opposite had happened. They were stronger than ever. The presence of the Holy Spirit could be felt whenever they were together.

The meeting today was charged with tension as David rose to speak. He greeted each one with tenderness. Before the gathering, Paulus had given him startling information and had requested that he be permitted to speak to the assembly. David now asked him to address them.

"I have been hearing things in the city." He stood before them, hands behind his back. "I am not part of the inner ruling body, but I have enough influence that I am privy to certain information. Earlier this morning there was talk about a plan of Justus Anthony's to rid the city of the Christians, and to do it this day." He paused as a ripple of shock moved through the crowd. He waited until he had their full attention again. "I found out as many details as I could to help prepare us. It's not sounding good. It will take a miracle to save us from his grasp, but more and more I'm coming to see that the God we serve is a God of miracles." Several amens greeted his declaration. He watched the group, noticing that every eye was fixed on him.

"The plan involves the legion stationed in the city as well as many of the temple guards. The order went out this morning that we are to be stopped and arrested as we leave our places of worship." He could see fear cross some of the faces, determination on others. Sweat began to form, both from the warm day and the tension, and he wiped his forehead. "There was not time to warn the other groups, so I shared this with David and we decided the best thing we could do was to pray fervently for the foiling of this plan. David, I'll let you handle this from here."

Paulus sat again as David outlined his plan for their prayer time. He reminded the believers of the times God had delivered His people, Israel, against all human odds. He encouraged them to confess any sin to the Lord and then to earnestly plead with Him for the deliverance of His people from the hands of their enemies.

"King David had numerous enemies, but he trusted fully in the Lord. I will read one of his psalms to you and then we'll pray.

"In you, O Lord, I have taken refuge;
"Let me never be put to shame;
"Deliver me in your righteousness.
"Turn your ear to me,
"Come quickly to my rescue;
"Be my rock of refuge,
"A strong fortress to save me.
"Since you are my rock and my fortress,
"For the sake of your name lead and guide me.
"Free me from the trap that is set for me,
"For you are my refuge.
"Into your hands I commit my spirit;
"Redeem me, O Lord, the God of truth."

"Now is the time for us to pray."

People fell on their knees all over the room, some in small groups, some on their own. When they finished praying, they left quietly, calmed by the time spent in prayer. Paulus left with Mattias and his family. He walked with them for several minutes then left them to return to his home. He was surprised when he arrived without incident. He began to wonder if he had not heard correctly or had been given false information. It was several hours before he heard what had happened.

∽ ∽ ∽

Once Centurion Petrius received the word to put the plan into motion, he gathered his cavalry together and gave a series of commands. The temple guards had also arrived and were given their orders: Slay all Christians. Rid our city of this cult, by order of Justus Anthony.

One cohort of soldiers hastened to the stables to retrieve their horses to ride out into the city to carry out the governor's order. There was excitement in the troops as they looked forward to a bloodbath. Things had been quiet, and they welcomed action.

As the first cohort approached the stables, the stable hands milled with frantic activity. Something was wrong. As they came closer, they could see men running across the fields behind the stable.

"The horses have escaped," one of the soldiers bellowed.

The rest broke into a run and soon received the news that earlier the horses had come charging out of the stable and across the fields. They were being chased and should soon be captured.

"How did this happen? Weren't they secured in their stalls?" The captain leaped from his horse to interrogate one of the stable hands.

The stable boy trembled. "Yes, sir, they were secure the last time they were checked. We don't know how they got out."

"This is unacceptable. We're on orders from the governor and need those horses now and that's an order." He grabbed the boy roughly and shook him.

"Yes, sir, we're doing our best. I'm sure they'll be back soon." His eyes were wild and even his chin was quivering.

The captain dropped his hand and paced the length of the stable. He turned sharply on his heel. "This is ridiculous," he shouted to his men. "Go with the others and get those horses back."

The soldiers began running across the field following the stable hands, but the horses were now out of sight. They met the first hands coming back defeated. The horses had disappeared. The soldiers continued to follow the course until they, too, could see there was no point in continuing the chase. Hoof prints in the muddy field were all that remained.

The soldiers returned to their captain in fear. He was a hard man and this would be a deep embarrassment to him. He would have to report back to the centurion in defeat.

When they returned to the stable, the captain was ordering the stable hands to be flogged for their carelessness in allowing the horses to escape. Some of the soldiers were snapping their whips in anticipation. If they couldn't round up Christians, they could at least enjoy a flogging.

Soldiers chased the stable hands until the last one was caught. The sound of whips slicing the air mixed with the howls of the afflicted. Some of the hands were mere boys and were begging for mercy. Their pleas mingled with cries of pain. The merriment finally ended when the captain ordered the soldiers into formation. They left the chastised stable hands and marched back to the temple.

When they arrived, they were surprised to see they were not the only group to return. Another band had mounted their horses only to find that some of them were lame. The soldiers checked out each horse and set aside the ones that they wouldn't be able to ride. They sought other mounts only to find that there were none available. They had retuned to the temple to see if they should ride with a smaller number or await further orders.

As the two units were discussing these unfortunate events, they could see more soldiers walking toward them. They were out of formation and were walking unsteadily. The story unfolded that their cohort had mounted their horses when one of the soldiers took violently ill. They stopped to help him and others began experiencing the same symptoms. They were unable to ride and could barely walk back to the temple.

The stories were repeated over and over as other companies returned. A swarm of bees attacked one lot, stinging both horses and riders, and another unit got hopelessly lost. They had taken a wrong turn and ended up far out in the country. Each cohort had experienced something different, but the result was the same: they couldn't ride.

≈ ≈ ≈

Word soon reached Justus Anthony. He reared up from his chair, his face dark as a thunder cloud when he heard the news.

"I demand an explanation," he roared at the messenger. But there was no explanation.

His wrath could not be contained. He shouted at anyone who came near. Humiliation was complete when the temple guards returned reporting empty streets. They had ridden through their assigned section of the city several times with the same result: no one was there.

Justus Anthony was in an agony of indecision. He had thought this might save Antipas, but the plan had failed. Now what should he do?

He sent word that the soldiers and guards were to return to their barracks and to tell no one what had transpired. The soldiers would obey the order, but not so the temple guards. They immediately met with the priests in the temple, and a plot was born to depose Justus Anthony for his inept handling of the situation and his inability to remove the Christians from their city.

As the news spread, unrest developed in the general populace who were worshippers of Zeus. A disturbance took place on the temple steps as the sun reached its zenith. Priests, traders, businessmen, merchants, guards; all gathered to protest the hesitation of Justus Anthony.

Word was brought to Justus Anthony about the disturbance. He knew he would have to do something and do it quickly. He met with his closest advisors, who pointed out that the only way out of this mess and the only way to hold his position in Pergamum was to sacrifice Antipas.

Outside, he could hear the noise from the crowd and knew he would have to face them. He hoped they would listen before they rushed at him in revenge. He rose from his chair, threw his cloak over his shoulders, and with a small group of his followers, left his room and appeared on the temple steps.

The crowd was chanting, "Justus, Justus, we want Justus," as he took the first step into the daylight. On sight of him, a hush descended over the throng. He faced them with his shoulders back, lips pressed into a thin line, brows curved downward. They were an angry lot and he knew he had no choice.

"People of Pergamum, followers of Zeus." At his words, all eyes were fixed on him. He took a deep breath. "Rest assured we will drive this religious cult from our city. When the leader is gone, then the others will follow." He raised his arm, fist clenched as he jabbed the air.

He could hear murmuring among the crowd. He was afraid that the noise would break out again, so he continued, "Tomorrow, at midday when the sun is high overhead, the evil leader, Antipas, will be sacrificed on the altar of Zeus, right here in the midst of our city." He felt his stomach muscles clench. "The gods will be appeased, and the believers in this sect will be devastated without their leader. Know, citizens of Pergamum, by this time tomorrow, the city will again belong to you and to your gods." He lowered his arm and stood before the people, hands at his sides, face deliberately blank.

Cheers rose from the mob. He should have been relived that he had appeased the people, but instead he felt a sadness that a good man had to die. What was it about Antipas that spoke to his heart? Perhaps with him dead, he could return to his normal life and forget he'd ever met this man.

He wrapped his cloak around him and turned to enter his chambers. His shoulders slumped and his body trembled as he regained his rooms. Servants hovered around him, hoping to grant his every wish, but he waved them away. He was weary and spent. Tomorrow would be a hard day.

∽ ∽ ∽

The priests were thrilled with the proclamation. It was well past the time that this situation should have been resolved. They were glad the governor had finally seen the need to remove Antipas from this life. There was a sense of triumph and glee in their evening meal celebration.

∽ ∽ ∽

Unseen by others, Paulus had been at the back of the crowd. He had mixed feelings as he rejoiced over the miracle that had protected all the church members this morning, for he realized there was no way to save his brother. Antipas would be a martyr for the cause of Christ. His life for all of theirs. That was a little like what Christ had done, His life for all of mankind.

He realized that Antipas would count it a privilege to give his life for Christ. Paulus had been praying that God would use him as He had used Antipas in leading the Pergamum church. God seemed to be nudging his heart in that direction. He was learning fast under David's teaching, but it would still be some time before he would be accepted by the people as a leader. But he was ready to do what God wanted him to do and to wait for God's timing.

Right now he needed to meet with the church leaders and plan their response for tomorrow. He knew he wanted to be there to support Antipas and to stand up for Christ, and he knew that many of the others would feel the same way. It was time to stand up and be counted.

David, Emin, and Mattias listened sorrowfully to all that Paulus had to say. They, too, were overwhelmed with how God had protected the church that day. They could not do less than rally around Antipas and stand before the religious and political leaders as Christ-followers.

The word went out until every believer within a wide circle heard the message. Paulus and the other leaders could do no more.

Sixty-Five

They came. They came one by one. They came in groups, both large and small. They came in wagons, by horse, on foot. They came in the afternoon, the evening, and through the night. They came with grim faces, determined faces, ready to do their part.

By sunrise they were entering the gates of the city, moving toward the temple and the altar of sacrifice. The streets were packed with the silent throng. They came out of houses, out of alleyways, through the market, down the dusty streets of the city where Satan held the citizens in bondage.

They gathered before the altar; a large, still crowd. No guards were needed, they were not here to riot, but to stand before this altar of Satan and defy his rule, to stand for Christ and everything that is right in this world. For truth and justice. For salvation and righteousness. For peace and freedom. For Christ and eternity. It was time for a public declaration of their faith, and they were here to make that declaration.

Word reached Justus Anthony that they were gathering. He trembled when he heard the news. He looked from his window and gazed on them.

To his aides he said, "Do they not know that I could have them killed for this?"

"I think they know, Governor, but they seem to be obeying a higher power."

"A higher power than their governor?" He shook his head as he watched.

"I've heard that they commune with this Jesus they worship and fear no other." The aide stood beside him.

"Remarkable. I envy them their faith." He put his hand on the window frame and bowed his head.

The aide said nothing but moved away from the window.

Justus Anthony turned away sadly to begin his morning rituals. The ordinary routines seemed futile and empty now. He felt that something good was leaving Pergamum today. Perhaps, if the sect survived, he would secretly seek information about their God.

Antipas slept fitfully. Since the visit from Paulus, the prison had been quiet. Brutus had not been to his cell again, nor had the two kind guards.

A young boy brought his meal once a day without speaking or making eye contact with him. It was the only time he saw any light, but that had ceased to matter. It was like the prison was holding its breath.

Antipas spent his time reciting passages from the Scriptures and communing with God. He had never felt so close to Him. It felt like He was right there in the cell with him. He knew his time on earth was not long now, but he had come to terms with that and was looking forward to seeing Christ face-to-face. He wouldn't have exchanged this prison experience for anything.

As he was meditating on a verse, his door was flung open and an aide of Justus Anthony's peered into the cell. He held the lamp high and covered his nose at the smell that emanated from the cell. The whole prison reeked and he was offended that he had been sent on this errand.

Antipas looked up with a calm demeanor, waiting to accept whatever the visit meant. The aide took one step into the cell, far enough to unlock the shackles.

"Get up," he cried, "You are to come with me."

Antipas was too weak to get up quickly and received a kick in the side to help him. He refused to react and tried again. He reached out for help but was shoved back.

"Don't touch me, you filthy rat. I'll smell for a week."

Antipas slowly reached a leaning position and the two exited the cell. The hall was dimly lit with torches. It was hard to see far in either direction, as the smoke hung like fog along the walls. It was an eerie procession that moved down the hall through the smoke, one standing erect and aloof, the other merely shuffling along, trying to keep pace.

They made several turns and ended in a section of the prison that Antipas had never seen. A battered door swung open at the aide's touch, and Antipas was surprised to see they were in a bathing room. He blinked rapidly in the bright light, shading his eyes with his hand. He hadn't known there were baths in the prison.

The disgruntled guide threw him a hard piece of soap and a few rags, and told him he would be back with new clothes.

"And don't try to escape. There's no way out, I can guarantee you." The door slammed and Antipas was left alone.

At first he just breathed in the warm, moist air and looked around, letting his eyes adjust to the light. Then he gratefully slipped off his soiled clothes and slipped into the water. He couldn't remember anything feeling this good. The water was reviving, even though he suspected this visit was not a good thing, that this was not for his comfort.

His hair was matted and slick with dirt. It took a long time to get it feeling clean. The water felt soothing to the healing scars on his back. His brain was beginning to revive as well. Just being out of the cell was releasing. Thoughts turned to his family and believing brothers and sisters. He prayed for each of them while the water did its work.

All too soon the aide came back carrying a clean set of prison clothes. Still prison clothes, but clean. He would take anything that would help restore his dignity. When he was dressed, the aide led him out of the baths.

He was surprised when they took a different turn on the way back. They weren't heading toward his old cell. Did this mean more floggings? Or a new form of torture? Or did Justus Anthony want to interrogate him again? Or maybe it was a new cell. His shoulders sagged at the thought of any change. His body was tired and his wounds still painful.

The two, prisoner and servant, at last approached a barred door. The two guards there leaped to attention. There was a whispered exchange between the aide and one of the guards. The guard was obviously angry and did not want to comply with the aide's request. The aide finally reached inside his cloak and pulled out a small scroll with a wax seal stamped with a ring.

The guard grudgingly accepted the scroll and looked at the seal. His face paled as he handed it to the other guard, who carefully opened it. He studied it in the dim light then handed it back to the first guard. When they had finished reading, they quickly unbarred the door and swung it open.

Antipas was surprised to see that they were entering a wide hallway lined with works of art and high windows. He recognized the route to the outside world. They were in the anteroom of the prison. He remembered that this was the place shown to visitors, to convince them of the luxury and humane conditions of the prison. Antipas noted that no one, outside of guards and officials, were allowed past these doors.

There were two guards posted on this side of the door as well. They looked questioningly at Antipas and his companion. The aide spoke to the guards, and with a nod from them, Antipas and his companion continued down the corridor into the main foyer.

People were milling around, seemingly awaiting their approach. He thought he caught a glimpse of Marcus but when he looked more closely, the ranks of people pulled together and he was not visible. He knew now that this was a portentous sign that all was not well from a human point of view.

What did this mean for him, he wondered. He was not afraid to die. He felt like Paul when he had said that it didn't matter to him whether he lived or died, either way he was a winner. If the Lord allowed him to live, he had more time to preach the gospel; if he died, he would be in heaven with Christ.

Thoughts tumbled around in his head. Memories of his mother's face flashed before his eyes. Would she ever be safe again? Eunice—surely God would be her strength and helper as she raised their son alone. She was strong, he knew. But the faces that filled his thoughts the most were the faces of Marcus and his father.

He hoped that if he died, they would somehow benefit by seeing and embracing the truth. It would all be worthwhile; the rejection as a young teen, the isolation from his family, the constant threat in later years, if these two would come into a relationship with the one true living God.

It was strangely still in the foyer. Eyes were averted as he and his guide passed by. The guards at the main entrance to the outside were alert and awaiting their approach. The doors were opened even before they reached the portal.

A breath of fresh air feathered across his face, and he inhaled. He was sure he could smell the fragrance of flowers. His knees were weak as his feet shuffled toward the entrance.

As he stepped out into the warm sunlight, he could not believe his eyes. The door exited onto the side steps of the temple, just above the altar to Zeus. He could see down the steps and along the main thoroughfare of the city. As far as his eye could see, it was thronged with people, silent people, eyes all focused on him. It took him a few seconds to adjust to the light and begin to pick out faces. He knew these people!

The faces were all familiar, all believers, all people that he knew and loved. They had come to support him, he knew instinctively. As he was led down the steps to approach the altar, the crowd became animated, movement first and then the cheering began.

"Antipas, Antipas," the crowd roared.

"Save him, spare his life," they continued, rising in volume.

The noise was like thunder as it rolled up the steps past the altar and circled around him and his captor. As the noise increased, others appeared on the top steps and began the descent to him. Justus Anthony walked slowly at the head of the procession. He stopped one step above Antipas.

His face was set with determination. His eyes were hooded and unreadable. At his approach the crowd fell silent, a pregnant silence as they awaited the events to unfold.

❧ ❧ ❧

Justus Anthony stepped down on the level with Antipas. He glanced at him then at the crowd. He knew there was fear on his face as he gazed out over the vast throng. No one had told him the Christians would show themselves publicly like this. No one had told him there were so many, a vast throng, in his city. He was afraid. What if their God sought retaliation? He would be the one responsible for the sacrifice of this man, the servant of this God.

Others had gathered on the stairs above them. All the priests with their most elaborate white robes were there, gloating. The city fathers were there, pompous in their regalia. The temple guards, with swords raised, flanked the regal group.

He was trapped. He couldn't back out now. The guards would throw him on the altar if he should reverse his position. He thought about running down into the crowd at the base of the steps and throwing himself at their mercy, but he wasn't sure if they would accept him or attack him. He would need to be hidden, defended, at a risk to their lives and his. Why would they even consider such a thing? He was killing their prophet.

As he hesitated, thoughts whirling through his head, a body hurled itself down the stairs toward him, voice raised in maniacal rage.

"Kill him, kill him. What are you waiting for? Rid the world of this worthless being."

It was Julian, Antipas's father. His turban had slipped to the back of his head and his hair was in disarray. His face twisted in a snarl. Two guards detached themselves from the group and surrounded him, pulling his arms behind his back and binding them.

"He's no son of mine. Throw him on the altar," he screamed as the guards held him.

He looked into the face of Antipas. For one moment reason seemed to play over his features. For one second of time, he seemed aware that this was his son. Tears streaked down his face. A look of longing passed from his eyes to Antipas.

Antipas leaned toward him and spoke softly.

"Oh my father, my father. It's not too late for you yet."

It almost seemed as though the father would reach out to the son, but the demon inside took control again. He tried to struggle out of the guards' grip, panting and cursing.

"Zeus will be avenged. Sacrifice him now. This man is a traitor and a thief. He stole my son. I'll never forgive him for that," he raged on and on.

The priests took up the chant behind them as the tableau played out on the step. Justus Anthony was frozen in time as he watched the interaction.

Some in the crowd began murmuring until a voice was raised above the others.

"Jesus is Lord." The words rang out over the crowd. Others took up the call until the street was filled with praises to God.

"Jesus is Lord."

"You can kill the body but you can't kill the soul."

"Praise God."

The words were distinct and carried over the heads of all those gathered below the steps. Finally the words reduced themselves to one word, chanted over and over again by the believers.

"Jesus, Jesus, Jesus, Jesus, Jesus, Jesus, Jesus, Jesus."

As the name resounded through the crowd and up the stairs, Justus Anthony was deeply moved. The priests nudged each other and whispered frantically, hands gesturing sharply. A darkness seemed to hover over the steps and just above the altar. The air became oppressive.

Justus Anthony became aware that the forces of the universe faced each other, but he was powerless to do anything. It was as though someone had taken all his strength and all his power of reasoning.

❧ ❧ ❧

Julian was being dragged away by the guards. Before he left, he spit in Antipas's face as a final insult to him. Antipas just stood there with pity and forgiveness on his face.

A light was gathering around him. Against the darkness of evil on the faces of his oppressors, he seemed to shine.

Antipas could see the faces before him with even more clarity than before. Paulus stood proudly right in front. Antipas's heart sang as he saw him. He could see a leader in Paulus, someone to carry on after today. Paulus saluted him gravely with love and tenderness in his eyes. Antipas responded, and an unspoken message passed between the brothers.

This was not lost on Marcus. He had not realized that Paulus had become one of "them." He wondered when this had happened. For a moment he wished he could join them, the three brothers again in harmony. But he was too ingrained in Zeus worship, its grip too tight for him to back out now.

≈ ≈ ≈

Eunice stood beside Paulus. She smiled bravely and lovingly at Antipas. God had already promised him that He would care for Eunice. He drank in her beauty, knowing what it must cost her emotionally to stand before him today with a smile on her face.

Mattias and Larium stood just behind her. What dear friends they were. He knew they would befriend both Eunice and Paulus. They already considered Simon a part of their family.

The biggest surprise of all was the face of the woman on the other side of Eunice. It was his mother! He had long hoped that she and Eunice would meet, and now here they were leaning on each other. How brave of his mother to stand here where both Marcus and his father could see her. Now that Paulus was on their side, she felt comfortable making a public declaration of her faith in the one true God and her support of her son; now two of her sons.

Other faces kept crowding in front of his vision. He studied each one, communicating eye messages. How brave they were to gather so publicly. They would never know how much this meant to him. Whatever happened in the next few minutes, it was made easier by their presence.

≈ ≈ ≈

A tense stillness stretched out over the city. The powers of Satan were locked in an eternal battle. Realization dawned on them that they could not win this battle. They could claim the life of Antipas—and they would—but they could not touch his spirit, and they could not stop the march of Christianity. Frustration and anger filled them.

The silence was broken again by Julian. The demon that possessed him threw him on the ground, writhing and whimpering in defeat. The man was broken. He gave one more moan then was quiet again.

The chief priest detached himself from the other priests and stepped down to stand right behind Justus Anthony. He whispered in his ear, gesturing with his hands. Justus pulled himself together and stood tall once again. He spoke to the crowd.

"Men of Pergamum, today we stand before you with a man charged with rejection of the great god Zeus, rejection of the worship of the emperor, rejection of the proud family into which he was born. The penalty for such treason, such arrogance, such defiance, is death by sacrifice." He took a deep breath, scanning the crowd and keeping his back to the priests. "The altar has been lit, the prisoner has been tried and found guilty. The religious and political leaders of Pergamum are united in their rejection of him."

The mention of the altar turned people's heads in that direction. Flames leaped from the top, the smoke ascending to the clear sky. A shudder ran through the crowd, but no sound was made. Their eyes turned back to Antipas, who was standing calmly, with the glow continuing to gather around him.

≈ ≈ ≈

Justus Anthony faltered again, but if he did not continue, his life would be over. The chief priest had made that clear. He had the temple guards on his side, and Justus Anthony would be no more. He must go on.

"Bind him and throw him on the altar, and may the gods be satisfied with this sacrifice," he said in a loud voice. Only he knew what it cost him to pronounce the words.

Guards circled Antipas, wrapping him in a cloth prepared in advance for sacrifice victims. Antipas remained steady while the cloth was being wound. They pushed him roughly as they spun him round and round, pulling the fabric tighter with each circle. As the cloth made contact with his face, the coarseness scraped across his jaw. He flinched as his nose was covered and it became difficult to breathe.

He made eye contact with one of the guards, who instantly cried out and fell back. He was not able to continue and was dragged away by other guards and replaced in the wrapping ceremony. The others quickly completed the wrapping, over eyes and head, and with one last tug and it was in place. Someone held him steady. The pressure on his arm was somehow reassuring. He felt it was strange that he could think that way when he was about to die. Now his life had been reduced to a dim light filtering through the fabric. He retreated to his inner self and embraced God's welcoming peace like a warm hug.

He could hear Eunice calling his name. How sweet it was that one of the last sounds he could hear was her voice.

"O maker of heaven and earth, surround her, love her, protect her. She is Yours now, Lord. She's always been Yours, I know. Thank You for letting me have her for a time."

From the top step, where his father had been taken by the guards, Julian once again cried out.

"Sacrifice him. He deserves to die. Let him go to his God."

Justus Anthony gave the order, and Antipas was lifted from the step and carried to the edge of the smoking altar.

Time stood still. The arms lifting him were surprisingly gentle, wrapping themselves around him. The heat was intense as they approached the altar. The smoke bent down and circled him, enclosing him in its fragrance. His vision was limited, but he could see the dancing light from the flames; ever rising, ever retreating. The smoke curled away and back again, at the whim of the wind.

"The time has come for the god Zeus to be avenged," shouted Justus Anthony. "Commit him to the flames!"

And with that, Antipas was thrown on the altar. As the arms encircling his body fell away, he was floating through space. Now the only sound was the hissing of the flame. It called to him, luring him on.

Then his body made contact with the altar. Searing pain shuddered through him, sharp and consuming. The flames welcomed and embraced him. He could make no sound. The only sound was the roaring of the flames. The cloth melted at the touch of the feverish blaze. Mercifully he could no longer feel. The flames licked the fabric away then devoured his garments. With great finality, they attacked his body.

⧽ ⧽ ⧽

Julian watched the flames consuming his son. His son. Oh yes, it was his son. Too late, the realization hit him. Too late for Julian. He trembled violently, speechless, consumed with horror. He crumbled in a heap on the step and was carried away, unconscious, by temple guards.

A cry broke out from the vast crowd. It was not what Justus Anthony or the priests were expecting. It was not a condemnation of the deed done, not the cry of grief and pain, it was a cry of victory!

"Jesus is Lord. Jesus, Jesus, Jesus, Jesus…" The crowd chanted His name over and over again. Arms were thrown in the air in praise of the one true God.

As the flames covered his body, the spirit of Antipas rose from the altar and soared heavenward. He was amazed that he could still see the crowd, still hear their chanting, still see individual faces. Then he heard the voice, the voice of the One he had been following for years, the voice of his Savior.

As he continued to rise, the things of this world faded as the eternal world opened to receive this true and faithful servant.

"Well done, faithful Antipas," numerous voices rejoiced as he was received into the bosom of his heavenly Father.

"Welcome to your reward."

As he entered heaven, he heard a great chorus chanting. "Holy, holy, holy is the Lord God Almighty, who was, and is, and is to come."

The sound reverberated throughout heaven, was flung across the centuries, reached the lowest depths of hell, reached into the hearts of men everywhere.